THE CHASE IS ON!

WHATEVER IT TAKES

NOVEL BY

THE AUTHOR THAT BOUGHT YOU
THE ACTION-PACKED THRILLER
"THE MOUSE THAT ROARED"

DWAYNE MURRAY, SR.

Published By

Madbo Enterprises
1444 East Gunhill Road, Suite #32
Bronx, New York 10469
Website: WWW.MADBOENTERPRISES.COM
Email Address: DEE64MAN@AOL.COM

Warning!
This is a novel of fiction. All the characters, incidents and dialogue are products of the Author's imagination and are not real. Any references or similarities to actual events, people, living or dead, or to locales are intended to give the story a sense of reality. Similarities in names, characters, entities, places and incidents are purely coincidental.

Cover Design/Graphics/Photography: Marion Designs
Email Address: MARIONDESIGNS@BELLSOUTH.NET

Cover Models:
Santrelle Woodruff, Cristal Stevenson, and Jasmine Alexis

Printing Company: United Graphics Incorporated

ISBN 0-9769855-1-9

Dedication

I dedicate this novel to my wife and biggest supporter Angela who has been there from the beginning to the end. She is just as much responsible and credited for the conception of this novel. She is invaluable to my endeavors for self-publishing and I could have never done this without her. "Ang" I love you and thanks for doing "Whatever It Takes" (pun intended) to see this book make it into the hands of readers. You have been my rock and again "I Love You"

To my sons Dwayne, Jr. and Daniel thanks for giving me your support and showing love and patience. Thanks for being the sons any father would love to have and I love you both always and forever.

A special dedication to the newest member of the Murray Family "Donte' Lamar Murray" born June 2, 2007. While this novel was in the embryonic stages so was my handsome grandson. Special thanks to Nataya Perry for presenting this gift to our family that I hope you believe to be a part of. Thanks for your support.

Acknowledgments

First I want to thank my *Savior Jesus Christ* for yet again giving me the strength, love, and guidance to complete my second novel. It is always through His Grace that this is possible.

To my wife *Angie*, words will never be enough to show my gratitude and appreciation for all of the love and support you have bestowed upon me during the making of this novel. All I do is for you and you are the ultimate friend.

To my sons *Dwayne, Jr. & Daniel*, who are both making us proud parents as 2007 college and high school graduates. You guys will never know just how proud I am of both your accomplishments and willingness to live out the dream your Mom and I had and continue to have for you both. You both are the greatest sons I could ever hope for and deserve. I love you both.

To *Christine Murray*, the mother of all mothers. Thank you for always being there with motherly advice and support when needed. I am truly blessed and thankful for always having you in my corner. No mother does it better!!!

To *Nyoki, Falomi*, and *Joshua* my sisters and nephew respectively what can I say but…you all are the greatest and I love you to death.

To the *Crafton Crew: Lorraine, Shaunte, Evelyn, April, and Shennie*. Thanks for the love and encouragement. Love you and See ya'll at the next BBQ.

To my in-laws who I love dearly *Robert* and *Margaret Crafton* thanks for your support and you two are the best.

To *Treasure E. Blue*, author of *"Harlem Girl Lost"* and *"A Streetgirl named Desire"* a special "Thanks" goes out to you for being the most unselfish brother I happened upon in this literary arena. You have been so supportive through all of this and I am glad to know you. When I think of the support you've tossed my way, it only solidify that fact that you are very generous, selfless, thoughtful human being with a kind heart. Thanks!

To my relatives **The Murray** and **Olivero** families for you support and encouragement throughout the creation of this book and also your past support with The Mouse That Roared. **Aunts Janette, Annette, Geogi and Barbara. Also Vickie, Sparrow, Gracie, Tito** and **Pleshette.** Thank you very much and much love.

To an outstanding editor **Alvin C. Romer**, who took the time to advise me on my **Whatever It Takes**, and offered support, positive feedback, constructive criticism, and helped bring this novel to fruition. I thank you for your patience and willingness to help me with my book.

To **Nakea S. Murray**, who had me hustling up and down the east coast with book signings and literary events. "Thank you" for all you support and know-how in relation to marketing and publicity. I'm ready to hit the scene and I am ready to go where ever you send me.

To all the members at **Coast-2-Coast Readers' Forum**…**Glamour, MsKiki, Hotchocolate, Ladyscorpio, Chocolatesirprize, Virgo, Greeneyedrican, Shyste, Inquisitive, Caligurl, Lee-Lee, Xtina, Khaleelah, Nicole098, Black Poe, Kerry E. Wagner,** and **Hunnigurl.** I am almost sure I missed a few, however I am shouting out the entire C2C family and all its members when I say, "Thanks for the abundance of love and support!"

A special shout to my friend and fellow author **Moses Miller** writer of the hot novel "The Trifling Times of Nathan Jones" for all the cold days we spent on the street pushing each other's work and always looking out for one another's best interest. You've got a friend Moses.

To my fellow authors **Renee Jones-Brown** and **Kymberle Joseph**, ladies keep doing your thing and it was a blessing when I got to meet you two.

A special "Thanks" to all the book clubs and literary sites that reviewed **The Mouse That Roared**, such as **RAW Sistaz, The Romer Review, Urban Reviews, ARC Book Club Inc., Reader Views, Book Review, People Who Love Good Books Book Club, Imani Book**

Club, OOSA Book Club, APOOO Book Club, and Book Pleasures. I am hoping you all will be so gracious to yet again review this novel ***Whatever It Takes.*** I do appreciate your services to me and other authors alike.

A heart-felt "Thank you" to my man ***Nelson*** who I met at the Harlem Book Fair 2006 to this present time has been real and a true book game brother. It's been a pleasure to work with you while promoting my book and along the way a true friendship evolved. "Thank you!" Also I want to shout out ***Bruce*** who always pushed my book on Sundays.

Thanks to ***Raheem,*** who never hesitated to give me a call when the supplies of ***The Mouse That Roared*** were running low. Thanks for your support and marketing of my book.

Here's yet another shout-out to all the other book vendors who showed me mad love and support in this hustling game. Shout out to ***Pargo of The Bronx, Henry on 125th Street, Musamba in Queens, Carvelas (DC Bookman) and wife Tiah in Washington,*** and of course my man ***Hakim in "Philly."***

Thank you to my book distributors at ***A & B Distributors and Baker & Taylor.*** Thanks for being available to answer my questions and concerns and for working with me to get my books into the hands of avid readers.

A very special "Thank you" to all my extended ***family, friends and All the Book Clubs*** *across America* for your love and support. I recognize the importance of each and every one of you and I am blessed to have you all in my life.

A thank you to ***Kimberly Martin*** of ***Self-Pub.net*** for all of your help in formatting this book.

To all the avid readers who purchased both of my books, ***The Mouse That Roared and Whatever It Takes,*** I want to sincerely thank you for your support.

Chapter One
The History of Steel

It was ninety degrees on the quiet tree lined block of Eastchester Road in the Bronx in the summer of 1981. In the backyard of their home 11 year-old Butch Steel and his 10 year-old brother Zig dug a 2 x 16 trench that would soon be filled with vegetables of all types. The boys had on shorts and work boots as they worked with great vigor as Pete and Simone Steel looked on with great pride. In systematic rhythm, the Steel brothers worked diligently as if they were well oiled machines and never got in each others' way always in sync.

Pete and Simone watched from the dining room window as dirt flied in the air. Pete said with great pride, "Baby look at our two sons, not even twelve years old yet, working and earning their keep like we have always taught them."

Simone, a registered nurse at Bronx North Central Hospital replied, "I thank God for them because even though we try to teach them all we know, they could have taken another path. Yes baby, we should be proud."

Pete, who was an electrician's foremen, hugged his wife and watched his boys complete their task.

"Boy! Look at the time. I have to go get dinner started."

"You do that sweetheart; I'm going outside and give my soldiers some cold lemonade." Pete kissed his dark and lovely wife on the cheek, and went to the kitchen.

*****

Butch and Zig dropped their shovels and sipped their lemonade in the shade. Their father assessed the ditch as he admired their work. "Good job boys, I couldn't have done it better myself. Your momma will love the job too, especially since she will be able to plant her vegetables. I need to ask you two a question. Do you think I'm hard on ya'll when it comes to chores around the house?"

Butch looked at his father with a slight glimmer in his eyes and answered, - "No Sir, we don't feel that way at all."

Zig, who sported a bald head and had the body of a 16 year-old, looked at his dad and answered, "No Dad I don't feel that way either."

Pete looked at his sons while he scratched his beard and asked, "Why is it important for a man to do his job?"

Without missing a beat Butch and Zig answered at the same exact time, - "Because if a man shall not work, a man shall not eat."

Pete clapped his hands loudly with pride towards his sons. He grabbed their sweaty necks and pulled Butch and Zig close to his chest, "That's what I want to hear! That's my boys, the Steel brothers'! Now ya'll go get washed up for dinner. Your mother will be calling us soon. But hold on before you two go, I need to say...

Before Pete finished his sentence, his sons looked up at him and responded, "Dad we know you love us, we love you too!"

Pete looked at his sons and sucked his teeth "Oh shut up. I wasn't even going to say that." A smile on his face, Pete nudged his boys towards the backdoor so they could wash up for dinner. Before he followed them inside, Pete's attention focused on Elizabeth, an elderly woman in her seventies who lived two houses down from his.

Elizabeth Smith had lived on the block for more than fifty years. She's widowed and had no children. Elizabeth was a retired school teacher who taught in catholic schools in the Bronx.

"Good evening Mr. Steel. I'm terribly sorry for disturbing you, but I haven't seen Tigger since yesterday morning and I'm worried because he always comes home for supper."

Pete always admired Elizabeth who still had so much energy and spunk even after the death of her husband five years ago. Pete walked over to Elizabeth and gently put his arm around the old woman's shoulder to say, "First of all young lady, what did I tell you about that Mr. Steel stuff?

The old woman blushed as Pete continued, - "I promise when we finish dinner the boys and I will search the area for Tigger. I'm pretty sure he found himself a girlfriend so there's no need for you to worry."

The old woman smiled with confidence and said, "You and your family have always been so kind to me. I want to thank you for that. I know you will find Tigger." Pete gave the woman a wink of his eye and went inside to join his family for dinner.

*****

Later after dinner, Simone stood on her stoop with Elizabeth by her side. Pete, Butch and Zig however walked up the block with flashlights in their hands in search for Tigger.

"Simone, my eyes are not nearly what they use to be, is that them walking this way?

"Yes Elizabeth they're making their way up the block now."

"Do they have Tigger with them? Simone, please tell me."

Simone, who had the vision of a hawk, looked up the block and turned towards a worried Elizabeth and responded, "No they don't have Tigger but I'm sure he will turn up."

The Steel men approached their stoop and saw the anguish on Elizabeth's face. Pete motioned to his sons to go inside as he gently explained to Elizabeth, "We looked everywhere and couldn't find him. I promise Elizabeth, if Tigger doesn't come home soon, the boys and I will nail posters to trees and telephone poles for you."

"Thank you for all of your help Pete and Simone, I better go inside just in case Tigger decides to come scratching at the back door."

Pete and Simone watched the old woman as she slowly walked to her home. Elizabeth looked both ways up the block in hoped that she saw her pet, but didn't.

*****

Saturday morning 6:00 AM to be exact, Zig quietly left the house from the kitchen entrance. Zig quietly opened the garage door and did his best not to wake his parents. Inside the garage Zig pulled out his brand new Apollo 5 speed bike with the banana seat. Zig slowly closed the creaking garage door, and looked up to his parents' bedroom window to make sure his light-sleeping mother didn't see him sneak out. To be caught that early out the house would be disastrous. Zig walked briskly while he rolled his bike down the driveway. Once he was at the curb, he jumped on his bike and sped down Eastchester Road towards his hideaway.

*****

An hour later Butch was in the kitchen as he helped his mother with breakfast. Butch always enjoyed that time with his mother on Saturday morning's. Simone mixed pancake batter when she noticed Butch had tossed bacon in the hot frying pan.

"Butch never throw the bacon into the pan okay? Always lay it in the pan gently so the grease doesn't pop all over the place."

"Yes momma. Am I doing it right now?'

Simone looked proudly at her independent son and answered, "Yes you are little man. Now use your fork and gently spread the bacon apart."

Butch did as he was told and flipped the bacon over with the fork like a professional, which bought a smile to his mother's face.

"Butch can you clean, cook and sew on your own?"

"Yes mama I can do those things very well."

"Butch do you need a woman to take care of you?"

"No mama I don't need a woman to take care of me because I have been taught to take care of myself, and carry my own weight."

Simone prided herself on how she raised independent young men. She didn't want them to rely on anyone for anything. Simone also used every chance to teach her sons lessons in life. Simone gave her son a long look and asked "Any man can take a wife Butch, but what makes her qualified to be yours?"

"She must be honest, loyal, trusting, strong and fearless", Butch stated.

"Butch, what if she doesn't have any of those qualities within her?"

"Then she can't come here to meet you mama, Butch replied"

Simone rubbed her son on the top of his head and said, "Very good grasshopper now go wake your brother up so he can eat."

Butch did as he was told and ran from the kitchen and upstairs to get his brother. When Butch got to Zig's room he noticed that he was already gone.

*****

Butch was pissed off because he knew his mom would send him out to get Zig. Butch wanted to enjoy his hot blueberry pancakes and bacon. Butch knew for a fact that reheated pancakes never would taste the same as fresh "right out of the skillet" pancakes.

On his bike, Butch rode fast to their hideaway. Butch and Zig used the hideaway to look at their father's nude magazines. Butch was determined to get Zig for messing up his Saturday morning breakfast. Butch cut across Eastchester Road until he came upon Pelham Parkway. Butch pumped his legs harder until he was 100 feet away from the wooded entrance of the Steel's hideout.

At the entrance Butch got off his bike and walked the rest of the way. He was going to sneak up on Zig and make him pay for having to eat re-heated pancakes. Gently Butch walked on dry leaves and twigs as he wiped away sweat that dripped down his face. The heat and humidity was already kicking during the early morning hours. Butch swatted away mosquitoes and flies as he made his way closer to Zig.

Butch ducked behind a nearby tree and spotted Zig's 5-speed Apollo bike. Zig begged his parents the whole winter for that bike because he knew no one else would have it by the summer. Butch knew Zig had to be close; his brother would never let that bike out of his sight.

Zig was in front of the muddy pond on his knees and his arm swiped down numerous times. Still not sure what the hell Zig was doing,

Butch crept closer so that he could get a better view. While Butch watched Zig from behind, he saw his brother swipe his arm from side to side and noticed a shiny object in his possession.

*****

Pete is awakened by the delicious aroma of his wife's pancakes. He entered into his bathroom to prepare for his morning shave. Pete prepped his skin with a very hot towel that he covered his face with.   Pete grabbed his shaving accessories and in a circular motion spread the lather smoothly and evenly on his face. Pete whistled the theme from "Shaft" and reached into his black leather shaving bag to get his stainless steel straight razor with the rattlesnake on the handle. Pete loved that razor because his father gave it to him as a Christmas gift, just before he died. He sucked his teeth in disgust because it's not there. "Simone have you seen my razor!" Pete shouted.

*****

Zig raised his visibly bloodied hand for another swipe. Butch ran from his concealed spot and yelled, "Zig you fucking bastard!"

Butch scared the shit out of Zig as he quickly jumped up and dropped the razor to the ground. In front of Butch was Miss. Elizabeth's cat Tigger dead with his stomach cut wide open. Totally pissed off at Zig, Butch ran and tackled him to the ground. The two brothers wrestled intensely. The aggression was evident between the brothers as they tried to get the advantage on each other. Butch knew full well that Zig was stronger than him. So Butch used all of his body weight to pin his brother down as he sat on his chest

Both of them breathed hard when Butch slapped his brother across the face, "You bastard how could you!"

Zig tried hard to get up while he screamed, - "You were late getting up this morning. I told you to go to bed early and I told you what time I was leaving!"

Butch slapped his brother across the face again and peered at Zig with anger in his eyes, "I don't give a damn you stupid selfish bastard. I planned this whole thing, I was the one who lured Tigger and caught him. You had no right doing this without me!"

Zig extremely exhausted, looked up at his older brother and somberly said, "Butch I'm sorry, please don't be mad at me. I was dreaming about it all night! I couldn't wait. Please don't be mad with me man."

Butch slowly got off his brother's chest and helped him to his feet, "Go dig a hole with a branch and bury it. I'll wash the blade and remember the story we will tell them when they ask us where we were. Do you understand?"

Zig picked the gutted Tigger off the ground and buried it like his brother told him to do.

Chapter Two
In a Blink of an Eye

At the First Baptist Church seated in the fourth row, the Steel family listened to Reverend Joe Glover as he gave an electrified sermon on appreciating the gift of life.

Reverend Glover, was in his sixties but looked much younger, wiped his forehead as the organist played in rhythm to his words.

The reverend in rare form laid down the word, "Brothers and Sisters the Lord says our view of one hundred years seems long and worth living, but with life all things must come to an end. I'm here to tell you that the true gift to us is eternity with The Lord Jesus Christ. So we must keep that in perspective today brothers and sisters. Spiritually we must ask ourselves what do we want? One hundred years on earth, doing what we want with no regards to whom we hurt or eternity with our Heavenly Father knowing that we will rejoice with him forever and ever?"

The packed church with about 300 members all shouted in unison that they wanted eternity as the reverend continued, -"Tomorrow is not promised to us Brothers and Sisters, this is why I say you must come forward and proclaim your love for the Lord. I ask you now, who wishes to be baptized and be cleansed on this day?

Butch and Zig, who wore brand new two piece suits, looked around the church as about twelve members got out of their seats and walked up to the front of the church. The boys continued to look on as the remaining congregation clapped and sang praises. Pete arose from his seat and walked into the aisle, while at the same time he looked down at his sons who had shocked looks on their faces. Pete kissed his wife Simone who cried on the cheek. An usher grabbed Pete's hand and led him to the front of the church where the other members stood.

Simone wiped tears from her eyes and looked at her boys who both seemed mystified about the baptism, "Tomorrow is not promised Butch and Zig do you understand? You must live and love for today"

The boys' nodded their heads up and down in agreement as they watched their father as he was slowly walked towards a large pool of water by the usher to be baptized.

*****

7

The members of the church filed out into the sun soaked backyard of the church. Simone held her boys' hands as they watched Pete shake Reverend Glover's hand. Goodbyes were said to the ushers and members of the choir. Pete walked down the steps and into the opened arms of his family.

"Baby we are all so proud of you! You have no idea what this means to all of us", Simone said.

"Well I didn't want to say too much about it but I'm glad that I chose to do it because in a strange way, Simone, I feel complete, - almost like a void has béen filled in my life", Pete responded.

Zig loosened his tie and asked his father, "Dad I'm really hungry can we get some Burger King on our way home?"

Butch agreed with his brother and added, "Yeah, I'm starving like Marvin and I have a taste for a vanilla milkshake."

"Butch what did I tell you about saying you're starving? You have a refrigerator and a freezer in the basement filled to the brim with food. So you are nowhere near starving, okay? Let's take a trip to Africa and I will show you starving. So if you want Burger King just ask for it?" snapped Simone.

Pete hugged his wife's waist in an attempt to calm her down, "Come on booby they didn't mean anything, leave my two bodyguards alone and let's enjoy the day baby."

Simone regained her composure and apologized, "I'm sorry fatheads we can go, and I'll even let you two eat in the backseat of your father's brand spanking new Pontiac Grand Prix."

"Please, you two better not even think about eating one French fry in my car."

The Steel family laughed as they entered their dad's car and drove to the nearest Burger King.

*****

It's 1:15 PM on Boston Road. Donald Baker a 35 year-old African-American computer analyst drove his brand new red Cadillac Elderado with his 10 year-old son Melvin in the front passenger seat. The number one hit song "Heartbeat" by female artist Tanya Gardner played on the radio. Melvin asked his father, "So when do you think I can drive the car?"

Donald looked at his son and replied, "Melvin you can't drive, you're too young. When you get older then I will consider teaching you how to drive."

Melvin gave his father an evil stare, one that no child should be able to get away with and snapped, "I think that's bullshit! You're always telling me that you'll do something and you never do it!"

"Hey young man you watch your mouth, and just remember your birthday is coming up soon, and with that kind of attitude you will be lucky to get a card" Donald reprimanded.

Melvin, who was an only child and spoiled rotten to the core, pushed himself back with such great force he caused the passenger seat to recline. Obviously disgusted with his father, Melvin played with the window rolling it up and down as they headed down Eastchester Road.

"Melvin stop acting like a baby! I said when you get old enough I will teach you how to drive, now stop playing with that window before you break it!"

Melvin disregarded his father and retorted, "No, it's hot outside!"

"Melvin I swear I will smack you across your behind! I said close that window the air conditioner is on!"

In a disrespectful manner Melvin took his sweet time and pushed the button that closed his window.

*****

The Steels' pulled up in front of their home coming from Burger King. Pete put the car in park and kissed his wife on the lips, "Simone I love you baby, but "your" kids are greedy. I can't afford to feed them boys!"

Simone looked at her husband with a smile on her face and said, "Oh Pete shut up! So they're "my" boys now huh?"

Pete checked the back of his car. He searched both on the floor and on the leather seats where his sons sat and admonished, "If I see one crumb in my car your butts are mine."

"Come on Pop we promised we wouldn't spill anything" said Butch.

"Man just get out of my car with your big heads looking like before and before"

Simone rolled her eyes, grabbed her purse and told her sons, "Come on kids lets go inside before your daddy has a fit about his car."

"That's right baby, ya'll know how I feel about my ride!" said Pete while he opened the car door. Simone looked inside and saw that Zig struggled with his seatbelt. "Pete open your door again, I think Zig's' seatbelt is stuck."

Pete opened the car door and saw that Zig was frustrated and angry. "Ok Hercules! Relax, I told you not to eat that double whopper, I mean, look at your gut." Pete grabbed the buckle of the seatbelt and pressed the button to release the latch but it didn't work. Pete pulled on the seatbelt a little harder as frustration mounted because he realized it was jammed.

Simone wiped ketchup off Butch's face then looked inside the car. She noticed that her husband was frustrated while Zig sweated profusely inside the hot car. "Butch go stand next to the steps while I go help your father." Doing as he was told Butch stood against the gate while his parents helped Zig.

*****

Two hundred feet from their home, Donald signaled to get in the right lane so that he could turn into his garage. Melvin from a distance saw the Steels' car up ahead was hell-bent to impress Butch. "Listen we are almost home, just slow down here and let me drive. There are no cars in sight come on!" screamed Melvin.

Not saying a word, Donald a half a block from his home, ignored his son. All of a sudden a crazed Melvin grabbed hold of the steering wheel and fought his father for control. "Oh shit Melvin, what in the hell are you doing! Let this damn wheel go!"

"No let me drive! Just… let…Me…Look out!" screamed Melvin as his father accidentally hit the accelerator and picked up speed. Donald lost control of the car. as it side swiped the Steels' car. With great force the car hit and dragged Pete and Simone all the way to the other end of the block.

Donald felt his car tires roll over the couple's bodies and realized the magnitude of what had happened. Donald felt light-headed and as if his heart was going to pound right out of his chest. He saw Pete reach up and slam his mangled hand on the hood of the car.

Melvin showed no remorse at all and screamed out, "Daddy, Mr. Pete is getting blood all over your car!" Donald regained his composure and took a long look at his son who was only worried about the blood on the car. Donald used all the strength inside him and smacked Melvin so hard across his face Melvin's nose spurted blood. "Say one more thing and I'll shut your damn mouth for good!" screamed Donald as he fumbled with his foot to locate the brake.

The drivers' side door was completely ripped off of the Grand Prix. Zig still inside the car screamed in horror as he watched his parents vanish before his eyes. Butch stood on the sidewalk and dropped his milkshake to the ground. He looked on in horror as the Cadillac hit a parked car and came to a complete halt, but not before it smashed his father like a pancake. His mother, who taught him everything he knew in his young life, was under the car as her right leg stuck out from under the left front tire. There was a long trail of blood that painted the black asphalt red.

People came out of their homes to witness the terrible carnage that had become a spectacle on their quiet street. The Steel's next door neighbor Alice Sanchez, ran out of her house still adorned with her house gown. Alice looked at the scene in disbelief as tears fell from her eyes. Alice with the presence of mind grabbed Butch who ran towards the Cadillac to get to his parents. Alice rubbed Zig's sweaty face and did her best to calm Butch down, "Ok baby you just look at me, Butch you hear me baby just look at me!"

Alice's husband Miguel ran out of his house looking for his wife. He saw her on the sidewalk as she held Butch and could do nothing to stop the tears that fell from his eyes. This was the same couple who he enjoyed a barbeque with last week. Miguel looked to his right where he heard cries that came from the Grand Prix. Miguel quickly ran to the car to check on Zig. Miguel pushed the button on the seatbelt buckle and unfastened it. He quickly had to grab Zig who was ready to run to the accident. "Stay with me big guy, ok? You just stay with Mr. Miguel."

Donald sat in his car which was now surrounded by practically every homeowner in the neighborhood. Donald looked over at his son who stared blankly out of the front window. Smoke billowed from the hood of the totaled Cadillac.

Sirens were heard from a distance as they got closer to the scene. Tisha Baker, ran out of her house with rollers in her hair, - "Donald! Melvin! Oh God! My family!"

*****

It had been about an hour and the street was flooded with paramedics, policemen, and firefighters who had converged on the scene. Donald sat on the back step of an EMS truck as he held a cold pack on his forehead, while his wife held their son in her arms right next to him.

Pete's only sister Karen, finally arrived on the scene. What ran through her mind was the telephone conversation she had earlier that morning with her brother and Simone. Karen was going to watch the boys while Pete and Simone caught a movie, but in a blink of an eye life had changed forever. Karen saw Butch and Zig with Alice. When they spotted her, the boys ran into her arms. Karen had tears that swelled in her eyes but tried her best not to let her emotions get the best of her.

Karen held it together as she hugged Butch and Zig close to her. Everybody watched in disbelief as three firemen used 'The Jaws Of Life' to pry Donald's car away from another vehicle. Witnesses stood in the street and all screamed at once when they saw Pete and Simone's upper torsos severed in half, fall to the asphalt. Butch heard the screams from the people as he felt his aunt pat him gingerly on his back. Filled with pure fear and curiosity, Butch pulled away from his aunt who used all of her strength to deter him.

"Butch you need to stay here with your brother and me. Let the paramedics and the police do their jobs." It was too late. Butch ran past two officers and ducked under the police caution tape. Butch was inches away from the mangled carcasses that use to be his loving parents. His heart dropped to his stomach like a ton of bricks.

Cops came over to Butch and pulled him away from the scene. The only thing on the little boy's mine was making blueberry pancakes with his mother, and handing his father the power tools whenever they did a side job for someone. While the white sheets were placed over his parents' dead bodies, Butch could see Zig was in the twilight zone as his eyes were fixated far beyond the scene. Two police officers took Butch by his hand back over to his aunt. For just about three seconds it happened: The eyes of Butch and Melvin's met and locked. It happened fast and short but for those three seconds each boy's face was burned into their brains and stored there for safe keeping.

Chapter Three
Auntie Will Love You,
I Promise

The Woodlawn Cemetery was hot and humid as the skies were filled with dark, thick black clouds. The brothers sat in front of their parent's maple colored coffins that laid above their plots. Butch and Zig looked on as Reverend Glover presided over the service. In all, about 100 people were at the service including electricians, doctors and nurses who in one way or another worked with Pete and Simone. The reverend finished his sermon and blessed Pete and Simone then asked everyone to pay their last respects.

*****

Only the immediate family and relatives were left. Roses were thrown onto each casket as they were slowly lowered into the ground. Karen looked on as she gently squeezed Butch's hand and pulled Zig closer to her.

The sound of the lowering device got louder and Zig like a jack rabbit jumped to his feet. He ran towards and dived on his mother's casket, "Momma please don't leave me! Please come back to us momma please!"

Family members gently removed Zig from the top of the casket, and took him to a limousine that sat a few yards away. Karen looked at Zig somberly and then she turned her attention to Butch. He stood still and stared at the back row seats were the Bakers sat.

Karen stood to her feet and gently rubbed Butch's head as the Bakers walked closer towards them. Donald held his wife's hand as they came face to face with Butch. Donald bent down on one knee to express his condolences,

"Butch your parents have been our friends and neighbors for years. We have barbecued in the summer and shoveled snow in the winter. In a very special way we have looked at you and Zig as our sons next door. You guys will never know how sorry we are. I feel terrible about the accident. Pete and Simone were great people and we are so honored to have known them. I pray to the Lord everyday for forgiveness and I can only pray that one day you guys will forgive me too. Butch I just…."

"Daddy why are you saying sorry it wasn't your fault. I was the one who grabbed the steering wheel, it was my fault", said Melvin who rudely interrupted.

Butch and Karen were shocked at Melvin's confession. The Steels looked at Donald who obviously by the look on his face, didn't want that little unknown fact known.

"Listen Donald, no disrespect to you and your family, but we have just buried the two most important people in our lives. I can appreciate you having the courage to pay your respects, but right now the kids have a long road ahead. So understand that now is not the time for this meeting. It would be greatly appreciated by the family", explained Karen.

Donald nodded his head in agreement while his wife and child looked on as he attempted to pat Butch on the head. Butch took offense to the gesture as he backed away from Donald. "Get the fuck away from me", Butch coldly told Donald with rage in his eyes.

The Bakers stood in complete shock at the anger that burned inside Butch's eyes. For a moment a cold chill ran through Donald's body as he knew Butch blamed him. Donald, along with his family, couldn't believe what Butch said to him. It was at that moment Donald realized Butch would probably never forgive or forget.

Karen took her nephew as the sky released raindrops from the dark clouds above. Lightning danced in the sky and a clap of thunder followed. Karen hurried Butch to the limousine but not before he burned a hole through Melvin's soul. Butch knew that Melvin was really responsible for the death of his parents. Butch also realized that Mr. Baker covered up the truth in regards to Melvin's involvement in all of this. While Butch was led away he swore to himself, "That motherfucker will pay for this sooner or later, but his ass will pay."

*****

There were about forty people inside the Steel's home that ate and grieved at the same time. Most of them were relatives that spoke with each other in a low tone, while some tried to give Butch and Zig some support. Zig held a plate of food that had barely been touched. Zig sat on the couch with blood shot eyes and a runny nose. Butch who hadn't said a word since he returned home, turned to his brother and whispered inside his ear, "It's okay to cry little brother, just let it out. Remember from this point on all we have is each other and we have to stick together."

Zig placed his plate on the table, turned to his brother, and gave him a huge bear hug, "Butch what are we gonna do? I miss them man, what are we gonna do?"

Butch had no answers, so he just hugged his brother in return. Butch then looked across the room and saw Karen as she spoke to a tall white man in his forties. Curious about their conversation, Butch decided to get a closer look and listen. Butch walked through the crowd of people who passionately patted him on his shoulder. He walked over to the window and pretended to gaze outside while in all reality he really eavesdropped on his Aunt Karen and the tall white man.

"Miss. Steel I want to express my deepest regret for your loss. I realize that this matter is extremely sensitive, and the only reason I couldn't put it off is because I have an important flight to catch and won't be in the city for the next four weeks."

Karen wiped her eyes with a napkin and said, "No Mr. Hatcher I understand, life has to go on, please continue.

"I have handled the Steel's financial accounts for the past fifteen years and I must tell you they were two highly intelligent caring parents who had their son's best interest at heart. I made a copy of some very important documents that you need to read", Mr. Hatcher explained.

Karen took the documents and examined them slowly. Karen also noticed Mr. Hatcher also felt the pain and loss from Pete and Simone's death. "I see a bunch of numbers and jargon but would you be so kind to explain what it all means?"

Mr. Hatcher smiled at Karen and obliged, "I will get to the bottom line for you Miss. Steel. Your brother left a financial security blanket for his children and named you their legal guardian, which indicates that this was all discussed many years ago. In regards to financial security, Pete set aside a one hundred and fifty thousand dollar home insurance policy that automatically pays off the remaining mortgage upon his death. The balance will go into a treasury account in the children's names with you holding power of attorney."

Butch listened intently. He paid little attention to the people around him as he waited for the man to continue.

"Pete and Simone also have what is very rare, an annuity that will pay you twelve hundred and fifty dollars per month until they reach twenty- one. After which the money will go into a special account set up by the bank. In addition, they also have an insurance policy worth two hundred and fifty thousand dollars that will take care of bills such as credit card, car note and private school tuition. Seventy-five thousand dollars allocated to Butch and Zig will automatically go into a college fund. The remaining amount will be paid out in one thousand dollar increments every month to maintain the home and lifestyle the boys have grown accustomed to. Finally Karen, Pete and Simone had very good jobs that they also set up what is known as K-fund accounts. Now you must understand that this money was set aside for retirement and it will be hit with a ten percent penalty for early withdrawal regardless of their deaths. The remaining balance will be divided among you and the boys. Therefore Karen, beginning the first of next month until the boys turn twenty-one, you will receive thirty-three hundred dollars per month with the house completely paid for. In my opinion, this is more than enough to give you and the boys some peace of mind."

*****

Karen along with Butch and Zig dried and put away the last dishes. Karen put the drying towel on the table then took Butch and Zig into the living room.

Karen wiped a few tears from her eyes before she spoke to the boys. "You two know aunt Karen has always been straight up with ya'll, so I won't stop now. I know nothing about raising kids and what it's like being a parent. I can never be your momma and I'm not gonna try because she will never be replaced. What I know is that I'm your only aunt and I love you two boys more than anything, and I really believe we can make it through this. What do you guys think about that?

The boys hung on to every word that came from their aunt's mouth. Butch moved closer to Karen and said, "Auntie we promise to listen to you and behave, please just be there for us please. We have no one else but you."

"Aunt Karen we promise to listen to you and do as you say, we swear. Why did they have to leave us like this?" Zig asked as he started to cry.

Karen hugged her nephews and told them both, "We will make it! We will be just fine. I promise to be the best aunt you two ever had. I will make sure you grow up to be the men your mom and dad always wanted you to be."

*****

The summer of 1983, June to be exact, Butch and Zig are 13 and 12 years –old. In their backyard, they tossed around an old NFL football with no air in it. The white garage their dad always kept freshly painted and clean was completely filthy and visibly rusty. The backyard where Simone proudly grew her fresh vegetables for her family was now reduced to a square plot with soil that was hard as concrete. The boys for the past two years have done their best to keep the outside of the house as pre-

sentable as possible, but it had been difficult with the shee
house.

Butch and Zig attended public school and discovered fron
letters from their private school principal that their tuition had ₁
due. They were often left to fend for themselves in the public school
system. Not only in the classroom because teachers lacked the ability to
control the other children, but in the schoolyard also.

Butch and Zig were large burly boys. To add to this affect, they often wore clothes to small for them which often made them open targets
for ridicule and after school fights.

Eventually students started to realize that when you messed with one
Steel brother, the other was not far behind. For sure, kids wised up quick
and accepted the fact that getting physical with the Steel Brothers always
resulted in getting your ass kicked.

Still just young teenagers, the brothers were weak mentally, not book
smart because they maintained a B+ average. No, the brothers were being
picked on mentally when it came to their appearances. You see, even
though the cash came in on time every month like the lawyer said it
would, Butch and Zig wore clothes that were old and raggedy. Butch and
Zig were going through their rapid growth stages. Their pants became
highwaters and their shirts became three sizes too tight. Their father
always made sure they got a haircut every other Saturday, but ever since
he's been gone it's been more like every four months. Both brothers
heads were matted and nappy, letters from school were sent home about
their poor personal hygiene. That's when the teasing started and with kids
in public school, they have no mercy. While the taunting got to Zig, Butch
made sure he never cried in school because that would be a sign of
weakness.

Through all of this, the thing that caused the brothers blood to boil
the most was when they had to look into Melvin's face. Accident or no
accident it put Butch and Zig into another frame of mind when they
watched the one responsible for their parents' death ride a new bike, play
basketball, wear new sneakers and receive brand new Britishwalkers every
month while they suffered in pain. Sometimes Butch would stay up at
night and think how unfair life was, but soon he realized what his father
told him was the truth- "No one helps you but yourself, so be strong and
pull up your bootstraps."

*****

Butch threw another pass to Zig who had the body of a college
football player. The red Cutlass Supreme that their aunt Karen purchased

...is past winter pulled up into the driveway. The boys got out of the way and saw that Karen was not alone. Her boyfriend Devon sat next to her and wore a stupid grin on his face. Devon a light-skinned brother five years younger than Karen, stepped out of the car. He wore brand new Air Jordan's with the sweat suit to match. Devon rocked a red Kango on his head and sported large square "Gazelle" glasses trimmed in 14 carat gold. Devon walked towards the back door and looked at the brothers. He had the nerve to walk in their home and not even speak to them. Karen grabbed from the backseat of the car bags with logos of Sachs Fifth Avenue, Macys and Tiffany's. Two other bags contained food from McDonald's and Beefsteak Charlie's. Butch and Zig looked at the bags and knew right away which one would be their dinner. Karen was decked out with Gucci from head to toe, gold earrings, a diamond ring, and six inch leather pumps to match. She smiled at her nephews and said, "Hey boy's how was your day? Come on in and eat because I need to talk to the both of you."

*****

Butch and Zig were done eating their quarter pounder meals and sat at the table with Karen. She started to talk to them, but before doing so, she tapped Butch on his shoulder. Butch's attention was somewhere else though as he was pissed because Devon sat his funky-ass in their father's favorite chair.

"Guys, I need you to pay attention to me. Tomorrow night your aunt is going away for the weekend like I did last month, and I need you guys to do as you did the last time. That means staying in the backyard, no messing with the stove, and don't answer the phone unless you hear our secret ring. Like last time, I will go shopping before I leave to make sure you have all your favorite snack foods. I will also leave you ten dollars each just in case of an emergency. Just like the last time, - do not open the door for anyone, understand?"

Zig looked to his brother for some guidance and answered his aunt," We understand and we will do as were told."

Karen turned to Butch who never took his eyes off Devon, nudged his leg, "Butch do you understand what I just said?"

Finally turning his attention to his aunt, Butch asked, "So are you going to Atlantic City again?"

"Well Butch if you need to know so badly, yes we are going to Atlantic City, is that alright with you?" Karen asked in a huff.

"Who are you going with? Is he going with you?"

"Butch don't worry about who I'm going with, just tell me that you understand what I said."

Butch looked at Zig who had his head downward to the floor and finally told his aunt what she wanted to hear, "Yes I understand. You are going away this weekend."

Karen smiled approvingly and responded, "Very good. Now go play your Atari while I pack my things."

*****

It was 11:00PM and the Steel Brothers were in their bedroom that hasn't been cleaned in months. The racing car curtains that were once white with multicolored cars were now dingy and the kid's bed sheets had a funky odor to them. In a nutshell the room was in disarray. Butch laid on his bed and read a Hustler magazine. He looked over to where Zig sat on the floor with his back turned to him.

"Zig what the hell! I know you're not doing what I think you are!"

Zig did his best to shield himself and answered, "Just leave me alone, Butch okay? This helps me get over them, just leave me alone."

Butch jumped out of his bed and ran over to his brother. He leaned over Zig to get a better view. "I told you about this shit Zig, what is wrong with you man!"

Zig turned around and had a fingernail file in his hand covered with his own blood. In order for Zig to cope with his anger and depression, he had been self- mutilating his body for the past 7 months. Those rituals have been undetected by everyone except his brother. Extremely angry with his brother, Butch grabbed Zig by his shirt collar, dragged him over to the dresser, and reached for a bottle of rubbing alcohol. Butch pinned Zig down and opened the alcohol bottle. He proceeded to pour it all over his brothers bloodied arms and admonished him, "This won't bring them back Zig, do you hear me? They are gone you have to accept that!"

The brothers tussled on the floor while Zig cried out, "Don't say that Butch! Please don't say that!"

Butch held down his brother and failed to see Devon who stood on the other side of the opened bedroom door.

"Listen guys your aunt said for you both to keep it down."

Butch shielded his brother from Devon's sight and looked closer at Devon. Butch realized that Devon had on his father's housecoat that they gave him for Father's Day. "Hey, what the hell do you have on? That belongs to my father you son of a bitch! Take it off right now!"

Devon looked at Butch like he was crazy and sarcastically replied "Motherfucker please!" then closed the bedroom door.

Butch's face was tomato red. He picked his brother off the floor and threw him on his bed. Butch turned the lamp off, laid his head down, and said to Zig, "I've had enough of your shit little brother. Your ass better get strong."

*****

It was 12:30AM and Butch was still wide awake while Zig slept like a baby. Butch couldn't get the image of Devon out of his head. He sat up in his bed because he faintly heard music from the other side of his door. Butch checked on Zig and quickly killed a water bug that crawled on his brother's bed. Butch walked to the door, slowly opened it and clearly heard Marvin Gaye's "Sexual Healing" being played down the hall. Butch looked back at his brother, and slowly walked out of his bedroom to walk up the hallway. Butch stopped at the bathroom where the music came from. Butch gently put his hand on the doorknob and turned it slowly until the door cracked open.

Through the slightly opened door, Butch not only heard the music, but also the moans of his aunt and Devon. Butch opened the door until they were in clear view; he looked on as Karen sat on top of Devon and grinded with intense passion while covered in soapsuds.

"You ain't nothing but a fucking slut!"

Butch scared the hell out of both of them. Karen quickly jumped off Devon and back into the tub covering herself from Butch. "What the hell are you doing out of bed Butch! Go get your ass back in bed I mean that shit!" Karen yelled while she grabbed a towel.

"You promised to love and take care of us in memory of our parents, Aunt Karen. Instead all you have done is treat us like bums while you live like a queen. You said you loved us right? That's bullshit! My parents left you a lot of money and you don't give us anything. The fucking money changed you. You're not my fucking aunt. I don't know the bitch I see in front of me."

Devon slowly tried to get out of the tub and said, "Little man just calm down, your aunt does love you."

"Shut your fucking mouth, you're as bad as she is, you son of a bitch."

Karen didn't like the look in Butch's eyes and tried to calm him down, "Butch listen, I promise I will be better to you and Zig. Baby please go back to bed. I promise we will talk about this tomorrow okay?"

Butch stared at his aunt as tears rolled down his eyes. Suddenly Butch experienced an outer body feeling. All the good times with his parents flashed across his mind. All the love that they showered on them ran through his body. Butch smelled the sweet scent of his mother's breath deep inside his nostrils. He could feel his father's strong arms that carried him to bed at night. Slowly but Butch came back to reality as he remembered the two coffins that held his parents inside and the fucked up life they presently lived.

Without any remorse Butch replied "I'm sorry bitch, there will be no tomorrow." Butch rushed towards the tub before Karen and Devon could react and smacked the radio into the tub of water. Butch stepped back and watched as their bodies convulsed inside the tub. Sparks flew everywhere. After their last few trembles of life, Karen and Devon both slid under the water dead with their eyes wide open.

Butch looked on as he saw smoke come from his aunt's head. Butch quickly turned around and saw that Zig stood directly behind him. Zig rubbed his sore arms and quietly asked, "What are we going to do now?"

Chapter Four
State Property

That morning found police and detectives swarmed around the Steel home while Butch and Zig sat on the couch. It had been two hours since Butch called the police and explained the crime scene to the 911 operator. Before he made his phone call though, he made sure Zig and him had their stories straight which was very simple. Zig would keep his mouth shut and just proclaim until the cows came home, that he was fast asleep since ten o'clock the night before. Butch would simply tell the cops that he was asleep also, and was the first to wake up to discover the bodies inside the tub.

*****

Two hours passed and many of the officers left the house except for six detectives and two women from social services. Zig did as he was told and keep his mouth closed. Butch told the same exact story eight times and never once broke a sweat. Even after he saw the bodies removed from the house, that didn't shake Butch at all.

One thing bothered Butch a little, and that was the sight of a black sedan marked "Sheriff Department" on the side. Butch never saw this type of car before and wondered why it was parked in front of his house. Butch watched intently as the tall well built man, who wore a black uniform, taped a yellow sheet of paper on the front of their door. After the men talked for a minute, the detective walked over to Butch and Zig with the two women from the Child Protective Services

"Fellas as you know already, I'm Detective Bronson and this is Ms. Burnett from social services. Listen guys, I know all about the horrible accident involving your parents, and now you have this to deal with regarding your aunt. I'm afraid that I have some more bad news, the man that I was speaking to and who put the notice on your door told me that you have to leave your home today by five o'clock."

Zig looked at the detective as if he was badly mistaken. Tears started to swell up in Zig's eyes. Hearing that they had to leave their home scared the hell out of Butch.

"This is our house mister! My mom and father paid for it!" Zig protested.

The social worker pulled out a tissue from her purse and attempted to dry Zig's eyes, but was pushed away. Zig turned angrily towards Butch and looked for answers.

"Yes son you are absolutely right they did. What happened though is that your aunt forgot to pay the property taxes. Zig, I know that all of this may be too much right now, but Ms. Burnett is going to help you and your brother find a place to stay for the night until she can possibly locate another family member" explained Detective Bronson who tried to lessen the blow.

Butch, whose mind raced a mile a minute held Zig's hand to show solidarity. Instead he winced in pain as Zig with his mannish large hand squeezed his brother's hand so hard, Butch was sure he broke a finger.

*****

It was much later in the day and the social worker had been unsuccessful in finding another relative where the boys could possibly stay. While Butch and Zig stood in the living room, the sheriff and six men have moved furniture and other possessions from the home. With each item that was removed, memories flashed in their minds when their parents purchased it. Butch stared out the front door and watched as his things disappeared inside the large green truck.

*****

The brothers stood outside and held duffel bags that contained some of their possessions. Butch and Zig watched as their front door was chained and padlocked by the sheriff.

Ms. Burnett opened the trunk of her car and placed their bags inside. While the other case worker escorted Butch and Zig to the car, a few neighbors came out of their homes and tearfully gave them hugs and kisses. Before they entered the car, Butch stopped and looked a few houses down and saw Melvin who sat on his bike and wore yet another pair of brand new Air Jordan's.

Their eyes locked for what could be the very last time. Melvin looked at Butch with a devilish smile on his face, while at the same time he waved bye-bye. Butch felt like a ton of bricks had been dropped on his head. He looked in disbelief at the cold-hearted Melvin as he got on his bike and sped off down the block.

*****

Inside the office of social services on Southern Boulevard, Butch and Zig sat in a large room that was filled with about one hundred other people mostly woman and their children. The room smelled pretty bad and the floors were filthy as children played on them. There was one television and the sound was drowned out by the wild children. Reruns of "Gilligan's Island" were on. While they took in all the chaos around him, Butch saw kids that were out of control while their mothers' wore looks of despair. Butch's face was intense as he stared at Ms. Burnett who tried to locate other family members. Zig prayed that she would come out of the office with the good news that someone had been located.

*****

It had been forty-five minutes since the boys first arrived, and Butch was worried. Ms. Burnett peeped out of her office every now and then with the phone to her ear but it seemed like she wasn't having any luck finding a family member. This pissed Butch off because he knew he had plenty of cousins. Every time a barbecue was given by his parents they all showed up to stuff their faces and pack up food to take home. Butch did his best to control his temper, but just the thought about what his father always said, - "A boy will look for others for help, while a man will look to help others."

Butch's stomach felt as if he swallowed an anvil because reality just kicked him in the ass. He was a murderer who killed his father's only sister. He was a thirteen year old murderer who could easily have been sent to Spoffard Juvenile Center and later on to prison for the rest of his life. For the first time Butch asked himself, "What the hell did I do to Zig and Me?" While he searched for an answer Butch felt a tap on his leg that caused him to shudder. A woman in her early twenties with numerous holes in her arms and burn marks on her face smiled at him with brown teeth,

"Hi baby you got a dollar for some food please?"

Butch moved his face away to avoid her sewage breath.

"Come on baby give me a dollar and I'll suck your little thing for you in the bathroom, I promise to do it good" she said..

Butch felt nervous because the women rubbed her scabby legs against his. Butch tried to move away again when Zig pushed the woman away from his brother and on to the dirty floor.

"Get the fuck away from us before I kick your ass!" said an angry Zig.

The woman picked herself up off the floor and yelled, "Don't push me you little motherfucker, I'll cut your ass!"

Ms. Burnett heard the commotion and quickly exited her office with a security guard to get the woman away from the boys.

*****

Inside Ms. Burnett's office fifteen minutes later, Butch and Zig sat down as she explained their situation, "Boys I want you to know something, I have been doing this for many years now and this has been one of my most difficult placements. You two have gone through so much pain and tragedy in such a short period of time that if I could, I would take you home myself. I have made tireless phone calls in an attempt to find relatives that would be willing to take you both in, but I have been unsuccessful. Guys, I feel I have made the best decision possible and that is to have you sent to a group home in Albany, New York. I'm so sorry but it was the best I could do to avoid both of you getting lost in this system."

*****

The brothers sat with Ms. Burnett and waited for another social worker from Albany to drive them to the group home. Ms. Burnett looked at Zig who had a blank stare in his eyes. Butch looked at a bunch of children who stood across the street that belonged to the PAL summer camp. Butch cried inside at the contrast. The PAL kids waited for charted buses to take them home to their families while they waited to be taken to a group home.

Ms. Burnett saw the anguish in Butch's eyes, "Butch listen to me, okay? I know you may see me as just a white woman from Long Island but understand something, most of my time is spent right here in the Bronx dealing with children just like you guys who don't deserve the hands they've been dealt. Butch, I look into a hundred young eyes everyday and see confusion and pain. When I look into yours I see not fear, worry or anxiety, I see determination and hope. I know about your parents and what they sacrificed to provide a nice life for you guys. When you boys turn eighteen according to legal documents, you will have access to your money which will give you both a fresh start. Butch you have to help and look out for your brother along the way."

Butch looked up at the woman who didn't have to give a damn, but somehow it felt like she did and replied, "We'll be ok I guess, and thank you for all of your help Ms. Burnett. I promise to do my best to get my brother and me through this."

Up the block they all saw the brown station wagon as it approached. A white man with glasses in his forties drove as the car stopped in front of the social service building. Butch and Zig watched as Ms. Burnett walked to the car window and spoke to the driver. When she was done Ms. Burnett handed him Butch and Zig's files. The kind woman helped the boys put their bags inside the car and opened the door for them.

Before they entered she grabbed them both by the shoulders and gave them a long hug, "Zig you listen to your brother. He will help you get through this. Always listen, be respectful, do as you are told, and stay out of trouble while you two are up there. Butch, you be a man okay? Use all of that energy inside you to make yourself useful you here? I promise I will check up on you guys from time to time to see how you're doing."

The car pulled away and began the long trip to Albany, Butch turned around and looked back where he saw Ms. Burnett stand in the distance. Butch never took his eyes off the woman until he could no longer see her. He turned to his brother who looked straight ahead. Butch remembered what Zig's reaction was the last time he held his hand and grabbed it again. Butch braced for the pain of another squeeze but got none as Zig grabbed on to his hand also.

*****

7:45 PM and the sun descended in the sky. It looked so beautiful because the sky was orange and mixed perfectly with the hundreds of trees that lined the countryside. A female staff worker approached the car and took their duffel bags. Butch and Zig followed her inside the Peachtree Boy's Facility.

The building was huge and covered one square block all the way around. It consisted of five stories and most of the windows were secured by gates in front of them. The lawn was perfectly manicured and the facility was surrounded by a ten foot high fence.

The brothers looked at the marble floors that were perfectly polished and trimmed with wood that smelled like fresh cedar. At the front desk an old woman sat who looked over paper work while classical music played lowly in the background.

The boys looked up the long hallway as a tall brunette woman came their way. The woman stood six feet tall and had a body built like an amazon. She wore black square glasses and a grey two piece suit. The woman stood two feet in front of Butch and Zig where she stared without blinking once.

"Butch and Zig Steel am I correct?" the brunette asked.

They looked at the woman who dwarfed over them. The brothers stood close to each other and nodded their heads up and down.

"I'm a smart woman but sign language I don't understand so I'll ask one more time, Butch and Zig Steel?'

In unison the boys answered, "Yes we are."

She peered at the brothers as if they were a piece of meat and said, "Come with me and never make me ask twice again."

Up the hallway the brunette lead the way then stopped in front of a room where a woman stood at a counter. Behind her were shelves upon shelves of what appeared to be grey clothes and black shoes. The woman came from behind the counter and without saying a word visually sized up Butch and Zig. After a few seconds she returned to the room and re-trieved four pairs each of grey pants, shirts, socks, underwear and under-shirts. She split them amongst the boys and gave them a pair of black skippy sneakers along with a toothbrush, toothpaste and towels.

"Come with me, there are a few things we will need to go over be-fore you get yourselves settled in" said the brunette.

Butch and Zig could barely see in front of them as they carried a mountain of clothes.

"This is not your home and we are not responsible for buying you fresh clothes every week, so you better make sure the ones that we have provided for you are well kept, do you understand?"

Zig did his best not to drop his clothes and answered, "Yes ma'am, I understand."

Butch for the first time blamed himself for the situation he and his brother were in, answered the brunette "Yeah."

The boys walked near the end of the hallway which leads to another door. The brunette allowed Zig and Butch to get a few feet ahead of her when from behind her back she revealed a 2-inch thick paddle that she used to smack an unsuspicious Butch across his back. Butch dropped his clothes and fell to the ground in unbearable pain.

Butch rolled all over the floor as his mouth opened but delivered no sound. Zig was petrified but summoned the courage to come to his brother's aid, but froze in his steps when the brunette pointed the paddle in his direction.

The brunette stood over Butch and said, "When you address me Mr. Steel you address me as your brother did, with ma'am do you under-stand?"

Butch held his back and caught his breath one gulp at a time. He looked up at the giant of a woman and mustered the strength and ans-wered, "Fuck you bitch!"

Butch had taken the bait. The brunette almost seemed happy to be called a "bitch" She raised her paddle towards heaven and began to come down with the speed of a 'Kamikaze' directly towards Butch's head when Zig quickly snatched the paddle away from the brunette's hand. Shocked and somewhat afraid of the strength of the young Zig, the woman quickly pulled a whistle from her jacket then proceeded to blow on it frantically.

Like bees swarmed to honey, the Steel Brothers were surrounded by four orderlies who held thick leather straps. Butch recognized the situation lifted himself up and slapped the paddle from his brother's hand on to the floor. His efforts were fruitless as the brunette stepped back and watched as the orderlies pounced on the boys with no mercy. The brothers yelled and tried to cover each other up but Butch and Zig felt the sting of the straps as it tore their skin apart.

The brothers took their beating and the brunette picked up her paddle and said to one of the orderlies, "Just make sure you don't hit them in their faces. When you're done make sure they are put inside the room at the end of the corridor away from the others."

Chapter Five
How Ya Livin

It was Thanksgiving Day and it has been five months since their initiation to Peachtree. Butch and Zig limped because of the beating they sustained the night before. They moved to a very long wooden table where about one hundred other boys sat. The dining hall was too large to describe. Six hundred children were assigned tables according to age groups as Butch and Zig were grouped with children of their age.

Boys at each table were instructed to stand and line up. They were made to march in one line through a large mess hall and then each child was handed a TV dinner like tray. The meal consisted of dry tough turkey slices, burnt stuffing, mushy rice, canned cranberry sauce and one hard slice of cornbread. Everyone was served and sat down while the Lord's Prayer was said by a Catholic minister. Butch looked across the table at his brother and remembered his last Thanksgiving with his parents. He remembered his mother's cooking, especially her homemade coconut sweet potato pie.

Butch hoped this would help him swallow the slop that was in front of him. He chewed on what tasted like diseased turkey when from the back of his neck he felt the hot breath of the brunette headmaster. Not daring to turn around, Butch just looked at his brother who had a terrified gaze on his face as she whispered into his ear, "You ain't in Kansas anymore."

*****

The Baker home was filled with the smell of fresh turkey, baked macaroni and cheese, fresh yams, cabbage, collard greens and stuffing. On a small separate table sat pies, cakes and cobbler that cooled off. At the dinner table sat 14 year-old Melvin with his parents Donald and Tisha who looked proudly over the feast placed in front of them. Donald stood up and motioned to his family to do the same as they held hands and said a prayer that included the well being of Butch and Zig.

Melvin looked up at his father and asked, "Why did you do that?"

"Do what son, say the prayer?"

"No not that. Why would you include them in our holiday prayer?" asked Melvin.

Donald looked at his wife in disbelief and answered his son, "Well son the Steel's were friends of ours and no matter how we might want to try, we can't let what happened be forgotten. We owe them that much respect don't you think?"

His mouth stuffed with a forkful of yams while sneaking a peek at the football game, Melvin swallowed his food and said, "It was an accident okay and besides people die every day I don't see them getting special treatment."

Melvin then ate some turkey that was smothered with gravy while his parents stared at one another very disappointment.

*****

It was Christmas day and the brothers moved slowly up the line as the brunette stood in front of a 9 foot high Christmas tree with eight assistants nearby. They handed one wrapped gift to each child that walked up to her. Zig was next on line and walked up to the tree, "Merry Christmas Ma'am."

The brunette stared at Zig as if he was nothing and reluctantly responded by handing him a wrapped gift. Zig walked back towards his seat and wondered what was inside, so he began to shake the box a little.

Butch was next in line. He walked up to the brunette with fire in his eyes. The angry teen imagined that he could get one punch in her face before her punk ass assistants could grab him.

The brunette gazed at him and said very discreetly, "Don't fuck this up Steel."

Butch swallowed the glob of salvia that was aimed for the brunette's face and managed to say, "Merry Christmas Ma'am" then his gift and walked away.

When Butch passed, the brunette smiled and continued handing out gifts.

*****

Zig sat inside his room and opened his gift that consisted of a cheap plastic chess set. He turned to his brother and said, "I can play like a general just like dad taught me, Butch."

Butch smiled at his brother because Zig seemed happier. Butch opened his gift and was dumbfounded because he was given a white baby doll with blond hair. "What the hell is this?" Butch yelled as he looked at the doll before throwing it against a wall in disgust.

*****

Inside the Baker home, Donald and Tisha looked on as Melvin opened his Christmas gifts that were mounted as tall as the tree itself.

Melvin received over one hundred various gifts. He looked around the scraps of wrapping paper and hoped to find more gifts. He had the nerve to look at his parents who smiled at their son while Melvin asked, "Where's my CB radio?"

*****

The year is 1986 and Melvin who's 16 years old attended Cardinal Hayes High School in the Bronx. He wore his high school jacket to show off the fact that he was the captain of the debate, chess, science, and history teams. Melvin strutted down the hallway of his school proudly but members of the football team walked pass him and purposely knocked him into the lockers. A large boy named John who was the team's offensive lineman said, "Get the fuck out of my way you jock wannabe motherfucker." Shamefully taken down a peg or two, Melvin bent over and picked up his books from the floor.

*****

On that very same day 175 miles away, a group of six 18-year old boys were scheduled for discharge from Peachtree Boys Facility. The state had no legal right to hold them at that age. The group entered the boys' shower for the last time. They called themselves the "Sick Six", because they were infamous for terrorizing younger boys by the order of the brunette who she felt needed discipline. The boys all muscular in size entered the shower with towels around them and held pantyhose filled with fresh bars of soap. Butch stood under the warm water that rinsed the dirt away from his body and looked behind him as he heard the entrance door close.

"Butch my man, how are you?" asked Casey a freckled face kid from New Jersey.

Butch moved from under the water and looked at the six teenagers as they formed a semi circle around him. Butch never said a word but quickly grabbed his drying towel and saturated it with water. Butch stood naked in front of the gang as he wrapped the towel around his fist while he braced for the first attacker.

"Come on Butch we don't have to do it like this man. I mean, you have been very smart to avoid an ass reaming ever since you arrived here. Forget about that now my friend and just take it, because we'll be gone tomorrow morning. All six of us will get a piece of your pretty brown ass today. Look Butch, Jeff even bought a bowl of lard so you won't feel it so much man", Casey said with a grin.

While his heart pumped faster, Butch did his best to hide the fear on his face as the six teenagers started to swing their soap-filled pantyhose.

Another teenager in the group named Peter quickly moved in and swung his soap but missed because Butch dodged his blow.

"Knock his ass out Pete, he ain't shit!" screamed Alvin a tall lanky kid from Jersey too. Butch backed up in the shower stall and did his best not to slip on the wet surface. Butch loosened the towel from around his hand and quickly tied one end into a knot again placing it under the running water. Barefoot and naked, Butch braced himself on dry tile and got ready.

Casey grinned at Butch and confessed his admiration, "You got balls my friend but now you are going to feel ours banging on your chin, Terry move in on his ass now!"

Terry rushed in while at the same time he swung his soap at Butch's nuts but instead caught his thigh, which resulted in a bad bruise. Butch cringed from the blow as he quickly swung his towel at Terry's head that struck him on the temple and sent Terry to the floor. Butch knew this would be his only chance to hurt at least one of his assailants. Butch pounced on top of Terry and rained blows all over his body.

Casey watched in frustration as Butch beat the hell out of Terry who was twice his size. Casey nodded his head towards Jeff who sat the bowl down that contained cooking lard.

From Butch's right side, Jeff raised his hose of soap and swung down and hit Butch in the back of the head. The blow shook Butch's skull as he rolled over on the wet shower floor while blood began to ooze from his head. Butch was dazed and confused as his vision was blurry. It was very difficult for Butch to focus on his assailants, who he heard laughing as they quickly picked him off the wet floor.

Butch's face was violently shoved into the wall while he heard the laughter and whispers of the teenagers behind him. They spread his arms and legs apart so that he resembled a human x.

"Now Butch, because you couldn't just give it up like a good boy, you won't even get the benefit of having lard to help ease the pain", said a Casey as he chuckled. Butch listened to the laughter of the boys behind him as he felt two hands spread his butt cheeks apart as Casey leaned against him harder. Butch closed his eyes and bit down on his bottom lip only to remember what his mother always preached- "Son watch what you do in life because you reap what you sow."

Butch shivered because he felt Casey's manhood pressed forcefully between his cheeks. Butch spit and cried as the inevitable was near. He did all he could to squeeze his cheeks together but Butch was too queasy from the blow to the head. Butch slowly turned around while he slid down to the floor and faintly made out a figure swinging what looked like a large club of some sort.

Butch rubbed blood away from his head as he tried to sit up and look at the "Sick Six" as they had fallen to the ground like dominoes. Butch looked at the drain where the water rolled down and strained his eyes because the water had turned red. All six teenagers screamed in agony while blood was everywhere. Butch held up his hands in a defensive manner because the figure walked towards him.

Butch felt like his head was spinning one thousand turns a second. He could no longer feel the water hit his body because the figure turned it off. Towels were wrapped around his lower torso and head as Butch grabbed onto the tree trunk arms that easily lifted him off the shower floor. The figure began to carry Butch out of the shower room as he looked down at the carnage of bodies that lay motionless from the savage beating that they received from the figure. Closer to the exit, Butch heard the echo of the voice of the figure that not only saved his manhood, but his life as well, "Everything is okay big brother, let's get out of here before she finds us. Don't worry big brother, Zig is here."

*****

The brunette paced and stared disapprovingly at the six teenagers who had bandages and bruises all over their bodies. She walked over to each individual and put inside their hands ten subway tokens, a three day hotel voucher, a Pathmark voucher worth fifty dollars, and three hundred dollars in cash.

"As of this moment you six are no longer eligible for residency at the Peachtree Facility. You will all take your belongings and the subsidies the state has provided and begin your lives in this world. In other words, get the fuck out of here!"

Ten orderlies escorted the six teenagers out the door and off the property. The brunette heard her phone ring. She gazed out of her office window as the teenagers disappeared off the grounds.

"Peachtree Facility, this is Miss. Sweet how can I help you? No, it didn't happen and I don't have time to explain. Listen, what the hell do you want from me? I guess they're more resilient than what we gave them credit for. You just make sure the payment is on time because a deal is a deal, understand?"

*****

Inside the living room of his home Donald Baker answered into his phone, "Yeah I know a deal is a deal, but you don't have a clue what I saw in Butch Steel's eyes when he was just fourteen years old. Those boys loved their parents hard. I've never seen such little boys with that kind of hatred in their eyes. I saw how they looked at my boy Melvin. Especially Butch, if looks could kill I wouldn't owe your ass one red dime Ms. Sweet because my son would be dead already. My son is a selfish ass teenager but I love him with all I've got so I'll send you the money but you make sure that you handle this shit ASAP. I already paid you good money to ensure the safety of my son. I know that bastard Butch has vengeance in his heart."

*****

Miss. Sweet peered out of her window and answered, "Don't tell me what you saw in Butch's eyes Mr. Baker do you understand? I see it every day from six in the morning until I leave this fucking place. So like I said just wire what is mine and maybe I'll see if I can do something else before the fucking Steel Brothers turn eighteen." Miss. Sweet hung up her phone and slowly turned around to leave her office when in front of her door was a bandaged Butch who leaned on Zig for support. The brunette took two steps back as the Steel Brothers both grinned at the same time.

Chapter Six
Do The Time, Don't Let The Time Do You

August 1988 found the Steel Brothers drenched with sweat as they stood inside the enormous kitchen of the Peachtree facility. Without windows and air circulation, Butch and Zig scrubbed hundreds of over-sized pots and pans with burnt food inside them. They used their shirts as bandanas and worked vigorously as 3:00PM drew near.

"Zig, remember what doesn't kill you makes you stronger, do you hear me? Our time is drawing near. This is just a test for the next two months, and once this test is completed we will be out of here" said Butch.

"Butch, what if they say I can't leave because I'm ten months behind you? What if they try to separate us?" Zig asked.

Butch passed a wet pot to his brother calmly and answered, "That won't happen Zig because when I turn eighteen according to the state, I will be your only known relative and considered to be your legal guardian. The state doesn't want to continue paying for your care when they can just pass you onto me. Besides, we both earned our GED's so that shows more proof that we are responsible people."

Zig looked at his prune fingers as a smile came to his face and asked, "Butch where will we go once we're free?"

"We have to find that lawyer that showed up after mom and pops funeral because I believe he can help us collect whatever money is left for us."

"Butch that was so long ago how will we find him?" Zig asked.

Butch grabbed another steel wool pad from the shelf and answered, "You let me worry about that little brother, okay? I'll find him, trust me."

*****

Three o'clock approached in the brother's stood at attention as Miss. Sweet examined the pots and pans that the Steel Brothers scrubbed since eleven o'clock that morning. Dressed in all black, the brunette studied the large metal spoons with a hawk's eye and looked for any blemish. Butch stared straight ahead and glanced over at Zig who picked at the self-inflected scabs on his arms. Blood oozed out of his brother's arm so Butch kicked Zig's foot in an attempt to stop him.

Miss. Sweet touched the pots to make sure they were all dry. Butch noticed the four orderlies that stood at the kitchen's entrance. Butch sighed with relief as she appeared to leave. Butch's heart skipped a beat as she quickly turned around and took notice to a spoon that hung over the sink. The brunette walked over to the spoon to examine it and noticed a speckle of egg on the tip.

"I said to the two of you how I wanted this kitchen spotless did I not?" implied Ms. Sweet.

Zig, with a worried look on his face, quickly said, "Ma'am we can clean that spoon until it's real shiny and make it look like new, I promise."

Miss. Sweet looked at the frightened Zig and smiled devilishly, "No I'm afraid that's not good enough, you'll have to do them all again."

Butch looked at her as if she had lost her fucking mind and angrily retorted, "That's bullshit! Do you know how long that would take us? It's just one damn spoon bitch! Why are you doing this shit to us? You know damn well how long it would take us to wash these pots again!"

"Well that's too bad Mr. Steel, because I have state inspectors coming today and I won't let you ruin this for my facility. I suggest you get a new supply of steel wool pads and soap", said Miss. Sweet.

Butch took two steps towards the woman and said through clinched teeth, "You're a fucking bitch and I hate you. I hope you rot in hell, you no good whore!"

The orderlies moved in as Butch reached for a large pot and began to hurl it towards Miss. Sweet who quickly ducked behind a nearby refrigerator. All hell broke loose as pots flew and crashed around the kitchen. Butch dashed towards the brunette with mischief in his eyes, but was tripped by two orderlies who beat him with leather straps. Another orderly rushed Miss. Sweet out of the kitchen while the fourth orderly held Zig in a choke.

"Hurry up and get them to the dungeon! Keep them there until the inspectors are gone and you know what to do with them next. Hurry up and get them out of here!" screamed Miss. Sweet.

The Steel Brothers were dragged away as Butch spat directly into the face of Ms. Sweet. She looked Butch directly in his eyes and simply smiled while licking the saliva off her lips.

*****

It was early October as Butch and Zig sat inside the library with about forty books stacked neatly in front of them. Butch was slightly swollen from this past month's beatings as he read a book on electronics while he glanced at a PC magazine. Butch spotted an article on how to find long lost relatives. He peered up at the calendar that was on the wall and calculated that he and Zig had thirty days until they received their ten tokens.

Zig sported two knots on his forehead but still studied three biographies all at once on General Douglas MacArthur, Napoleon Bonaparte and Genghis Khan. Zig took a break and began to study an encyclopedia that was opened to a section on guns. The brothers felt her presence but never looked up at Miss. Sweet who stood at the entrance door.

Miss. Sweet who was with her chief orderly asked him "What have they been up to for the past five weeks?"

"Nothing Miss. Sweet, they have been on their best behavior and all they do is read all day. They have been perfect borders.

The dictator looked at the boys calm demeanor and said, "That's what bothers me, why the change?"

*****

The time neared for the Steel Brothers' release as Butch and Zig spent most of their time in the library or inside the gymnasium working out together. Since they've arrived at the facility, the brothers have grown in size and weight. They both stood six feet tall as Zig outweighed his brother by thirty pounds. Both are ripped throughout their bodies with very little body fat and as each day passed their stamina increased from the two miles they ran every day. While they ran on the outdoor track field, the brothers sometimes took a quick glance up at Ms. Sweet's office window where they caught her every now and then as she watched them.

Rain or shine the brothers ran eight times around the track. Everyday Butch made sure he strapped around his waist the white baby doll Ms. Sweet gave him purposely on Christmas Day. Butch knew her nosey ass always watched them from her window; Butch wanted her to see him run with the baby doll by his side. Zig always asked his brother why he ran with that ugly doll, but Butch never answered him.

*****

Ten days were left before their release and Butch looked out of the library window and saw Margaret, the facility groundskeeper. After one of many beatings by the orderlies, Margaret felt sorry for Butch and would check on him secretly when he was inside the dungeon. Margaret was in her mid-forties but had the body of a vibrant young woman. Butch could tell she had the fever for him and he was damn determined to use that to his advantage. After she instructed three other gardeners where to take their lawn mowers, Margaret looked up at the library window where she saw Butch standing with his grey shirt half unbuttoned which revealed his

37

bare chiseled chest. Margaret nodded her head towards Butch in agreement.

Butch walked over to Zig who read about the civil war.

"I'll be right back little brother."

"Butch come on man you promised you would let me explain what Napoleon's biggest mistake was when he went up against the Russians."

"Zig just give me ten minutes. I have to go to the bathroom when I come back you can explain all of it to me."

Zig smiled at his brother and nodded his head in agreement.

*****

Inside a fifth floor broom closet Margaret rubbed and kissed Butch all over his face while he rubbed and squeezed her large breasts. Margaret breathed hard while she tried to keep her moans low. Margaret quickly unzipped her jumpsuit as it fell to her ankles. Margaret frantically pulled at Butch's zipper as she unzipped his pants and removed his manhood and placed it in her hands.

Margaret bit on Butch's lip and moaned, "Oh baby I missed you so much, you have no idea how pissed I was when you were in solitary last week. Oh shit, how I long for you baby. Hurry baby give it to me, I want all of this." Margaret said as she tugged at Butch's manhood.

Butch proceeded to give it to Margaret hard and fast like most eighteen year olds would. He grabbed onto her wide hips as the feeling consumed him. Butch listened to the moans of the woman as they became longer and louder. Butch enjoyed the ride.

*****

They both stood inside the closet and got dressed but Margaret couldn't keep her hands off her young lover as she said, "Damn baby I'm going to miss you when you leave, will you miss me?"

Butch tucked his shirt into his pants, wiped his face, and glanced at the woman "Yeah baby I'll miss you too, but we have to hurry, okay? Did you bring that for me?"

Margaret reached into her pocket and pulled out three small balloons. She placed them gently into Butch's hand, "Of course I did baby but please you must never let this get out."

"I will never tell anyone baby" said Butch as he slid his tongue in and out of Margaret's mouth for the last time.

*****

Two days until their release, Butch and Zig received handshakes from numerous teenagers that still had years to do before their release. The Steel Brothers gave away some of the things they had collected over the years such as work gloves, magazines and brand new winter socks, Miss. Sweet entered the room with orderlies that caused the small circle around Butch and Zig to dissipate.

"So the day is coming fast upon us when the infamous Steel Brothers will be exiting my facility. You know Butch, if it were up to me your brother would still remain with me for a little while longer", said Miss. Sweet.

No word was spoken as the brothers stood at attention and looked forward and remembered that this was small bullshit compared to what was awaiting them in two days: freedom and a life of opportunity.

"It's a harsh world out there Butch, do you really think you have the brains and courage to handle what's to come? I mean, you're fully responsible for your brother now with mommy and daddy being maggot food, who will you turn to?" Ms. Sweet asked.

Never blinking an eye, the brothers continued to look ahead and never responded once to the woman who grew agitated by the brothers' silence.

Closer to Butch, Miss. Sweet got directly into his face, "You and your brother will be nothing but pieces of shit. I promise the both of you that in three years you two will end up in a state penitentiary being fucked up your asses."

Still the brothers refused to look at the woman, Butch didn't blink or say a word. He just smelled the garbage breath of his tormentor. Miss. Sweet moved away from Butch. The brunette who was red faced and angry left the room with the orderlies.

*****

The day had arrived and the Steel Brothers with the same duffel bags they arrived with stood in the receptionist area and waited for their paper work to be completed. Still quite warm for Halloween day the brothers wore new clothes and white sneakers, while they held new jackets provided by the state. Up the hallway with a man by her side, Miss. Sweet carried two brown envelopes.

In front of the brothers the brunette stated, "Inside these envelopes you will find release papers, ten subway tokens, a voucher for a three night stay at a hotel in the Bronx, and three hundred dollars. You are now members of the human race, and the staff here at the Peachtree boys' facility wishes you all the best."

Butch and Zig were escorted to an awaiting van that would drive them to a train that would take them back to the city. The brothers walked out the doors and into the still warm October sunshine while

Butch softly rubbed his brother's neck. The brothers looked forward to their new future.

*****

Miss. Sweet buttoned her jacket and walked to her black station wagon that would take her home. She removed a pack of Chesterfields and matches from her coat pocket and felt a sudden brisk wind across her face. The woman covered her mouth as she saw little children dressed in Halloween costumes as they walked near the facility door.

"Get away from that door we have no candy! Go somewhere else for treats!" she yelled at the children while she reached for her car keys. Miss. Sweet looked for the car door key and unlocked it to enter the car. She stuck the key in the ignition and started the car up. With her headlights on, the brunette placed a cigarette in her mouth and lit it.

Miss. Sweet slowly began to drive off when suddenly she slammed on her brakes and put the car in park. Miss. Sweet wondered why she never noticed it as it hung right in front of her. The brunette stared at a dirty baby doll that swung from her rearview mirror. A puzzled look on her face, the woman grabbed hold of the doll that hung by a wire. With the lit cigarette in her mouth she became angry because of the prank. Miss. Sweet quickly yanked on the doll and pulled the body from the head. The body of the doll swung towards her and splashed gasoline in her face which ignited the cigarette in her mouth. In an instant Ms. Sweet's face and hair were in flames. The woman screamed and whaled inside the car as the flames spread quickly throughout the interior of the car.

The little trick or treaters all screamed and ran to their parents. The car was engulfed in flames as Miss. Sweets' hands and face melted away as she banged on the door window for help. Staff members ran from the facility with fire extinguishers but they stopped in their tracks and watched in horror as the station wagon explodes sending car parts and smoke into the atmosphere.

*****

Butch reflected back to their stay at Peachtree Facility and how every lesson their parents taught them came into play. Deep in thought, Butch remembered the burning desire to kill Miss. Sweet who did everything in her power to break Zig and him down. In the end though Butch was the triumphant one and felt no remorse for Ms. Sweet's possible demise. Butch believed she had it coming to her and besides in his eyes he was a hero. By possibly ridding Peachtree of Miss. Sweet, perhaps other boys wouldn't have to endure what they did. Butch was full of himself now because Miss. Sweet thought she had all the power and control. She deviously used every chance to cut the Steel Brothers down. Many times she succeeded but in the end, the brothers stood strong and united ready to handle anything that came their way. Butch looked out the window as the train moved smoothly across the tracks and he mentally began to put his "To do list" together.

Zig slept like a baby on his brother's shoulder, while Butch pulled out the miniature bible that his late father gave him before his death. He read the story about David and Goliath as the train headed in the direction of New York City.

Chapter Seven
Hey Sisters, Soul Sisters
Go Sisters, Soul Sisters

The evening of July 2006 found the Bronx still baking from the 101 degree high temperature from earlier that day. The twenty-four hour McDonald's restaurant on Burnside and Tremont Avenue was practically empty as Tim Henderson the night manager, along with two workers, tended to the restaurant. It was 3:30 in the morning, and the only people that ate were two woman both African-American in their mid- thirties. The women drank coffee while they shared a quarter-pounder value meal. If one were to look closer it would be easy to ascertain that they were a couple by the way they cuddled each other.

Tim was currently on the waiting list for the nursing program at B.C.C. He lived with his mother who was a registered nurse at the Bronx Veterans Hospital. The job at McDonalds was only temporary for him. Tim was about twenty-five and was a dark skinned brother. Tim studied a chemistry book while his two workers Delores age 19 and James age 20, talked to each other in a low tone, Tim looked back at the warmer and saw that the employees had enough burgers, fries, fish fillets and apple pies to satisfy any customer who may have strolled in with the munchies.

"Listen Delores in about fifteen minutes go to the freezer and start getting the breakfast food ready, okay?" asked Tim.

"Sure no problem, Tim" answered Delores.

"By the way, how's the baby doing?"

"Oh my goodness Tim, she is getting so fat for six months. Tim, are you still going to bring me the college application for the fall semester?" Delores asked.

"Yeah Delores I almost forgot about that, I'll get it to you, I promise. I can't stop a young sister from marching ahead."

Delores smiled and began to do as Tim had asked. James drained and cleaned out the deep fryer when three men in their late twenties entered the restaurant. The men wore shades, sported bald heads, and were dressed in black dungarees with white tee-shirts to match. They were six feet tall with ripped muscles from head to toe and wore menaced looks. Tim took notice and watched as one of the men sat at a table right by the entrance door while the two other men walked towards the counter.

Tim pushed his text book to the side and stood at the register and asked nervously, "Good morning gentlemen, welcome to McDonalds can I take your order?"

Two of the men stood next to each other as one of them who sported a seven inch scar on the left side of his face calmly answered, "We need a twelve piece of extra crispy and two large mashed potatoes with gravy."

"Sir, I'm sorry but we don't have that on our menu" answered Tim who looked behind him and saw that Delores and James looked a little nervous, too. Tim did his best to hold his composure and listened to another request from the second man who had a goatee.

"Oh we're sorry my man, what we meant was let us have three whopper with cheese value meals, and three apple pies."

The third man lit a cigarette by the entrance door as beads of sweat formed on Tim's head and Delores began to rub her hands together frantically.

"Sir, all I can serve is what is on the menu above my head. So if you would like something it would be my pleasure to serve you", asserted Tim.

The scar faced man grew impatient with Tim and said, "Okay partner you don't have chicken or whoppers, but I do know what you have. In the back room you have a black safe that contains the day's receipts and cash."

All at once the two men at the register pulled weapons from their pants and stuck them in Tim's face, while the man at the door pulled a black sawed off shotgun. He pointed it directly at the two women customers who held each other as tears swelled up in their eyes.

Tim shook uncontrollably while Delores and James leaned against each other and looked at the floor. The two men glanced at their watches and cocked their guns while Scarface mashed Tim in the face, "Go lock the door and turn the lights out over the tables. If you make any sudden moves I'll blow your fucking head off", declared Scarface.

Tim did as he was told and fumbled with the keys that were attached to his beltloop. Tim walked over to the door and couldn't help but let the tears fall from his eyes as the third man looked on. Tim locked the door and walked back over to the counter where he used a special key that controlled the lights. Tim sweated profusely as he dimmed the lights and waited for further instructions.

"Ok school boy, we're all going to the back where the safe is. If all goes well everyone is going home, but school boy if you play with me it will cost you dearly", growled Scarface.

The goatee man pointed at his partner by the door and said, "Get those bitches and bring them too."

The man pointed his shotgun at the two terrified women and demanded, "Let's go ladies and don't make me ask twice."

The two women gathered themselves and walked slowly in front of the man with the shotgun. They continued to walk behind the counter and stood with Tim, Delores and James.

"School boy, these lives are in your hands so lead the way to the safe and then we all can get out of here", said Scarface softly.

*****

The five civilians shook and whimpered as Scarface looked at his watch, "School boy, time is at a minimum so get that motherfucker open right now!"

Tim noticed the safe had a digital keyboard on the front of the door. He looked at the four people on the floor and then at Scarface, "Sir please understand okay? I'm just the manager not the owner. The only person who knows this combination is the owner, and he won't be in until ten o'clock this morning. Sir, please I swear, if I could open the safe I would do it, I swear."

"School boy are you a righty or lefty? Tell me what your best hand is when you play ball", asked Scarface.

Tim looked around the room for some guidance but only saw four panic-stricken faces as everyone looked nervous. Tim held his right hand up and answered, "My right hand sir is the one I use."

Scarface looked at Tim with a demonic smile on his face and nodded his head slowly. Then in an instant Scarface raised his weapon and fired a single shot that made a hole the size of a quarter through Tim's hand.

"Oh shit! Tim yelled as he fell to his knees and held his bloody hand. James, who was on the floor cowered in a nearby corner and covered his ears from the loud blast. Delores had crawled over to a pain-stricken Tim who drifted in and out of consciousness. Delores grabbed an old uniform and wrapped it around Tim's injured hand.

"Mister please, he's telling the truth! He doesn't know the combination. It's the honest truth only the owner knows it mister!" pleaded Delores.

The brown skinned woman who clutched her friend pleaded, "Please sir I have a husband and child at home. I have one hundred and forty dollars in my bag. It's yours if you want it. Just take it and let us go, this man needs a doctor."

Scarface reassessed the situation and looked at one of his partners and said, "Listen this cat don't know the combination like the rest of the managers have, so let's just get this over with. Take everything each one of them has, take them to the freezer, quickly tie them, lay the pipe to the women, kill their asses, and then get the hell out of here. It will be getting light in about an hour so let's do this"

"Why don't you just take the money and just go? Why do you have to do this to us? That girl is just a kid!" screamed the dark skinned female hostage who stood to her feet.

The robber with the shotgun walked in her direction and ordered, "Who the fuck told you to get up? You better sit your ass back down!"

"No! I'm not going to let you rape me! Just leave me alone! I don't want to die, please don't kill me!", the dark skinned woman yelled while she pulled at her hair.

"Grab that bitch and shut her up man!" ordered Scarface.

The robber with the shotgun doing as he was told quickly ran over to the woman with his weapon raised as if to strike her. Closer to her, the robber reached out with his free hand to grab the woman. The dark skinned woman with the quickness of a rattlesnake grabbed the man's wrist and broke it in two places which caused the bone to puncture through the skin.

"Oh shit my wrist! The robber yelled as the dark skinned woman quickly grabbed the shotgun and blasted the robber's head off his shoulders that splattered brains and blood all over the supply room walls.

"Kill that bitch!" Scarface screamed as he ran towards Delores with his hand gun drawn.

The robber with the goatee was dumbfounded by what he's just witnessed. He was too slow with his response and by the time he did, a 10" "Bowie" knife is shoved under his chin that killed him instantly. The brown skinned female quickly removed the knife and watched Scarface as he dragged Delores to the front entrance of the restaurant.

The two women looked at a scared Tim as the dark skinned woman told James, "Stay with your friend and keep pressure on that wound. You guys are going to be fine! Do you have a cell phone?"

James nodded his head yes and did his best not to look at the dead bodies that surrounded him. James quickly pulled out his phone and showed it to the women.

"Good. Now dial the police and tell them where to come, hurry!",
yelled the brown skin woman.

Scarface used Delores as a shield as he frantically banged on the exit
doors but couldn't get out because they were locked. He looked up at the
sky behind him and saw that it started to get a little lighter even though it
was just a little before 4:00 AM.

Both women reached inside their shirts and pulled out their Detective badges. They moved away from each other with their guns drawn to
get a beat on a nervous Scarface.

"You two bitches better let me walk out of this fucking restaurant or
I'll kill this girl I swear I will!"

The dark skinned detective squatted herself behind a set of tables
and chairs. "You got sixty seconds to try because I can see it in his eyes.
You got sixty seconds."

The brown skinned detective sat her weapon on the table and calmly
said, "Listen brother I know this seems bad but listen to me, I know
about the other McDonald's you guys robbed. I also know you have not
killed one person yet, but your friends are dead in the back and you're the
last one standing."

Her 9mm berretta in hand, the dark skinned detective said, "Hurry
up you got forty seconds, his pupils are beginning to dilate, he's gonna do
the girl"

The brown skinned detective boldly stated, "Come on partner, I
know for a fact you'll get eight to ten for the robberies, but if you pull that
trigger it's the death sentence. Please just lower the gun from her head.
She's a little kid with a baby; I know you don't want to kill her."

"You got twenty seconds left then all hell will break loose; he's
sweating a lot more, look at his arm pits" warned the dark skinned
detective.

"You shut the fuck up bitch! I ain't going to any jail! This bitch is
going to hell with me!"

It was clear Delores was consumed with fear as she urinated on herself. Delores cried which agitated Scarface as his index finger twitched on
the trigger of his weapon as the barrel of his gun pushed on the girls'
temple.

The brown-skinned sister made one last plea, "Brother don't go out
like this, think about what you're doing."

Drops of sweat fell from his nose and Scarface felt he had no hope.
He gently squeezed the trigger of the 44 caliber magnum a little more. The

brown skinned detective never looked at her partner and simply asked, "Jesse do you have him?"

Jesse James laid on the floor, still under the table, and marked her target. "I got him."

"You ain't got shit bitch! We are going to hell! Die Bi...."

BANG! BANG! Echoed inside the dining area as two bullets exited Jesse's weapon. One bullet removed Delores bamboo name earring before entering Scarface's mouth. The second bullet pierced his right eye and exited his skull only to shatter the glass door behind them.

His one eye still open, Scarface crumbled to the floor with his gun still clutched in his hand, but miraculously he never pulled the trigger. Delores near shock fell to the ground and held her ears. Brenda quickly rushed to her side and kicked the gun away from the dead Scarface.

Jesse back on her feet, holstered her weapon and looked down on her dead prey and yelled, "Guys it's all over. You two can come out now!"

James helped Tim from the back of the restaurant then looked at the scene in front of them. They both hurried over to Delores who sobbed in Brenda's arms.

Jesse looked at her watch and could hear from a distance that police sirens were near asked, "Tim how's your hand?"

"Officer I will be fine, I just want to thank you for saving our lives. I know for a fact those men would have killed us."

Jesse gazed out of the shattered door and saw the sky as it got brighter when she said to Brenda, "Damn I know already that it's going to be another hot one today."

The detectives gathered the civilians together and led everyone outside to squad cars and an emergency EMS truck that arrived on the scene.

Chapter Eight
Clocking Out

Jesse James and Brenda Simple were in Captain Ben Gordon's office at the 46th precinct. The two women received praises from their fellow officers on how they finally brought a stop to the McDonald's chain robberies. Jesse, a dark chocolate sister with a body like an athlete is 36 years-old and has been on the force for twelve years. Jesse was the first and only female to serve on a reconnaissance team in the Gulf War. She received a medal for bravery that resulted in the rescue of four fellow marines in the heat of combat. A sniper and weapons expert she once killed an enemy soldier with a single shot 300 yards away in the blinding rain.

After she served her tour, Jesse decided to follow in her father and grandfather's footsteps by becoming a police officer. Jesse was aware that both of them died in the line of duty, but she threw caution to the wind and became the leader of the vice squad. After several years of hard tactical street work, she passed the detective exam with flying colors and was reassigned to the homicide division. Street smart and hard-boiled, Jesse was not one to be fucked with. She could hold her own with anyone and commanded respect.

Right next to Jesse, cleaning her glasses, was 36 year-old Brenda Simple; also a twelve year veteran who was beautiful, bright and when pushed could be unforgiving. A graduate of Spellman College in Atlanta, Georgia, Brenda finished at the top of her class majoring in Chemistry. While working for DuPont in 1990, Brenda's father Hal Simple suffered a major stroke which forced Brenda to run her father's auto mechanic shop.

After the death of her father, and then her mother two months later, Brenda faced and accepted the responsibility to raise her then three-year old sister Vanessa. Four years later Brenda decided the auto repair business wasn't for her anymore so she sold the shop, bought a small single family home in the Bronx, and decided to take the police exam. She became the fastest ranking female officer in her department; Brenda took her detective exam six years later where she scored in the top three percent of her class. After Brenda joined the 46$^{th\ precinct,}$ Jesse and her had been partnered together for the past four years.

Totally different with their lifestyles and personalities, the two women meshed together like peanut butter and jelly. They shared some common beliefs: Never leave your partner behind; while on the job be relentless; fear no one; and bring their asses in dead or alive.

"Detectives I read your reports and I must say you two did your homework on this one. Very good detective work, but I still feel you two should have went to the hospital just to be checked out", said a concerned Captain Gordon who is a thirty-year veteran on the force.

"Captain, we're fine and thanks for the concern. We just want to get home, it's been a very long night and I know my baby is hungry", said Jesse.

Captain Gordon, a burly sized-white man chuckled at the detectives, "Yeah I can't blame you, but please be on point with the press. I have a funny feeling they'll try to put some type of twist on this whole damn thing."

"Don't worry sir, we'll make sure that they only get a taste, and not the whole meal" responded Brenda.

On that note, Brenda and Jesse left the captain's office and got ready to go home. They both had a loved one that waited at home.

*****

Brenda entered her yard and threw away all the circulars on the ground. Proudly she unlocked the door to her single family brick home located on Pelham Parkway South in the Bronx. Brenda's house was immaculate and had the scent of apple-cinnamon. As usual she laid her keys on her cherry stained dinette table as she sifted through her mail. Brenda took off her sneakers and placed them inside of her closet. Just before she put them away Brenda sprayed them with 'Frebreeze'.

Brenda headed to her kitchen to start her coffee maker. She noticed it was 7:18AM., so Brenda opened a nutrigrain bar and walked upstairs.

Slowly she cracked the bedroom door to look in on her heart and soul: seventeen, and soon to be eighteen year old baby sister Vanessa. Vanessa has a beautiful full-size canopy bed with her bedroom walls adorned with photos of renowned dancer's that she has studied since the age of five. Such photos of Gregory Hines, Fred Astaire, Savion Glover, and Michael Jackson. Vanessa is a light sleeper and sensed her sister's presence inside her room.

"Good morning baby sis, it's about that time. Go downstairs and fix yourself some breakfast, and I'll help you iron some clothes" said Brenda.

Vanessa sat up in her bed with cold in her eyes. She was so beautiful she could easily be a runway model. Vanessa gave her sister a crazy look.

"I can iron my own clothes! Besides, I really don't feel like going in today anyway.", replied Vanessa.

"Vanessa do you have any idea the kind of strings I had to pull to get you this summer job? Do you realize that there are hundreds of kids your age that would love to have your job? Vanessa for the last time, get up from that bed and get ready for work."

In a huff, Vanessa kicked the covers off of her and sucked.

"You know what Vanessa? Suck your teeth again and we can stop off at the dentist if you want?" Brenda said.

*****

Jesse got out of her red Dodge Charger and walked across the street into the courtyard. Jesse lived on Tiebout Avenue on the east side of the Bronx. Like clockwork, Jesse saw Roy the building's super as he swept the large well kept courtyard.

"Good morning Jesse what's up with you?"

"Hey what's up Roy, I'm doing good and you?" Jesse asked.

"Couple of people came by looking for you last night. Just wanted to let you know" Roy reported.

Jesse surveyed the courtyard and didn't see anything suspicious. "Thanks Roy, I believe I know who it was."

Roy nodded his head and continued to sweep the courtyard.

*****

Jesse entered her apartment and was knocked flat on to her butt. Instantly she held her hands to guard herself from the 10-inch tongue that tried to lick her face. Finally able to regain her balance, Jesse was face-to-face with her baby. Light brown; 42 inches on all four legs, weighing 245 pounds an English Mastiff that is to a dog what a lion is to a cat named Apollo. Jesse grabbed him by his large head and tried to keep him still, while Apollo was so happy to see her he left slob all over her hands.

"Ok baby, mommy's home. That's right I know you have to go take a big shit."

The gentle beast shuffled and barked loudly around Jesse while she removed her holsters and her cannons. Suddenly Jesse heard a knock at her door. Retrieving one of the Berettas, she held her finger to her mouth and Apollo was instantly silent. Jesse Quietly walked over to her door and listened for a second. Jesse looked down at the base of the door to check if she saw any shadows. Not seeing any she gently cocks her pistol.

"Yeah who is it?"

"Jesse it's me Tut, open up."

Jesse looked through her peephole to make sure her neighbor was alone and opened her door. Jesse's neighbor was a four foot-two inch, 70 pound man named King Tut. Jesse had known Tut for eight years.

Always neatly dressed and well groomed, King Tut was a 40 year old graduate of Fordham University with an undergraduate degree in Business Administration. The most impressive degree he obtained was a Doctorate degree in street knowledge. Anything happening on the streets Tut knew about it. Tut entered the apartment and was greeted by Apollo, who nudged the seventy pound man with his enormous head.

"Jesse please put this mutant dog up before he consumes my little ass."

Jesse closed the door behind her and laughed, "Well don't start nothing little man and it won't be nothing. What's up Tut, what you doing up so early?"

Tactically climbing on Jesse's couch, Tut expressed some concerns with Jesse, "At three o'clock this morning some dudes came by and knocked on your door. What worries me is that he didn't just send his men this time, but Hunger came with them. Now I know you feel that there is nothing to worry because the two of you being childhood friends, but Jesse he only makes visits when shit gets critical."

Jesse mulled over what Tut reported and wanted to ease his concern, "Listen friend, I don't want you worrying about this. Hunger knows he better not fuck around too much and get me pissed off. I promised him he would get what was his, and now he just has to wait."

"Jesse how much you owe him?" Tut asked.

Jesse reached out and rubbed Apollo across his head while she calmly answered, "I owe Hunger sixty thousand Tut, but like I said, he will get his money."

Tut stared at Jesse as if she has lost her mind, "Jesse you can't be serious right? How the hell did you let yourself get this deep in debt to him? Jesse you only make forty plus a year, and you got bills up the ass, what could you have possibly done to get this deep?"

"Well five thousand on the Seahawks versus the Steelers; fifteen thousand on the Mavericks versus the Heat; a little poker, and some other stupid shit; but hey that's my problem not yours. Look I don't want to talk about this shit anymore. Let's go get some breakfast", Jesse snapped while she changed the subject.

"Jesse, you just can't brush this shit off. Listen, I have twenty thousand in the bank, let's give it to them. I'm pretty sure it will buy you some time."

Jesse smiled at her friend and wondered to herself what this person saw in her, Jesse calmly replied "Hell no Tut, I could never take your last… and besides, Hunger will get his money. Now come on let's eat. Apollo is about to explode; besides he's been a good baby for not pissing on mommy's floor."

Jesse got her keys and put Apollo's leash on his neck. Jokingly she said to Tut, "Come on Tut, mommy will push boo boo in the swings."

Tut rolled his eyes towards the ceiling and said, "Yeah Jesse very funny."

Jesse and Tut were headed out the door when they came face to face with Hunger.

"Good morning my beautiful black sister, I see you're about to go for your daily little walk. Do you mind if we chat for a minute?"

Hunger stood six feet-three inches tall with a body chiseled from granite. Hunger was a brown skinned brother with hazel eyes and braids that came down to the middle of his back. Along with Hunger were two of his associates who were just as big as he was. Hunger wore jogging pants and a white wife beater and sported a ¾ inch thick platinum rope chain around his neck. "Come on sis you don't have to be at work for a while. I promise this won't take long."

Tut had a look of concern on his face as Jesse opened her door for Hunger and his guards while she pulled Apollo out of the way. "Tut I will catch up with you. Why don't you just go home I'll be fine," declared Jesse.

"No sis, this won't take up much time; Tut can stay, it's cool" said Hunger.

Tut looked at Jesse and couldn't understand how Hunger knew his name because they had never spoken before. Tut looked discreetly at the table where Jesse's Beretta's laid and made sure he stood there.

"By the way Jesse, how's your partner Brenda doing? What about her beautiful little sister Vanessa? She's only seventeen but what a long future she has in front of her" Hunger stated.

"Hunger in five months I will be able to borrow fifty-two thousand from my annuity account, and while we're waiting for the five months to pass, I can get my hands on five thousand tomorrow. During the five month wait I will give you six hundred a month which is another three thousand. That should set us straight, but you must understand those close to me have nothing to do with this." Jesse explained.

Hunger looked at his men and over to a nervous Tut with a "Who me?" look on his face, "Jesse baby stop! You're my sister and I love you girl, don't ever make that insinuation babygirl. It's just that the streets have eyes and if the streets see that I'm giving lay-away plans it won't look good on my behalf; do you understand sis?"

Jesse thought to herself she could never be Hunger's sister and hated when he referred to her as so. Jesse also knew that she didn't want to get other people involved. "Hunger that's the best plan I can come up with. So if you have a better one I'm willing to listen to it."

Hunger looked at Jesse and with the reflexes of a rattlesnake, smacked an unexpected King Tut across his face that knocked him to the floor and on his back.

Apollo barked violently, Hunger's guard pulled out a nickel- plated magnum and pointed it directly at the gargantuan beast. Jesse pulled his large head against her thigh and said, "Hunger don't hurt the ones I love brother, because it will only cause shit to get twisted, okay? Now, I said you'll have your money, but doing this only makes me want to get personal. How's your sister Sharon doing up at Riker's in protective custody? What about your baby brother Jeff in Spoffard? He's with the fourteen-year old kids' right? I heard the seventeen-year old age group can be brutal. Now let's do this right, and everyone will get what they want."

Hunger nodded to his guards, "Sis you know this is not what I want to do, but the streets are watching. I'll see you soon."

Jesse watched them leave her place and locked her door. She ran over to Tut who laid on the floor and held his throbbing head.

"Tut baby I'm so damn sorry, I never meant for you to get involved" Jesse lamented compassionately.

On his feet, Tut looked at Jesse evenly and said, "Reconsider my offer Jesse. You don't want this getting out of hand. Unless you have another plan you need to take Hunger's crazy ass seriously."

Jesse helped her friend to the couch and pondered her next move.

Chapter Nine
25 Years and Now It Is Time

In the beginning Butch and Zig worked odd jobs for about two years. They worked for the Sullivan Seafood Company for the past fifteen years. Butch and Zig started as maintenance workers but quickly advanced to overseeing the entire shipping and receiving department. They were responsible for shipments that went out to over twenty-seven different states in America.

They recalled the smell from the fish while they rode on the train. The brothers never complained or missed a single day in fifteen years on the job. Sixty-eight year old Eddie Sullivan founded his company before the brothers were born and grew so fond of them that he passed over his only son Lance to promote them.

The brothers never owned a car or went anywhere for a vacation. Butch and Zig saved every penny from their earnings, wasting nothing. The brothers always remembered the standards that their mother laid out for them in regards to women. Never got involved in a serious relationship and never indulge to anyone about their very private lives. Both brothers were in excellent physical shape and never caught a cold in twelve years. Once a year on this very day since their release from the boy's group home, Butch and Zig paid one visit to their parents' grave and laid eighty-one roses near their tombstones.

On this evening though, a new chapter would begin to unfold in their lives. Butch and Zig managed to save a substantial amount of money and were ready to move forward. This was a chapter that had been closed for the past twenty-five years and could no longer remain dormant. The brothers had goals and objectives that needed to be attended to and the time was at hand. Their boss approached his office so the brothers stood tall like soldiers and waited for him.

"Hey guys what are you two still doing here? You usually disappear as soon as you clock out, what gives?" Eddie asked.

"Mr. Sullivan, my brother Zig and I first off want to express our appreciation for your kindness and generosity for these past fifteen years. You have been nothing short of a gentleman which I can say proudly, and will take to my grave."

Eddie looked at Butch with puzzlement and asked, "Butch what are you talking about and why are you thanking me?"

Zig cleared his throat, "Mr. Sullivan we are here to let you know that Butch and I are officially resigning from the company."

"We can understand how this may seem sudden to you Mr. Sullivan, but due to circumstances that we can't elaborate on, please accept our gratitude for all that you have done for us", said Butch.

Eddie Sullivan held paperwork and did his best to control his hands that trembled as the news sent shockwaves throughout his body. How in the world he replace these workers who knew his business as well as he did?

"Butch and Zig listen, how about I raise your salaries from sixty-eight thousand to eighty thousand? We can keep the same agreement of paying you in cash off the books. I mean, I never knew why you guys wanted to be paid that way; but listen; I can let things stay the same. Please reconsider your decision because as smart as my son is, I know he can't replace you two" responded Eddie.

Zig looked at his watch then over at Butch who reached his hand out to Eddie, "Take care Mr. Sullivan and I believe you have an envelope for eight days pay, including four weeks of vacation?"

Eddie Sullivan shook Butch and Zig's hand for the final time. He walked into his office to calculate what he owed the brothers, took the cash from his safe, and placed the money inside two envelopes. Back in the hallway, Mr. Sullivan gave the Steel Brothers their last pay.

"Butch and Zig I want to thank you for all that you have contributed to this company for you shall be missed" said Eddie.

"Mr. Sullivan inside this envelope is all the computer discs containing the records and transactions that have been processed since you gave us that responsibility. Anyone with minimum skills in the distribution field will clearly understand what we were doing. Once again sir, good luck and take care" said Butch.

Eddie Sullivan stood with his mouth half open at his office door as the Steel Brothers turned and walked out of his company for the last time.

*****

On a train station platform in Brooklyn, Butch and Zig waited for the number 2 train to take them to 96th street in order to pay an old acquaintance a visit. Butch reached inside his shirt pocket and pulled out a piece of paper that read, "John Hatcher, Esq. 425 West 95th Street, Penthouse Suite"

Zig looked at his brother put the note back in his pocket and asked, "Butch, are you sure you can get into his suite? I mean, it's very secluded in the building."

Butch answered with confidence, "It took some working out but like I have always said to you, money and greed is a very powerful combination."

Their train rumbled into the station and the two of them waited for the doors to open so that they could get down to the business at hand.

*****

9:23PM and on top of the 44th floor high-rise roof were Butch, a sweaty Zig, John Hatcher, and his wife Candice. Butch looked over at his sweat soaked brother, "Zig this is why we do four hundred push-ups a day. Just hold on for a few minutes. I really believe this won't take long."

Butch stared at the terrified Hatcher couple, and said, "First off Mrs. Hatcher you have nothing to do with what is happening right now. You're just in the wrong place at the present moment. How your husband answers my questions will determine if you will be watching reruns of "Murder She Wrote." Please don't take this personal."

Close enough to John Hatcher so that their noses almost touched, Butch scowled, "Mr. Hatcher we are not going to play games with each other. I'm going to ask you a few questions and all I want is honest answers. If you tell me the truth there is a great possibility things will turn out fine. When my aunt passed away from her accident many years ago she was in charge of my parents finances. I have discovered that after my aunt died you were left with power of attorney, giving you authority over what solely belonged to my brother and me."

Hatcher scanned the New York skyline and then the concrete that was 500 feet below him. The retired lawyer swallowed and answered meekly, "Yes you're right, but I had you and your brother's best interest at hand, so I tried to invest the money into aggressive mutual funds but the market crashed resulting in a huge lost. That is the honest truth I swear on my children's eyes."

Butch looked alarmingly at a composed Zig and stated, "Zig did you hear that? Mr. Hatcher said he had our best interest at hand. Tell me why you don't believe him Zig."

Bracing himself Zig answered, "Because I know the truth and the truth will be told tonight."

Butch stroked Candice's grey hair that blew from the summer breeze, "No Mr. Hatcher this is what you did: When Candice got sick ten years ago you decided that you would get you a little lady on the side, and

56

from that little lady a lovechild was created named Tony. You gave, and continued to provide a good life to your bitch and bastard son. When your whore began to get greedy, you had to find a way to keep her quiet for the sake of your marriage and your prominent law practice. The motherfucking money that my parents worked so damn hard for, you used on your fucking child right Mr. Hatcher?"

The man who seemed so nice and sincere twenty-five years ago looked at Butch then at Zig stoically and made his final request. "Butch it's obvious that I did a terrible thing to you both. I only ask that you please let my wife go. She had nothing to do with this. Please Butch, I promise she won't say anything to anyone, I beg of you."

Mr. and Mrs. Hatcher almost shit their pants when Zig temporarily lost his grip of the rope. The Hatcher's were strapped to one another inside a chair that was strategically placed on the concrete ledge of their high-rise roof. Zig, with the strength of an ox held the chair steadily with the rope while Butch continued.

"I heard you say earlier she had nothing to do with this, but your wife just ended up at the wrong place at the wrong time and she will be going along with you for the ride."

"You no good sons of bitches! You and your brother are nothing but fucking animals and I hope you both burn in hell, you crazy fucking bastards!"

Butch looked at the man for the final time and responded calmly, "I have never killed or hurt anyone that didn't deserve it. I'll see you in the next life Mr. Hatcher, and I hope it was worth fucking with the Steel Brothers. Zig, make their asses scream."

Zig could feel the rope as it burned his hands when he finally released it and let the couple plummet to their deaths.

Butch didn't bother to look at the carnage below as he grabbed his brother by his arm and led him to the service elevator that would take them to the street .They would calmly go home and brainstorm about carrying out their next mission.

*****

1:00A.M. Saturday morning found the brothers in their two-bedroom apartment in the Bronx

The apartment was modest looking but clean enough that you could eat off the floor. The furniture looked like something a grandmother might have given them. Inside the living room sat a 20 inch television with an antenna with no cable box.

The Steel Brothers were about fifteen years behind technology. There was a rotary telephone on the kitchen wall, without a voicemail system. The brothers got up from the table and threw away their empty cartons that once contained mixed fruit from the Korean market. They sat back down at the table and began to discuss how they would spend the $745, 000.00 in cash that sat on the kitchen table.

"Zig listen up because we will only get one chance to make this happen, and I'd rather have one strong chance then to have many weak ones."

"Butch, I will not to let you down. I want this as bad as you do." Zig said.

"This money is what we worked hard for the past fifteen years. It will be used wisely. We will need many things, but I will first list the necessities. Most importantly we will need ten laptops networked together with wireless internet access and camera surveillance. We will also need six high powered cameras with zoom lenses along with night vision capacity. We will not work out of this apartment therefore we need to rent another one, preferably in the Bronx near the Hunts Point section. Zig I will need you to obtain four unregistered vans. I know a man who can get us passports with access to four continents and he can help us establish an offshore bank account. We will need to look at apartments in Canada just in case if we have to relocate. Most importantly Zig and I give this task to you because of your impeccable expertise. We need an arsenal of automatic and semi-automatic untraceable weapons. Can you handle this? Butch asked.

Zig saw in Butch's eyes the look of will and determination. "Butch, please leave the vans and weapons to me. I'll let you handle everything else. I say this because of your knowledge and expertise from the books you've been reading."

Butch looked at his brother and softly asked, "What about the four individuals we discussed five months ago? How is that coming along, and how long can they be trusted?"

"Yes Butch, they are all in place and are ready to meet with you at a moment's notice. As far as the trust factor goes, they can be trusted up until when we no longer need them."

"Fair enough then, you will set the meeting up in two weeks which gives us some time to finalize some things and get our heads in the game. Put the money in even bundles, wrap it in rubber bands along with saran wrap, and return it back to the safes."

In agreement, Zig asserts "Sure Butch whatever you say. Your plan sounds like a masterpiece."

"Thanks Zig, but it will not be a masterpiece until everything is completed. Listen, it's getting late and we have to run our seven miles in a few hours, so we better turn in when we're done. " Butch commanded.

"I agree bro, and like you always say, healthiness is the closest thing to Godliness."

*****

Butch stood in his room that contained only a twin size bed, a five-drawer dresser, and a bookshelf. On top of the bookshelf laid a radio that was set to the Bloomberg radio station. Butch never blinked once as he stared at a video game magazine cover that was framed and hung from his wall. The magazine cover featured Melvin Baker with his wife and two teenage children.

While Butch stared at the framed picture his eyes began to twitch. His hands closed tightly and created a huge fist. Butch's teeth grinded so hard his jaw began to hurt. The picture of Melvin Baker angered him to a point of no return; but on the other hand the thought of payback almost made him ejaculate where he stood. Payback was going to be sweet.

*****

Zig listened inside his bedroom to the creaky sound of Butch's bed. He waited and listened until he was sure that his brother was lying in his bed. Satisfied that he was, Zig quietly reached under his mattress and pulled out a manila envelope that contained photos. Zig looked at the mangled bodies of women at crime scenes that had been murdered in sadistic ways. Zig got the pictures from some guy he met at a porn shop in Manhattan. Zig began to look at the photos while at the same time he masturbated.

Chapter Ten
The American Family

Inside the large split level brick home on Mosholu Parkway in the Bronx were the African-American Baker family which consisted of 37 year-old Melvin, his wife and high school sweetheart 37 year-old Joyce, their 18 year-old twins Keith and Michelle, and adopted 9 year-old daughter Penny. Melvin had become an international millionaire as he was the co-creator of the number one video game on the market. He was extremely smart and savvy when it came to computer software. Melvin had earned so much money over the past few years that he bought enough of the company's stock to become a partner. However, Melvin didn't get to his upper status without cut throat tactics and pure selfishness, an attribute that had been a major ingredient that made up his character. Inside his den while in the dark, Melvin assessed his different assets online with his laptop.

The family checking account contained about nine hundred thousand dollars. Melvin tracked the spending that his wife had done within the last month, which consisted of daily visits to day spas, shopping malls and five hundred dollar per week hair salon visits for both her and Michelle.

"What the fuck is this woman doing with my damn money? This just doesn't make sense, who spends this much damn money on hair? This fucking shit is going to stop" proclaimed Melvin angrily.

Melvin struck another key on his laptop and his face lit up as he began to smile from ear to ear. He looked at his offshore account that had just posted his share of the video game that he co-created. The account had a balance of twenty six million dollars. Melvin quickly logged in with his password to transfer one million dollars into the family checking account. Like a kid who just got a new bike, Melvin patted his feet and smiled gleefully when he almost jumped out of his skin.

"So baby when is this big payoff coming to us, and when can mommy see it?" Joyce asked.

Melvin quickly and secretly pressed a key on the keyboard that closed the screen.

"Joyce I have asked you a hundred times about knocking on the door, I hate being snuck up on."

Joyce had on a white Versace jogging suit, walked slowly up to Melvin and slid herself on top of his lap.

"Oh come on baby don't be mad at mommy, you know I don't mean to."

Joyce unzipped her jacket and revealed her large firm breast to Melvin which he proceeded to feel with his left hand, as his right hand still remained on his keyboard. Joyce stuck her tongue inside her aroused husband's mouth and began to grind her large backside on top of Melvin. He started to get lost in the ecstasy as Joyce slowly opened her eyes and saw the balance of the family account which showed close to two million dollars.

Melvin aroused, slowly opened his eyes and saw that his wife paid little attention to him, because her eyes were fixated on the laptop screen.

*****

On the livingroom floor with her teddy bear was 9 year old Penny Baker who watched reruns of "The Jetsons" on a 60-inch plasma television while she ate Oreo cookies with a glass of milk. Penny was a brown skinned girl with shoulder length hair and soft brown eyes. She started to dip one of her cookies when Michelle entered the livingroom while on her cell phone.

"Oh shit Trina you serious? The "Mobb Deep" video is on now? Okay let me go girl, I'll talk to you later because I have to see it."

With no regard to Penny, Michelle grabbed the remote control and quickly changed the channel to BET where the video had just started. Penny with half a cookie in her mouth looked up at Michelle with total disappointment on her face.

"Hey I was watching that Michelle, that was rude."

"Oh bitch please, go watch that stupid shit upstairs in your room" retorted Michelle.

"That's not fair, this is my house too, and this is the family room" said Penny.

Michelle shook her head from side to side to the beat of the music and responded, "You're family by name only little girl so be gone."

Penny stared at Michelle who danced to the music, picked up the remote control and pointed it at the screen. Michelle looked at her with burning eyes and angrily asserted "Little girl if you do, I swear I will bust your skinny ass from here to the other end of this house!"

Penny peered at Michelle who was three times her size and gently put the remote down. Penny looked at her older tormentor with a hint of anger.

"I thought so, now take your ass to your room like I said", Michelle demanded as she began to roll up her three hundred dollar fresh hairstyle.

On the couch Michelle watched the next video then jumped up with shock and bewilderment as she felt a cold thick glob on top her head. Penny poured a combination of milk and cookies over her. Michelle quickly stood up and glared at Penny. Her three hundred dollar hair-do was done and Michelle saw red.

"Bitch you better run because your ass is dying in this house right now!"

Penny surveyed the livingroom and ran to the staircase that would lead to her room. She was yanked back violently by her long thick hair and thrown to the floor. While milk and cookies dripped from her chin, a crazed Michelle straddled Penny and repeatedly slapped her across the face.

"You just fucked with the wrong person you little bitch! I told you not to mess with me!" Michelle stated.

Penny shielded her face from Michelle's long fingernails and curled her body into a tight ball to minimize the pain of Michelle's blows.

Michelle looked up at the livingroom entrance and saw her brother Keith as he held his ipod with a smirk on his face.

"Oh shit, Little Orphan Annie did that to your weave?" Keith playfully asked.

Michelle had a handful of Penny's hair in both of her hands and got in one last kick to Penny's leg before she went to see the damage for herself.

"If I can't get this shit out of my hair bitch, I'll be back to finish kicking your little ass", promised an angry Michelle.

Michelle stormed out of the living room while Penny struggled to get up from the floor. Minor scratches were on her face and her hair somewhat jacked up, Penny calmly picked up the remote control and turned the television back to the cartoon network.

Keith looked at Penny and shook his head, "Raggedy Ann you really wanted to watch your show I guess, huh?"

*****

Around nine o'clock that night Melvin was in the shower as his wife Joyce came in to use the toilet. She sat on the toilet and decided to ask her husband a question, "Melvin you are a successful video programmer with a major company, why are we still living in the Bronx?"

"What's wrong with living in the Bronx? The neighborhood is quiet, the people are nice and most importantly, we attract very little attention to ourselves", Melvin replied while he rinsed his body.

Joyce considered Melvin's answer and continued, "I'll give you that, but my other issue with you concerns our account. I saw the amount on your laptop, and I know your new video game sold one million copies Melvin, and your share has to be larger than that. Now I'm your wife and have been with you when you had nothing, so why are you hiding things from me?"

Melvin rinsed more soap from his body and answered, "Listen Joyce, I think you're being paranoid. When have I ever complained about the shit you spend on these kids and yourself? I'm not stupid. I see the bank statement once a month, and see the beauty parlor visits, day spa treatments, five star lunches, and Donna Karen shopping sprees. So before we get into an argument Joyce, get up in the morning and watch the other women on this block get up and go to work every day, while you sleep to noon and shop every hour after."

Melvin hit Joyce below the belt. Joyce had no rebuttal. Therefore, she got up from the toilet and headed out the bathroom, but not before deciding to speak anyway. "All I'm saying Melvin, is that I know we have more money then what I saw on that screen earlier and I know you are not open with me about the money"

"Ok Joyce, why don't you go count your Gucci bags and add up the clothes in your walk-in closet", Melvin retorted..

Joyce was furious with Melvin so she flushed the toilet and made the shower water piping hot. Joyce closed the door with a smirk on her face as Melvin cursed up a storm.

*****

It was 2:35AM and Melvin examined his offshore account on his laptop. He plugged a barcode gun into the laptop as it downloaded software. After the download was completed, Melvin shut down his laptop and placed it inside a fireproof safe. Melvin got dressed and dialed a telephone number on his cell phone.

"Hey its Melvin listen, we have to do this now, okay? Yes, I know what time it is. I have a clock right in front of me, but that's too bad. We have to do this now before morning. Okay, we will be there in about an hour, and don't worry I'll have your money."

*****

Melvin drove his Escalade fast with no traffic north on I-95. Right next to him in the passenger seat was a half asleep Penny, confused as to why Mr. Baker took her out so late at night.

"Where are we going so late Mr. Baker?" Penny groggily asks.

"Don't worry baby. We will be back home real soon, and if you keep this our secret, I promise I will get you whatever you want."

"I want a new tea set for me and Mr. Snuggles."

Melvin glanced at his adopted daughter and responded, "You're a good girl Penny. You're the only one that doesn't give me trouble. So yes, I'll buy you the biggest tea set we can find. You just have to promise to be brave and keep this our secret, alright?"

Penny hugged her teddy bear and said, "I promise, Mr. Baker."

*****

Adam Coast sat in his small office in New Rochelle and was on his fourth can of coca-cola. Adam heard his front door buzzer ring. He checked the monitor and saw it was Melvin and Penny.

Adam pressed the intercom button and said, "Come on up Melvin." Adam walked to his staircase where he could see his guests as they approached. Adam saw how sleepy Penny was, he offered a suggestion, "Melvin I have a couch in my office, why don't you let the little girl rest there for a moment while I speak to you?"

Melvin walked Penny to the couch and closed the office door half-way. He then turned to Adam who appeared to be very concerned about the little girl's presence.

"Melvin I'll tell you what I said last week, I think what you're about to do is insane. When we're done I want my money, and I never want my name ever mentioned by you again do you understand me?" Adam boldly exclaimed.

"Like I said to you last week man, what happens here stays here. Believe me when we're done, I won't need to see or speak of you ever again. It's three-thirty and I want to hurry back before someone notices we're gone so let's stop talking" Melvin demanded.

The men entered the room where Penny was sleeping. Melvin tapped her gently on her shoulder, "Come on sweetheart this won't take long. I promise tomorrow you will have that tea set you want"

Penny rubbed her eyes and followed Melvin and Adam to the other room. "It's going to be okay sweetheart, I promise" Melvin assured Penny.

*****

Inside a make shift examining room, Melvin stood over Penny as she laid on the left side of her body, while a harness held her right arm up towards the ceiling. Adam tried his best not to look at Penny's large brown eyes as he removed a syringe from its packaging. He filled the syringe with a liquid that would be applied near her armpit for a local anesthesia. Adam used an alcohol pad to clean the area and said to the scared girl, "Penny this will sting a little, but it will help in making sure you won't feel any pain for a while."

Penny looked to Melvin for refuge as she braced herself for the stinging pinch of the needle. Adam stuck the needle right below Penny's armpit and slowly injected the anesthesia. He removed the needle then walked over to a table and started to set up a laser pen that was attached to a machine with knobs and buttons.

Adam pulled a white curtain in front of Penny's face and turned on the machine. Ready to use the laser on Penny's numb skin, Adam promised, "This won't take long Penny, just look at your father and I will be done soon."

Adam sat right next to Penny and told his little girl, "I'm here sweetheart. Soon you will be back in your bed."

*****

Penny sat inside the Escalade with a gauze pad under her arm while Melvin and Adam stood outside the truck talking.

"Good job Adam, and for your work here is what I promised you", said Melvin.

Adam took the thick envelope from Melvin and agreed, "Looks like fifty thousand to me Melvin. Like I said, never mention what took place here tonight, and likewise I won't either."

Melvin opened his vehicle door and looked at Adam with a smile, "Have a good life and with that money go buy some clothes, you look like a bum."

*****

It was 4:45AM and Melvin sat on the floor by Penny's bed while she slept without a care in the world. Melvin checked the hall and was satisfied that everyone was still asleep.

Melvin turned the laptop on and plugged the barcode gun in. He then lifted Penny's arm and removed the gauze pad. Penny moved a little but went right back to sleep again.

Melvin lifted her arm again and used a penlight to examine the work. to his utter surprise Penny's arm is practically healed and Melvin was sure it could be scanned. Melvin pointed the gun about two inches away from the barcode tattoo under Penny's arm. Melvin pressed the trigger on the reader which scanned Penny's armpit from left to right.

Refocused back to his laptop, Melvin smiled from ear to ear as the numbers register to the software which prompted Melvin to "Press Save." Carefully following directions, Melvin opened his offshore account and clicked on the link that said "Change Password."

Melvin downloaded the barcode into the password box and pressed "ENTER" and watched the blue indicator load at the bottom of his screen. Finally everything was complete. Melvin unplugged the barcode gun, shuts down his laptop and replaced the gauze back under Penny's armpit.

*****

Melvin was in the kitchen drinking orange juice when he jumped out of his skin from Joyce's voice.

"Melvin what is this shit!" Joyce yelled while she dragged Penny to the kitchen with her arm up in the air.

Melvin walked over to the table, retrieved a box and a police report to show to Joyce, "Calm down and let her arm go. I can explain everything if you relax and shut up, Joyce."

"Don't tell me to shut up Melvin! Look at this shit under her arm, what the hell did you do to this child?" Joyce demanded.

"What I did Joyce, if you must know; I took safety to the next level. A detective I met told me about a new program that can help parents track their children if they ever turned up missing. Here look at the kit and the police report if you don't believe me.

Joyce, looked at the box and read the police report, turned to a silent Penny then back at Melvin, "Listen I don't know what you're up to Melvin but I should have been told about this shit. I never heard of any shit like this, and tonight when I get back, you better be ready to explain it to me."

Joyce stormed out of the kitchen and slammed the box down on the table, while Melvin winked at Penny and sent her out the kitchen to follow Joyce upstairs. Melvin walked over to the sink to put his glass inside it. He peered out the window admiring his garden when he noticed a black mini van sitting across the street. It dawned on Melvin that this was probably the fourth time he saw that minivan outside his window. Melvin thought it was strange that he had never seen the person that drove the vehicle; yet there it was again. Melvin decided to get a closer look and started to go outside when in an instant the van pulled away and sped down the street.

"What the hell was that all about?" Melvin asked himself out loud.

Chapter Eleven
Two For The Price Of One

Monday evening inside the basement of the 46th precinct, Sergeant Stevie Simpson, leader of the narcotics division gave his team last instructions on the upcoming raid of drug kingpin, Mr. Frost.

"Okay everyone this is it so get in the zone. Everyone here knows Jesse and Brenda. They have been granted access because of their knowledge of the area and I feel they'll add pop to our bang."

The narcotics division prepared themselves as Jesse and Brenda made sure they had everything they needed. Jesse put on her vest that had an African spearhead on the front, checked and holstered two 9mm Berettas along with an 8-inch hunting knife that she slid inside her side pants pocket. Jesse also hid brass knuckles under a pair black Nike baseball batting gloves.

Brenda wore a black skull cap along with rose colored sunglasses. This sister holstered two 9mm glocks, and on her waist she carried a 50,000 watt taser gun along with a can of pepper spray. To top it off Brenda camouflaged her vest with a 'Donovan McNabb' jersey.

"Jesse and Brenda, I need you two to stand back and be alert. You both read the report on Frost and his crew. They are not afraid to fire first and have no problem killing based on the twenty-seven homicides they've accumulated already. We watch each others' back and front, no heroes, we work as a team, and everyone goes home safe tonight", instructed Sergeant Simpson.

The crew headed out to their awaiting cars while the sergeant patted every member of his team on the shoulder as they exited the building.

*****

The narcotics team sat in four separate cars on Creston Avenue and 187th Street. A large corner house three stories high was under surveillance. Jesse and Brenda wore ear pieces so they received updates and the sergeant's commands. Jesse, who used night binoculars, spotted two Suburban vehicles up the street. Jesse was sure that Simpson noticed the Suburban's too.

Jesse also saw a light come on from one of the windows, which meant someone was already in the house. The place was dark since the stakeout began which lead them to believe no one was inside the house.

The two SUV's pulled up to the house. The entire team watched as eleven people including Frost, a Dominican man in his forties around six feet tall and completely bald emerged from the truck.

"Oh shit hell no, look" Jesse said quietly.

In Frost's arms are a set of twin boys that look to be three years old. Close behind him was a Spanish woman around eight months pregnant. A group of five men and two very-hard looking Dominican women carried brown shopping bags. Frost surveyed the block while he removed keys from his pocket. The other four men surrounded him like secret servicemen protecting the president.

Jesse paid close attention to a man that seemed very familiar. His back was turned to her so she couldn't get a good look at his face. Brenda then taps Jesse on the shoulder because verbal transmission was coming through.

"This is it people, get ready. Let them all enter the house, but as soon as the door closes we are rushing in. We can't give them time to get settled. Take caution, there are children with them. If we can do this clean then great, but be aware these guys are ruthless. Eva you are assigned to the children, and when you get the chance you get them out of the house ASAP", ordered Simpson.

Eva Hernandez, a 40 year old Spanish woman with eleven years in the narcotics unit responded, "That's a copy Sarge I will extract children at all cost if possible."

Frost and his posse walked up the concrete steps of the large red house. Everyone on the stakeout was waiting for Simpson's command. Jesse and Brenda unlocked their car doors and got ready.

Once the last person entered the house, Sergeant Simpson kissed his crucifix and surveyed the surrounding area. While a few people were on the street, Simpson commanded through his transmitter, "Move In!"

Simpson placed the warrant in his back pocket and lead four members of his team to the front door while two other members ran towards the back of the house. Simpson pressed his transmitter and commanded, "Jesse and Brenda follow behind us let's go!"

"Showtime sis!" exclaimed Jesse as the two of them exited the Charger and ran towards the front door where Officer Henry Tate, a white officer who sports a razor sharp crew cut, was at the front door with a battering ram.

Officer Tate with all of his strength slammed the steel ram against the door and knocked it off the hinges. Sergeant Simpson lead the way with his weapon drawn shouted, "This is a raid nobody move!" He saw Frost's crew as they took cover throughout the large house.

Jesse, with heightened awareness saw the man reach inside his shirt screaming, "Come on fuckers!" The crazed man brandished a weapon and acted erratically. Jesse dropped to one knee and fires once hitting the man in his head, sending him sprawling to the floor.

"Frost don't do this man, give it up!" yelled Simpson as he cautiously ran towards the back of the house.

The narcotics team split up into pairs as Brenda yelled, "Sam on your nine!" At that moment a tall hairy man with a machete rushes towards Sam, a Spanish officer with six years in the unit.

Sam fired two shots that blasted the machete-waving man in his chest that killed him instantly. Sam, a little shaken turned to Brenda, kissed his two fingers and placed them near his heart, a gesture thanking Brenda. In response Brenda winked her eye at Sam silently expressing, you're welcome."

Simpson kicked the machete away from the man's body and motioned to Officers Ben Crate and Henry Tate to check upstairs. He indicated to Earl Wallace and Eva Hernandez to check the basement. Meanwhile, Clive Warner and Sam Peterson, both with three years in narcotics have just picked the lock on the back entrance of the house and entered cautiously.

Eva swiftly moved up the steps towards the basement door and held her hand up in a wait position. Behind her was Earl who led an old woman about 70 years old out the basement door. Simpson pointed towards the entrance door and motioned to Earl to get the old woman outside the house. Earl grabbed the old woman gently by the hand and led her quietly down the hallway. Out of nowhere the old woman pulled a .22 caliber handgun from her robe pocket and fired two rounds into the back of Earl's head. He instantly collapsed to the floor.

"Oh God, no!" screamed Eva as the officers turned and saw their comrade on the floor with blood oozing from his head. Absent of any hesitation, Simpson cocked his weapon and fired four rounds into the old woman that killed her instantly.

Eva rushed to her partner's side and screamed on her radio, "This is zebra one-three we have an officer down! Seeking medical assistance right away at one-two four Creston Avenue, Officer down! Repeat officer down!"

Blood was heavy on her hands and tears streamed down her face; Eva quickly got to her feet and ran towards the staircase. En route she pushed Simpson out of the way. Eva made her way between Ben and Henry who were squatted at the top of the stairs. Eva with all her experience let her emotions take over. Ascending to the top of the steps, Eva yelled "Game over Motherfucker's!" In a flash there was a thunderous explosion. It blasted through a bedroom door that Eva that Eva stood in front of. The impact ripped half of her head off.

The once beautiful wife and mother of two fell backwards down the staircase. Simpson yelled, "Call for Back up! Clive! Sam! Call for back up now!"

The officers covered each other while Clive ran back out the backdoor entrance. Gunfire rained down from a window above and hit Clive in the shoulder. Clive fell to the ground in agonizing pain and screamed out, "I'm hit!" Sam carefully reached out and grabbed his wounded partner by his arm and pulled him back into the kitchen.

"Sarge they're buried upstairs in the rooms! We need back up now!" Sam frantically warned.

"You just keep pressure on his wound and hold your position, back-up is on the way!" the sergeant answered.

Simpson reached for his cell phone but looked at it and noticed, "Fuck I have no signal!"

Sam looked at his phone and noticed the same, "Sergeant, I have no signal and I didn't hear a response on Eva's radio either."

Jesse looked at her phone. It too had no signal. "Listen everyone they're jamming our frequency from somewhere inside the house and from above they're keeping us at bay. At the same time, they're not allowing us to leave. Brenda, I need you to cover me while I try to get to the trunk of my car."

Brenda held a gun in each of her hands agreed, "Sergeant playing by the rules ain't working, and with all the gunfire blazing I don't hear a siren coming from anywhere. Keep your team back and covered, do not initiate anymore gunfire until we say so."

Simpson didn't want to risk any officers lives especially following what happened to Eva, Earl, and Clive but he knew they had to do something. Simpson looked at the two detectives and said, "Whatever we can do to take these bastards down let's do it."

Jesse checked her two Berettas and admonished "Keep them upstairs, and hopefully I will get them to come to us. We must remember they have two children up there so stay on point."

Jesse and Brenda cautiously walked towards the door. They stepped over the dead bodies of Earl and the old woman. Slowly approaching the door, Brenda eased out of it quietly but not before she looked up above at the rooms that were dark.

Brenda indicated to Jesse to come out as they walked close to the wall of the house. Brenda motioned to about ten civilians to leave the area. After the people dispersed and cleared the streets, Jesse took a chance and ran towards her Charger 70 feet away. While Jesse made a dash for her car, Brenda heard glass break above their heads. Not taking any chances Brenda fired in that direction with the hope of taking the attention away from Jesse.

After Brenda fired her gun, she pushed her body up against the wall, and noticed her partner had made it to the car.

Jesse who was out of breath opened her car trunk and revealed an arsenal of licensed weapons not issued by the police department. Jesse realized she had to think quickly and grabbed a tear gas launcher, semi-automatic assault rifle, five flash grenades, and two pair of night vision goggles. Jesse put everything around her shoulder and whistled to Brenda that she was ready.

Jesse crawled to a nearby tree that stood thirty feet from the house. Brenda fired six shots above her head which was reciprocated back at her. Brenda was relieved to hear police sirens that got closer, but still had to get Jesse safely back to the house.

Jesse took her partner's cue, as she proceeded behind a car directly in front of the house. Jesse placed the other weapons and accessories on the ground, took aim with the launcher and sent tear gas into each window with pinpoint accuracy. Not wasting time Jesse took the equipment off the floor and dashed back to the front door where Brenda still provided coverage.

Safely back inside the house, Jesse and Brenda ran for cover behind a wall and yelled to Simpson, "Get ready!"

Jesse and Brenda put their goggles around their necks. Then Jesse released the safety switch on her assault rifle. The tear gas was doing its job because people could be heard upstairs coughing and gasping for air.

"Please, police me pregnant with baby!" Coughing her head off the Hispanic woman begged. "Please my sons sick please!"

Simpson pointed his gun up the smoked filled staircase and shouted, "Come down with your hands up!"

The upstairs floor was completely dark and Jesse heard the sounds of a crying child as they got closer. The pregnant woman was now in view as Brenda saw the white dress she had on.

"Hurry up and come down with your hands up!" Brenda commanded.

The crying woman led her children down the steps as Simpson and Henry quickly grab and got them out of harm's way.

Jesse heard multiple steps above and knew others would follow. Airing on the side of caution Jesse screamed out, "Everyone take cover!" as she pulled the pins on two flash grenades and threw them upstairs. A bright flash lit up the top level of the house. When the smoke cleared Jesse and Brenda saw Frost and two of his men at the top of the staircase. Jesse was absolutely shocked because the man that seemed so familiar to her was none other than her bookie Hunger.

Brenda noticed that all four men were injured but still held their weapons.

Without hesitation, Jesse yelled, "They're armed!" and fired her assault rifle that killed two of the assailants at point blank range.

Brenda saw Hunger regain his bearings, so she fired off two shots which hit him in the head. The violent death of Hunger actually bought a smile to Jesse's face.

"Sarge they're down, but don't harm Frost! I'm sure he will have a lot to say, right?" said Jesse as she pulled out her knife and sliced Frost's Achilles tendon which caused the man to scream in agony.

Brenda saw two women on the floor covering their mouths as they cried.

"Get your asses up off that floor and stop that fucking crying. Shut up! She demanded.

The other officers made it up the stairs to process the scene. Simpson heard six uniform cops rush in with their guns drawn. "Hold your fire!, We're fellow officers! I have an injured man down there; get him some help, now!" Simpson yelled as he flashed his badge.

*****

The crime scene on Creston Avenue was roped off with yellow tape. Sergeant Simpson was being consoled by Captain Ben Gordon who just arrived on the scene. Also by Simpson's side are the surviving members of his narcotics unit. It was a solemn moment as Eva and Earl were taken to the city morgue while Clive was rushed to Union Hospital for his wounds.

Jesse and Brenda were examined by EMS workers for upper respiratory problems. Jesse stared at the six dead bodies that laid covered on the ground waiting to be moved. Frost's pregnant girlfriend and two kids were taken away in a squad car. Jesse couldn't help but to feel relieved and at ease as she studied the covered bodies and wondered which one was Hunger.

Brenda never turned to face Jesse and said to her calmly, "Jesse, he may be gone but you still have a problem. You have to get yourself some help because there is hundreds of Hungers out there waiting for you to believe you can win."

Jesse wore a shocked look on her face and began to ask, "Brenda how…"

"Jesse, I love you which means our relationship goes way beyond the job we do. You are my sister; therefore I am your keeper, which allows me to look out for you."

The two women just stared at all the action going on at the scene. No more words were spoken between the two as Captain Gordon approached and patted them both on the shoulder.

Chapter Twelve
Confessions

As Jesse walked up to her apartment, she wondered what would become of Eva and Earl's families. They must be going through hell, she thought. Jesse knew she would have to take out her uniform. She hated this task because it always meant she had lost a comrade and a friend. Jesse remembered the one time she met Eva's kids at the precincts' Christmas party last year. Jesse did something she hadn't done in a long time: She entered her apartment, kneeled by her couch and prayed.

*****

After she took a hot shower, hoping to have washed away last night's crime drama, Jesse sat on her couch with Apollo's large head in her lap. She was startled after hearing a frantic knock at her door.

"Go away! Jesse yelled with her eyes closed.

"Come on Jesse, it's Tut I know you had a rough one, but I need to show you something!" King Tut responded from the other side of the door.

"Come back later Tut, I'm so fucking tired man!" Jesse begged.

"Damn Jesse, I know you're tired. Open the door! Come on man, hurry up I'm serious!" Tut pleaded.

Jesse gently pushed Apollo's head off her lap, got up and walked to her door. "Hold on Tut, I'm coming."

Jesse was not prepared for what stood on the other side of her door. King Tut was wearing a brand new white two piece suit with white gators to match.

"Oh shit, you look like tattoo from "Fantasy Island" where's your boy Mister Rourke?" Jesse jokingly asked.

Kind of getting tired of her midget jokes, Tut took Jesse by the hand and said, "Yeah, yeah very funny. Just lock your door and come over please" Tut gently ordered.

Jesse kissed Apollo on the head and locked her door, "This better be good because I had a very long night, and the only reason I'm being humorous is to forget about the craziness last night."

As Tut led Jesse inside his apartment he told her, "I heard what happened, and I'm sorry about your friend Eva. I have a check ready to give to the family if you don't mine taking it from me?"

Looking around Tut's apartment which is immaculately clean and in perfect order, Jesse took notice to all of the African artifacts that adorn his livingroom wall.

"Tut I love your place; it holds so much history which we don't reflect on anymore."

"Thanks Jesse, the art always reminds me that we were once kings and queens, not just captives", says Tut.

Jesse twitching her nose to the air, looks at Tut asking, "Damn your place smells good, what's that?"

Smiling at Jesse, Tut says, "Follow me young lady, and I'll show you."

Tut directed Jesse to the diningroom where her mouth dropped wide open. Spread along the diningroom table were various types of food such as pancakes, strawberries, cooked apples with cinnamon, scrambled eggs, croissants, grits, beef sausage, freshly squeezed orange juice, freshly brewed coffee, and two white envelopes.

Jesse turned and gazed at Tut. She wanted to say something sarcastic, but couldn't because she was overwhelmed by Tut's love and concern for her.

Not saying a word, Jesse allowed Tut to lead her to a chair like a true gentlemen. Jesse felt warm inside because she hadn't been pampered by a man in years.

Tut sensed this and broke the silence; "Listen, this cost me half of my hustle money."

Jesse laughed out loud then grabbed a spoon and made Tut's plate first, "Thank you my friend, but a sister could get use to this."

To add a little ambience, Tut used his remote control to turn on his CD player. Earth, Wind, and Fire's "Reasons" played softly in the background.

*****

After Jesse and King Tut were done with their meals, Jesse had a comforting look on her face. She smiled at her friend, "Tut that was very nice and you didn't have to go through all this trouble, but damn it was good."

"You see Jesse, there's a lot you don't know about a brother, but it's cool because with time you will" Tut expressed.

"Tut where are you going with this?" Jesse asked.

"To a place where you can relax and do you and only you Do you wanna go baby?", Tut asked.

"Tut come on, how long have we known each other? You know I love you, but I'm not built for what you want baby."

Tut took a sip of orange juice and said, "Jesse I understand the persona; the guns, the knives, the three hundred sit ups and push ups, the fearless personality and that two hundred and fifty pound dog. All those attributes make up Miss. Jesse James. I also know that you're a woman who aches to be loved. I see a woman that wants to let her guard down and not have to worry about being taken advantage of."

Jesse sat across the table bewildered and speechless. After a brief moment she was able to speak; "Tut where is this coming from?"

"Jesse, everything that I say comes from my heart, and if you just put your fears behind you I'm pretty sure you'll feel the same way too."

Jesse did her best not to stare into Tut's green eyes and admitted, "Unfortunately my life is screwed up and this job, that dog and you is all I have. I'm so afraid that if I let anything change in my three ring circus, including our friendship, shit will never be the same again."

"Jesse, I understand what you're saying and I respect it, but I can never hide the feelings I have for you. Do you see those two envelopes right there?"

Jesse afraid to look, but can't help herself - "Yes Tut I see them" she answers coyly

"Jesse, those are two tickets that are open to go anywhere in this world you want to go. Just open your heart and allow yourself the freedom to love. You and I can go spend the most romantic two weeks that anyone has ever shared. Only if you let your heart lead yourself to me" said Tut.

The two of them sat in silence for about a minute. Then Tut broke the silence, "I'm sorry, I know you need some rest and time to get your head straight about your friends Eva and Earl. Come on I'll walk you to your door, and don't worry about Apollo I walked, better yet he walked me earlier before you came home."

"Always looking out for me, huh? Thanks a lot Tut" Jesse said..

Tut unlocked his door and watched Jesse leave. Tut reached in a vase nearby and removed a pink rose that he gave to her and asked, "Jesse, do you know why I'm giving you this rose?"

"No Tut I don't", Jesse answered.

"Because I want this rose to see what true beauty really is" Tut answered proudly.

"Tut I really never knew how much of a sweetheart you are. You are truly the best.

*****

Jesse sat inside her apartment and wondered if she could ever see King Tut in the same way again. Jesse admitted to herself that she felt very alive during breakfast and Tut really had her emotions swirling inside and out. Jesse felt Apollo as he pushed his head against her leg. Jesse still with rose said "Apollo mommy loves you too."

*****

Inside her kitchen Brenda was bobbing her head up and down while she listened to the SOS Band's, "Take Your Time". She prepared a grilled chicken salad sandwich for Vanessa and herself. Brenda glared up to the ceiling toward Vanessa's bedroom with a mean look on her face. She took a broomstick and banged on the ceiling yelling, "Turn that whatever your listening to down, Vanessa!"

*****

While Vanessa danced to the song "I Luv My Chick" by Busta Rhymes, Brenda angrily rushed to her sister's room. Brenda was going to bust in Vanessa's room but decided to sneak in and scare her instead. Brenda had to admit that the beat was hot that came from the boom box in the room. Carefully she opened the bedroom door and Brenda was amazed at how well Vanessa danced with so much rhythm, style, and grace.

Vanessa had on shorts, a t-shirt, and tube socks. She was sweating as she shuffled all over the floor. While spinning around, doing full splits, cha-cha-cha moves, and flaring her arms, Vanessa performed moves like a true professional dancer.

Startled Vanessa jumped back and held her chest, "Oh my goodness Brenda, how long have you been standing there?"

"Long enough to know that I need to get you back to church."

Vanessa wiped her head with a towel and uttered defensively "Oh here you go; I'm just dancing to a song. It's not like I'm in a BET uncut video."

Brenda checked out Vanessa's CD collection and said, "Whatever Miss thang. Wash your hands and come help me in the kitchen."

Giving Brenda a twisted look, Vanessa answered, "Yeah, sure old woman, what's the matter the Advil, ain't kicking in yet?"

*****

Brenda and Vanessa ate salad and drank ice-tea. Brenda lowered her Bose radio system.

"Vanessa I know you think I'm bossy and old fashion because of the way I hover over you sometimes. Baby you have to understand I love you and only want the best for you. I work these streets every night, and there are some real dirty people on them who mean a lot of us no good. I don't want any of that negativity touching you. So you're going to have to get use to my over protection for a little while. "

Vanessa gazed at her sister and tried to feel the sincerity of her comment, "Sis, I know this, and even though I walk around here with my little attitude at times, I'm not stupid. You're a single woman who happens to have a dangerous job with the added responsibility of myself and this house. Brenda, you know if I could, I would pay half of the bills with you."

Brenda reached out her hand to her sister and said, "Vanessa in September you will be a senior, and from the first day of your freshmen year, all I have stressed to you was to graduate. Yes, it can get tight around here, but that's for me to worry about not you. Just graduate Vanessa, I can't stress the importance of an education to you.

"Brenda, I know that, and I look at your wall everyday admiring what you have accomplished, even after losing momma and daddy. Listen sis, I'm not pregnant because I take my virginity seriously! I don't come in here all times of the night. I make sure I keep this house clean and study hard every night. Brenda I have a question. I'm seventeen years old and your little sister but we have not once done anything that sisters do with each other, not once. We don't do each other's hair, go to a club together, double-dating, or even hang out at the mall. Brenda why is that? Why do you treat me like I'm your daughter, and not your baby sister?

Brenda turned her head to Vanessa to explain, "When I was much younger than you Vanessa, momma and daddy were my backbone and rock. They instilled in me courage and determination never letting anything hold me back. Our mother, on her deathbed, made me promise that I would not run and hide from my responsibilities to you. To this day I haven't. So yes baby you have been treated like a daughter, but it is only because it is all I have ever known how to do."

Vanessa rested her hands on her sister's shoulders and told her, "You're my backbone and rock too, so never forget that I love and appreciate everything that you sacrifice for me. Don't you ever forget that, but you have to do me a huge favor?

Brenda who was very concerned said, "Name it."

"Let's have some fun before your arthritis and social security checks kick in?

Brenda punched Vanessa in the arm and expressed to her, "Alright now, I had enough with your "Old folk's comments.""

Brenda got up from the table and ran to the livingroom. She returned moments later with a CD in her hand. Vanessa was curious to know what CD Brenda was going to play. Brenda turned up the volume and ran back to the middle of the floor.

"Oh my goodness Brenda, what are you getting ready to do?" Vanessa asked with glee.

The CD player started rocking "Pump It Up" by Joe Budden's and Brenda did the only dances she knew- The Patty Duke, The Running Man, and The Smurf. Vanessa fell to the kitchen floor dying laughing with tears running down her face. All jokes aside, Vanessa knew all the dances Brenda was doing. Vanessa thought to herself that her sister had some skills but continued laughing because Brenda was working hard and sweating.

Chapter Thirteen
Information Is Power

In a large three room apartment located on Woodycrest Avenue in the Bronx, Butch studied the four walls inside the bedroom. On the walls were various photos of the Baker family involved in everyday activities in their lives.

Butch studied photos of Joyce attending her tennis club, hair salon, health spa treatment center, the supermarket, the bank, and her Friday matinee at the Cineplex. Butch watched Joyce like a hawk while he snapped his pictures of her. He noticed how Joyce goes out without any protection, and she never used a cell phone. What Butch did admire though, was the fact that Joyce never drifted off of her scheduled activities during the week. Joyce was a creature of habit and Butch planned on using that to his advantage.

On the other wall were pictures of Keith doing what teenage boys usually do with their time, such as hanging out at the Palisades Mall, shooting hoops at the park, going to the movies with his boys, and spending time with his girlfriend. The one thing that was relayed to Butch by one of his men was how possessive Keith was when it came down to both his brand new Mustang convertible, and his very pretty girlfriend. Butch thought of the car he never had the chance to own, and the girlfriend he missed out on just made him angry as hell towards that family.

Butch then looked at the other wall where there were pictures of Michelle who was captured doing nothing but shopping with her friends. One of Butch's other men reported that Michelle is very loud in public making herself the center of attention. Butch took notice to how in some snap shots Michelle always walked in front of her friends; like she was the leader and they were the followers. Her selfish behavior reminded Butch of her father Melvin. Butch was also informed that Michelle never paid attention to her surroundings when she was alone. She was always too busy talking on her cell phone even when she drove.

Finally, Butch's body tensed up as he stood in front of the color photos of Melvin Baker. Butch walked closer to the wall and rubbed his fingers smoothly across the pictures of his source of pain. Butch touched the picture of Melvin walking into the Manhattan office building where he made his fortune. That son-of-a-bitch wore a two-thousand dollar Armani suit while driving what had to be a one hundred thousand dollar custom made Escalade. Butch wondered to himself if Melvin even remembered the summer of 1981.

Melvin was blessed with a family that Butch thought one day he would have. Butch was amazed how in the few weeks of surveillance, Melvin spent no time with his family. Butch had photos of Melvin having power lunch meetings with his associates. They were eating swordfish sandwiches and drinking imported water. Just the thought of Melvin's life .pissed Butch off even more.

Butch smiled as he looked at a group of photos that caught Melvin's frequent visits to the "Affinia Hotel" with numerous female companions. Butch could have sent the photos to Joyce who would have surely took care of Melvin's ass but he stopped himself because Butch wanted Melvin more.

Butch looked at the photos of Melvin as he left the cemetery after he paid his respects to his dead parents who passed away ten years ago. Butch remembered how much kindness Donald tried to show them at their parents' funeral twenty-five years ago and smiled because it was Donald who tried to ruin Zig and him while at the group home.

Finally Butch studied five photos that always confused him and made him wonder. On a daily routine at least five times a week, a woman Butch didn't recognize always came by the Baker's home first thing in the morning, and left late in the evening. The lady didn't resemble a cleaning employee or a nanny, and besides, Butch thought to himself, why they would need a nanny? Their kids were eighteen years old. Whoever she was, Butch knew he would stick to the plan, and there was no way some unknown bystander would get in his way.

Butch walked over to his laptops and hit a button that uploaded live images from various wireless cameras. On the screens were live dates and times with the location of each camera. The Woodlawn Tennis Club, Palisades Shopping Mall east and west entrance; 275 Park Avenue front entrance; parking lot spot #188; Baker residence front, back, side, garage entrances; and the Bronx apartment.

On the laptop, Butch pulled up a log that had documented times of when members of the Baker family would arrive and leave from various locations. Butch got up from his chair Butch and moved over to a small safe where he removed a pile of ripped- up papers.

Butch had been able to get his hands on important pieces of mail that Melvin carelessly threw out. Butch was pleased with himself for being able to gather all of Melvin's information. Butch couldn't believe that someone with Melvin's savvy in software could be such a dumb-ass with his personal information.

The torn and somewhat dirty documents were spread throughout the table. Butch pieced together paper from Melvin's Chase bank accounts that included account numbers. Another ripped paper was an e-mail from Melvin's e-gold account. There was a credit card statement that Butch had got the account number and used on a few occasions, just to see if Melvin was on top of his financial business. The credit card remained open and Melvin never disputed the charges.

Finally Butch pushed the documents to the side and gently rubbed one document close to his face inhaling deeply. Butch looked at the document, which was an offshore account in the British, Virgin Islands. He smiled at the transfer of twenty-five million dollars from Melvin's software company.

Butch wondered how Melvin could be so stupid and lackadaisical with important documents, but at the same time be so on point when it came to this account. Butch discovered Melvin didn't have an average security password on this account, but a highly sophisticated one.

Butch spent most of his nights trying to break the password to Melvin's offshore account. He became angry and frustrated when he couldn't figure it out. It ate Butch alive that a punk-ass like Melvin could out think him. One day after retrieving more trash from Melvin's yard, Butch's eyes lit up. In the garbage bag was a box that once contained a barcode gun.

From additional research, Butch found out that this was new technology that businesses were now using to secure large sums of money. He strongly believed that the barcode gun held the key to what soon what be his.

For the first time in a while things were feeling right to Butch, as his plans and hopes took a turn for the better. Butch studied the laptop screens and saw that nothing was happening at the time. Butch decided to visit Zig in the next bedroom and challenge him to a game of chess.

*****

Butch opened his brother's door to make his challenge when he stopped at the entrance in disbelief. Zig is butt naked and covered in his own blood from head to toes. All of Butch's positive feelings were overtaken by despair. He could not contain his feelings as the tears fell. Zig's bare body trickled with blood from superficial created by their father's straight razor.

"Zig haven't I been there for you during our times of struggle?"

Zig looked down at the floor and softly answered, "Yes Butch, you have always been there for me and that's why I feel so ashamed right now."

Closer to his brother with sorrow in his eyes, Butch asked, "Zig, you have to tell me what's wrong with you. I can't help you if you don't tell me what's wrong, so please brother talk to me."

Zig felt the compassion illuminating from his brother's eyes, "Butch I swear nothing is…."

Like a rattlesnake striking at a mouse, Butch dashed across the room, grabbed his brother by the throat and slammed him up against the wall so hard that plaster crumbled from within.

"Hell no, don't tell me that nothing is wrong! Look at your fucking self in this mirror!" Butch demanded as he used all of his strength to pull the strong like an ox Zig towards a mirror and made him look at his hideously scarred body.

"Butch stop! This helps release the pain. Try to understand my pain! I want my mother and father back! Butch I miss them so much man!" Zig screamed while he tried to get away from his brother.

With his 19 inch biceps around Zig's neck Butch took him down to the floor. Butch squeezed tighter around Zig's neck and shouted," That's bullshit Zig! They have been gone for twenty-five fucking years, and guess what? They're not coming back!"

"Don't say that Butch! Don't you say that!"

In an attempt to calm Zig down, Butch stroked his brother's head softly, "Zig listen to me. In a very little while we will transfer our twenty-five year pain to the one who deserves it. We will leave this place and go far away forgetting all the loss and pain. It will just be you and me living a fruitful and pleasant life, but little brother, I need you man. I need you to be the General that I know you to be. You can't do this to yourself anymore because when you do this, I lose my focus. Like I said before, we will only get one chance, so staying focused is so very important."

The grip got loose from around his neck and Zig replied "Butch I can be the General you expect of me. I won't let us down. I just miss them so much."

Butch released Zig from his grip, got to his feet and looked down on the floor that was covered with blood.

Gently touching Zig's bruised body, Butch rubs his brother's bald head saying, "You have to get some help little brother. You can't do this to yourself anymore, right?"

Zig shook his head up and down and said, "I promise no more Butch."

Fire blazed inside Butch's eyes because he didn't believe his brother. Butch grabbed Zig by his ankles, and dragged him out the room towards the bathroom, "You must be cleansed from this bullshit Zig!"

"Butch please, no man! I swear no more!!" Zig yelled while he held on the door in an attempt to keep out of the bathroom.

Butch yanked Zig's ankles with all his strength and was able to pull his brother closer to the bathroom. Butch turned on the bathroom light and dragged Zig inside.

Butch held Zig in the bathtub while he filled it with warm water and epson salt. Butch proceeded to pour isopropyl rubbing alcohol directly onto Zig's open wounds and used all his strength to keep his brother still.

Zig slowly began to keep still and adapt to the pain.

It had been two hours since Zig's cleansing, and Butch adjusted the blowing fan on his brother's bandaged body. He walked over to his lap top computer and logged on to the internet for a search engine. Inside the search box Butch typed the word "Self Mutilation." Many definitions popped up and Butch had to decide which to choose from to help Zig with his dilemma.

Chapter Fourteen
The Last Supper

Thursday evening found the Baker family as usual on their own throughout their home doing their own thing. Keith sat inside his room and played his Xbox 360 on his 50 inch LCD flat screen, while on the phone with his girlfriend India.

"So, what's up Ma, we're going to the hotel tomorrow after the movies, right? No India, I don't want to see that, let's go see, "Waist Deep", cool?" Keith asked his girlfriend.

Keith peered to his left at his opened door and noticed that Penny stood there with her tea set.

"Hold on a minute baby, what is it Raggedy Ann? What do you want?" Keith asked.

"I have no one to play with Keith, can you play with me please?" asked Penny.

Keith held his hand over his cell phone and looked at Penny who wore a big pink bonnet, an oversized plaid dress and fake pearls. "Not right now Raggedy, I'm on the phone. Why don't you go ask Michelle, I'm pretty sure she would."

Keith focused back on his girlfriend as he slowly pushed his door closed until Penny was no longer in his view.

Inside the master bedroom was Joyce who looked through five different clothing catalogs while on the phone with her mother Bernice.

"Mama it's not like I'm some damn hood rat, okay? I've been here with him when his ass was working in the mailroom making fourteen thousand dollars a year. Now all of a sudden he wants to keep secrets and shit?" said Joyce sarcastically.

While Joyce listened to her mother she picked up and studied a pair of Versace shoes.

"Mama, what does me not having to work have to do with the price of coffee in Brazil? When I got pregnant I gave up my whole young life taking care of those kids so that his ashy ass could pursue his dreams."

"Then to top it off, after my accident on the horse ten years ago that destroyed any chance of me having anymore children, I gave in again to his wishes and adopted. Now guess who gave up another piece of her life again to raise another one? That's right mama, good old Joyce."

"Well you know what? From this day on Joyce does what the hell she wants, and will get what she wants. Tonight Melvin will know that I want out of the damn Bronx! I know his ass has money and damn if he won't start spending some of it! I'm driving out to Scarsdale to look at property, and you know what mama? He will build me an eight bedroom house on that property with a guest house attached to the side for you. His mother and father left this earth penniless while he was sitting on stocks and bonds. Well that won't be happening to you."

Joyce spotted Penny at her bedroom door and waved her in. With a smile on her face Penny ran and joyfully grabbed Joyce by one of her legs. While Bernice spoke on the other end, Joyce kissed, tickled, and made funny faces that made the little girl laugh.

"I'm just going to say this last thing mama, Tomorrow isn't promised to anybody, so from this point on I'm living. I have in my possession a brand new MasterCard with a twenty-five thousand dollar spending limit. Damn if I'm not coming to pick you up tomorrow so we can go shopping."

Joyce smiled down at Penny while she rubbed her fingers through Penny's soft hair and admired her big brown eyes.

Joyce playfully tugged at the 9-year old's nose and held up one finger to Penny gesturing for her to hold on.

"Listen Mama, I have to go but you just be ready around noon tomorrow. Alright then Mama bye-bye" said Joyce as she flipped her phone down.

"Now what do you want half-pint, huh? You want to play make up?" Joyce asked Penny who quickly shook her head up and down in agreement.

*****

It was 7:35PM when Melvin walked through the front door with three bags of food from Boston Market. "Hello everybody I'm home! Can everyone come to the dining room please?"

Melvin began to sit his dinnerware on the table when he turned his ear to the stairs. He could hear everyone began to come down to the dining room. Melvin loosened his tie, unbuttoned his collar and saw that Penny was the first to arrive.

"Hello young lady and how are you?" Melvin asked.

Her hair freshly done by Joyce earlier and with a little blush on her cheeks, Penny answered "Hello Mr. Baker, I'm fine thank you"

"Being that you're here first, would you mind helping me prepare the table?"

Penny nodded her head yes and skipped around the table setting the plates and silverware in place. Everyone entered the dining room while Melvin directed them to have a seat.

The food sat on the table as everyone took their seats. Melvin looked around at his family and said, "It has been nine months since we all sat at this dining room table together as a family, the last family dinner was on Thanksgiving Day and that's a damn shame. Sometimes I believe we all, including myself forget how good we have it here in this house. Everyone drives a brand new car and wears new clothes with not a care in the world, but what I also see is a family that is divided living in their own world."

Keith looked at his watch and his cell phone, "Dad the food is getting cold. I really need to take this call, so do you mind if we can eat?"

Joyce looked at her son and snapped, "Forget that damn phone! For once in your damn live Keith, will you care about someone besides yourself? Damn!"

Michelle rolled her eyes at her mother and said, "Mama you don't have to yell at Keith, I mean we never do anything as a family anyway, so why all of a sudden is tonight such a big deal?"

"You know why it's a big deal, Ms. Smartass? Because regardless of how unimportant you may think this is, your father obviously felt that this was something he needed to do. So Michelle do me a favor, shut your mouth before I walk around this table and smack the shit out of you, Joyce warned.

Michelle stared at her mother with a nasty look and Joyce stared back even harder, "Keep looking at me like you want some hear? I swear to you I will bust your nasty attitude acting ass, and give you a one way ticket to "Foot in my assville" you hear Michelle? Now keep playing."

Melvin didn't like the fact of not being able to continue, stepped in, "Please Joyce and Michelle let me finish. I know we have not done much as a family and I fault myself for that. I truly believe we have time to change all that so guess what? I have first class tickets to Florida, and passes to Disneyworld theme parks along with passes to Universal Studios. We will spend ten days there getting to know, love and appreciate each other. There will be no arguing or fighting, because if it is, I promise I will take away every electronic device you both love so much."

Keith had his mouth open and asked "Pop when are we planning to do all of this?"

"We will be leaving in two days so after dinner I suggest everyone start packing", answered Melvin.

"This Saturday, are you kidding?" August has just begun; do you know how hot and crowded that place will be during this part of the year?" Michelle implored.

"Come on man! I can't just pick up and leave, I have plans with India this weekend", responded Keith.

"Melvin this is nice and all, but don't you think it's a little much to get ready for this in just two days?" Joyce questioned.

"I want to go!" shouted a jubilant Penny.

"I know I'm springing this on everyone, but that's what's so exciting about it. In two days we will be leaving so we must pull together and make it happen. I don't want to debate about this, and it's not like anyone here besides myself has a job, so please no more excuses. I truly believe this trip is what this family needs to bring us closer" stated Melvin.

Penny jumped up from her chair and carefully began to remove the lids from the containers containing various side dishes.

Michelle looked at Penny who started to put food on everyone's plate, got up from her chair and helped her. Keith turned his phone off and began to put chicken and meatloaf on everyone's plate. Joyce looked at her daughter, and as a peace offering, gently rubbed Michelle's hand.

Everyone sat down and got ready to eat when Penny jumped up and went around the table to give everyone a kiss on the cheek.

*****

Joyce lied next to Melvin in their bed. She turned slowly towards him and said, "Melvin I know sometimes I can come off as snotty and bitchy, but I think what you did tonight was wonderful. I just want you to know that even though I may not say it much, I truly appreciate what you have brought to our lives. I'm going to stop complaining about everything including about living in the Bronx. I do realize that we are blessed. I will work hard to change the way I have been thinking lately."

Joyce retrieved the new credit she told her mother about and in front of Melvin, used scissors to destroy the card. Joyce walked back over to the bed and slowly removed her nightgown which exposed her shapely body. Back in the bed, Joyce removed Melvin's pajama pants and got on top of him giving him some much deserved passionate sex.

*****

Michelle was in her bed while she read the current issue of Vibe magazine. Michelle heard three light knocks at the door and answered "Come in."

The door slowly opened as Michelle peaked over her magazine and noticed Penny with her teddy bear.

Michelle sighed deeply, "Yes Penny."

"Michelle I know you're probably still mad at me, and you don't like me as a sister, but I keep hearing noises outside my window. Can I sleep with you?" Penny begged.

Michelle clearly saw that Penny was really scared. She put her magazine down, slowly pulled back her sheets and said, "Come on Raggedy...I mean Penny, you can sleep with me tonight."

Penny ran, jumps on the bed, and snuggled closely to Michelle. Penny was asleep instantly. Michelle felt remorse and acknowledged It, "I'm sorry" while she stroked Penny's hair gently. Michelle stood up and took one last look before she turned the lights off.

Chapter Fifteen
On My Command,
Unleash Hell

Friday morning at 9:00AM Butch and Zig stood in front of four men who went by the names of Blue, Green, Red and Black. The men all wore a short sleeve blue shirt with blue Levi jeans to match. They all sported a pair of black framed glasses. All the men had bald heads and were of a dark complexion. Butch provided the men with leather shaving bags that contained what they would need to complete their assignments. These men lacked emotion as they listened to Butch and Zig.

"Gentlemen, all six of us are wearing Tag Heuer chronograph watches that are synchronized to the second and you all know that time is of the essence for this to work precisely as planned. The preparations we've taken for the past sixteen days must pay off" Butch said as he instructed the crew.

"I've opened a bank account for each of you on this team. When this assignment is completed an amount of fifty thousand dollars will be wired into each account. We will also give you a passport so that you may choose to travel out of the country. You will lay low while this situation dies down", Zig added.

Butch walked over to a table and picked up four sets of keys. He gave a pair to each man, "Everyone will meet back here at the designated time, except for my brother and me. You all know what needs to be done once everyone is here, so please don't deviate from the plan. The time is now nine-fifteen and thirty four seconds, do you all understand?"

The four men looked at their watches and nodded their heads in agreement. Butch saw the coldness in their eyes and wondered where in the hell did Zig find these men? Butch decided not to ask because he didn't want Zig to think that he had no confidence in him.

Blue, Red and Green exited the apartment Black stayed with Butch and Zig. Butch pulled Zig to the side and whispered "Revenge is a dish best served cold and we are about to pull that shit from the motherfucking freezer."

*****

The Woodlawn tennis courts were basically empty because of the heat and humidity outside. Joyce moved like a star athlete is on the court.

She was hitting backhands as the feeder spat out lime green tennis balls at rapid speed. Joyce had on a powder blue two piece shorts suit and Nike tennis shoes. Joyce played like she would definitely qualify for an amateur tennis tournament if she wanted to compete. After about her two hundredth ball, Joyce ran to the other side and shut off the ball feeder.

Joyce sat on the bench and patted her face with a matching blue towel. While catching her breath, Joyce took sips of her very cold Propel energy drink. Joyce got the attention of two workers, "Excuse me! I'm finished with the feeder!" Joyce put away up her tennis rackets and the rest of her belongings and headed straight to the sauna.

*****

Joyce sat inside the sauna wrapped in white terrycloth towels and noticed two women holding their own conversation. Joyce got up from the bench to pour water over the hot rocks to make more steam. As she returned back to the bench she joked, "My goodness it feels like a sauna in here." Instantly the two women laughed and agreed with Joyce. She returned back to the bench and started to think about all the packing she had to do for their trip to Florida.

While Joyce relaxed in the sauna, she couldn't help but to appreciate how well-off she truly was. Joyce realized her family was dysfunctional and her husband was a liar, but it was "Her" family and she loved them dearly. All of a sudden the sauna door flew open and a huge man stood in the steam. The two other women also noticed the man while Joyce informed him, "Excuse me sir, but this sauna is for women only. The men use the other one at the end of the hall."

The man totally ignored what Joyce told him. He quickly walked over to the two women and with very little effort he slit their throats from ear to ear. Joyce was in shock and quivered in the presence of Mr. Blue. He quickly pulled out a tranquilizer gun, firing once, and hit Joyce in the side of her neck.

The drug was fast-acting as Joyce wobbled on her feet. Mr. Blue picked her up and moved her out the sauna in a dirty towel bin.

*****

Inside the Whitestone Multiplex Theater, Keith and his girlfriend India sat in theater #7 feeling very lucky that they were able to catch "Waist Deep" before it went to DVD. Keith surveyed the theater and noticed that they were the only two patrons present. India removed two Subway sandwiches, candy, chips and soda from her canvas bag as Keith helped her get things in order.

"Baby, you know if it was up to me I would rather be here this weekend with you slapping skins together in the Poconos" Keith revealed.

"Boo, it's cool; don't even sweat it. I think you and your family getting away for a week is so cute. We have our whole lives together to make our own plans, so let's just enjoy this day and cherish it okay baby?" said India.

Keith gave his girlfriend a long wet kiss, "I can't wait to get back so we can start choosing colleges together. Hopefully if you can keep up with me we'll graduate together, and you can work for me" Keith mused.

With a piece of sandwich in her mouth, India had to cover it so that food wouldn't spit out from her laughter. Keith looked up at the screen and silenced India because the previews were about to start. While Keith sipped his soda, he noticed the theatre door opened behind him. A bald-headed large man with glasses walked down the aisle. Keith hugged India and pulled her close to him. Keith tried to ignore the fact that the whole damn theater was empty but this cat sat right behind them.

The movie was started and India kissed Keith on the cheek. She then took a sip of her soda when she felt a tap on the back of her chair. India felt eerie with the man sitting behind them but she tried not to pay him any attention. She felt another kick, but this time it was more deliberate. India sucked her teeth and looked at Keith.

"Damn Keith let's move because this man keeps kicking my chair." India whispered.

Keith noticed that India was quite irritated so he turned to face the man when a cloud of reefer smoke was blown in his face on purpose.

"What the fuck is your punk ass turning around for bitch?" Mr. Green shouted at the young teenager.

India was very nervous and calmly whispered to Keith, "Baby lets' move, okay?"

"Bitch, shut the hell up and move your tender ass on my lap so you can feel what a real man has" Mr. Green lustily groused.

Keith about seven inches shorter and seventy pounds lighter, looked down at his girlfriend, then back at his tormenter, "Listen Mister we're just trying to watch the movie, we don't want a problem with you.

Mr. Green took his large plastic cup of soda and tossed the drink in Keith's face. "Sit your stupid ass down motherfucker while I take your whore to the men's room" he stated vehemently

Mr. Green pulled India by her shirt trying to get her closer to him. India quickly jerked away from him with disgust and shouted, "Get your damn hands off me before I call the police!"

"Bitch you ain't worth my time!" said Mr. Green as he pushed India so hard that she fell backwards and hit her head on the cement floor.

Keith wiped the soda from his face and saw his girlfriend on the floor. "You motherfucker, I'm gonna kill your ass!" Keith took a miscalculated swing at Mr. Green. Keith was yanked around his throat with one arm, while Mr. Green took a syringe from his pocket and removed the cap with his teeth. Mr. Green injected the liquid into Keith who tried to fight back. Mr. Green smiled with satisfaction as the liquid took effect and Keith was knocked out.

Mr. Green surveyed the projector room and the entrance doors. He lifted Keith over his shoulder and quickly removed him from the theater via the screen exit. Mr. Green continued to his min-van while India was left in the theatre unconscious.

*****

Michelle held bags of new clothes she planned to wear in Florida. She sat down at a table to enjoy the rest of her strawberry flavored water. Michelle was simply admiring the people that walked by her inside Green Acres Mall. Michelle spotted in the window of a young girl's boutique a short set that would look great on Penny. Michelle went inside the store and charged about two hundred dollars worth of clothes for Penny. Barely able to carry all of her shopping bags, Michelle made it to the doors that led to the mall's parking lot. Michelle searched through her purse, and was able to get her hands on her cell phone to call her friend Bernice.

"What's up girl, are you ready or what? Hurry up and wash your big ass, we have to hit the spa before I get on that plane, girl" Michelle gushed.

Finally approaching her white Acura RSX, Michelle clicked her automatic car starter while she mentioned to Bernice, "Girl you should see the outfits I bought my baby sister. What baby sister? Penny girl, who the hell do you think?"

While Michelle placed her shopping bags inside her trunk, a black mini-van driven by Mr. Red, slowly rolled up behind her and stopped. Michelle still on the phone suddenly noticed the shadow the vehicle created, "Wait a minute Bernice hold on for a second."

Michelle could barely move because the side of the van was inches away from her body. Not aware of what she did, Michelle flipped her phone and hung up on Bernice. Michelle tried to look inside the passenger door window while she yelled, "Excuse me, can you move your damn van, you have me pinned against my car!"

The person did not respond. Michelle managed to slide her body between the two vehicles and made her way to the driver's side and knocked on the tinted window. Still the driver didn't respond, "Listen dumb ass, I know you can hear me. If you don't move your car I will get security and have your raggedy shit towed."

Michelle banged harder on the glass with her fists and yelled "Listen for the last time can you please...."

The window rolled down and Michelle's expression changed as she was now face to face with the crazed-looking Mr. Red. "Excuse me, can you please move?" pleaded Michelle who was in awe of the size of Mr. Red's head.

Still no response, Michelle turned her head to locate a security officer when Mr. Red said, "Hey, you."

When Michelle turned back, she was caught directly in the face with pepper spray. Instantly feeling the burn, Michelle grabbed her face while screaming, "Oh shit, my eyes! Somebody help me!"

Acting quickly, Mr. Red jumped out of his van and tossed Michelle violently inside the van. He punched the screaming girl in her thigh and rolled up his window to muffle her cries. Mr. Red took Michelle's phone and smashed it against the dashboard; breaking it into little tiny pieces.

"My eyes burn, please somebody help me please!" Michelle begged as she tried to sit up in the van. Tired of hearing the whiney teenager, Mr. Red made his way to the Cross Island Expressway, and delivered another blow to the side of her head knocking her out cold. Mr. Red checked his watch and smiled because he knew he was clearly on schedule.

*****

On the 23rd floor of the Hightower Building on Park Avenue, Melvin is surrounded by his colleagues that work with him at Sunrise Electronics Corporation. Melvin stood next to his partners Chung Lee Wong and Tommy Pang while workers and friends took pictures as they all celebrated the success of their new video game, "Battle Planet Rising"

After hugging his partners, Melvin peered into the faces of his workers and expressed "Everyone should know by now that I'm not big on long speeches so, I won't start now. I just want to say how proud and privileged I feel to be a part of such a great group of people with such powerful minds as yours. Without you, and the two gentlemen by my side, my dreams would have never materialized. For that reason, I just want to say thank you so very much."

The people applauded as Melvin hugged Chung and Tommy before leaving for his office. Melvin smiled from ear to ear, as he received praises from everyone. "Come on everyone eat, this is a party!" Melvin replied before he called home.

After calling his house and everyone's cell phone number, a puzzled look came across Melvin's face. He wondered where his family could be, but decided not to let it concern him. Enticed by the laughing people outside his office, Melvin planned to have a few drinks before he headed home to get ready for the family trip.

*****

With briefcase in hand, Melvin exited the elevator and walked to his BMW 760Li Sedan. Melvin checked his cell phone for messages and saw he had none. Melvin thought to himself why his nanny Eunice was not at home with Penny which heightened his concern. He always instructed Eunice that he wanted Penny to spend the majority of her time inside the house.

Fifteen feet away, in the backseat of the mini-van Butch and Zig were salivating at the sight of the man who changed their lives twenty-five years ago. Butch never blinked while he watched Melvin walk towards his car. Zig was squeezing the van door handle so tight that he almost ripped the leather off of it. Mr. Black peered through the rearview mirror swears that he saw the Steel Brothers' eyes roll up in their heads. Mr. Black reached over to the passenger seat and checked the 50,000 volt taser gun making sure it's ready for use.

Melvin got closer to his car as the tears rolled down Butch's face. Visions of his parents being drug under Donald Baker's car fill his head with vivid memories of their death. Zig still believed he could smell his mother's blueberry pancakes she always made every Saturday for breakfast. Melvin was fifteen feet away from his car, and Zig softly whispered, - "Now."

With those instructions, Mr. Black quickly and calmly exited the van and walked towards Melvin.

"Excuse me Melvin Baker; may I have a word with you please?" Mr. Black asks diplomatically.

Melvin stopped four feet in front of the man and answered, "Do I know you, and how do you know my name?"

Never taking his eyes off Melvin, the calm Mr. Black aimed the taser at a panic-stricken Melvin who tried to turn and get away. Mr. Black then fired the taser gun that released two coiled cords into Melvin's back. The 50,000 volt darts hit Melvin in his back as he quickly fell to the ground and began to have spasms. Dislodging the wires, Mr. Black then tossed the gun back into the mini-van, retrieved an incapacitated Melvin, and handcuffed him with a thick Ty-wrap.

Mr. Black situated Melvin in the backseat. Melvin groggily moaned as he sat between the Steel brothers in the backseat. Mr. Black returned to the driver's side of the van and started the engine to quickly exit the parking garage.

Melvin wobbled back and forth between the Steel brothers. Butch put his face inches away from Melvin's eyes hoping the man would recognize him twenty-five years later. Zig stared at Melvin then slowly stuck his tongue out gliding it across Melvin's face as if he was a lollipop..

After taking a long deep sniff around Melvin's neck, Zig began to weep louder

Every so often Mr. Black would take took a peek at what was going on in the backseat. When Mr. Black saw Zig lick Melvin's face he quietly said to himself, "Oh shit, these brothers are fucking crazy."

Chapter Sixteen
Demons, DVD's, Batteries and Refugees

Inside a dimly lit room in a Bronx community center, Jesse sat in a circle of people who suffer from gambling addictions. The group listened to a man named Herod introducing himself, "My name is Herod, and I have a gambling addiction. Last year I owned three McDonald restaurants, two Bentley automobiles, a beautiful home and a loving family. I lost all of those possessions while creating three hundred thousand dollars in debt. I'm currently employed at a Brooklyn White Castle working the night shift. I haven't heard or seen from my family in nine months, and I miss…." Herod said as he broke down in tears.

Herod was comforted by group members while Jesse mustered up the courage to stand up and speak. "Hello everyone, my name is Jesse James and I have a gambling problem. In no way shape or form have I lost as much as Herod, or received so much pain because of it, but I truly believe that if I don't do something about my addiction I most certainly will suffer great losses. I see myself as a strong person but evaluating my current situation how it is out of control, I know I'm not invincible. I really hope with your support you all will be able to help me help myself."

The group gathered around to show Jesse and Herod support. as Brenda, Vanessa, and King Tut offer support by standing in the back of the room clapping softly.

*****

The meeting was over and Jesse shook her last hand when she headed for the door. She felt good as she came out of the group. Jesse felt even better once she stepped outside because Brenda, Vanessa, and Tut waited.

The four friends walked up Fordham Road which was crowded with shoppers and vendors alike. Vanessa stopped and looked at a new version of Nike's in a Footlocker window as Brenda said, "Okay Miss. Thing, the last time I checked your closet you had twelve pairs of brand new sneakers, so let's go."

"Brenda, you really looked through my closet?" Vanessa asked incredibly.

"All the time baby, I mean you never can be too sure about baby sisters", Brenda honestly answered.

With a roll of her eyes, Vanessa continued to look at the sneakers while she sipped on soda.

Tut walked close to Jesse as if he was her second skin, "Jesse, I'm really proud of you for seeking help. Remember there is nothing wrong admitting that you have a problem."

Jesse also noticed how close Tut walked next to her, "Thanks Tut, I'm glad you all came to lend support. Oh shit, there's my boy Abdul, my movie man."

Jesse walked toward the curb of the sidewalk and greeted Abdul. "What's up playa, how's my boy doing? I know you got some hot shit for me today."

Everyone gathered around Abdul as he replied, "Jesse my sister, how are you and that monster dog? Here, look at what I have for you."

Jesse looked on as Abdul pulled from his personal stash "Snakes on a plane"; "Ghost Rider"; "Crank"; and "Rocky Balboa." Jesse was too hyped, "Oh no, you didn't just hook a sister up! This shit won't be in the theater for months!"

Abdul smiled as if he just pleased his own mother. He handed Jesse the DVD's and said, "I got the hook up with a man who gets crystal clear promotional copies."

Brenda watched Jesse as she took the movies from Abdul and asked, "Hey Abdul, I'm Jesse's partner Detective Simple, do you have a vendor's license? In addition, did you know piracy is against the law here in the United States?"

Abdul quickly looked at Jesse and wondered to himself "What's up with your girl?" when Jesse intervened, "Abdul pay my sister no mind she just got her 'friend' today okay? Thanks a lot Abdul, tell wifey and the kids I said hello." With that, Jesse grabbed Brenda by the arm and pulled her away from Abdul.

"Brenda listen, don't do that shit okay? I've known that man for seven years and all he has ever done is take care of his family the best way possible."

"News flash Jesse, he's breaking the damn law. You taking those movies imply that it's alright to break a law. You took an oath to up hold the law, so please Jesse." Brenda replied.

"Oh please, go take your squeaky clean ass home. Always so high and mighty, you don't know shit about how I do things? I'm not trying to catch porgies baby, I'm going for the great white fucking shark", Jesse bellowed.

"Come on ladies, people are starting to look at us and Jesse, you know how I have a complex about being stared at." Tut admonished.

"Aunt Jesse stop screaming. Let's just go get something to eat, please", Vanessa pleaded with the brawlers.

A Chinese woman in her sixties pushed a cart filled with batteries, Krazy glue, trinkets, and water, "Jesse my friend how are you today!"

"Hey Ms. Lu, how you doing ma, what are you doing out here in all this heat?" Jesse asked.

Ms. Lu placed batteries in a plastic bag and handed them to Jesse, "I know you have no boyfriend so I make sure you always have new batteries Jesse."

Jesse, Vanessa, and Tut stood with their mouths open as Jesse screamed, "Oh no you didn't Ms. Lu, you are crazy! I don't handle my stuff like that!"

Tut and Vanessa busted out in laughter while Jesse grabbed the old woman gently around the neck and gave her a hug. While all this went on, Brenda watched while not flashing a smile.

Ms. Lu pulled Jesse's head down and whispered "Jesse help comes right?"

"Yes Ms. Lu it sure does, on a white horse so don't worry" Jesse answered.

The old woman waved goodbye to everyone as Jesse turned to her friends, "I'm hungry ya'll let's go!"

Brenda looked at the sky and replied, "I don't have an appetite anymore, Vanessa we're going home."

"No Brenda, come on let's go eat and enjoy the day", said Tut.

"Brenda, I'm hungry and besides, I wanted to do a little shopping so yeah come on don't do this", agreed Vanessa.

"Wait a minute everybody, let Brenda go home and think about what she saw today, because you know what Brenda? You're acting like a fucking rookie who just got her cherry popped. So please, do me a favor and go home. Vanessa, don't worry, you know aunt Jesse will come get you so we can watch these flicks. Brenda one more thing before you go home, one day maybe not tomorrow, you will face the decision of doing something that's not in your fucking comfort zone. I got your back though" Jesse stated.

Brenda grabbed Vanessa by the hand and began to walk in the opposite direction. King Tut reached out and pulled Jesse's hand as she looked at her partner walk away.

"Come on baby, let's enjoy the rest of the day because you have to work tomorrow", Tut insisted.

Jesse looked down at Tut, Jesse shook her head and walked towards the Grand Concourse.

*****

Friday, 6:30PM found Jesse and Brenda along with four plain clothes officers who sat in two vehicles across the street from a beige house on 184th street and Valentine Avenue. Two Chinese men had entered with two young girls that looked to be approximately 14 years old.

In the backseat of Jesse's car sat Ms. Lu who cried and pointed her finger at the house. Brenda looked at the old woman and gave her a napkin, "Its okay ma'am we will do everything in our power to make sure all goes smoothly. Try not to worry, we need you to stay in the car no matter what, do you understand?"

Ms. Lu wiped her eyes and looked at Jesse, "Jesse, you know everything I tell, yes? Please Jesse, you make me a promise."

Jesse checked her vest, two Berettas, and adjusted her shades. "When have I ever let you down Ms. Lu? You have nothing to worry about because I keep my promises."

Brenda grabbed her radio and chirped the officers in the other car. "Guys let's get on top of our game. Jerry and Don, you two take the side and back entrances. Our man just entered the home with two girls, so be aware of a possible hostage situation. Corey and Maurice stay on our nine and three; let's make this neat as possible. Are we ready?"

At the chirp of the radio, Jesse and Brenda heard "That's a copy Detective Simple whenever you're ready it's a go."

Brenda kissed her locket that held a picture of Vanessa, and pressed the button on her radio "Let's hit them and forget them."

Jesse and Brenda exited the vehicle as Ms. Lu lowered herself in the backseat. Jerry and Don quickly ran to their positions. Jesse with warrant in hand rushed to the front door and yelled, "This is the police and we have a warrant, open this motherfucker up!"

Corey saw people stop across the street to observe what was going on. "Jesse, we're ready?"

Jesse adjusted her weapons and responded, "Let's do it now!"

On that command, Maurice slapped the "Slug Buster" on the doorknob, and began to pump quickly until he heard a snap. When he removed the device, the officers looked at the 10-inch hole, and quickly kicked the door open.

Guns drawn, the officers rushed inside the house and the first thing that hit them was a strong stench. To guard themselves from the oppressive odor, they placed their hands over their nose and mouth. Jesse quickly scoped the house and spotted what looked close to 5,000 DVD's that were wrapped in plastic. Also found were hundreds of boric acid sticks used to kill roaches.

Jesse spotted a man run into the bathroom. "Police! Don't you move!" Jesse yelled as she aimed in the man's direction.

The officers cautiously moved to other sections of the house when a Chinese man around 40 years-old exited a bedroom and demanded, "Get back now! I will kill young bitch right now!" He held a 12-inch butcher knife to the girl's throat. The girl cried hysterically, was covered with dirt from head to toe, and wore nothing but a bra and panties.

Jesse still focused on the bathroom door, yelled, "Brenda, if one drop falls from her neck, blow his fucking ass back to Chinatown!"

"Pay attention to your door, I got him dead to rights!" Brenda yelled back.

Maurice and Corey returned to the living room and surrounded the man. Corey reported "No more bad guys inside Brenda, but we got a fucked up situation in the back bedroom!"

Jesse turned her head to look at the livingroom. The bathroom door quickly opened and revealed the other man who screamed, "You die now bitch!" Acting on pure instinct, Jesse moved away from the bathroom door and dove to the floor as the man held a lighter up to a can of roach spray. If Jesse didn't respond as fast as she did, the 2-foot stream of blue flame would have caught her right in the face.

While on the floor, Jesse blindly fired her berretta inside the bathroom and hit the man six times in his shins and knees. When the man hit the floor, Jesse slowly peeped inside the bathroom and could see he was immobilized. "I got his dumb ass now save the girl!" Jesse yelled, as she entered the bathroom. Jesse kicked the can and lighter away from the man and stepped on top of his wounded legs which caused him to scream in agony.

"Let me go, or I kill now!" the man continued to scream as the little girl urinated on herself. Their weapons drawn, Corey and Maurice watched the man spin towards them. Brenda in an attempt to keep the man calm said, "Listen to me! Calm down! Look at the two men, they are lowering their weapons!"

The man, who was confused, began to panic. Maurice and Corey placed their weapons on the floor. "Okay now you give me the girl right?

Let her free, I promise we won't hurt you, but you have to let her go" Brenda demanded.

"Let me go now! I kill now! Move away from door now!" the man yelled. Brenda, who lowered her weapon to the floor, never took her eyes off the little girl who sobbed uncontrollably.

"Look no guns right? Now you be nice and let that girl go" said Brenda evenly as she was on her knees while Jesse aimed her gun at the back of the man's head.

The man lowered the knife away from the girl's throat. He slowly smiled then yelled, as the blade was bought back to the girl's throat. "Fuck you, she die!" Unbeknownst to the man, Brenda removed her two shot Dellinger from her ankle holster and fired a shot that hit the man dead center in the head killing him instantly.

What seemed like slow motion, the man fell to the floor while Maurice grabbed the little girl and covered her with his shirt. Corey rushed to the bathroom and looked at the bleeding man as he muttered, "Call me doctor please!"

Corey turned the Chinese man on his stomach and responded, "Oh I don't know yet partner, let's see how I feel in about an hour."

Jesse tapped Brenda on the shoulder and asked "Boo, are you alright?"

"I'm cool, what about you? That bastard almost cooked you."

"I'm fine, but Corey mentioned that something ain't right in the back bedroom. Let's check that out. Wait a minute, Brenda hold on." Jesse said as she grabbed her radio.

"Jerry and Don all is clear, we got'em, but before you come in call for back up and child welfare."

"Roger, Jesse" responded Don.

Maurice sat by the little girl's side as the other officers entered the back bedroom finding twenty young girls shackled by their ankles to each other. Flies and roaches were everywhere as the room smelled like death. On the floor were hundreds of empty containers of noodles and rice that the girls had eaten. Jesse covered her mouth and walked past the girls who sat on the floor to open the window for fresh air. Jesse walked around and looked at the malnourished girls who ranged in ages from twelve to fifteen. They grabbed at Jesse's hands and legs crying for help.

"Let's get them out of these cuffs, Brenda demanded as she comforted one of the girls.

*****

Valentine Avenue was swamped with police cars, EMS trucks, health inspectors, child welfare workers, and four media vans. Jesse and Brenda stood by their car with Jerry and Don. Ms Lu cried and prayed to the sky, as she held her 14-year old granddaughter.

The reporters walked towards Jesse and Brenda and asked them, "Can you answer some questions?"

Maurice led Jesse and Brenda to their car as he shook his head and stated "No comment! Come to the stationhouse where you'll be informed."

Jesse started her car up with her partner by her side. Brenda cleared her throat and retorted "Great white shark, huh? Jesse I'm sorry"

With the car in drive and turning the volume up, Jesse blasted "Made You Look" by Nas.

"Fuck sorry tramp, I'm hungry and you're treating me to Amy Ruth's"

They pulled away from the scene and Brenda responded, "No problem my sister and I love you too."

Chapter Seventeen
Think Clearly and Choose Carefully

The mini-van door opened and Butch and Zig both removed a groggy Melvin whose head was covered with a black mask. Weak but coherent, Melvin felt the tight grip of his assailants as he was able to say a few words from under the mask, "What do you want from me, and who are you people?"

Butch checked out how well Melvin was dressed. Two-piece Armani suit with Italian leather shoes to match. Butch couldn't help but to remember how Zig and he had to share their clothes right down to their underwear. Butch indicated to Zig to take Melvin over towards some trees. Butch thought it was funny how Zig yanked Melvin violently causing him to stumble over tree roots.

Butch tapped the mini-van glass and Mr. Black asked "Yes Sir, what can I do for you?"

Butch pulled out a one hundred dollar bill and placed it inside Mr. Black's hand, "I need you to leave this vehicle with us. About a quarter mile past the gate is the main road where you can get a cab. When you catch your cab, you are to go straight to the spot. Stay there with the others until we contact you, is that clear?"

"No problem, I'll be standing by", Mr. Black said.

Mr. Black walked away until Butch could no longer see him. Butch then proceeded to walk over to where Zig and Melvin were. Butch stood directly in front of Melvin and said, "I will remove the mask from your head motherfucker. You will do nothing, and say nothing except listen, do you understand?"

Melvin was quiet until Zig jerked him by the arm. Melvin then nodded his head up and down in a 'Yes' gesture.

"Very good bitch, because I hate repeating myself. If you fail to follow my directions, I will get my axe and chop your motherfucking head off your neck. Are you sure you understand?

Melvin's knees almost buckled as he bobbed his head up and down again.

"I will trust you are a man of your word, so here we go", Butch said as he slowly removed the mask.

Melvin blinked rapidly as he adjusted his eyes to focus better and study his surroundings. Melvin was able to see hundreds of trees around him. As he turned to his right, he was face to face with Zig. Right away Melvin saw rage all over the man's face and death glare from his cold dark eyes. To his left stood Butch held the mask in his right hand, and an axe in the left. Butch stared hard at Melvin as he dropped the mask to the ground and slowly raised the axe over his head.

Butch held the axe high with both hands. He twisted his body and began to swing the axe directly at Melvin's head. Scared as hell, Melvin held his hands up to guard his face and screamed as death was just inches away.

Butch swung the axe right over Melvin's head and hit the tree instead. The blade of the axe was embedded in the large tree behind his head. Melvin fell to his knees, clutched his head in his hands, and shook like a baby.

While on his knees, Melvin realized he was in the middle of a cemetery surrounded by tombstones. Still in a state of fear, Melvin was held by the collar and yanked to his feet by a "Bad Intentions" Zig.

"Melvin just like that, death was coming right at you but you were given a second chance. You should feel fortunate because good people like Pete and Simone Steel were not as fortunate," Butch reminded him.

"Melvin, you remember Pete and Simone Steel don't you? Motherfucker, I said don't you!" Zig screamed.

Melvin was really confused and finally mumbled "But I don't understand. What do you want from me?"

Soon as the words left Melvin's mouth an irate Zig backslapped him across the mouth so hard Melvin's top and bottom lips bust wide open as blood flowed freely.

"No, not like this I told you!", yelled Butch.

Butch took a napkin from his pocket and handed it to Melvin. "Melvin I'm sorry about my brother, but twenty-five years of waiting to fuck your ass up has taken its toll on him. As I promised you earlier, I will explain who we are, why you're here, what you should do, and what you will give us. Time is critical, so let's get moving."

Butch led the way across the humid and damp cemetery grounds with Zig walking behind Melvin taunting him every few feet. Melvin looked around with the hope of recognizing someone he may have known. Melvin looked on the ground for a possible weapon of any kind and Butch whispered to him, "Bitch that wouldn't be wise, and besides if all goes well there will be no need for further violence."

Butch came to a halt. He looked at Melvin straight in the eyes and said, "Melvin these two tombstones were placed here twenty-five years ago, and the names on these tombstones belong to the greatest people I have ever known, my parents. To this day I never understood or accepted why they had to be buried here at such a young age."

Like a ton of bricks landing on his head it all came back to Melvin because he finally realized who these two men were- "Oh my goodness, the Steel brothers."

Zig whispered into Melvin's ear "In the motherfucking flesh you son of a bitch."

Butch kneeled down to the tombstones and gently wiped away the dirt as he turned to Melvin and demanded "Get on your fucking knees and don't make me ask twice."

Melvin felt the hot breath of Zig on his neck and never hesitated to do as he was told. Melvin finally got the courage to read the engravings on the tombstones, and with the tone of a mouse whispered, "It was so long ago, I was just a kid for goodness sake."

"That may be true and it may not be true motherfucker. The fact remains that during our parents' funeral your family seemed so sincere and remorseful about what you took away from us until I heard the phone call between your father and Miss. Sweet. From that moment I realized what was being done to Zig and me. I swore that everyone would taste the venom of the Steel brothers and motherfucker the reapers are here", Butch stated with conviction.

Melvin realized he would not be able to negotiate with these men, like he had with so many businessmen in the past and replied "Listen I have no idea what you want from me. I just want to go home to my family, so please tell me what I need to do to make that happen."

Butch looked at his brother Zig who clearly wanted to kill Melvin and answered, "Melvin, I will explain to you what you must do to gain your freedom and sustain your life. I want to make this very clear to you so it's imperative that you listen and think out your responses clearly. The axe that missed your head will be on time if you don't do what we ask. Do you understand?"

Melvin nodded his head, and then is kicked violently in his leg by Zig, "We don't speak sign fucking language you bastard, so when my brother asks a question you answer him!"

Absorbed by the blow to his leg, Melvin answered, "Yes I understand."

"First Melvin, I know about the offshore bank account. I also know how much money you received from Sunrise Electronics, but I won't reveal that at this time. Between now and two hours you will give me the barcode scanner that I know holds the code to the money. Are you following me?' hissed Butch.

Melvin remained on the ground in disbelief and answered, "Yes I understand. I will turn the money over to you, but I how can I trust you will let me go?"

Butch reached from behind his back and pulled out a folder from his pants and calmly displayed photos of Joyce, Michelle and Keith so Melvin could see them. "Because they need you motherfucker, that's why" Butch said to answer Melvin's question.

Melvin touched each photo with his hand and took notice to how they all had bruises on their faces. Tears began to swell up in Melvin's eyes and he wondered to himself why didn't they have a photo of Penny? If they had all of this information, then how could they have let Penny slip through the cracks? Melvin focused back on the photos and couldn't hold back the tears any longer as he realized that his family wouldn't be on a plane tomorrow morning.

"What have you done to my family? How do I know they are still alive?" Melvin tearfully asked.

Butch ignored Melvin's questions. "Secondly Melvin, I want you to stand and face my parent's graves issuing them a heartfelt apology on behalf of you and your parents. I want you to get your emotions together, and do this shit correct."

Melvin tried to gather his composure and stumbled to his feet. He turned and faced the graves like he was told. Butch and Zig looked at the man they pursued for most of their young adult lives. A sense of joy took over their bodies, as everything finally was falling into place.

"Melvin this can all be done and you can be back with your family you claim to love so dearly. Recognize the magnitude of your selfish actions, say you're sorry, then turn the scanner over to us and we're done. You have my word" Butch said.

Melvin looked at both Butch then Zig and mustered up as much mucus as he possibly could and spat out a white glob that landed on the tombstones.

"Fuck you and your parents you sick motherfuckers! I'm going to give you the money in exchange for my family, but that's where it ends!" Melvin courageously screamed.

Rage blazed in Zig's eyes as he leaped on Melvin's back and proceeded to beat him to the ground, while Butch stared at the DNA slowly running down his parent's tombstones.

"Zig stop! Get off of him right now!" demanded Butch.

Zig was dumbfounded at his brother's request but delivered one last blow, "Look what he did Butch! Look what he did to Mom and Pops!"

Butch walked over to Melvin and offered wisdom, "Pride kills the strongest of men Melvin, so let's go get the money to free your family. I'm sorry you found it so difficult to apologize to my parents, and I'm sure they would have appreciated it. Come on Zig; let's take his dumb ass home."

The Steel Brothers led Melvin back to the waiting mini-van while Melvin cried, "If my family is not alright and harmed in any way you bastards better have some place to hide with that money!"

*****

Melvin sat inside the mini-van in front of his house and watched the brothers quickly change into uniforms that looked like satellite TV. repairmen. While the sky turned orange from the sunset, Melvin reflected on his home he bought eleven years ago for his family. Melvin always felt a since of pride because he was the first person in his neighborhood to pay off his home early. Melvin realized all the missed opportunities of spending quality time with his family invaded his mine. How he wish he'd done things differently. Not sure if they were dead or alive, the tears of regret fell down his face.

"Melvin you can try to scream, yell or run if you like, but understand if you choose to do so, I promise your family will be dead in three minutes" Butch reminded him.

Melvin hoped that Penny and Eunice were not inside the house he replied, "I won't try anything stupid, but please don't harm my family!"

"I'm going to take the Ty-wraps off Melvin, and you will lead us into your home. So you better recognize what's at stake"

Butch retrieved a laptop and some cables while Zig carried a 30-inch flat screen plasma television. Both Butch and Zig wore uniforms; they also had on black leather gloves to avoid leaving fingerprints. Nonchalantly, Butch and Zig walked behind Melvin with bad intentions in their hearts.

*****

Melvin sat with his legs and wrist tied together with just enough slack to move them slightly. He watched Butch and Zig complete their hi-tech mini-network. Butch placed the laptop in front of Melvin and was satisfied that he would be able to type in the code to transfer the money into their account.

"Well Mr. Baker, it is now as they say- showtime" said Butch as he pressed F1 on the keyboard which turned on the plasma television. Melvin's eyes were fixated on the screen. He knew there was something sinister the brothers wanted him to see. Melvin was overwhelmed with feelings of doom. On the T.V. screen, in three separate chairs, Joyce, Keith and Michelle were bound and gagged.

Butch inserted a transmitter into his ear and started speaking, "Gentlemen take your positions now." Melvin was so afraid for his family that his heart felt like it would beat right out of his chest On the T.V. screen Melvin saw four men that wore black jumpsuits and ski mask who stood behind each member of his family. Each man held a semi-automatic weapon in his hand.

"Melvin, where is the barcode gun, and hurry because your family needs you" said Butch.

"Behind that family photograph is a safe, just swing the picture to the left" Melvin instructed.

Butch pulled a 12-inch knife from his pants leg and pressed it against Melvin's throat, "I really hope no booby traps are behind that picture Melvin."

Butch indicated to Zig to check out the picture. He watched his brother slowly swing the frame open that revealed a sunken vault. Zig smiled at his brother and turned the dial.

"The combination is eleven to the right, thirty-seven to the left and sixteen to the right. Just turn the handle, open the door and the gun is there" said Melvin.

Butch held his hand up to Zig not to proceed and then declared, "Melvin, if for some reason that safe has a silent alarm, and I hear cop cars near this house, I will be very disappointed."

"There is no alarm, I assure you of that" promised Melvin.

Butch pointed his finger at the safe and observed his brother turn the dial. While this was going on, Melvin saw Joyce nod her head at her children which made Melvin think she attempted to keep them calm. With all the hope in his soul, Melvin tried to make himself believe this ordeal would be over soon.

Butch had the barcode gun and connected it to another laptop. Melvin jumped with the sound of Zig's deep voice, "Log onto your account motherfucker!"

Melvin was logging on to his account when he remembered when the doctors revealed that Joyce would have twins. It was a happy moment in their lives. Once Melvin opened his online account, he was shocked at how savvy Butch was with navigating through restricted areas online. On one laptop Butch created an account, while on the other laptop he hacked into the barcode's password system. There was no doubt in Melvin's mind Butch knew what he was doing.

What Melvin noticed was that the actual amount in his account was not revealed. Melvin asked himself, "What if I was to give this asshole most of my money, but not all of it? There's a good chance I could use the rest of the money and get my family out of the country starting a new life. Damn this too risky because what if this son of a bitch knows? Also, where is Penny and what if he has her in hiding somewhere else? What if ..." Melvin was snapped back to reality by Butch's voice, "Melvin, this is it, the moment of truth. I need to ask you one final question. How much money will be transferred into my account today?"

Melvin looked at his family who were all terrified, swallowed his saliva and answered, "I'll be transferring twenty-four million dollars."

Butch stared at Melvin for a moment then erupted into a fit of rage, "You selfish, stupid bastard! You have to be the biggest fucking idiot in the world right now! Did you think I was fucking with you Melvin! Everything that is important to you is riding on your stupid ass doing the right thing, and you manage to fuck that up too!"

"No, wait I made a mistake! Please, I wasn't trying to fool you!" replied a red-faced Melvin whose eyes were filled with fear.

"Fuck you Melvin, all I have done is treat you like a man, giving you reassurances, and calling your sorry ass Mr. Baker instead of Mr. Cocksucker! You know what Melvin? I hope you enjoy the million fucking dollars!"

Zig violently grabbed Melvin from the back and tied him up with rope. Zig duct taped his mouth and positioned him directly in front of the plasma screen. Melvin started to cry hysterically as his idea backfired on him.

Butch had nothing but hatred and anger towards Melvin. He adjusted the microphone to his mouth and talked to his men through the transmitter, "Mr. Black one million divided by five is two-hundred thousand. That is what each finger on Joyce Baker's right hand is worth to me, I want those fingers!"

Zig held Melvin's head in place so he could not turn away. Joyce was horrified when Mr. Black held her right hand. He slipped a cigar cutter around her thumb and pressed firmly until her thumb was on the floor.

Melvin tried to scream but couldn't. He watched his children who shook uncontrollably as Joyce's beautiful brown complexion turned red. Joyce convulsed inside her chair while Mr. Black emotionlessly slipped the cigar cutter over another one of her fingers.

Within two minutes Joyce's fifth finger was cut off and fell to the floor as she was barely conscience. The blood continued to flow from her fingerless right hand creating a red pool beneath it. Mr. Black peered at the camera installed inside the room and waited for further instructions.

"Mr. Black pick up her fingers and place them inside a cup of ice. Also please wrap her hand with a towel" Butch ordered.

Melvin in a state of shock was slapped in the face by Zig demanding him to, "Wake the fuck up! My mother and father were awake when they laid under your father's fucking car!" Zig then hit Melvin so hard on the side of his face; he ruptured Melvin's eardrum that caused blood to drain from his ear.

Butch was satisfied because the money transfer was almost completed. Butch then whispered in Melvin's good ear "I never planned on letting you and your family see the next rising sun. If you would have had the decency to simply apologize, I would have ended this quickly with very little pain. You spit on my parents grave motherfucker which basically means you have no remorse. You will witness first hand what twenty-five years of a man burning with vengeance is all about."

Zig returned with a large pitcher of water and placed it on the coffee table. He grabbed Melvin by his shoulders and threw him to the floor; one foot away from the television screen. Zig then placed Melvin in between his large tree trunk legs. He squeezed hard so that Melvin could only sit still and watch.

Butch spoke into his transmitter again, "Gentlemen, it has been a very long and grueling few weeks, but we have accomplished what we set out to do. You all have been diligent in following commands and asking no questions. You all have been loyal and we now come to the end of this mission. I will offer some relief for all of this stress."

Melvin at this point shook like a leaf. "Comrades take a good look at little Michelle. I may be wrong, but I believe she has yet to experience the painful yet mesmerizing feelings of the first strokes of sex. Who would like to give the young lady her first taste?"

Without hesitation, the four masked men quickly walked over to Michelle who tried to move away from the entourage of sex craved men. One of the men untied her and removed her from the chair. The men laid the young girl down 'spread eagled' on the floor, removing her pants and panties.

"Melvin, I really want you to hear this, so listen up" said Butch as he used a remote to turn the volume up on the television.

Melvin tried to bury his head in his chest but was yanked as Zig made him keep his head upward towards the screen. Melvin sadly looked at his baby daughter attempt to scream as her legs were spread apart by two of the men. Melvin remembered the joy on her face when she passed her driving test on the first try, and how she jumped in his arms completely overjoyed.

Keith violently thrashed his body in his chair, and was punched in the face four times by Mr. Black knocking him out temporarily. Mr. Blue and Mr. Green pulled out their penises, and yanked Michelle's backside upward so that her backside was exposed to them.

Butch noticed how Joyce was going berserk in her chair when he said through his transmitter, "Wait men! Let me show this motherfucker what true love is. Brothers hold your horses; it will only take a second. Mr. Black remove the gag from Joyce's mouth I want to hear what the bitch has to say."

"Melvin this is love, okay? Not that bullshit you tried to pull tonight"

"Please...Please...Please not my baby! She's so young and innocent! Leave her be, I beg of you! Whoever you are tell these men that I will sacrifice my body for as long as they want me, but please don't hurt my baby, please!"

Butch looked at Joyce on the screen then at Melvin and said to his men "Give her what she's begging for."

Mr. Blue and Green quickly removed Joyce from her chair. They stripped her naked, gagged her, and laid her on the floor face to face with Michelle. Each man took turns and brutally shoved themselves into Joyce as blood began to trickle from her rectum.

Butch looked on in amazement because while all of this was happening Joyce never cried or screamed. Joyce wiped the tears away from a shocked Michelle's eyes in an attempt to soothe her daughter's pain.

Butch watched the scene and turned to Melvin, "That's love my man, that's stone hard motherfucking love. You are a true asshole because you have a strong woman and your selfish ass took her for granted. Your selfishness and greed is why you are here, and your family is there. You're the reason your wife is being fucked by four of the biggest cocks in the Bronx."

Melvin never felt such deep pain and helplessness. He did love Joyce and his kids but much of what Butch said was true to his character. Now Melvin could no longer hold back as he wept like a child.

Zig, who is in a trance, was aroused as he watched Mr. Green thrust his manhood in and out of Joyce. Deep inside Zig's dark mind was his desire to cut Joyce on her ass and watch the blood ooze out. Just that thought alone made Zig ejaculate inside his pants and he was happily satisfied.

Chapter Eighteen
Calm before the Storm

Inside her bathroom Brenda was washing Vanessa's hair as they listen to a local hip-hop station. Not able to stand it anymore, Brenda left her sister temporarily under the warm water to change the station. Brenda smiled when she found the smooth jazz station.

While her eyes were still closed and warm water ran through her hair, Vanessa yelled, "Brenda come on now, I was listening to that station! Turn it back!, we agreed you would open up various genres."

"Vanessa the love of my life, for the past two hours I have listened to this shit trying to be as opened-minded as possible, and I still don't understand what the hell they're saying. Now all I ask baby sis is for you to let some variety into your life for a little while okay?

Vanessa sucked her teeth while Brenda massaged her scalp with shampoo and replied, "Open my mind to jazz? How's this for opener's, George Benson, Sounds of Blackness, Wayman Tisdale, Norman Brown, Chris Botti and David Benoit, just to name a few, duh!"

Brenda was shocked as hell that Vanessa knew these jazz artists, "Oh shit."

"Yeah, now what? Get back to scratching my scalp you ain't done yet. When you put the conditioner in, turn back to my station so that you'll be able to run off some artist, now get to scratching" Vanessa joked.

*****

Brenda and Vanessa sat on the livingroom floor eating popcorn and watched "The Inside Man". Brenda looked over at the coffee table and took notice to the utility bills. Brenda watched her sister drool over Denzel's said, "Vanessa, I have to budget all the bills in this house. I know you have the Spellman College catalog in your room. It will be very difficult based on my salary to pay the tuition."

"Brenda please don't apologize to me because I may not say this much, but I count my blessings everyday when I walk in this house. I know it's hard on you doing everything yourself, so the last thing I want you worrying about is Spellman. It was just my little dream to go to the same college you attended. Don't even sweat it Brenda, because Bronx Community College is a twenty minute bus ride away. Besides, once I find me a job I can contribute money to help around here. After I earn my associate degree I can maybe enroll at Spellman for my Bachelors. So stop looking sad and pass me the remote. You're making me miss my Boo."

Brenda handed Vanessa the remote and got up off the floor. "I'll be right back; you don't have to pause the movie. The white guy in his crew got away."

Vanessa had popcorn hanging from her lip retorted "Oh Brenda, come on sometimes you can be so juvenile!"

Brenda laughed while she ran to her bedroom and heard Vanessa say, "So what, I'm watching it anyway."

Brenda returned to the livingroom and stood in front of the television blocking Vanessa's view.

"Come on Brenda get out the way!"

"Pause the movie Vanessa, I have something to say, it's very important.

"See now Brenda you are working my last nerve!"

Brenda placed her hands on her hips and answered, "Well smart ass I'm so tired of you calling me an old lady. I wasn't going to show you this today but I figured with you surprising me with your jazz knowledge I might as well show you."

Brenda revealed a white envelope from behind her back as she gleefully stretches out her hand in the direction of her sister. Vanessa reluctantly takes the envelope with a hint of suspicion.

"Oh go ahead and open it, hurry up" said a anxious Brenda.

Vanessa used her fingernail to rip the flap open. She looked inside the envelope and removed two tickets. Vanessa read the tickets and screamed, "Oh know you didn't Brenda! These are tickets to Summer Jam! Everybody who is somebody in the rap game will be there!"

Vanessa ran to her sister and hugged Brenda around the neck, "Oh my goodness Brenda thank you so much! I love you so much, I love you and did I say I love you!"

"You went to work every day without being late or absent. I also know you paid last month's cable bill, so I just wanted to say thank you and spread the love. I figured you and one of your homies could have some fun before school starts" replied Brenda.

Vanessa smiled at her older sister and admitted to her "You're my home girl Brenda! The only person sitting next to me at Sumner Jam will be you big sis."

Brenda was surprised but gladly accepted the invitation, "Oh my goodness, let me go to the bookstore. I need a hip hop dictionary so I can understand all this mess."

The two sisters laughed together on the couch. Brenda got up to get ready for work. She looked back at Vanessa who no longer paid attention to Denzel but the concert tickets in her hand.

*****

Jesse drove north on the Hutchinson River Parkway towards an old marine buddy's house. King Tut sat by her side while Apollo took in the cool breeze out the back window of Jesse's car. She reached 90 miles per hour on the wide open road and she loved every minute of it. Jesse was wearing a blue tee-shirt and a pair of Nike shorts. Tut couldn't help himself as he admired her strong chocolate colored thighs that seemed to entice him to kiss and massage them.

Jesse took a sip of her energy drink and caught Tut as he stared. "Please, don't even think about it, I'll crush you like a grape."

Tut with a sly grin on his face responded, "Oh please do baby, because it would be a pleasure to go out like that."

Jesse laughed at Tut's statement as she gave the car more gas at 100 miles per hour.

*****

Jesse, Tut, and Apollo got out the car and took in the beauty of land that surrounded them. Jesse pointed to a ranch style house and noticed that the door was slowly opening. A tall figure stood at the entrance that wore a straw hat with sunglasses.

"I want you to stay here because this dude doesn't look like my friend Randu at all" cautioned Jesse.

Uneasy about how far and secluded this ranch was, Tut had some concern, "Jesse be careful. I hope you remembered the directions on how to get back home. This place is like Timbuktu."

"Tut please the damn car has a navigation system. Just sit tight and keep Apollo calm."

Jesse slowly walked towards the house waving her hand in a friendly gesture and tried not to startle the man at the door. "Hello, my name is Jesse James and I'm looking for my friend Randu."

Jesse got no response from the man and continued to walk cautiously All of a sudden from behind an old truck she heard footsteps. Jesse drew her nickel plated .45 handguns. Jesse aimed it at Randu, who stopped in his tracks with his face painted in camouflage and his hands in the air. "Damn girl your ass is still fast as a jaguar. Put that cannon away before you take my eye out!"

Jesse lowered her weapon with a disgusted look on her face and yelled, "Randu man I'm telling you, one day I'm going to blow your ass back to Kuwait for doing that shit!"

King Tut let out a sigh of relief as he watched Randu as he grabbed Jesse by the waist and lifted her off the ground. With a twinge of jealousy, with Randu just did to Jesse didn't sit too well with Tut.

Randu stood five foot-eight inches tall with very muscular legs. The brother had about a half of percent of body fat and was well chiseled.

"Jesse, where the hell you been? You know we have to train every other month" Randu reminded Jesse.

"I know Randu, but the city can get pretty rough sometimes and duty calls. By the way, who the hell is that standing at your door with not enough manners to speak?"

"Oh Jess that's my father, he comes to visit me once a month, and the reason he didn't wave was because he's totally blind, and half his hearing is gone.

"Randu I'm sorry I didn't know."

"Oh girl please, don't even worry about it, hold on. Hey Pop go inside, I'll be in the house later! Pop I said go inside!"

Randu watched his father go inside, and again faced Jesse. "I see you bought your little friend with you and Apollo. Why don't their asses like me? Your friend mini-me acts like ya'll a couple or something."

Jesse glared at Tut and Apollo who stood a shaded tree, "Come on Randu, I have asked you about calling him that. His name is Tut, and if you took the time you could learn a lot from him. Tut is one of the smartest cats I know, and besides he's good people he's just quiet around you"

"Yeah okay I'm sorry. Listen; are you ready to go to work, or what?"

Jesse removed her shirt, and revealed a sports bra that matched her shorts and 'Red Wing' boots. "Let's get this shit popping baby."

*****

Jesse gripped her pistol in her hand and adjusted her skull cap on her head. Jesse held her head down and waited until she heard the sound of Randu's whistle. After Randu blew the whistle, Jesse ran towards some red cones. Jesse maneuvered through the cones and noticed a large cardboard cut out of a masked man that held a pistol. Without hesitation, Jesse squeezed off one round hitting the image directly in the head and watched as it fell to the ground.

To her right another image popped up with a man holding a lady hostage. Reaching for her hunting knife on her thigh, threw it with such force, half the blade stuck out from the other side of the image. Jesse was careful to his the assailant and not the hostage. She was on point.

Jesse knocked down three more images with one shot each. She then sprinted over to the swimming pool, undress and dived in.

*****

After the completion her twentieth lap in the pool, Randu checked his stop watch as she exited the pool. Never drying off, Jesse ran to a pull up bar for better conditioning. In one graceful leap, Jesse grabbed the bar and proceeded to do chin ups with precision and grace.

Tut watched Jesse go through her drills and thought to himself, "I have to make this sister mine.

Her triceps were bulged and face drenched in sweat, Jesse completed her fiftieth pull up. She released the bar and ran over to a log that was lying on the grass to do sit ups.

"Jesse time is a wasting hurry up!" Randu shouted.

Jesse felt her stomach muscles cramp up but refused to stop as she completed her one hundredth sit up. Jesse picked herself up off the grass and ran towards a twenty-five foot wall that had a thick rope hanging from it. Jesse ran with all the energy she had left and let out a loud grunt, as she grabbed onto the rope. Every muscle in her body was used to pull herself up the wall.

Tut looked on and was amazed. He couldn't help but to shout out, "Come on baby you can do it!"

"Ain't no babies on this playing field my man! Come on Jesse, climb that mountain girl!" Randu yelled.

Tut was furious with Randu. Daggers could almost be seen shooting from Tut's eyes as he mumbled under his breath, "Fuck you, dumb bastard."

Almost up the wall Jesse temporarily lost her grip which caused her to momentarily lose traction, but she hung on and pulled herself to the top of the wall. Jesse took in one deep gulp of oxygen, as she regained her balance and quickly climbed down the wall.

Randu pressed the button on the stop watch and walked over to Jesse with a bottle of cold water. "Not bad Chocolate Thunder, you had nine seconds to spare. Why don't you go inside and shower. I'll keep them company. Not bothering to debate, Jesse patted Randu on the shoulder and did just that.

Randu slithered over to Tut and Apollo with a devilish smile on his and patted the dog on his head. "Why do you need to make this a freak show? You know she will never be yours."

"Isn't it time for your steroid injection asshole? Your chest is losing its peak. Don't underestimate me motherfucker. Your ass can get dealt with very easily. Randu it's obvious that you recognize Jesse and my connection and you're threatened by that. Yeah, she comes to you to keep her skills intact, but she relies on me for the support of a man. Seriously I'm tired of playing these games with your ass. Grow the fuck up!" Tut demands after setting Randu straight.

"You got a big fucking mouth for a little motherfucker who has to stand on a stool to piss, bitch" Randu said while he took digs at Tut's limitations.

"I have the heart of a lion and courage of three motherfucker so anytime your medication kicks in, come get at me", Tut reassured

Randu slowly removed his blade as an attempt to scare Tut. Apollo stood on all fours and growled ready to protect Tut.

Randu saw Jesse walking back towards them and said, "You ain't man enough homey."

"Yeah whatever partner, stop focusing on my size and try to reach my level of a man."

Jesse waved to the both of them while Tut and Randu smiled and waved back.

*****

Jesse started her car for the return trip back to the Bronx. "As always soldier, it's been real as hell and thanks for everything."

"Never a problem Jess and you have the number so holler at a fellow leather neck" Randu encouraged.

"I'll holla at you soon Randu. Hey, tell your dad I said feel better." Jesse replied as she drove towards the driveway.

Jesse turned right heading towards the "Hutch" and reveled from her outstanding performance asked, "So what did you think about the drill Tut?"

"I'm proud of you and was very impressed Jesse, you're a strong sister"

"Thanks boo that's what's up" Jesse said proudly.

Jesse merged in with traffic and headed home to get ready for work.

Chapter Nineteen
Penny For Your Thoughts

Four painful hours passed since the gang rape of Joyce Baker. Poor Michelle was in a catatonic state as she laid in one spot motionless. Joyce was hunched over naked in her chair with duct tape on her hands and ankles. She felt helpless while she looked at her son, Keith. He had been severely beaten all about his face while in and out of conciseness.

All the men sat together in the Bronx apartment and waited for further instructions. They openly talked about how good Joyce felt inside and poked fun of the children. Mr. Black wondered what's next as he looked at his watch and then at the wireless camera.

*****

Butch sat on the couch in Melvin's home and admired the scene on the television screen. He looked at Melvin who no longer wore a face of sadness but one of anger and vengeance that Butch readily recognized.

Butch wiped his face with a paper towel and tossed it on the floor. He looked at the laptop that exhibited the large sum of money of their new found wealth. Butch walked over to a bound Melvin who sat between Zig's legs. Butch got inches within Melvin's face and said, "Twenty-five years in the making motherfucker. You caused the slaughter of the only two people in the world who loved us, and now I will return the favor. Is there anything you want to say Melvin?"

Melvin looked Butch straight in the eye and answered "I pray you motherfuckers both rot and burn in hell. All the vengeance in your hearts along with my fucking money won't bring your dead parents back. You and your brother will pay for what you've done tonight, I promise."

Surprised by Melvin's response, Butch said, "Unbelievable Melvin, even with death at your doorstep you don't even ask to say goodbye to the family you claim to love. You're still a dumb selfish son of a bitch. Well so be it, because we can't change who you are right?"

Zig lifted Melvin to his feet so he wouldn't miss anything on the TV screen. Melvin glanced down at the laptop and was shocked because the screen read, "Are you sure you wish to complete this transaction?"

There were two boxes that read yes and no. Melvin couldn't believe Butch, who was so savvy on the computer, didn't notice the final action.

Until Butch clicked "yes" or "no", the money transfer would not be complete.

Butch and Zig stood on each side of Melvin as Butch spoke into his transmitter "Take them out of their misery gentlemen but do us the pleasure of doing them one at a time."

Melvin watched the screen as his son Keith's throat was cut slowly from right to left. Keith's eyes rolled inside his head while his body jerked until it moved no more. Melvin whispered silently "I love you son."

Mr. Blue yanked Michelle by the hair as Melvin watched his daughter who was still in a trance. Mr. Blue plunged a 8-inch blade into her temple that killed her instantly.

Melvin realized that what he watched was real. Melvin was numb as he witnessed the brutal deaths of his children. The hardest to watch though was Joyce's death as Mr. Black stabbed her in the heart, twisted the knife, and ending her life. When Joyce lifeless body fell to the floor, Melvin experienced a tremendous agonizing loss. He was a man now without a family.

Each man wiped his weapon clean and put it back into their respected holsters as they stood over the carnage that was once the Baker family.

Zig pushed Melvin's flaccid body down on the couch then listened to his brother as he gave final instructions, "Men first of all Zig and I appreciate you all for voyaging down this dark and evil road with us in the name of payback. We will take care of the apartment and we need you all to lay low for a few months. Now men, as we have promised, your reward awaits you inside the livingroom."

The four men stepped over the bodies and headed towards the livingroom. Butch watched from another wireless camera installed inside the living room and continued, "On the wall in front of you is a pad that contains numbers. These numbers must be removed and taken to the location we discussed so that you can receive your rewards."

Mr. Black led the way while the other men followed him to a green pad that hung on the wall. Along with his comrades, Mr. Black ripped off the first sheet of paper that has the number "10" written on it. Mr. Black continued to rip off sheets of paper that reads "9, 8, 7, 6, 5, 4, 3..." Feeling very uneasy, Mr. Black stopped removing sheets from the pad. Mr. Black looked into the camera and had a dreadful feeling in his gut. Mr. Black quickly ran for the door while he pushed through the others.

Zig wore a smirk on his face as Mr. Black fought to unlock the apartment door. Zig dialed a number on a cell phone that rung just once.

Butch and Zig showed no remorse when a massive explosion caused the television screen connection to be lost.

"Melvin I'm not a bad guy. I just don't like sharing. I'm sure you can understand where I'm coming from. Well motherfucker, this is the moment of truth and we are going to make sure the last things you see are the Steel Brothers" Butch gloated.

Melvin showed no emotion as he checked the laptop again. Still the transaction was not confirmed. Zig breathed like a wild animal that hadn't eaten in days, as he anticipated killing Melvin. The brothers both removed their knives and placed them on Melvin's throat. When the brothers were going to slice his throat from 'A' to 'Z', they were all startled when someone entered the room. Eunice walked in with Penny who had her teddy bear in her arms. "Oh Mr. Baker what's going on!"

The brothers removed their knives from Melvin's throat and quickly rose to their feet. Melvin screamed at the top of his lungs "Eunice and Penny get the hell out of here now! Run now and don't look back!"

Butch was absolutely shocked because he had no idea who these people were. Butch was sure he monitored everyone who lived in the house. Butch snapped back into reality and yelled, "Don't let them leave this house!"

Zig looked at Melvin with a menacing stare and sliced him across the throat but missed the man's jugular vein by half an inch. Butch and Zig watched Melvin keel over sure he would bleed to death. They turned and ran after Eunice who was behind Penny.

Melvin was able to see Zig as he gave chase along with his brother after Penny and Eunice. While a large amount of blood continued to drain from his throat, he looked up at the laptop screen and saw the blinking cursor that still waited for confirmation,: "Are you sure you wish to complete this transaction?"

Melvin's hands and ankles were still tied but he used every ounce of strength he had to see the computer screen. Melvin with the tip of his tongue was able to navigate the cursor to the box marked "NO."

Melvin still used his tongue and was able to click "Enter." The screen asked one final question, "Are you sure?" Melvin experienced dizziness as blood continued to leave his body, was able to click "Yes.". A new message is on the screen: "Transaction terminated!" Melvin's head slowly fell to the table as he whispered, "Run Penny run."

Eunice and Penny ran towards the kitchen door. Eunice instantly stopped as Butch's knife pierced through her back. She turned around slowly and saw a crazed Butch glaring at her with evil eyes. In a feeble attempt to pull the knife from her back Eunice fell to the floor. Butch then turned his attention on a terrified Penny who still had her teddy bear in her arms. Penny never took her eyes off Butch and frantically reached for the doorknob when her secret with Mr. Baker was revealed. When Penny reached to unlock the door, Zig who stood behind his brother, saw the barcode tattoo in plain view.

"Come her little girl I won't hurt you, I'm your uncle Roy", Butch cooed calmly as he lied to the little girl. A terrified Penny got the door open and quickly ran outside while she screamed, "Help me! Help me!" She headed in the direction of the Grand Concourse which is five long blocks away.

Butch attempted to run after Penny, but his leg was grabbed by Eunice who still had life within her. Angry as hell Butch looked down at the woman, lifted his foot, and stomped down on her head. The impact was so strong that it crushes her skull and popped her left eye clean out the socket.

"Shit, come on Zig, we have to grab everything and get it to the van!"

Feverishly the brothers ran into the living room and noticed Melvin was still moved while he attempted to say something. Butch nodded his head at Zig and watched him grab the fatally injured man by the neck. Zig gave Melvin one last look and twisted his neck violently to the left breaking it. Zig tossed Melvin's dead body to the floor like yesterdays garbage and worked with his brother to place their equipment inside canvas bags.

Butch never paid attention to the laptop screen closed it putting and put it away with the rest of the equipment. The brothers quickly examined each other from head to toe. Butch saw that their hands and boots were still securely covered with gloves and plastic.

"Lets get to the van, she couldn't have gotten far", said Butch as he grabbed his brother and pulled him in the direction of the kitchen door.

Butch lead the way out of the kitchen as Zig sneakily bent down and picked up Eunice's eyeball and placed it inside his pocket. At the door, Butch surveyed the scene, and to his surprise the house-lined block was so quiet, he was convinced no one had heard a thing. Gently closing the door behind them, the Steel brothers calmly walked to their van.

Zig who was a bit edgy looked at his brother, "Butch, come on brother, let's get the hell out of here. We have everything that we need."

The van was in drive and Butch replied "Somebody fucked up, man! Why didn't we know about that girl? No problem because she is about to die anyway!

"Butch, what are you talking about man? We have what we came for. Melvin is dead and we have the money, so why do we need to find that girl? Besides, she could be anywhere right now. Let's just stick to the plan and get the hell out of this city, tonight!"

Butch slowly drove off the Bakers' property and said "What the fuck did I tell you when we started this mission, Zig? Nobody escapes the wrath of the Steel Brothers. We will find that little bitch and eliminate the Baker family bloodline, end of fucking discussion!"

Strictly by hunch, Butch turned the van towards the Grand Concourse in search of the last Baker.

Chapter Twenty
Please Let Me Introduce Myself

Inside Captain Ben Gordon's office, the clock read 9:35PM. Jesse and Brenda sat silently while the Captain looked over the reports of the McDonalds robberies, the drug bust involving Frost, and the Korean sex ring where little girls were smuggled into the states and sold for sex.

Captain Gordon looked intently at the women and finally broke his silence, "In my thirty plus years on the force I just want to say that I have never been so proud and honored to be associated with two detectives such as you. You might think I don't realize what kind of pressure you two are under but believe me ladies I most certainly do.

Captain Gordon reached into his desk and pulled out two citations for outstanding detective work that have been signed by the city's mayor.

"Your dedication, skills, and love for the job means more than these pieces of paper, but take it for what it's worth, it's coming from the mayor" said, Captain Gordon.

Jesse and Brenda reached across the table and accepted the awards. "We couldn't work for a better captain and besides I speak for Jesse when I say we love what we do sir" Brenda reported.

"Captain, Brenda speaks for herself. Is there any extra cash from the mayor in your desk?

Jesse jokingly asked.

Everyone chuckled as Sergeant James Russell knocked on the door, "Excuse me Captain."

"Yes Sergeant, what can I do for you?"

"Sir, I don't know if you've heard, but over in the four-one district an apartment exploded earlier, and the firemen said they pulled out seven bodies."

Captain Gordon looked at Jesse and Brenda and asked, "Terrorist acts?"

"Sir, I know it's not our district. I just figured we might be able to offer some help" offered the sergeant.

"Ladies, don't forget what we discussed. I really mean what I said; now get out of my office. I want to give a buddy at the four-one a call."

Jesse and Brenda took their awards and walked over to their desks.

*****

Penny clutched her teddy bear as she walked down the well lit streets on the Grand Concourse doing her best to keep a brave face. People on the street paid little attention to Penny as she neared the Kingsbridge Road train station. Penny thought about what she saw at her house and did her best to hold back her tears. She remembered how the school bus took this same route on a class trip to a local police station, but she couldn't recall the exact location.

Penny turned her head quickly because of the loud noise behind her and walked a little faster from the snow cone man who just tilted over his cart.

*****

It was 9:50PM and the black van with the tinted glass drove slowly down the Grand Concourse near Kingsbridge Road. Butch and Zig slowly scanned the street for the little girl who could identify them.

"Butch, chances are that little girl will be scarred for life, we need to get home and get ourselves ready for the next phase." Zig said nervously.

"Zig this will be my last time saying this to you, there will be no next phase until that little girl is dead. You say she will be scarred for life? I didn't see fear in her eyes tonight, what I saw was a little girl who had the heart and courage to run out the fucking door!"

"No problem Butch, we'll do it your way man. I have no problem killing her but I just feel…never mind."

Butch clutched the steering wheel tighter as he approached Fordham Road when he spotted his prey.

"Zig listen to me very carefully because there she is."

Butch pointed at the little girl as she walked past Poe Park. Zig adjusted his gloves and gently unlocked his door. Butch slowed the van down a bit. Zig carefully opened his door and stuck his leg out in order to get himself ready.

"Zig don't fuck this up, grab her quickly and get her ass in this van. Don't look around just grab her, and if she screams smack the shit out of her" Butch inserted.

Zig opened the door wider and positioned himself behind the little girl. Zig made his move and snatched the victim by her long black hair. Zig had the girl in his arms when he noticed his mistake.

"Poppy! Poppy help me!" the little Spanish girl screamed as she fought to get free.

Around twenty feet up the block, the girl's father along with six other Spanish men were on the run as they heard the little girl's screams.

"Alicia! Daddy's coming baby! I kill you motherfucker!" promised the man as they all ran to rescue the little girl.

"Zig drop her! Run man run!" screamed Butch as he brought the van closer to his brother.

Zig dropped the little girl to the ground and jumped inside the van. The father tended to his distraught daughter as his friends gave chase after Zig.

Once inside the van, Zig locked the door and yelled, "Get the hell out of here Butch. Oh shit! That wasn't her!"

"Son of a bitch! Hang on and get down!" Butch screamed as bottles smashed against the van as they speed down the Grand Concourse. In order to get off the busy street, Butch made a hard right towards Jerome Avenue and Kingsbridge Road past the old armory.

*****

Meanwhile, Penny stopped to rub her aching knees. The long walk up the Grand Concourse was no joke, she reminded herself. Still with her teddy bear, Penny looked at the subway station at "182nd & 183rd street" Very afraid and confused, Penny felt lost and the tears began to swell up in her big brown eyes.

"Little girl, what's the matter are you lost?" asked a teenage girl along with two female friends.

Penny suspiciously answered, "No I'm not lost. I was just going to my friend's house."

The girls formed a semi circle around Penny as she looked around and hoped someone would come in their direction. The girls stood a foot taller than Penny and stared her up and down. No one paid them any attention, and the girls backed Penny up against the dentist office wall on the corner of 182nd Street.

"Little girl, you got money in your pocket? You better not lie because if we find something you're gonna get fucked up."

"I don't have any money! I'm not lying!" Penny promised.

The three girls searched throughout Penny's pockets and found nothing. One of the girls punched Penny in the face and knocked her to the concrete while she held onto her teddy bear.

"Bitch, that's for not having any money on your ass!"

Penny held the side of her face, withholding her tears. She listened as the three girls stood above her and laughed out loud. Penny saw on the ground a piece of sharp glass. She knew the girls would try to hurt her. Penny went for the glass and with on swift motion, cut one of the girls on the leg.

"Oh shit my leg!" the girl screamed as her friends stopped their laughter when they saw the blood.

While the girls were focused on the bloody leg, Penny saw her chance to escape. She squeezed between the girls and ran top speed towards Ryer Avenue. When Penny looked back she saw the girls as they pointed and screamed in her direction. Penny was so afraid her heart seemed like it was beating in her ears. She knew the girls would hurt her if she didn't continue to run. Penny frantically looked up and down Ryer Avenue. Suddenly Penny saw two lights with huge round green domes on them. She clearly remembered them from her class trip. Penny took off in the direction of the green lights.

*****

The detectives sat at their desks and watched the 10 o'clock news. Jesse and Brenda paid close attention to the broadcast on the tragic deaths of seven people inside a Bronx apartment relative to some sort of explosion. The anchorwoman described the scene in detail. The victims had been burnt unrecognizable and DNA testing along with dental records would be needed to identify the bodies.

Jesse took a bite of egg roll and was shocked when she noticed what was in front of her. Brenda with her back turned to Jesse said, "Wow, I wonder what happened over there in that apartment? It sounds very suspicious to me. Doesn't it seem fishy to you Jess? Are you death? "

Brenda turned around and was shocked by the sight of 9 year-old Penny Baker who stood at the precinct door with a dirty teddy bear in her possession. Her face, hands and clothes were filthy as she took a few steps forward and said, "My name is Penny Baker, please help me." As if her little life batteries gave out, she fell to the ground on her hands and knees in pure exhaustion.

"Oh shit! Somebody get that medic out of the bathroom, now!" Jesse screamed as she rushed to Penny's side. Jesse lifted her off the ground and carried Penny to a nearby bench.

*****

Inside their Bronx apartment, Butch and Zig listened to the radio as the news broke about what they did earlier. Instantly the brothers began to take off their clothes and placed them in black garbage bags. Butch sat at the table with nothing on but his underwear. Butch located his laptop and Melvin's barcode scanner.

Inconspicuously Zig walked to the kitchen with Eunice's eye in his hand.

"Brother, I think you better go flush that shit down the toilet and wash your fucking hands before you come back to this table", Butch demanded.

Zig froze right on the spot and without looking at his brother responded, "Sure Butch no problem."

After Butch connected all the wires and cords, he booted up the laptop. While he waited for the computer to complete its 'Start' mode, Butch reminded Zig, "Make sure you dispose of those bags first thing in the morning."

Butch signed in with his username and password. While waiting for the blue bar to complete the log in, Butch thought about why he didn't know about the little girl. The log in was complete and now Butch connected to their Swiss bank account. Zig stood over his brother's right shoulder and waited to see the money inside their account. Butch looked up at his brother and said "We have to decide what island we're going to build our mansion on."

The secured website showed that Butch had $1000.00 in the account. Coldness ran through his body as if he had been dropped butt naked in the Antarctic Ocean. Butch refocused his eyes on the laptop screen and gritted his teeth so hard he almost chipped two of his teeth.

"Zig, didn't you see me hit enter when we transferred the twenty-five million dollars into this account?"

"Yeah bro' I did, and I saw you hit the enter key as the blue bar moved across the screen. You did everything you were supposed to do, what happened?"

Completely confused and dumb founded Butch exhaled and did his best to keep his composure. Butch stood up and paced around trying not to lose his temper and toss the laptop against a wall. Butch returned to the laptop and noticed he had an e mail from Merrill Bank of Switzerland. He clicked and opened the e mail. Butch and Zig read it about five times.

"Butch, please explain to me what this shit means."

"In a nutshell, the bank is saying that the transaction was aborted and the money is floating in fucking cyberspace. The bank says we have until noon this Monday to re-enter the code, or the money will be sent back into its original account."

"Butch do you think the code is still in the barcode gun? If it is, all we have to do is load the gun into the laptop and transfer it to our account."

Butch thought Zig might be right so he quickly connected the barcode gun into the laptop. Butch took a deep breath and pressed the blue button on the barcode gun. On the small screen they saw "Please scan and enter barcode"

Once again doing his best to maintain his cool, Butch placed the gun down and asked Zig "How much money do we have left?

"We have five hundred and fifteen thousand dollars left, Butch. I made sure everything I bought was used and untraceable. I want to ask you a question. When the barcode gun displayed please scan and enter the barcode, that means something has that code printed on it right?"

"Yes Zig but that can be anything from a can of air to a box of zucchini, what's your point?"

"Butch I know I'm not as smart as you, but I have stuck by you through thick and thin I may not be as quick witted as you, but I'm not stupid. So please do me a favor? Speak to me like a man and not like a slow brother, okay? "

"Zig I love you, and I will give my life for you because that's what brothers do. If I have made you feel like less than a man, I apologize. This is not the time to get all sentimental in shit. I'm trying to figure out what the fuck went wrong and you're asking me shit like this. Is there a reason why you feel the need to defend yourself against stupidity?"

"Butch in all your haste and frustration about the money, I noticed something that you haven't registered in your mind yet. Just know that Melvin's ass still lives even in death. Think hard Butch. When the little girl was pulling on the kitchen door trying to get out, do you remember what we were staring at? Under her right arm was a red tattoo that looked exactly like a barcode number. I would bet my life that that slimy selfish motherfucker did that."

"Brother, we have a half a million dollars in the closet and I don't know how far we can run with it. As we speak, that little girl could be inside some police station describing what she saw tonight. When the police find out who her parents were, they will have Fort Knox-type protection around her. You said we should take what we have left and move out of this city. From one man to another do you still feel that way?" Butch asked.

Zig looked Butch straight in the eyes and answered "Hell motherfucking no! We've come to damn far to turn back now. Let's use every second until noon Monday to figure out how we can grab the girl. We'll get the barcode number then kill her little ass."

"Zig I need you to get the other equipment while I figure out what district police station she could be at this moment I don't know if I'll be right, but we have to sit and scope. We have less than two hours to get out of here, because those cops aren't stupid. They are starting to put pieces together as we speak."

Zig began to walk away but not before Butch grabbed him by the arm. "I love you Zig, please don't ever forget that."

*****

Penny sipped from a can of orange soda and was surrounded by Jesse, Brenda and Captain Gordon. She placed the soda on the desk and pushed her hair away from her face and said to Jesse softly, but with great certainty, "They killed my daddy."

Captain Gordon looked at Penny with great compassion then turned to Jesse and Brenda, "No sleep tonight. Let's get to work."

Chapter Twenty-One
Wits versus Wits

It was 11:59PM Friday night and inside the police station questioning room, Penny told Jesse, Brenda and Captain Gordon everything that she witnessed earlier. Brenda tried to be as delicate as possible so that Penny wouldn't get rattled and possibly crumble asked, "Sweetheart when was the last time you saw your family?"

Penny took a bite of her pizza, swallowed and answered "I saw them this morning before Ms. Eunice took me to the museum and the park. Then I saw Mr. Baker with those men tonight, like I told you. We were supposed to go to Disneyworld tomorrow, please call Ms. Joyce, she will come get me."

Captain Gordon nodded his head to let Penny use the phone. Jesse then picked up her cell phone and asked "Do you know Ms. Joyce's phone number Penny?"

"Yes I do its nine-one-seven, five-five…"

Before Penny could finish Captain Gordon's cell phone rang.

"This is Gordon."

Silent for about three minutes, the Captain listened to Detective Frank Cannon who he sent to investigate the Baker home. While Penny continued to ear her pizza, the captain said to Detective Cannon, "You and your partner stay there and make sure not to touch or move anything. I will be there with the CSI unit."

Jesse and Brenda stared attentively at their commander. He listened some more then hung up the phone "Penny sweetheart, I want you to enjoy that pizza. I have to speak to these pretty ladies for a minute. They will be right back."

Captain Gordon, Jesse, and Brenda stepped outside then he whispered to them "Listen very carefully. Inside the Baker's home two dead bodies have been found. One is a woman in her late forties and the coroner confirmed that the other is Melvin Baker. The coroner knew it was Melvin Baker because he subscribes to his video magazine. I think this woman may be this Eunice that Penny told us about. "

Brenda who is a bit confused needed to ask," Captain should we know who this man is?"

"You would know him if you had kids who played video games. Melvin Baker is part owner and a major video designer at Sunrise Electronics Corporation in Manhattan. He is the sole creator of the most popular video game out right now. He made that company millions. The Japanese owners offered him partnership recently. Trust me this wasn't an ordinary break in. Whoever did this came looking for something, and when they couldn't get what they came for all hell broke loose. I think Penny and Eunice walked in on the situation and in the process Eunice was killed. Somehow they fucked up and let Penny escape. Ladies this is a very important case and I hope you don't have any other cases pending. I will need the both of your full attention on this one"

Jesse put a stick of gum in her mouth and said, "We're on this one captain. Just tell us what the plan is."

"I'm placing Penny in your care until we get more information. Child welfare will have to be bought in and updated but not until we can insure her safety. She saw the murderers and right now I want her protected by you and Brenda. I'm not sure that Child Protective Services can protect her from the guilty party. So for now I feel better if you both watch over Penny. So, ladies let's get to work but be patient with Penny. Start by showing her some photos. I believe she got a good look at those assholes."

Brenda accepted the responsibility but asked, "Captain who is taking the lead with the investigation?"

"Brenda we will do this a little differently this time. Detectives Cannon and Jones are seasoned veterans and excellent detectives. They will do the preliminary investigations passing everything to me which in turn, I will pass to you. I respect the both of you so don't think you are being used as babysitters. I need Penny protected, and nobody can hold it down like you two."

"No problem captain. We'll keep Penny calm and find out what she saw. Our cells are on so keep us updated, Jesse said.

Captain Gordon and the CSI unit left as. Jesse and Brenda returned to the office only to find Penny fast asleep.

*****

Inside the parked van about half a block away from the 46th precinct entrance, Zig watched from the backseat with his zoom-lens camera out of the window. Butch was in the driver's seat, with a mini-boom microphone positioned slightly out of the window. Butch adjusted the volume on his headphones as his eyes widen because Captain Gordon and the CSI team exited the station.

"Zig start taking the pictures now!"

"Don't worry brother I got'em."

While Zig took the pictures, they were automatically downloaded onto a laptop already in his midst.

Butch pointed the microphone towards the officers, satisfied that it will pick up on any audible sound. "I have two detectives there as we speak named Frank Cannon and Benjamin Jones. They have been ordered to sit tight and not touch anything inside the residence. I need you guys at the top of your game making sure every potential piece of evidence is collected."

The officers got into their cars and drove off, but not before Butch recorded everything they said.

Butch turned to Zig, "She's inside brother, that much I'm positive about. The morning shift will be arriving about seven o'clock. If they don't bring her out for whatever reason by six o'clock, we go to plan B Zig, but if all goes as planned we just strike on my command. Zig, what's inside the duffel bags?

"Two full body Kevlar forty-nine grade armor suits, two Tavor Tr-21 assault rifles, forty clip magazines, silencers, Kevlar boots, hats, gloves, face masks, and tear gas."

"Brother tell me how in the hell did you got your hands on an Israeli weapon? Never mind little brother, everyone has a specialty, and I guess yours is getting shit."

"Butch, if we have to go to plan B, I want you to know that I'm ready."

"I know that, but I think plan A will come into focus. Zig this is do or die"

*****

Brenda turned on the computer that's on the desk. Ready to get more information, they gently tap Penny on her shoulder and wake her up from a sound sleep.

"Sweetheart we know you are really tired, but do you think you could help us a little bit more?" Brenda asks.

Penny stretched then wiped her eyes and told Brenda," I don't feel like talking anymore I just want to go home? Why isn't Ms. Joyce, Michelle and Keith here to take me home? Mr. Baker and Ms. Eunice are hurt, we need to go see if they are okay."

"Penny there are friendly policemen over there right now checking on them. It would help us so much if you would cooperate with us and look at some pictures. How about this, I have a pack of licorice for you to eat while you scan some of these pictures" Jesse bribed.

Enticed by the candy, Penny nodded her head up and down while she took the sweets from Jesse.

"Sweetheart, I'm going to show you some pictures. I need you to take your time and look at the faces. Now sweetheart, the two men that you saw at your house, if you see their picture are you sure that you'll remember them?"

Penny took a bite of her Twizzler's, and indicated yes.

A sudden knock at the door found desk personal employee Daisy Green on the other side with a serious look on her face.

"Detectives I'm sorry to bother you, but there is a family at the front desk that I really think you need to see. Also desk Sergeant Williams has some information that he only will share with the two of you."

Brenda looked at Daisy, and nodded her head. Jesse got up from the desk with instructions for Penny. "Penny you stay here with Detective Simple. I'll be right back."

Jesse walked down the hallway with Daisy. As they get closer to the front desk, Jesse saw a man and woman along with a teenage girl who had a bandage around her head.

"Good morning I'm Detective James, may I help you with something?"

"Good morning detective, my name is Carl Francis, and this is my wife Alice. Our daughter India has told us a horrifying story in regards to her boyfriend Keith Baker. She says, they were attacked in the Whitestone Multiplex Theater yesterday afternoon. My daughter should be in a hospital bed right now, but is too frightened to leave my side. India has been asking about the whereabouts of her boyfriend Keith. We have known him for about two years now."

"Mr. Francis I can see that your daughter has been through a terrible ordeal. I want to take your statements and see if we can help find her boyfriend. Please have a seat and I'll be with you shortly. It's the early morning hours and we're short staffed right now."

The Francis' took a seat as Jesse walked over to desk Sergeant Williams who leaned towards Jesse and whispered, "I just got a call from a friend at the five-two and he told me that two Caucasian females were found Friday in a sauna room at the Woodlawn Tennis Club with their throats cut so severely that they looked like Pez candy dispensers. That's not all though, my buddy did some asking around, and he found out that you have to sign in to use the sauna. The two women were not alone

Jesse, the third signature belonged to an African-American woman who went by the name of Joyce Baker."

"Hey Pat, thanks for the heads up. Damn good work. This shit is starting to get thicker by the moment. Listen; let me know if you find out anything else. Do me a favor Pat, make a pot of coffee and see if that family wants a hot cup of Joe while they wait"

The Francis family sat as Jesse walked over to them and sat on the bench next to them, "I know it's very early and you all must be exhausted. Sergeant Williams is our best coffee brewer; please have a cup while you wait. India with your parents in the room, would you be up to answering some questions pertaining to your boyfriend Keith?"

While her head still pounded from the bad fall she suffered, India looked at her parents then at Jesse, "If it helps to find Keith, then yes I will."

Jesse gently rubbed the young girl's shoulder and said, "If you please, everybody follow me to the back."

The Francis family got up from the bench and followed Jesse to one of the interrogation rooms. Jesse opened the door and let the family in then said, "Have a seat and Sergeant Williams will bring you some coffee. I'll be right back."

Jesse returned to the room where Brenda and Penny continued to look at photos. Jesse took Brenda to a corner in the room and said "Brenda you gotta hang with Penny because I got something popping in the next room. When I'm done I'll give you the 411. How's our friend doing?"

Brenda slid her fingers through Penny's hair and answered, "She's doing just fine. Who you do you have in the room Jesse?"

Penny looked at photos while Jesse waved her finger at the little girl, "I'll get at you soon just watch our friend Penny, here."

Brenda acknowledged the clue, "Okay Jesse no problem, I'll see you in a minute."

Jesse closed the door and walked over to the other room to question India.

*****

It was 3:47AM on Butch's watch when he saw Captain Gordon. He turned on the microphone and positioned it in the window again. Butch noticed that Captain Gordon had a notepad in his hands. Zig snapped pictures while Butch continued to eavesdrop. While this was going on the Francis family left the station while the captain entered.

"Good Morning" said the captain. That was the only dialogue Butch's microphone received.

"Zig, at five o'clock we get dressed and armed, ready to take the girl. Whoever gets in the way just dies. Like I said earlier, we're not taking any fucking prisoners."

"Butch, I understand clearly what must be done. We go in, get the girl, scan the numbers then, drop her little ass."

"This is it Zig. That's the fucking plan."

Zig put his camera down and stated, "There comes a time as a leader when you must stop thinking and bring the pain. You must not let your mind cloud your better judgment. I understand that this is not just about money, but more about ending our years of pain. Butch let's just relax and wait. If things don't happen like we expect, then it gets bloody, but let's just enjoy the quiet of the night and let them choose their own fate."

Butch placed the microphone back inside the car and slowly turned to Zig, I couldn't have said it better myself.

*****

Captain Gordon stood outside his office and looked in on Penny who had fallen sleep again on his office sofa. The captain slightly closed the door and pulled Jesse and Brenda into a room next to his office.

"This is the situation and it's a very dreadful one so please listen up ladies. I have an open line with the coroner's office, and he assured me that within the next twenty-four hours he will have some type of identification on the seven bodies. He stressed patience due to the damage to the bodies."

Jesse shook her head slowly in agreement and said, "Captain, I just questioned a girl who says she was injured when a man attacked her and her boyfriend at the Whitestone Multiplex Theater Friday afternoon. You will never guess who the boyfriend was- Keith Baker, the son of Melvin Baker. I showed her photos but she was so distraught she couldn't make a positive ID. All she could let on was how the man threw a cup of soda in Keith's face, and how large he was when he stood up."

Perplexed and concerned the captain asked, "Brenda were you able to get anything out of Penny?"

"No sir, I didn't. She just looked at the photos with a dazed look on her face while asking for Joyce Baker."

"Which leads me to another bombshell, Jesse revealed, "The five-two had a double homicide at the Woodlawn Tennis Club Friday afternoon in the sauna room, but the log sheet shows that there were three women in that sauna at the time. Two Caucasian women had their throats slashed and were left in the sauna room. The third name on the log sheet was Joyce Baker."

Captain Gordon's jaw almost hit the floor as he questioned in disbelief, "You have to be fucking kidding me?"

"I wish I was kidding sir, but the more that this comes into focus the more it looks like what you said- a kidnapping and robbery gone badly."

"Jesse and Brenda whoever is responsible for this is still out there, and until we apprehend them, Penny is a target. I will use every resource necessary, even if that means involving the media. You better believe by then this shit will be all over the news. Frankly, I don't know if I will be able to hold them off that long because we're talking about a very influential man in the video game industry."

"Captain what's our next move?" Brenda asked.

"I want you both to get Penny out of here ASAP. I really don't care who she stays with, I just need to know where, so that I can have a car parked there for protection. I don't want you two worrying about the progress of this case because I will keep you informed of everything. Just keep Penny in your eyesight at all times, and be vigilant because this massacre was carefully executed. The bad guys are still out there."

"Brenda you have Vanessa at your place, so Penny will stay with me, but we can divvy up the time to watch her. I mean, Vanessa will be cool if she's alone at certain times of the weekend, right?" Jesse asked.

"Sure, Vanessa is real good with being home alone. She knows the rules. Besides she knows how to contact me in case of an emergency. I'll just hang at your place for now."

"Captain we need to stay in contact, but using regular phones during the weekend is not smart" advised Jesse.

"I got that covered Jesse; about a month ago we had a major bust involving a group of pushers who were using disposable and untraceable cell phones. They won't need them anymore, so I guess we'll take advantage of their availability. When those phones ring we'll know that it can only be one of us."

Jesse checked in on Penny, then looked at her watch, "Its four-thirty Captain. If we're going to move her this is the best time."

"You're right, but ladies, I believe you are both the right cops on this job however; we do this by the book. There's a lot going on with this case, so your main priority is to protect Penny."

The three of them proceeded to wake Penny when Captain Gordon's cell phone began to ring. "Hello this is Gordon. Okay Larry thanks a lot my friend I owe you a dinner."

Brenda looked at her Captain's flushed face and asked him, "Captain what's the matter?"

"Get Penny out of here guys, that was a buddy of mine. An Acura was found at the Green Acres Mall with the doors unlocked. They ran the license plates. The car belonged to a "Michelle Baker"- Melvin Baker's daughter Keep your heads up and your fingers on your triggers. Let's go!"

*****

Inside the van Butch said, "Start putting your gear on Zig, its five o'clock."

No questions were asked as Zig did as he was told when Butch quickly grabbed him by the hand, "Wait Zig, look!"

From the tinted glass the Steel brothers' watched Jesse and Brenda lead Penny down the precinct steps towards a car. They also saw Captain Gordon near. Butch breathed faster and louder then started the van. "Fuck it, if they all must die then so be it."

When everyone entered her car, Jesse pulled away from the curb. Unbeknownst to Jesse and Brenda, the Steel brothers' trailed only a half a block behind them

Butch, who kept a good distance behind the Charger, said to his brother "Get the "new" crew ready Zig."

Already in the process of Zig dialed a number and responded, "I'm already on it Butch, and I guarantee they'll have no problem killing those three bitches on the drop of a dime."

"Good, we didn't come this far to give up without a damn fight. That money is ours Zig. We paid a heavy price for the past twenty-five years and I want what's owed to us. Ain't no "wanna be" hard dyke cops or some little bitch gonna stop us from getting paid. This shit is on and anybody, I mean anybody or anything that gets in the way, will be dealt with swiftly with a shotgun blast to the head. You with me bro?"

Zig simply answered, "Click, click boom."

Chapter Twenty-Two
Let's Get To Know A Little About Each Other

Brenda sat in the backseat with Penny. She was fast asleep and drooling on Brenda's lap. There's not much talking going on at this hour of the morning, but surely this little girl and her circumstances weigh heavy on Jesse and Brenda's minds. In such a short time Penny has won their hearts over. Already Jesse and Brenda were dedicated to do whatever it took to protect this child. Penny has her whole life ahead of her, and someone out there is willing to end it at all cost.

Brenda was experiencing a transference issue with Penny. Her little sister Vanessa was around Penny's age when they're parents died. Brenda's motherly instinct kicked in as she felt 'extra' protective over Penny. At that moment Penny switches her position and asks, "Are we there yet?"

Brenda wiped the slob from Penny's mouth and answers, "Soon baby, go back to sleep."

In the driver's seat, Jesse evaluated her feelings towards Penny. She always wanted children, preferably boys but she kept those desires to herself. Jesse admitted to herself that she strangely begun to fall in love with Penny's sad brown eyes. Jesse smiled to herself when she remembers holding Penny's soft tiny hand. Jesse thought to herself, "Hell no! No one is gonna harm a hair on her head because motherfuckers will have to go through me first!"

"Jesse, did you say something?" Brenda asked.

"No, just thinking out loud I guess. Home sweet home." Jesse said as she brought the car to a stop in front of her building.

*****

The sun made its presence known through Jesse's living room window. Brenda took Penny to the bathroom with a fresh towel and washcloth. Brenda was surprised that Jesse's bathroom was actually as clean as hers. Brenda bent down to Penny and asked, "What do you like better sweetheart showers or baths?"

"I like showers better. Is he gonna bite me?"

Penny turned her head to the bathroom door because she heard heavy breathing and growling noises. She also saw something moving around in the darkness from under the door. While Brenda prepared the little girl's shower, Apollo stuck his enormous head through the bathroom door. Startled by his massive size, Penny held Brenda around her leg and asked, "Is he gonna bite me?"

Brenda looked back at Apollo and stretched out her hand and patted him on the nose, "No baby he's a good dog he won't bite you."

"He only bites bad girls who don't listen!" Jesse yelled from the living room.

Brenda reassured Penny, "Don't listen to Jesse, she's only playing." Brenda turned the shower on and adjusted the water to Penny's desire. "Okay make sure you wash up good and when you're done we have some fresh clothes for you."

Penny, still felt leery of Apollo so she closed the door as Brenda returned to the living room to read more about the Baker family.

"Jesse, I'm going to leave for a minute. I need to take care of a few things at home. I want to make sure Vanessa is alright and give her some stuff to do while I'm here with you and Penny. I'll update her what's going on and get my personal cell phone in case she needs to contact me for anything."

"That's a good idea, but once you get back here we have to remain unseen. Also, while you're out there bring back some kids food you're better at that than I am. The more we keep Penny happy the less we have to answer questions about her family. Take my car, and when you return ring the bell three quick times, then two long times."

Getting ready to leave, Brenda wondered, "Have you been going to your meetings on Tuesdays?"

While she sat her guns out for routine cleaning, Jesse answered, "Yeah, I haven't missed a meeting but to be honest with you, Brenda every time I walk pass the OTB I get the itch."

Brenda grabbed the car keys and responded, "If you don't use me Jesse like the counselor said, then what's the use of my support? I'll be back soon just make sure Penny's okay in the bathroom."

*****

Penny came out of the bathroom smelling like jasmine. She wore clothes Brenda picked out from the precinct's clothing drive last week.

"Did you wash up good and scrub between those stinky toes?" Jesse jokingly asked.

"Yes I did" Penny answers chuckling a little. "But why does your dog keep staring at me like that?"

"He doesn't trust you yet, so he's just feeling you out. Remember that Small Fry, never trust anyone right away. Always feel them out. Are you hungry?"

Jesse asked.

"Yes, my stomach is making grumbling noises."

"Inside the freezer is a snickers candy bar, go get it. I always freeze my snickers and have it with a glass of milk." Jesse offered.

Penny looked at Jesse strangely and asked, "A candy bar?"

"Yeah a candy bar. Are you hungry?"

Penny nodded her head and walked to the freezer to get the candy bar.

Penny returned to the living room and didn't say a word as Jesse worked on her guns. Penny removed the candy wrapper while she observed Jesse and thought to herself that Mrs. Joyce would never allow her to eat candy for breakfast.

*****

Butch was able to get information on Jesse by running her license plate number on a secure Internet site. Butch and Zig read all the information on Detective Jesse James.

"Damn Butch I didn't know sixty dollars could get you so much shit on people off the Internet."

"Most people don't have any idea how open they leave themselves once they start paying bills online. It looks like Jesse James has done some time in the military. Badge of courage, only black female in a reconnaissance unit, credit card debt and never been married. Father and grandfather served on the police force and she is a twelve year vet. Zig, we might have to call our friend "Cleopatra Jones" or "Foxy Brown" with this type of bio, but you know what? All that shit don't mean anything because she'll be dying for the cause."

Zig quickly adjusted himself in the car seat and pointed at Brenda as she walked over to a blue four door sedan parked in front of Jesse's building.

Brenda spoke to the two brothers who were clearly plain clothes cops. Zig produced a miniature pair of binoculars and took a closer look inside the car.

"Butch, it looks like they've got babysitters for the rest of the weekend."

"They're already dead little brother they just don't know it yet."

The brothers watched Brenda as she entered and started the car. Zig communicated on his "two-way" radio with one of his associates, "Follow her and gather as much information as possible. We want to know every stop she makes." The car was in route and Zig snapped photos of Brenda with a black Passat following close behind.

*****

Penny was in awe of all the guns, clips, knives and other weaponry on Jesse's table. "When will we let Ms. Joyce know where I am because she'll worry about me?"

"Penny, we're working on that right now but for now, you have to trust us and let the police do their jobs in trying to find her" Jesse explained.

"Something happened to the Bakers right? That's why I'm here with you and Brenda."

Jesse thought to herself "How can I explain this shit to a child?" Jesse was never known to be a bullshit artist and she wasn't going to be one now.

Jesse looked Penny square in the eyes and explained, "Penny those men you saw at your home yesterday killed Mr. Baker and your nanny Eunice. We also believe those same men might have something to do with why we can't find the rest of your family. The reason you're here with me and Brenda is because we need to make sure those bad men won't hurt you too. So there it is, you asked and I told."

*****

Brenda entered her home and believed she was not followed, walked in her living room yelling, "Vanessa are you home? Vanessa are you here?" Brenda looked at her watch that read 7:50AM. Brenda turned her head towards the top of the staircase where she heard footsteps.

At the top of the steps rubbing her eyes was Vanessa who asked, "Where have you been? You should have been home hours ago."

"Vanessa, I don't have a lot of time. Just do me a favor and get my duffel bag and those two cartridges. I need you to bring them downstairs then I can explain the situation."

Vanessa was a bit concerned as she hurried to her sister's room.

*****

Brenda checked her duffel bag one last time, and then gave Vanessa a big hug and kiss on her forehead.

"Vanessa remember what I told you. There is no reason for you to leave this house or to answer the door, so please just do as I say and I promise to give you more details about this case when it's over. Ms. Davis is always home, so only in an extreme emergency are you to go there do you understand?"

Vanessa was worried and told her big sister, "Brenda please just be careful. I will be worried about you so try to call me from time to time."

"I'll be fine. I promise on Monday we'll go shopping for BET uncut outfits for summer jam."

The sisters bust out with laughter and went for another hug. "I love you" Brenda declared.

"I love you back." Vanessa said.

*****

Brenda waved to Vanessa as she entered the car. The man inside the Passat picked up his radio and reported, "I'm at her house on Pelham Parkway. She made no other stops on the way. She either has a niece, daughter or sister who lives with her. Whoever she is, she is hot."

"That's a copy, it's her sister. You know the plan, so get that done then you can come back to base. I need you to park the car away from the building", ordered Zig.

The man in the Passat responded, "Copy that" then does as he was instructed.

*****

Jesse, Brenda and Penny all seemed to be warming up to each other as they played "I Declare War" on the dinette table. Penny won another hand as the private phone rings. Brenda and Jesse knew it had to be an update from the station.

"No cheating. I'll be right back", said Brenda as she took the phone inside the bathroom.

"She won't Brenda", said Jesse as Penny and her look at Brenda's hand with smiles on their faces.

*****

Inside the coroner's office in Manhattan, Captain Gordon stood next to three badly burned bodies as they were covered with heavy plastic. "Brenda is the kid next to you?" Good listen to me okay? The DNA tests just came back and Brenda the bodies belong to Joyce, Michelle and Keith Baker. Are you all doing alright? Brenda, when you get Jesse alone and only then will you explain the situation to her. When you bring Penny in I'll have a child psychiatrist and a state certified social worker on hand. Tell Jesse I said hello. I'll see you two when you come in on Monday."

"Captain, just a minute. The report we heard mentioned that there were seven bodies found in the apartment. Do you have any idea who the other four individuals were?"

"Nothing has come back yet, but it could be any moment now. Once I hear the results I will let you know. Keep this line open and I'll talk to you soon take care Brenda."

"Thanks captain, goodbye." Brenda flipped the base of the phone down and looked in the mirror. The tears fell from her eyes. Brenda understood the rules of never to let personal feelings interfere with the job, but this was different. A little girl who never harmed a soul who had been adopted by a family that could have possibly offered an unbelievable future was massacred. The odds were great that whoever carried it out wanted her also.

Her face rinsed with cold water, Brenda looked in the mirror and said. "You want to kill her I know you do. It won't happen because I'm her guardian and nobody is going to touch her. Not on my fucking watch."

Brenda wiped her eyes one more time, then left the bathroom making sure she had a smile on her face, "Okay I know it's been a minute since I left, so don't tell me…Jesse! I know you've lost your damn mine!"

To Brenda's horror she saw Jesse teaching Penny how to load and unload a clip into a Beretta handgun.

"Mary Poppins please calm down. There is nothing in the clip or chamber and the gun is on safety. She kept asking me so I showed her. What's' your problem?" Jesse asked.

Brenda looked at her partner as if she had lost her mind. Brenda shot back, "Jesse she's a child that's the problem. The last thing she needs to know is how to load a clip."

"Ms. Brenda I'm not afraid, look I can do it" said Penny as she did it again which Jesse smile and Brenda cringe.

Jesse realized that Brenda was dead serious. She gently took the gun away from Penny, "Let me have that Small Fry before Ms. Brenda has a heart attack. Penny go in the living room and watch whatever you like on my television."

Penny grabbed a bag of crispy cheez doodles and headed to the room as she was told. Apollo followed behind her and sat at Penny's feet.

"Jesse may I speak to you for a minute please?" Brenda asked.

With a long sigh, Jesse answered, "Are you gonna dig into me again?"

Brenda with a serious look on her face responded, "No I need to discuss the assignment with you. Let's go to the kitchen please."

Jesse put away her arsenal and answered "Sure partner come on."

Both women walked to the kitchen while Penny watched the Cartoon Network and fed Apollo cheez doodles.

Brenda turned on the faucet, got closer to Jesse's ear and whispered, "Jesse I know I can be a pain in the ass at times, but I just wonder about your judgment."

"Brenda I would never do anything that would hurt that girl. It's just that she kept asking me, so I showed her. I'd rather her ask me and get taught right than to find one at a friend's house and not know how to handle it. Besides, being that I satisfied her curiosity chances are she'll never pick one up in her life."

"Jesse you may be right about children and curiosity, but I still expect you to be careful especially with Penny. Anyway I need to update you about the case. Remember when the Captain called me when I was in the bathroom."

"What did he say?" Jesse asked with a curious look in her eyes.

"Partner, the tests came back from the lab and three of the victims in the explosion were her family members. Jesse, her whole family was wiped out on Friday."

Jesse who was conditioned to the shit that went on in the street prided herself with also having a strong 'hood' mentality. "Brenda I can't explain why but I have a feeling in my gut that the next few days will be very dark. Partner we will definitely be put to the test on this one. That man was worth a fortune. I'm not sure if those bastards got what they wanted, but I'm sure they want Penny dead. Either they want her because she saw their faces or...

"Maybe they didn't get what they wanted Jesse and somehow could be the missing piece. This means once they get what they want they'll kill her anyway. Why would they need her?" intoned Brenda.

"Brenda, I'm not good at speaking to children on their level. I think you need to just grill her a little bit more. I mean, not hard but just enough with the possibility she can tell us something."

"We'll let her watch her cartoon show, then we'll both go in cautiously and with compassionate" Brenda suggested.

Brenda and Jesse poured themselves something to drink as Penny carefully turned the volume up on the television after she heard some of their conversation.

*****

Inside their parked vehicle, Butch and Zig concentrated on the capturing of Penny Baker. The van reeked of bad odor as they couldn't think of anything but the money. Zig turned to his brother and said "Can you pass me the bottle please?"

Butch passed Zig the bottle and instructed him to dump it out when he was finished.

While Zig unzipped his pants and urinated inside the container, Butch said "Zig, I'm not a bad person and I'm not an animal. The only thing I ever wanted was simply to be loved, and I got that in abundance from Mom and Dad. They were the salt of this earth. They never complained about anything or asked for a handout. No not my parents. Momma paid her own way through school while that bitch Melvin called a mother sucked off his weak ass father. Daddy went to an apprentice school dominated by white kids, where most hated the fact that he had the nerve to think he could be an electrician. He did it even with all their bullshit. Yes he did it."

Zig dumped the urine in the street and continued to listen to Butch.

"Our parents fed many of people who never had the decency to show up at their fucking funeral, never gave them a call during the holidays or even remembered their anniversaries. They taught and preached to me the right things to do because I was the oldest to forgive and forget the shortcomings of others. Their hearts were in the right place but you know what Zig? I can't forgive anymore. I'm all fucking out! That piece of shit smiled at us when we went upstate to that hell hole of an orphanage. His father "Mr. Can't Do No Wrong" tried to have us set up because he knew his family was fucking wrong. They fucked up our whole entire lives.."

Zig looked at Butch while tears ran down his face. He rubbed Butch on the shoulder to calm him down but Butch continued bitterly.

"When he killed our parents that shit changed everything. Melvin earned the right to feel my motherfucking wrath! That's why his ass is dead now! Fuck his wife, fuck his son, fuck his daughter and fuck that little bitch they got holed up in that apartment. She will never get the chance to continue the Baker family bloodline, you know why Zig? Because I'm going to personally cut her fucking head off!"

Zig sat quietly and watched his brother's bulging fist as he clutched the steering wheel excessively tight.

"The bible my father told me says, "Do not judge others because you will be judged harder. Well, no problem because I don't want that job. I want the position of the executioner, and I don't care who's in the way when I come knocking. Let God sort them out" said Butch.

Zig looked through his binoculars at the cops who ate sandwiches and said, "I hear you brother. God will sort those bastards out first. You know what's funny? They don't even realize they're eating their last meal."

*****

Penny sat in front of Brenda and Jesse. She wore a pair of overall's and a "wife beater" undershirt. Brenda learned how to do hair at a young age so she had Penny's hair in good shape. It was divided by two well-brushed and greased afro puffs.

"Penny we promise to play some more card games, but we need you to answer a few questions." Brenda requested.

"I never could draw very well in school, but I know that if I ever see those men again I would remember them. Miss Brenda are they out to get me?" Penny asked.

"That's why we're here Penny we want to protect you from those men, but tell me baby, did you ever see your daddy argue with anyone?"

"No Miss Brenda, I never saw that, but Mr. Baker and Ms. Joyce did sometimes and it got really loud."

"Jesse leaned forward and asked, "Small Fry why do you refer to them as mister and miss all the time and not as mommy and daddy?"

"Because they aren't my real mommy and daddy. They were my adopted mommy and daddy. They told me a long time ago that I could call them mister and miss as long as I wanted."

The detectives stopped momentarily with their questions and looked at each other with the unexpected news that Penny just sprung on them. They did their best not to look shocked.

"Well, that was very nice of them to take you into their family Penny right?" Brenda asked.

"I really miss them. Do you think you could call your friend Mr. Gordon and see if he has found Miss Joyce, Keith and Michelle?"

Jesse rubbed Penny's face and said, "Small Fry hopefully by Monday we will have some answers about them alright?"

Penny stretched her arms out as she yawned and revealed to the detectives the barcode tattoo under her right armpit. Brenda gently grabbed Penny by the arm and held it up so that she got a better look. Jesse rubbed her fingers across the mark that could've passed as a tattoo. She looked at Brenda then at Penny; "Small Fry tell me about this mark under your arm."

Penny had a worried look on her face as she felt her eyes began to water, "I'm I going to get in trouble with…"

Brenda soothed Penny, "No, sweetheart you could never get in trouble with us. We're your friend's baby."

Penny hugged Brenda tightly around her waist and looked into Jesse's eyes, "I didn't mean in trouble with you two, but with the bad men who want to hurt me."

Jesse looked at the frightened child and sat Penny on her lap. "Penny I know there's a whole lot of stuff going on right now and your scared. Sweetie, you witnessed some bad men do some very bad things to the people you loved and cared about. It's okay to be afraid. I would be too if I were you. Brenda and I will not allow anything to happen to you but you have to trust us. I promise those bad men will not lay one finger on you baby, but Penny you have to tell us about that tattoo under your arm"

Chapter Twenty-Three
Preparation Is Critical

It was Sunday morning and the sky was overcast. There were high clouds that moved in the same direction as the wind blew. Butch and Zig have sat for thirty straight hours inside their vehicle. Zig ate a nutrigrain bar and drank Gatorade. The brothers peered across the street at one of the plain clothes officers who returned with a breakfast special for his partner and himself. Another sip of his drink caused Zig to remember all the war books he read as a kid in the orphanage. He shook his head at the stupidity of the two officers. What the hell did they teach these dumb bastards at the academy? Zig knew he could have easily walked up to the car and silently killed the lone cop within a few seconds undetected.

Zig felt like a leader for the first time in a while and made sure he had all the bases covered as far as the invasion. He looked up an ex-marine who placed an ad on the Internet that for a small fee of fifty-thousand dollars, would assist in jobs like this. Most would call him a mercenary for hire who had no problem taking orders for the weekend. All together Zig had the mercenary bring five of his associates along. The first thing established was that this was his show, and he was solely in charge of how everything would go down. He also let the mercenary know in a round about way that the Steel Brothers were no punks, but were men who could hold their own.

Yes, Zig felt pretty important right about then, because it felt like he was about to move from his big brother's shadow. Make no mistake, Zig knew his brother was smart, savvy, strong and tough, but when it came to creating corpses they were a formidable team. If Butch was the fire under the pan then he was the grease.

His watch read 7:15AM and once again Zig smiled because at this very moment he felt every base has been covered, and he had everything he needed to make this work. What also circulated in his devious mind was that his prey was unaware that they would never see Monday morning.

Zig took the last sip of his Gatorade and thought about his parents' tombstones that were so prominent in his mind. How it felt like yesterday that they left him. What could have been different if that fatal day never took place? Maybe he could have given his parents grandchildren. All of those questions and thoughts filled Zig's head and it began to stress him out. Zig discreetly pulled a finger nail file from his pocket and began to pluck at his skin until little spots of blood were visible on his hand. Sighing slowly, Zig closed his eyes but was bought back to reality by a hard punch on his bloody hand.

"Zig I told you about this shit right! Get your fucking head into your business because this is it, man! Do you understand me? This is the real fucking deal!" screamed Butch who pierced his brother with a cold dark stare.

*****

Penny walked around the dinette table and neatly stuffed napkins in the front of Brenda and Jesse's shirts. The two detectives looked at each other with smiles as Penny poured each woman a glass of orange juice. The microwave bell rang and Penny retrieved two Swanson French toast entrees for Jesse and Brenda.

Penny then poured herself a bowl of Cap'n Crunch Berries cereal and bowed her head, "Dear Lord thank you for the food we are about to receive. We are grateful Lord. Thank you for keeping me safe with Miss Jesse and Miss Brenda; please take care of them because they are my friends. Lord please let Ms. Joyce, Keith and Michelle be okay at home waiting to come get me on Monday. One last thing Lord please let Mr. Baker be with you in heaven, Amen."

Penny prepared her cereal and threw Apollo three crunch berries that he gobbled up in seconds. Penny saw Jesse and Brenda stare at her with many different emotions in their eyes when she said, "Hurry up and eat before your breakfast gets cold."

Brenda snapped herself out of a trance and said "Penny this is so nice and it smells good too."

Jesse picked a piece of French toast up with her fork, stared at Penny and said, "Small Fry are you sure I'm going to make it through the night after eating this?"

Everyone laughed while they listened to "The Sunday Classics" on 'WBLS.

*****

It's noon in Baltimore, Maryland and King Tut sat inside his hotel room almost ready to attend the African artifact exhibit at the convention center. While he put the final touches on his black pinstripe suit, Tut placed the iron and ironing board back inside the hotel closet. He turned the volume down on the television set, climbed on the bed, and retrieved his cell phone. Tut called Jesse for the tenth time this morning and got a little frustrated as Jesse's phone went straight to voicemail.

"Jesse listen sweetheart, it's Tut, and if you get this message that means you got the other nine. I'm just calling to see if you're alright. If you don't want to talk, just leave me a message letting me know you're cool. Later and stay safe, Tut."

Before he took his shower, Tut walked over to his suitcase and unzipped the side compartment. Inside the compartment was a gift bag from Zales. He removed a small purple box that housed a one carat pear shaped diamond ring.

Tut admired the ring for a few minutes and carefully placed it back in its safe haven "If this doesn't prove it then I guess it wasn't meant to be."

*****

At 3:00PM inside the 46th precinct, Captain Gordon studied the profiles of the four men who were identified with the Baker family in Friday's explosion. Somewhat confused, Captain Gordon couldn't link the four unidentified dead men to anything. Not even a lousy parking ticket. The Captain was baffled and wondered what their connection to the Baker family was.

As he studied the profiles more Gordon thought to himself "What if these guys were hired to help abduct this family and when they served no other purpose they were disposed of along with the Baker's?"

He picked his up his exclusive phone and called Jesse and Brenda. "Brenda this is Gordon, how is everything over there? Listen I just wanted to give you guys some additional info on the four other bodies in the explosion. These guys were regular stiffs who seemed to have been suckered into the Baker's kidnapping scheme. No families, no priors, no arrest and no parking tickets. That's what's messing with my head."

"Yes Captain, we're all fine. She made us breakfast this morning. She's a sweetheart and on top of that, intelligent too.

Captain, they were pawns being used by the real assailants. I felt all along the perpetrators were merciless. The plan Captain is for us to be ready for our escort by six o'clock. No, we haven't been outside, but I take it they have a bad case of constipation right about now. When this is over, we'll be the first to thank them back at the station. Yes sir, I will tell Jesse and thanks for calling."

Eric Benson from the CSI lab just knocked and entered Captain Gordon's office. "Captain just wanted to give you a heads up. The napkin we found in the Baker house had some sweat and a strand of hair on it. The DNA didn't match the two victim's sir."

"So it could have belonged to one of the assailants. Until we can match it to a sample we still have no leads. Thanks Eric, I will definitely keep that in mind." After Eric left the Captain's office Gordon paged Cannon and Jones.

Within two minutes Cannon and Jones entered the Captains office. "You paged us Captain?"

"Yeah, I just got word from Benson from the lab that the DNA found didn't match any of the victims. I need you guys to run this DNA in every base known to mankind. If the bad guys were in any city or state system, I want to know about it. This may look like a crumb but it may be the break we need. Get on this right away and keep me posted."

*****

It was 8:00PM and Penny bounced around the apartment especially after she drank three cans of slushy coca-cola's. Jesse sat Penny down on the couch and explained to her what their next steps would be.

"Small Fry, tomorrow morning Brenda and I will be taking you back to the police department. Some important people will be there to ask you a whole lot of questions. These people will also answer any questions that you may have about your family. Some of the things you might hear may confuse you but you don't have to worry because we will be there with you the entire time" Jesse explained.

"Sweetheart the men that you saw at your home on Friday are still out there and we are not sure where they could be. We don't want you to worry. Jesse and I are here to get you to the station safely" Brenda added.

Penny got up from the couch and grabbed her teddy bear. She stood directly in front of Brenda and Jesse and asked them, "Friends are suppose to tell the truth to each other and you both said that we're friends right?"

"Of course we're friend's Small Fry, do you think I would have eaten your breakfast this morning if we weren't?" Jesse joked.

"Of course we're friends' sweetheart, this has to be one of the best weekends I've had in a very long time, and it wasn't because of Jesse. It was all you"

Brenda said.

"I know you think because I'm nine years-old and carry my teddy bear that I'm a baby, but I'm not afraid. So I want to ask you both a question, and if we're friends, you will tell me the truth."

154

The smiles on Jesse and Brenda's faces faded because they believed they knew what the spunky little girl was going to ask. What they were about to do was strictly against protocol but Jesse and Brenda felt with all this child had been through, and would probably go through, the last thing they wanted to take away from her was the trust that had been established this weekend.

"Ask us anything you want Small Fry go ahead," Jesse prodded.

"I know Mr. Baker is gone forever but are the rest of my family gone too?" Penny asked never taking her eyes off Jesse and Brenda.

Brenda looked at Penny somberly as if she were her own child and softly answered, "Yes baby they're gone too."

While Penny put on a brave face, it was clear she wanted to breakdown and cry. Penny nodded her head and said, "Thank you for the truth. I'm going to the bathroom to wash up so I can go to bed now."

Penny walked away and began to cry. She dropped the teddy bear to the floor near Brenda's feet.

*****

Penny turned the water on full blast and placed the stopper into the drain. She walked over to the door and locked herself inside. While she sat on the toilet Penny took off her sneakers and broke down in tears because her whole family was dead.

*****

Brenda and Jesse sat quietly in the living room and thought about poor Penny as their hearts ached for her. They quickly lifted their heads up when they heard the bathroom door open. Penny came out of the bathroom wearing her pajamas and held her dirty clothes in her arm. Brenda got up from her chair and took the clothes from Penny and placed them in a duffel bag. The two women watched as Penny climbed on the couch and pulled the sheets over her body. While Penny began to close her eyes, Jesse broke the silence.

"Small Fry is there anything you want to say or ask us baby?"

Never bothering to open her eyes, Penny answered, "Miss Joyce taught me to be nice to people but I want you to hurt them for taking my family away from me. I want you to hurt them real bad."

Penny eventually fell asleep. Jesse and Brenda both began to get their arsenal ready.

*****

It was 11:00PM and the brothers were still inside the vehicle on surveillance duty. They looked over their weapons and made sure they had everything in place as the time quickly drew near. Zig picked up his radio and asked, "Car number one are you ready on my command?"

"This is car number one, we are ready. Over."

"Men switch your radios to group mode." commanded Zig.

"Switching to group mode, over."

Zig then checked in with cars two and three to ensure they were ready also.

Butch cleared his throat and stated, "Zig I want to close my eyes for a little while. Wake me at midnight so that I may let you get an hour rest, also."

"Sure, no problem Butch. In one hour I will wake you up."

While Butch slept Zig looked into the rearview mirror and was petrified by what he saw. He thought his mind played tricks on him until he heard...

"Baby you don't have to be afraid. Turn around so we can see you" Simone said soothingly.

Zig looked toward his fast asleep brother for help, but to no avail he got none. Zig slumped his head into his chest and began to sob uncontrollably.

"Son, we don't have much time because Butch's mind is already made up, but you still have a chance. Why don't you turn around and listen to us" pleaded Pete.

Zig turned around slowly as the tears poured from his eyes. Zig now faced his parents who have not aged a day since 1981. Simone had on a beautiful white dress and still had the same slanted brown eyes that always bought a smile to Zig's face.

Pete wore a blue suit and looked at his son. Pete smiled showing his pearly white teeth and clean shaved face, "Son what have you and your brother done? Do you think this is going to bring us back or change what has happened? Zig, that family didn't do anything to us; Melvin was a ten year old boy who did something stupid. It was our time son, do you understand?

His head downward with shame, Zig whispered, "But I miss you so much. He took you both away from us. We were lost and Aunt Karen lied to us. What were we suppose to do? Nobody took care of us, and everything you left us was taken away."

Simone looked at her son and said, "No baby that's not true at all. You and Butch were left with plenty. Money comes and goes Zig, but the knowledge and wisdom we taught you would have lasted you both a lifetime."

"Son, we saw everything you and Butch did to those people. You took the lives of your Aunt Karen, Miss Sweet, our lawyer along with his wife, the Baker family, those four men, and now the little girl? Please understand that you two will have to pay for what you've done, but it has to stop. Stop before more lives are destroyed! You both are not the sons we raised!" Pete bellowed.

Pete and Simone look at each other searchingly for any semblance of hope. They knew that their time was almost gone. Simone made one last request "Son, eternity is a long time and I don't know if you will be spared, but you can still try and do the right thing for once in your life. To hurt that pretty little girl is wrong! She is pure and innocent. She has never done anything to you and your brother worth taking her life. You took enough from that little girl. Zig, I hope you do the right thing."

Zig looked intently at his parents and reached to touch them, but can't because just as quickly as they appeared they faded away out of sight.

"No, please don't leave me again! Please don't leave me again!" Zig yelled repeatedly while he shook Butch violently.

"Man what the fuck did I tell your dumb ass? I said gently wake me up. Gently!"

Tears streamed down Zig's cheeks as he tried to tell Butch he saw their parents.

"Zig, man what's wrong? What happened?" Butch asked.

Zig couldn't answer because of his sobbing.

Butch reached behind the seat to get a Gatorade. His hand touched the rear seat and a weird feeling came over him.

A puff of smoke passed Butch's nose and he could swear he smelled his father's aftershave lotion. Butch and Zig stared at each other silently while they both experienced feelings of overwhelming guilt, but neither of them would admit it.

Chapter Twenty-Four
Protect The Child

It was 3:00AM and the hour of doom had arrived. Butch and Zig shook hands before Zig retrieved his radio from on top of the dashboard, "Men listen up. All I have to say is spare no one."

On that command Butch smiled as he watched team number one spring into action. Carl and Dexter are two African-American ex-grunts in their forties. Their bodies are chiseled as if they were body builders in a former life. The two men slowly approached the unmarked police car. The officers have the car windows rolled down as Carl bent down to politely ask them a question,

"Excuse me brothers we're from Brooklyn and know nothing about the Bronx. Could you point us to the nearest subway station?"

The officer rubbed his eyes from exhaustion, and answered "Yes go up two blocks and…"

Without provocation, and with deadly intent Dexter fired four times with a silenced weapon that hit each officer twice in the head, killing them instantly execution style. Dexter wore black leather gloves, reached inside the car and laid each man's head to the side to make it look as if they're asleep. Carl rolled up the car door window and nodded at his partner who did the same.

"This is Team One. The roadblock is removed." Carl reported into his transmitter.

"That's a copy Team One. Proceed to the rear of the building and watch the door" ordered Zig.

Butch watched his brother carry out the plan with pride and said,, "Zig send up Team Two."

"Team Two proceed to the fourth floor, apartment 4C and apprehend the girl. You must do so as swiftly as possible, and I hope you studied the profiles of the two females that should be with her."

Team Two, Roger and Danny, are both Caucasian and extremely tall. They both wore black to ensure they were not seen. Roger and Danny quickly ran through the courtyard and entered the building via the lobby entrance. Danny quickly picked the lock of the front door. Both men entered the hallway quietly to begin their walk to Jesse's apartment.

"This is Team Two we are on the second floor and proceeding to the targets apartment," reported Roger.

*****

The night-light was the only source of light inside the apartment. Jesse and Brenda played two-handed spades. Penny was fully dressed and fast asleep on the couch. The detectives knew they had to move Penny soon and took no chances with her life so by Penny's side was an extra bullet-proof vest. Apollo laid quietly at Jesse's feet as she slammed down the little joker. Brenda smiled as she came back to win the book with the big joker.

"Damn hussy, you get me sick. That shit put me in the hole" said a dejected Jesse.

"You ain't ready for me yet baby, why I got to be a hussy?" asked Brenda who added up the final score.

Jesse shuffled the cards, when Apollo quickly jumped on all fours then slowly walked to the door growling deeply. Jesse motioned for silence as she slowly got up from her chair and pointed at Penny. Brenda reached for her weapons, quickly snatched Penny up from the couch and gently tapped her face.

"I'm sleepy Ms. Brenda." Brenda covered the girl's mouth while she slowly walked to the bedroom where the fire escape was located. Jesse holstered both of her Berettas and grabbed an assault rifle. She removed the safety latch and turned the television on making sure the volume was turned down. On Channel 3 Jesse saw the front of her door because of a security camera.

Jesse observed two Caucasian men as they stood at her front door. One man, Danny, held a silenced sub-machine gun, while Roger held the same type along with a lock picking device.

"Get to the roof and cross over to the other side of the building, Brenda. We have a little time to get a jump on these bastards because my roof door is locked from the inside. Small Fry, stay with Brenda and don't worry, I'm right behind ya'll" whispered Jesse, as she crouched behind her bedroom door.

Brenda grabbed Penny by the hand and lifted the latch on Jesse's security gate to unlock it. Brenda lifted the window and stuck her head out cautiously. She looked up and down to make sure no one was on the fire escape. Brenda climbed out on the fire escape first then began to pull a terrified Penny with her. The girl resisted and shook her head no. Brenda mouthed silently "Its okay baby."

Penny somehow found the courage to climb out on the fire escape with Brenda's help. Brenda hugged Penny, and pointed upward. "Come on baby, you can do this. Just take one step at a time."

Jesse felt the breeze from the open window hit her back. Confident as Brenda and Penny made their way up the fire escape, Jesse focused her attention back to the front door.

The clicking sounds of the locks came to an end and Jesse saw a small beam of light enter her apartment. A squeaky sound was heard as the front door slowly began to open. Jesse had her finger on the trigger of the rifle as she licked her lips and watched Roger enter the apartment. Jesse held her ground as she waited for both men to enter. Roger was in a crouched position as he held the door open for Danny who quietly entered and closed the door behind him.

Jesse heard the door close and raised hell, "Tear his ass up!"

That command was all that the dog needed as Apollo leaped from the darkness and locked his 10 inch wide jaws onto Danny throat. The force of momentum knocked Danny to the floor, while in one tug; Apollo ripped the unsuspecting man's neck wide open. Roger startled, fell backwards towards the wall and aimed his rifle in Apollo's direction. He readied his weapon to squeeze off a round, but Jesse fired first and hits Roger twice in the head.

"Apollo stay!" Jesse screamed as she turned and ran towards her fire escape. Jesse quickly climbed up to the roof and yelled "Oh fuck!", as shots are fired from below by Carl and Dexter who just missed her leg. Jesse leaned over the fire escape and fired back. She missed her target, but managed to get their attention.

"Oh shit! Call the police I hear shots!" someone shouted from their apartment.

Jesse made it to the roof and looked behind her. She witnessed one of the men on the second floor of the fire escape as he continued to climb. Jesse threw the rifle around her arm and hurried to the other side of the building roof. She acknowledged Brenda on the other roof who held the door open for her.

"I got your back Jess, let's go!" Brenda screamed as she looked back at Penny who was crouched in a corner behind her. While Brenda watched Jesse run towards her, little Penny shook like a leaf. The 9 year-old was convinced she would meet the same fate as the rest of her family had.

Jesse made it to the other side of her building and leaped over a small ledge that connected the adjoining building. Jesse ran past Brenda into the building hallway as Brenda slammed the roof door shut. Jesse rubbed Penny on her face and asked, "Small Fry are you alright?"

Able to nod her head up and down, Penny answered, "I think so."

"Jesse let's move and call for back up."

Jesse reached for the private phone that Captain Gordon gave her and shouted, "Oh fuck me! I left it in the apartment, do you have yours?"

While they ran down the stairs Brenda responded "Jess, I fucked up too! We have to get to the car."

Both Jesse and Brenda left their phones and Penny's bullet-proof vest inside the apartment. Jesse looked back at Penny who had terror etched on her face. Jesse momentarily stopped between the fourth and third floors. She snatched off her bullet proof vest and tossed it to Brenda.

"Get it on her now! Pull the straps as tight as possible!" Jesse commanded.

Brenda made her hold up her arms to put the vest on. While she did Brenda felt sorry for Penny because the little girl was fully aware of what was taking place. Brenda put the last touches on the vest and nodded at Jesse to get moving again. They all proceeded down the stairs with caution. Jesse stepped backwards with her gun pointed toward the roof entrance. She could hear the assailants as they pulled and banged on the roof door, which meant Carl and Dexter weren't far behind.

The women head down the steps as Brenda yelled "Don't!" She pointed her gun at an elderly man who had just opened his door, and was scared shitless.

"Sir, return back into your apartment and call the police! Tell them shots are being fired on Tiebout Avenue, hurry!" Jesse commanded.

The old man observed the three of them and quickly closed his door to hopefully make the phone call.

"Brenda keep your head on a swivel baby. We have to look all around us because for the time being, we are on our own."

While Jesse led the way, Penny held the belt loop of her jeans. Brenda walked down the steps ready to fire at a moment's notice.

At the front entrance of the door, Jesse carefully peaked out of it in order to look as far as she could up and down the street. The sky was still dark at 3:25AM and Jesse knew she had to use the darkness to their full advantage. As Brenda watched the rear, Jesse grabbed on to Penny and pulled her closer to her back.

"Brenda, this looks too easy, so stay on guard and watch everything. I'm pretty sure our bodyguards have been taken out."

Not able to hear anything from upstairs, Brenda turned around to look at Jesse. "Penny will stay with me on the sidewalk while you get to the car. I'll have your back all the way to the car, but once you get inside you'll be on your own" Brenda cautioned.

Jesse in agreement, opened the creaky door as slowly as possible, and positioned her assault rifle in her hand. The sweat started to seep through her black wife-beater as Jesse gave Penny a quick smile. Jesse slid out the door and assumed a defensive stance while she ran beside a parked car.

"Baby stay close to me. We're going to get you out of here," Brenda promised Penny.

"Penny, I need you to hold onto my belt and when I get down you do the same." Brenda said to Penny as Jesse indicated to them to exit the building.

Penny's beautiful brown eyes were wide as half dollars. Her breathing was shallow and her body trembled. All Penny could say to Brenda's command was, "Okay."

Brenda quickly exited the building with Penny at her side. They meet Jesse at the side of the car then survey the street. Eighty feet away from her car, Jesse looked up the block and saw it clearly under the street light. Jesse sucked her teeth in disgust and pulled out her car keys which contained an electronic starting device.

"Jesse, don't start that car you hear me? We have no idea where those cats are. I got your back, but you can only start the car when you get inside" cautioned Brenda.

Jesse raised her rifle and took a deep breath. In stealth like mode Jesse made her move towards the car. Brenda pulled Penny in front of a parked car and crouched on the side of it in order to protect both Penny and her partner's back.

*****

Inside their vehicle the brothers wondered what was took Teams One and Two so long when a frustrated Zig picked up the radio, "Team One what is your fucking problem?"

"This is Team One; we are on our way down the fire escape. They went across the roof into the beige building on the corner in front of you."

Zig peered at Butch who was very pissed off and asked, "So why in the fuck didn't you follow them down the steps, Team One?"

"That wasn't an option. They quickly got away from us and locked the roof door. We were going to blast the door but decided not to in order to avoid attention," reported Carl.

"Listen, get your asses to that building now. Take the front and side entrances because we haven't seen anything. They can still be there as we speak. Is that a copy?" Zig commanded.

"That is a copy" replied Carl.

Butch was about to say something to his brother but stopped and pointed at a white car twenty feet in front of them.

"Zig, look straight ahead of you, there she is." Zig focused his eyes on the white car then spotted Jesse as she got closer to her car. Zig slowly opened his glove compartment and removed a small black box that had a switch on it.

"Zig take your time and do it right. Don't fuck this up man" said Butch as he took a strong mental picture of Jesse who was now ten feet away from her car.

Brenda watched her partner as she got closer to the car and pointed the weapon at nothing in particular, but was ready to shoot anything that got close to her friend. Brenda quickly glanced to her right in the direction of the building entrance but spotted no one.

"Penny, we're almost out of here baby. Just sit tight and stay close to me."

Penny did as she was told and scooted closer to Brenda almost like a second skin. Brenda wiped the sweat from her forehead, and cocked the trigger on her gun while she covered her partner.

Jesse was near the front of her car when she lowered her weapon so she could open the door. She felt for the alarm button on the key chain and pressed the button softly which made the car lights flash quickly.

Zig watched as Jesse slowly reached for her door with her key pointed at the cylinder. Zig saw that the key was inside the door lock when he said, "I got your ass freak."

Butch glanced at his brother and screamed, "No Zig not now!"

It was too late. Zig flipped the switch and ignited a fiery inferno inside Jesse's car. Orange and yellow colors brightened the dark indigo skies. The explosion crescendos as the car went up in flames.

"You dumb ass! Zig, I told you to wait until she got into the car! What the fuck is wrong with you man? You fucking blew it!"

The explosion was so loud it shook people's windows. Apartment lights clicked on as tenants looked out of their windows to see what was going on. The explosion knocked Jesse backwards to the ground. Butch watched in frustration as Jesse made it to her feet. He saw her quickly retreat back to where Brenda and Penny were.

*****

"Jesse no!" Penny screamed as Brenda jumped to her feet and pointed her gun in all directions as Jesse got closer to them. Brenda looked back inside the building hallway and spotted a figure that hid behind the steps by the mailboxes.

Brenda grabbed Penny by the arm and shielded her, "Jesse ambush! Ambush move!"

Brenda and Penny quickly ran towards 182nd street. On her left Brenda saw another man as he climbed down the fire escape with a weapon in his hand. The assailant raised it in their direction with only a single intent in mind. "You fucking bastard!" Brenda yelled as she let off three rounds, that just misses the assailant's head. The bullets ricocheted off the fire escape to define the seriousness of the moment.

Jesse was five feet away from Brenda and Penny when she yelled, "Go! Run to the three-three-three projects at the bottom of the hill! Brenda take the back steps that lead to Webster Avenue!"

Brenda literally began to drag a petrified Penny towards the hill. Jesse saw the other assailant as he jerked the building door open while he held a silencer gun in his hand. Without hesitation, Jesse raised her assault rifle and blasted off a round of ten shots that shattered the door window which caused the man to take cover.

Brenda began sprint down the hill towards the 333 projects, when she shouted, "Jesse on your left! On your twelve from the fire escape!"

Jesse understood exactly what Brenda meant and squeezed off a few rounds not sure if she hit him or not. "Keep going I'm right behind you!" Jesse yelled as she gained on Brenda and a petrified Penny.

*****

Butch banged on the dashboard in complete disgust. He yanked the radio from Zig's hand and screamed, "Team One get the fuck back to your vehicle, turn on your GPS system, and find us! They were right in front of you! Damn it, they're nothing but women!"

Butch looked at his brother with disgust "Look at all this attention, stupid! Team Three, let's go right fucking now! Do not let those fucking dykes get to Ryer Avenue!"

Butch started the engine but kept the lights off. As Butch peeled off behind Team Three he looked over at Zig, who sat quietly in his seat when Butch yelled, "You can sit there and look sad if you want to motherfucker! You hired these dumb bastards, with your retarded ass!"

*****

Brenda and Jesse each held Penny by her wrists as they were almost down the hill. They were slowed by Penny because of the size and weight of the bulletproof vest. Jesse and Brenda collectively lifted Penny off the ground to gain some speed. Brenda, with sweat all over her face screamed, "Oh shit here they come Jesse, we might have to split up!"

Jesse adjusted the rifle that was strapped on her shoulder and looked down towards the foot of the hill. Jesse lowered Penny to the ground and yelled, "Come on Small Fry I know you can run faster than this!"

Respect for Jesse and with a new sense of determination, the little girl with brown eyes that tear nervously answered, "I can." Penny began to run down the hill while her little arms were swung back and forth. As Penny picked up speed the August summer breeze pushed through her afro puffs as she moved down the hill with Jesse and Brenda.

Brenda turned and noticed the vehicle that contained Team Three had just made it over the hill, and was now right behind them. Brenda never lose stride, turned quickly and fired three times which busted the windshield to pieces. Unfortunately Brenda missed the driver, but still caused a distraction that made the driver lose control of the vehicle. He side swiped a parked car, slowing him down enough to give the detectives an opportunity to gain some distance. While at the same time Butch and Zig had to slow down because of the minor accident.

Frustrated and vividly upset, Butch slammed on the steering wheel and grabbed his radio, "Come on, shit! Drive the fucking car! Don't let them get to Ryer Avenue, that's where the precinct is! Team One, turn down Valentine Avenue! Cut them off! Fire on the bitches but the little girl I want alive!"

Team Three straightened their car out as they continued down the hill in pursuit of the targets. Team Three member Bob pulled out his weapon and checked, "I'm getting real tired of this motherfucker barking orders at us man."

"Just stay focused partner, and don't worry about that shit alright? Besides, when all of this is over we'll be getting paid", said the driver as he began to pick up speed.

At the foot of the hill Jesse grabbed Penny and pulled her behind her. "Brenda I can't fucking believe no one has heard this shit and called the cops! Come this way we have to get them off us!"

They finally made their way through the lobby of the 333 projects. Jesse led the others through a backdoor exit that would take them to Webster Avenue. Brenda saw the banged up car that gave chase after them and decided to pick Penny up and run down the long wide steps toward the street.

*****

"Yeah Butch, this is Team Three, they just ran into the building on the corner in front of me!"

"No they did not! There are steps leading to Webster Avenue that has a twenty four hour gas station! Make the fucking left on the corner and cut those bitches off, we're right behind you!" screamed Butch.

Doing what he was told, the driver for Team Three made a hard left turn, and sped down Foley Street in an attempt to cut the woman off.

*****

Brenda, Jesse and Penny made it to the bottom of the steps as Brenda spotted the all night gasoline station. She couldn't help but to feel a bit relieved with the hope that the attendant would call the police.

"Jesse look ahead! Let's get inside so I can call for back up. Watch our backs Jess! These motherfucker's are out for blood!

"Stop cursing Ms. Brenda" admonished Penny who no longer cried.

"Look if we're going to make this move, then let's go! We have no time to waste! Ready? Let's go!" Jesse commanded.

They all ran towards the gas station that was just a few feet away. They got closer to help when they were stopped in their tracks because Team Three had just pulled right in front of them. Bob hanged out the passenger side window with his weapon pointed directly at them. Three rounds whizzed by Brenda's face. She returned fire and hit the front of the car but missed the car's radiator. The three females quickly turned and run in the opposite direction when they spotted a newspaper truck making his daily stops.

They could hear the screeching tires of the red sedan as it got closer to them. Jesse ran at top speed towards the newspaper truck that had slowed down considerably. The truck driver tossed a stack of newspapers in front of a closed bodega.

Police! Stop this truck right now! Jesse demanded while she flashed her badge.

The driver, a black man in his fifties held his arms above his head with a terrified look on his face.

"Please don't shoot me; please!"

"Do you have a cell phone sir?" Jesse screamed, as Brenda and Penny made it to the truck.

"No ma'am, the owner is cheap, he won't give us one! Please don't hurt me I have a family!"

"No one is going to hurt you! I need to commandeer your truck. I need you to find a police officer and report that two female detectives just stole your truck and need help. You make sure you give them the plate numbers, now go!"

The old man watched Jesse as she drove away with his truck. The man ran for cover because Butch and Zig were on the scene and fired at the vehicle. After the truck and van continued further down the street, the old man prayed while he crouched behind a parked car.

*****

At sleep at his home while next to his wife of thirty years, Captain Gordon was suddenly awakened by the sound of his phone. Gordon adjusted his eyes and saw that the clock read 4:07AM as he struggled to find the receiver.

"This is Gordon and it better be important."

His wife Susan turned over so that she faced her husband and listened to his voice. She noticed the unmistakable urgency.

"You have got to be fucking kidding me! Nobody touches anything until I get there, and Sergeant Cross, I'm giving you full authority until I get there."

"Benjamin what's going on, sweetheart?" Susan asked.

"We have a bloodbath in the Bronx in front of Jesse's apartment building, and my two detectives along with the little girl, Penny are nowhere to be found. Susan honey, I have to go and don't wait up" said Gordon as he kissed her on the lips.

The Captain had a bad feeling in his gut as he quickly got dressed and headed to the Bronx.

Chapter Twenty-Five
Manhunt

Jesse and Brenda did an excellent job keeping Penny safe over the weekend. They managed to keep her occupied with fun and games even though this case was far from an amusement park setting. Penny's entire family was executed and Jesse and Brenda were fully aware those responsible wanted Penny dead also.

Jesse and Brenda promised the little girl they would protect her at all cost. Everything seemed to be going as planned until they tried to move Penny. Still unsure of the bad guy's motives, it was clear they wanted Penny. The one thing they underestimated though was the will and determination of Jesse and Brenda doing whatever it takes to protect Penny Baker.

At 4:45AM the majority of neighborhoods in New York City were quiet and still, but on Tiebout Avenue, between 182nd and 183rd Street, it was pure pandemonium. Residents in the area looked out their windows at the plethora of police vehicles with flashing lights. The police sealed off the area. No cars were allowed in or out.

There were about forty uniformed and plain clothes cops in the area. Gordon arrived on the scene to identify the executed officers assigned to escort Jesse, Brenda, and Penny later that morning. Clearly the officers at the scene were devastated by the deaths of their friends, Officer Ervin Torrey and Corey Claxton six year veterans.

Captain Gordon noticed that Sergeant Anthony Cross was distraught. He walked over to the sergeant and placed his arm around him and said, "I know this will not be easy, but who said it ever was. I need you on top of your game sergeant. We have a major incident on our hands, and I need you to take the fucking lead because it's your backyard. These men and women are under your command. If they see defeat in your face instead of the look of confidence and strength, what kind of effect do you think that will have on them? I need you to round up your troops, get your helmet on and get in the fucking game, do you understand sergeant?"

"Captain you are right. It's just that those guys were more to me than colleagues" Cross answered while he composed himself.

The Captain patted his man on the back in an attempt to inject confidence as he watched Cross react demonstratively to the reprimand. Gordon took another look inside the car at the two fallen officers then reached for the phone to call either Jesse or Brenda. Still with no answer, Gordon looked up in the direction of the fourth floor very concerned about his detectives. Just then Gordon spotted Jesse's car up the street. He called their phones again and neither of them answered.

Gordon approached Jesse's car and looked inside. It was difficult to see inside the car because of the tinted windows. What concerned Gordon the most though was the smell of burnt leather upholstery. Gordon commanded to a uniformed officer, "Break this window open now!"

The officer raised his nightstick and smashed the passenger side window, as smoke escaped from the car. The officer stepped back so that Gordon could investigate the inside of the vehicle for anything of use.

"Sergeant Cross is this block secure as I asked?"

"Yes Captain, no one will be allowed to leave or enter without proper inspection, Sir."

"Very good, I need you and six other officers to come with me right now."

Cross gathered six police officers and followed Gordon inside Jesse's building.

*****

The team entered the building and walked up to the fourth floor with Gordon leading the way. They stopped at Jesse's apartment door that appeared to be intact with no clear evidence of a break-in. Gordon prepared himself and then knocked on the door four times waiting for a response. There was no answer so the captain knocked harder and more rapidly.

"Jesse this is Gordon, are you in there?"

Gordon looked at his sergeant and the officers around him as he removed his gun. He ordered two of the patrolmen, "Bust it open but be very careful, they're one of us, do you understand?"

The officers nodded their heads as they gathered momentum and moved forward with great force. With the door busted open they entered the apartment slowly, and with caution.

Their weapons were drawn and they used flashlights while proceeding cautiously into Jesse's dark apartment. All of a sudden they heard a deep ferocious growl. Gordon pointed his service revolver in the direction of the savage sounds. An officer shined his light which reflected off of a pair of large silver eyes that resembled glass.

"Sir, we have a large animal here" said the officer.

"I need everyone to stay calm" Gordon advised while he searched the wall for a light switch. Gordon finally found the switch and gently clicked it in the on position. "Alright nobody move" ordered Captain Gordon once the light revealed in full glory what was in front of them.

In front of the officers stood a proud mammoth beast, with slob drooling from his mouth and dry blood that covered part of his face. The officers looked down on the floor and noticed Team Two members Roger and Danny dead. The officers focused back on the brute. "Listen up men, Jesse always talked about her dog. I don't want the dog harmed so here is the plan. This kitchen has two entrances, one here, and another leading to her living room. Officer Knight, I need you to make it to the living room while I get closer to this door. On my command we will both very gently close those doors."

Apollo watched Officer Knight as he walked towards the living room as Gordon momentarily distracted the dog, "Easy big fella. Where's Jesse big guy?"

Apollo stood on all four legs and tilted his head. He glared at Gordon with suspicion as if he recognized his master's name. The dog turned his head quickly in the direction of Officer Knight who stood at the other entrance. Knight cautiously grabbed the doorknob while Gordon smiled at Apollo who growled intensely.

"Knight close your door now!"

Apollo turned away and quickly charged towards the living room. Gordon then quickly closed his door trapping the beast inside. Gordon took a deep breath and focused back on the two dead bodies that laid on the floor when he commanded Sergeant Cross, "While I check the apartment I need four officers to start going from door to door in this building. Somebody had to hear something this morning, and I want to know what."

The command was carried out as Gordon began to look around Jesse's apartment in hopes of finding some leads. On his way to Jesse's bedroom the captain found on the coffee table the two telephones he gave them. Gordon grabbed the phones squeezed them in his hands, while thinking aloud, "Come on ladies where are you? Reach out to me please."

Gordon felt a breeze that came in from Jesse's open window as the curtains rippled from the wind. Gordon stuck his head out of the window and he looked up towards the roof then back down towards the alley. He didn't see anything unusual so he went back to the living room to speak to his sergeant.

"Listen to me Cross, I need animal control here within the next half hour so that this dog can be temporarily put to sleep, and taken to a shelter. I also need you to get your men together for an impromptu meeting with me downstairs as soon as possible, you got me?"

"Yes Sir, I'm on it right now."

"Good, while you're doing that, I'll get a crime unit down here for these bodies and this apartment checking for any and everything. You come outside with me and have two men guard this door making sure nothing is moved, and no one enters without me knowing first."

"Yes Sir, I got you" said Cross.

The two of them left the apartment but not before Gordon knocked on the kitchen door where Apollo whimpered. "Hang on pooch help is on the way."

*****

It was 5:25AM and the sun had risen. Captain Gordon stood in front of practically every tenant that lived inside Jesse's building. Men, women and children, most still in their night attire stood at attention. Many of the tenants were fond of Jesse and were very concerned about what happened in their building.

"Ladies and Gentlemen, we have a situation here and we need your help. I realize you all have things to do this morning. My officers will be interviewing each and every one of you. The quicker you tell all that you know, the faster you all can get back to your normal routines. Tell my officers everything you possibly saw and heard. You may think it's not important but let us be the judge of that. Once we gather enough information, we will be on our way. I know this is frustrating to many of you, but your cooperation will go a long way in meeting all our needs and be greatly appreciated."

The people did as they were asked as Gordon watched his officers go to work.

*****

Jesse pushed her foot hard on the gas as she sped north on the Major Deegan Expressway. She looked at the gas gauge and speedometer that read empty and 70 miles per hour, respectively. Little to no traffic on the Deegan, Jesse looked at her side view mirror and spotted three vehicles- a red, green and finally a black mini-van that gained on them.

"Brenda here they come!"

From the rear door window Brenda saw the vehicles as they all separated into three different lanes. Brenda tried to keep her balance inside the truck and looked back at Penny who was obviously afraid and held on for dear life. Brenda grabbed bundles of newspapers and placed them around Penny to create a fort to protect her from any possible collision. Brenda adjusted the bullet proof vest around the little girl and said "Baby you stay right here and don't move, understand?"

"Ms. Brenda I won't move" Penny replied while she buried her head in between her legs. Out the rear door window, Brenda observed the men inside the red car load their weapons as they picked up speed and accelerated to the right side of the truck. Brenda pulled her glock from her waist and rushed to the front of the truck to lay on the floor careful only to stick half her body out.

Jesse looked up at the signs that were overhead and noticed that they just passed exit #11, Van Cortlandt Park South. Brenda with both hands on the butt of her gun, closed one eye slightly and waited for the car. The red car pulled up alongside them as Brenda quickly pushed her hair away from her eyes and mouth to fire. Brenda hit the driver's side door, and almost caused the car to swivel off the road.

"Jesse you have to speed this motherfucker up baby, come on!" demanded Brenda, who fired two more shots that knocked the driver side view mirror off the car door.

"This is as fast as this shit will go! Oh shit!" Jesse yelled as shots were fired that pierced the back door of the truck busting the window on the right door.

Brenda retreated back inside the truck and checked to see if Penny was okay inside the makeshift fort. Jesse tried to switch lanes because up ahead there was an Amoco truck coasting at a slower speed. Brenda grabbed the assault rifle and made her way to the back of the truck. Carefully, Brenda looked out the shattered window and saw the red car as the black vehicle was nowhere in sight. Brenda looked at Penny, who covered her ears, "Just stay down baby and don't move!"

Brenda stuck her rifle out of the back door window and was violently thrown to the floor of the truck as Butch slammed the side of it in an attempt to knock them off the road.

"Brenda I can't see them! They're trying to get us off the ramp!" screamed Jesse as she read the sign, "Exit #12 Henry Hudson Parkway/Sawmill Parkway." Jesse did her best to keep control of the truck; as she saw the green car as it gained on them. The truck was rammed again on the left side by Butch. Jesse frantically honked the horn because she is picked up speed and approached an empty school bus directly in front of her. Jesse noticed that Butch had fallen back, which meant one thing: He was going to try and tailspin them.

"Brenda ya'll better hold on tight! Get down with Small Fry because I have to get out of this shit right now!" Jesse yelled as she gained on the school bus.

"Jesse be careful but do what you have to do!" responded Brenda as she got down next to Penny.

Jesse could see the green car in the right lane. Jesse knew she only had one chance to do this right. She noticed that "Exit 13" was coming up, so she had to make her move, "Brenda hold on to Penny!"

With the back of the bus right in front of her, and the ramp for exit #13 coming up quickly, Jesse sharply turned the steering wheel to the right and swiped the green car that caused it to smash into a concrete divider. Carl, the passenger was tossed from the front windshield window and landed fatally on the freeway.

Butch missed his chance to tailspin the truck and looked at the demolished car that carried Team One. He quickly exited the highway still in pursuit of Jesse, Brenda and Penny.

"Motherfucker, come on man this shit is ridicules!" screamed Butch as he wheeled the minivan in the direction of Van Cortlandt Park. Butch spotted the red car that carried Team Three from the rearview window. Butch grabbed his radio and yelled "Take out the tires! Do not fire inside the truck, just take out the tires!"

"Butch if they shoot the tires it could cause them to lose control of the truck possibly killing everyone inside," Zig advised.

"Zig just shut up man! I know what the fuck I'm doing! Just sit there and don't say a damn word! If you had fired her car up when I said, we wouldn't be in this shit, so keep your mouth shut!"

Not saying a word, Zig held onto his door handle because of the sharp turn Butch had made. Butch saw the smoke that sputtered from the exhaust of the truck and calmly remarked, "They're running out of gas."

Inside the truck Jesse quickly pumped the accelerator and looked at the fuel gage that read "E" Jesse glanced to her left, and while the speed of the truck decreased, she spotted a closed warehouse that was about three hundred feet away.

"Jesse why are we slowing down, they're right behind us!" Brenda asked.

"Brenda, the gauge is on empty. We are out of gas!"

"Jesse call me crazy but I don't hear any sirens and I know some-body had to see the accident on the Deegan. Still we have to get going, they're right behind us!"

The truck continued to sputter as it came to a halt. Jesse looked at her partner and asked, "Brenda how much ammo do we have left?"

"The rifle is still juiced up, the glocks are fully loaded and I have two clips in my pocket. What do you have in mine Jess?"

"Brenda we have to get to that warehouse because that's our best chance of getting out of this shit. I'm pretty sure the troops know we're on the run, but take a look where at we are, this area is so isolated. That warehouse is where this battle will either be won or lost sister."

"Jesse, it looks like it's about a block and a half away. Penny is scared to death, and they have a clear shot on either side of the truck."

Jesse wiped sweat from her face while she unfastened her seatbelt. "Brenda they're not going to shoot, this I'm sure of. We have what they want and they're going to let us go inside."

Brenda kneeled down in front of Penny and rubbed the little girl gently across the cheek, "I'll lead Penny out the front window while you cover us."

Jesse began to thrust her strong legs against the driver's side win-dow. The door was jammed from the collision with the black mini-van. Jesse took a break from kicking the window and asked Brenda, "What are they doing?"

Brenda took another look and answered, "Nothing, just sitting there."

Jesse raised her legs again with more force this time she kicked the whole pane of glass onto the street which caused a crashing sound.

"You and Penny get up here!" Jesse commanded.

Brenda grabbed the little girl by her hand and softly said, "Swee-theart, I know you're a little frightened, and that's okay baby, but we can't stay here. Now I want you to stay low and close to me, because we're getting out of here."

Penny shook her head no, "I can't they're going to kill me."

"Small Fry listen to me; remember when we promised that we wouldn't let anything happen to you? Well, we don't break promises, but you have to listen to us. Now come on baby sis, you can do this" Jesse encouraged.

Carefully Penny climbed over bundles of newspapers and grabbed onto Brenda's out-stretched hand and bravely approached the front of the truck.

Butch and Zig sat in their van and watched in silence when Butch grabbed the radio, "Listen to me Team Three, this is almost over. Allow them to get out of the truck because they can only go so far. If for any reason they try to go in another direction, that's when we take action."

A voice on the other end responded, "That's a copy, we'll let them move."

"Zig get ready. The barcode gun is in the black duffel bag in the backseat" Butch ordered.

Without any hesitation Zig did as he was told.

Brenda carefully escorted Penny to the front of the truck where Jesse waited. Brenda handed her partner the assault rifle while she removed some glass particles that sat atop the dashboard.

"Brenda let me go out first and cover the front of the truck, if a engine is started on either car, I'll hear it. You help Penny get out and cover her at all times. When you begin to make your way to the factory door, stay in front of the truck using it as a shield. I'll be right on your rear, got it?"

Brenda patted Jesse on her arm and replied, "Got it." Brenda watched as her partner quickly climbed out of the glassless window. As Jesse jumped to the ground, she quickly dashed to the right side of the truck and peered out to check on the whereabouts of Butch and Zig. In a crouch, Jesse hurried to the left side where she could clearly see the red vehicle that held Team Three.

Brenda helped Penny climb on the drivers' seat. Penny assisted by lifting her right leg and sticking it out the window. Penny was very scared and asked Brenda, "Are you coming with me?"

Brenda smiled at Penny and stated, "I'll be right behind you. Besides I don't want to stay in this truck alone." That last remark put a small smile on Penny's face.

Jesse continued to keep her eyes on the black mini-van while Brenda assisted Penny out the window and to the ground.

Satisfied that Penny was clear, Brenda climbed out the window and jumped to the ground slightly spraining her left ankle. Brenda gritted her teeth and mouthed silently to Jesse, "I'm okay."

"Alright ya'll there's no time to waste. Get moving now!" Jesse commanded to Brenda and Penny.

They adjusted the vest on Penny as she looked at her new guardians. Penny thought confidently that they wouldn't let any harm come to her like they promised. She held onto Brenda's belt loop and looked up at Jesse with an "I'm ready" nod of the head.

Jesse turned her back to Penny as she squatted into a defensive stance. "Stick with Ms. Brenda Small Fry and do what she says. Do you hear me?"

"Yes Ms. Jesse, I hear you."

Jesse locked her eyes on the red car while Brenda clutched Penny by the wrist. With her glock cocked and ready to blast, Brenda walked backwards with Penny close to her. Brenda's main objective was to protect Penny, but she didn't want to leave Jesse by the truck alone. Deep inside, Brenda had confidence that Jesse would make it to the warehouse safely.

"Walk quicker baby, and stay close behind me."

Penny commanded her little legs to go as fast as they could as she sucked air into her body and trudged on, "Yes, Ms. Brenda."

Quickly, Brenda shuffled Penny and herself to the right so that they could get closer to the side of the warehouse. As Brenda clutched her weapon with two hands, she gritted her teeth and noticed that Jesse had made her move to catch up with them.

His radio in hand, Butch pushed the button and intoned, "Team Three when they enter we'll give them forty-five seconds, and then after that, we're going in."

"That's a copy", responded Team Three.

"Butch, I thought we agreed that we would keep the strategic moves and commanding of the men to me", said Zig who looked for clarity.

Butch stared in his brother's direction and responded- "Command what Zig? With all your commanding we have gone from eight men down to four! As of this moment you have been removed from your duties. I have too much at risk, and time is running out so you are no longer in command my brother. I am not about to let you blow my twenty-five million dollars."

"So now it's your money huh, Butch?" responded Zig.

"Listen motherfucker, like I said time is running out and the fucking money will be entering back into Melvin's damn account, so you can think what the hell you want, okay? From this point on I'm the head mother-fucker in charge!"

Butch picked up his binoculars to look at his prey. He smiled as he noticed that Jesse, Brenda, and Penny all stood at the front entrance of the warehouse. Jesse yanked on the door but is unable to open it. Butch watched as Brenda pushed them to the side. Jesse covered Penny's ears while she spun the little girl away from the door. Butch heard BANG! BANG!

Having fired into the door, Butch continued to watch as Brenda and Jesse together pulled on the door to get it open. Butch looked on as the two detectives retreat inside the warehouse with his twenty-five million dollar ticket. Butch smiled to himself as he was damn sure they would never exit the building again.

Butch retrieved the radio, "Get ready because this time shit is going to be done right" he said while he stared at Zig square in the eyes.

The two vehicles started up and both began to roll slowly towards the warehouse where a twenty-five year plan would finally come to a head.

Chapter Twenty-Six
The King Returns

6:35AM and Tiebout Avenue had turned into a police command center as police vehicles lined the block from one end to the other. Two members from the crime lab had brushed down Jesse's car for prints and any other evidence that would be helpful. Other members were inside Jesse's apartment collecting evidence. At the captains request all news media were restricted to each corner and not allowed to enter the block.

News helicopters hovered above in the sky while bomb sniffing dogs were led by their masters. Jesse's building is being guarded by at least ten officers headed by Detectives Jones and Cannon along with four other detectives. They questioned not only tenants who resided in Jesse's building, but they also questioned people from the building next door and the owners of the single family attached homes across the street.

Next to his superior Chief Robert McIntosh, who is surveying the block, Captain Gordon explained, "In a nutshell sir that's what I'm dealing with here. My two best detectives are nowhere to be found, and on top of that, we have a nine year old-child who is our chief witness to a multiple homicide that included her father. On top of that sir, I believe that the assailants involved in her father's death are involved with the current situation we are in right now. Also found dead were her mother, brother and sister. They were found in another section of the Bronx burned to death with four other people, who I personally believe were hired to help in the death of the family."

Chief McIntosh, who is a short and burly Irish man with forty years on the police force, removed his hat and rubbed his stubby fingers through his white frizzy hair. He took his Captain to the side and said, "Ben listen to me very carefully. I understand and feel your concern for your two detectives, but you have no justification for holding these people captive in their own neighborhood. You have the block under heavy surveillance which is acceptable, but get in a few more minutes of questioning and let these people get on with their lives."

"Sir, with all due respect, I have two dead officers with families that I have to deal with. They were disposed from here with multiple bullets in their heads, including two bodies from Detective James apartment who I believe tried to kill our detectives. All that has transpired this morning, not one person claims to have heard or seen anything. Can you believe that?" Gordon responded.

"Ben these people are frightened to death. Don't expect them to come forward with anything. You just have to take what you have, roll up your sleeves, and find James and Simple before it's too late. Listen to me Ben, I have to say this. Ninety-one percent of the adults in this block work, pay taxes and vote. On top of that, we have an election coming up next year. The last person I want to answer to is our commissioner. He's been coming down on us hard about the excessive overtime and you have the entire force out here with you. More money means me getting my ass chewed out. If his popularity falls so does my fat ass. Now come on Ben let these people go and let's find your detectives" McIntosh said as he patted Gordon on the back.

The two highly ranked officers walked back to Jesse's building and noticed a very small man that walked up the street pulling a suitcase on wheels. The man got closer to the building when he stopped to look inside Jesse's car that was visibly torched. The man laid his luggage on the ground and used it as a step. He then peered inside the vehicle with utter disbelief and serious concern before he was asked to move away by officers..

King Tut happened upon the police activity as he returned from his trip. Tut walked directly up to Gordon and McIntosh. "Excuse me officers, my name is Tut and I live inside this building; I had to park my car two blocks away and maneuver my way through your barriers. Let me ask you a question, though. Is Jesse James okay?"

Captain Gordon looked at the well dressed and vociferous Tut, and asked, "How do you know Detective James?"

"We have been neighbors in this building for the past nine years and have become good friends. Sir obviously something tragic has happened here today. I'm not here to cause you any problems, but I just need to know if Jesse's hurt or in any danger? Tut pleaded.

"Right now I can't answer that question sir, but answer this for me- when was the last time you've seen or spoken to Ms. James?"

"Captain is that right? The last time Jesse and I spoke was five days ago when she helped me pack for my trip to Baltimore. I've tried calling her on numerous occasions this weekend on her cell to see how she was doing, to no avail. Now I see her favorite car is burnt to a crisp and you have no clue if she's okay? Since you have no information about my friend, tell me, where's her dog Apollo?"

"Mr. Tut, due to a police situation the dog had to be sedated and taken to a city kennel, but I assure you he's fine. Excuse me a second" Gordon told Tut as the Captain turned his attention to one of his officers.

Tut looked up at his building and then at his watch. He moved a little closer so that he could eaves drop better on what the officer had to say to Captain Gordon.

"Captain, I don't know if this means anything or not sir, but I just heard over my scanner that there was a car wreck on the Deegan where two occupants were killed near exit thirteen."

"Officer Wilson you're right, what does this have to do with the situation here?" Chief McIntosh intoned.

Officer Wilson has worked many years with Captain Gordon. Gordon had taught him well under his leadership. He has also taught his subordinate to follow his gut instincts. Officer Wilson's intuition heightened after he heard about the car accident over the scanner. It was very early in the morning with minimal traffic, so it was difficult for Wilson to understand why it was such a fatal accident

Officer Wilson was not fond of Chief McIntosh. He decided to tell the Captain about the accident with McIntosh still on the scene. "Well sir, it's just that the report over the scanner says that the two men were wearing Marine dog tags, and semi automatic weapons were found inside the vehicle they were driving. Also, highway patrol reports came across the scanner saying they had a school bus driver who was on the Deegan at the time of the accident. The bus driver reported that it didn't look like an accident."

Captain Gordon knew how most of his team felt about the chief. He knew it took a lot for Wilson to discuss the case in his presence. They all knew McIntosh was an ass kisser, and they all limited his involvement in their day to day cases.

Captain Gordon placed his hand on the officer's shoulder and said, "Officer Wilson, good job we will definitely take your information into consideration. You may return to your post until we need you."

Officer Wilson, visibly upset calmed himself and answered, "Yes sir and you're welcome."

Tut watched Wilson return to his car. He turned to Gordon and asked "Excuse me Captain Gordon, but I'm exhausted and I need to get to my apartment. Can I go upstairs now?"

Chief McIntosh nodded his head in agreement as Captain Gordon turned and answered "Sure Mr. Tut you go to your apartment. Please reframe from going to Jesse's apartment. It's a crime scene and I want nothing compromised in there."

Tut grabbed his luggage and went upstairs as Gordon waved Sergeant Cross over, "Get all of the information you have gathered, and report back to me with it immediately. Let the people know we are done for now. Get all their names in contact information in case we need to question them further. Keep Jesse's apartment, her car and our two comrades' vehicle roped off because it's still a crime scene."

*****

Captain Gordon and his team continued to collect evidence, and brainstorm with each other. The team worked together but they felt a significant loss of not knowing if Jesse and Brenda were alright. Some officers had anger in their eyes while others had tears. They were all hurt by the execution of officers Torrey and Claxton.

They all wanted revenge on the degenerates responsible. The day heated up and so were the emotions of the officers. Being the good leader that he was, Gordon called to One Police Plaza and requested additional counselors from the EAP unit.

Gordon looked at his watch and it was 7:05AM. He began to disperse different units from the scene but before he did Gordon looked at the faces of his men. They all were visibly distraught over the events that led up to that present moment. They all stood at attention while they're Captain addresses them

"Jesse and Brenda are a part of our team. They single handedly closed many cases with their heroism risking their lives to protect others. I love these women as if they were my own daughters. I need you to love them as if they were your sisters. You will scour every street all the way down to one-three-eight, including The Major Deegan, The Bruckner, The Hutch and The Whitestone. We will be getting help from other departments, but understand that this is our responsibility. You all have photos of Jesse and Brenda. They are hopefully still in possession of a little girl named Penny Baker. If and when any of you come across, or think you have a clue to their whereabouts, you will immediately contact me! Ladies and gentlemen, go find our family members!"

The officers quickly entered their vehicles and left Tiebout Avenue as King Tut who changed into fresh clothes, exited the alleyway without being spotted. He walked to his car parked two blocks away.

The muscles in his legs tensed up with every step, Tut dismissed the strain from his mind. He could only think about Jesse. Tut removed his keys from his pocket and pressed his keychain that opened his door automatically. Tut climbed into his customized Elektra 225 with leather interior and started the engine.

Tut pulled out and checked his silver colt 45 revolver, to make sure it was fully loaded. He put the gun away and pulled away from the curb. While he drove, Tut had a bad feeling in his gut. He realized life would never be the same for him if anything happened to Jesse. He thought to himself "God help any motherfucker who harms one strand of hair on Jesse's head, because that son of a bitch will have to answer to me!"

Tut remembered what the officer said to Captain Gordon and drove in that direction with the hope he would find the love of his life.

Chapter Twenty-Seven
Enter the Dragon

The sun baked the streets with its rays and the cops roamed the area in search for Jesse, Brenda, and Penny Baker. Captain Gordon had all bases covered from one end of the Bronx to the other. King Tut was fully loaded and in pursuit of finding Jesse. Butch and Zig along with their crew had the girls cornered in a warehouse. They can almost taste twenty-five million dollars on their starving tongues and they wouldn't stop until they got it.

Butch and Zig stood in front of the door that Brenda blew a hole in. They turned their attention to the red vehicle as the doors opened. Getting out of the car were four men, which made Butch look at his brother in disgust.

"Oh shit who the fuck are those other guys? Hey Butch, I had no idea he had two more guys inside the car."

"Zig what the fuck are you talking about? How the fuck can the right hand not know what the left is doing? You asked me for absolute control of this part of the operation, and I gave it to you, now look at this shit!"

The four men were clean cut and wore army fatigues as they got within a few feet of the Steel brothers. One of them spoke up, "Butch come on brother, don't be so hard on Zig. He had no idea that I always roll with my own back-up. As far as these guys, don't worry about that because I have them covered."

Butch studied the face of the man that commanded the floor and cleared his throat to speak, "Let not one hair on the head of the little girl be harmed until I get what I need. When she is found and captured, bring her to me immediately! As far as the two officers are concerned, eliminate them on sight."

Butch sipped some water, checked his guns and continued, "Right about now I believe the whole City of New York's Finest are on a major manhunt for those three individuals inside this warehouse. They will send everything the department has at us in order to get their detectives back safe and sound. Time is not on my side so make this shit quick."

Three of the men removed and checked their weapons as the leader nonchalantly leaned on the door and proclaimed, "Well men I guess it's time to enter the motherfucking dragon."

Butch was not impressed that this bastard gave orders. He was even more pissed that Zig was about to listen to him.

Zig opened the door which made a long creaking sound. Everyone entered the dusty and damp three story building on full alert. The men were pretty convinced that Jesse and Brenda weren't stupid. They had chased them since the wee hours of the morning. Teams One and Two were dead and they didn't want to be next. They were all sure including Butch and Zig, not to underestimate the detectives.

*****

Penny sat inside an empty closet wiping sweat from her eyes. Penny saw only a slight gleam of light that came from under the door. Penny did her best not to move and used all her mite as she fought to keep her emotions under control. At that moment Penny felt it was time to be brave and keep it together like Jesse and Brenda.

Penny recognized how they protected her up to this point, so she began to think about what could she do to help her friends? Again Penny adjusted the oversized vest on her chest and the only thing she could think about was if her friends would lead them all to safety.

*****

Butch and Zig along with their four accomplices were finally inside the warehouse. Butch wasted little time to give orders, "From what I can see there are only two ways that lead to this entrance, the one to our right, and that one straight ahead. I need you two men to cover the right, and you along with your partner can cover straight ahead. My brother and I will be behind you. There are only three floors, so they shouldn't be hard to find. Remember I don't give a fuck about the cops! It's the girl I want alive."

*****

Jesse was crouched behind an old desk left behind by the last occupants. Jesse looked across the large floor of the warehouse and wondered if her partner was okay. Jesse knew they were each on their own, and that they were the last line of defense for Penny. For some reason and Jesse didn't know why but Tut's two vacation tickets to anywhere crossed her mind. She realized that there was a distinct possibility that she may never make it out of this warehouse. This resulted in increased swearing to herself that she wouldn't take life or love for granted again. While sweat beads formed on her forehead, Jesse squeezed the trigger a little tighter as she heard footsteps approaching.

*****

The strong smell of turpentine permeated the air. Brenda held her glock and looked quickly at her watch and wondered if Vanessa got up in time to report for her last week of work. Brenda remembered that Summer Jam was in two weeks and blinked her eyes rapidly with the hope that she could push her sister out of her mind, knowing that possibly there would be no tomorrow. All of a sudden as Brenda crouched behind a large crate, she observed the door knob as it began to turn slowly.

*****

Inside the south staircase, Butch led two of his accomplices to the second floor exit where he opened the door slowly, and peeped through so that he could navigate the scene. He looked back at his two men nodding his head to let them know that it was clear. With guns in hand, Butch made sure the men entered ahead of him.

While the warehouse floor was clearly visible due to the light from the windows, Brenda scoped her prey like a lion in the bush. She observed three men who split up as they searched the area. Brenda waited precisely for the right moment to strike. She crawled slowly on her belly slithering along the floor with the intent to hide behind a brick column.

*****

Zig and his men entered the third floor with bad intentions at heart. Jesse watched with heightened intensity as she took dead aim at one of the men. Shock waves rocked Jesse's body when her eyes fixated on the second man who stood beside the other. In her disillusionment she shifted her body accidentally knocking over a brick, which bought attention in her direction.

"Here we go!" yelled one of the two accomplices as he fired at the desk with a silenced assault rifle that ripped wood into splinters.

Jesse sat on her butt while she clutched her gun with two hands. She took a deep breath and sucked in as much oxygen as possible, as she slid quickly from behind the desk towards a brick column. She peered through the glare of the sun and dust particles that filled the air. Jesse spotted a man who tried to peek from behind a crate. Jesse not wanting to waste ammo fired once striking the man's ear. It was an absolute bloody mess as the man screamed in pain.

"Oh shit, my fucking ear!" yelled the man as he quickly ducked back behind the crate and held his blood soaked face.

"Listen we don't have to do this! All we want is the girl, and we are done!" Zig promised, who checked his automatic hand gun to make sure his clip was fully loaded.

Jesse scanned the area with rapid eye movement a technique she learned in the military. Jesse remained on the floor and retorted, "Listen up brothers! You better recognize that I'm a surgeon with this mother-fucking gun and there are only two ways your punk asses are leaving today. Either with a bullet in your head or one in your heart. It's your fucking choice."

Zig listened to Jesse while his assailant bled from his injured ear. Zig pointed in the direction that would place the other man on the other side of Jesse. "Have it your way baby, but don't say you didn't have a choice to either live or die!"

Zig fired which made Jesse stay down for cover. A wounded Bob made his move toward the column, but not fast enough as Jesse saw his black steel toe boots moving to her right. Without hesitation, Jesse fired twice and hit Bob in his left ankle and heel which caused him to fall to the ground.

"I'm hit! I'm hit!" Bob screamed as he fired recklessly in Jesse's direction. As noise and the smell of gun powder filled the atmosphere, Bob continued to fire his rifle until all he heard was the clicks of the trigger.

Bob was sprawled out on the dusty floor and yelled, "Listen some-body fire on this bitch so I can take cover!" Silence took over the room and Jesse didn't leave any part of her body visible. She watched Bob make an attempt to crawl for shelter.

"Why don't one of you motherfuckers go get your boy!" Jesse challenged the other men.

Zig squatted down behind a steel bin. He looked over at the other assailant who reported to him "Listen, I got this! Go upstairs and help the other crew, and when I'm done with her ass I'll join you to kill her fucking partner! Now go. I'll cover you!"

The man fired his rifle in Jesse's direction which caused debris to fly in all directions. Zig made his move quickly towards the exit. Jesse wiped sweat from her face with her wrist and tried to zero in on Zig but couldn't.

The exit door slammed causing a loud bang. Silence once again over the room but the tension remained as the man spoke out "Jesse I always felt using a gun was the easy way out when it came to killing someone! I am a firm believer in sticking a blade into a person's stomach while looking into their eyes so that I can see what's going on when they transcend on to the other side, ooh-rah!"

Jesse placed her glock and rifle on the floor beside her head. She listened to the voice that she once called her fellow "Leatherneck" and "Grunt." Jesse spat black dust from her mouth as she shouted, "I need to take care of something first!"

"No baby, you need your energy. I don't want any excuses!" the man yelled as he calmly walked from behind a column.

Jesse watched her soon to be combatant slowly walk over to Bob, who continued to lie on the floor and bleed from his wounds. Jesse watched as her challenger walked over to Bob while he checked the chamber of his gun. The adversary said, "Nothing personal Bob, and I promise to make sure your share goes to that pregnant wife of yours."

"Come on man, I'm not that bad off. Just get me on my feet and we can both kill this…"

Echoes from the barrel of the gun were heard as Jesse watched Bob's body jerk violently before his date with death.

Jesse quickly rose to her feet when she heard the clip from the man's gun hit the floor. Jesse immediately saw Bob on the floor with a hole the size of a plum in his head.

"Baby you had to know I always wanted to stick this in between your legs, right?" said Bob's murderer.

Jesse came from behind the desk and slowly walked towards Randu a man who she believed to be her brother, her recon partner, and a fellow marine.

Randu waved his 12-inch hunting knife. He welded it back in forth from one hand to the other. "Cheer up baby, don't act so surprised. Everybody has a price. Those VA checks don't help with shit when you're trying to take care of a blind father. A hundred thousand dollars helps a whole motherfucking bunch, and besides with Bob's share, two hundred thousand sounds just right. Besides I gladly kill a bitch who would rather fuck a midget instead of a real man."

Behind her back, Jesse removed her other glock and took out the clip. She gently dropped them both to the floor. Jesse rolled up her pants leg, never taking her eyes off Randu, and retrieved her 10-inch Bowie "Beefy Bear" knife.

As both ex-marines walked toward the middle of the floor, Jesse moved her body from side to side to loosen her legs. "I find it very disrespectful that you smile at me Randu."

"Don't take it personal baby; I just had so much respect for you until you chose that dwarf over me. Every time you came up to the crib you made my shit hard. You come up in your shorts and tight tees showing that big ass. You were a big tease and I didn't appreciate that shit. I had to whack off to relieve the tension. After I kill you I will carve out your ass and mount it on my wall with all the other animals I killed. Then I can bang your ass anytime I want! Ooh-rah that bitch! So baby you ready to die?"

Jesse brushed her silky hair away from her face and looked at Randu straight in his eyes and answered in a soft tone, "Every fuckin day."

*****

On the second floor Brenda stood behind the column, and fired a shot in the direction of a brown skin brother whose name was Shane. Brenda hit a large radiator as she heard a long hissing sound that escaped from the piece of steel.

"Come on girlfriend, I know those fumes have to be getting to you! Just tell us where the girl is, and it's over just like that!" promised another brother who went by the name of Quincy.

Brenda did her best to get her bearings and turned her attention to the exit door. Just then the door slowly opened and revealed Zig who held a gun in his hand.

Butch saw his brother from behind some crates and yelled "Zig, get downstairs and find the girl! We're running out of time!

Finally, Zig's name was revealed to Brenda as she watched him do as he was told. Brenda realized that she had to act fast because they were determined to find Penny. At that moment Brenda made her move.

Brenda hoped Shane maintained his position behind the radiator. Brenda bent down and grabbed a bottle of turpentine that sat by her feet. She stuck a piece of paper inside the bottle and lit it with a lighter her father owned many years ago. The flame flickered brightly causing embers to fall on Brenda's hand as she got ready to take her shot.

Brenda tossed the bottle across the warehouse floor. Butch and Quincy watched the flying bottle tumble in the air. The bottle flew directly in Shane's direction as Butch screamed, "Get the hell out of there!"

Shane was not able to respond to Butch's directive as the cocktail quickly descended near his body.

Brenda peeked from behind the column, and watched as Shane covered his head. He dashed to his left with the hope of getting out of the way, but instead he was caught in the back by the cocktail. The bottle shattered into little pieces which gave birth to a large blue flame that instantly engulfed Shane's entire body.

"Oh shit, help me!" begged Shane as he wildly dashed across the floor which only fed the flames. Shane ran in circles, and then stumbled to the hardwood floor screaming incoherently.

"I'm coming Shane!" yelled Quincy as he removed his jacket to help his buddy.

"No, get the fuck back!" screamed Butch as he watched Quincy carelessly leave himself in the open.

In a blink of an eye, Brenda quickly jumped from her column, and before Quincy could get to his friend she released three rounds in succession that hit Shane in the head and in the side of his neck.

Quincy fell back onto the floor, and was is able to scramble back behind some crates and watch his friend of eighteen years succumb to severe flesh wounds.

"I'm gonna kill you bitch! I swear on my fucking mother, I'm gonna kill you!" screamed Quincy as he frantically cocked his automatic weapon while he gritted his teeth.

*****

"Little girl I swear I'm not going to hurt you!" Zig yelled as he quickly walked the first floor of the warehouse in search of Penny. As Zig constantly looked at his watch and rubbed his fingers through his head he checked an old women's bathroom.

*****

While she sat inside the closet where her friends told her to hide, Penny could hear the loud monster-like voice of the man who was partly responsible for her family's death. Curled up like a ball, Penny couldn't help but to tremble like a leaf. From the other side of the door she could hear Zig's loud footsteps as they got closer closer.

*****

Randu attempted to press his right knee onto Jesse's throat as he stood over her. The blades of their knives made squealing noises because of the pressure each combatant applied to one another. Randu had begun to gain an advantage as he pushed down with greater force. The blade began to get closer to Jesse's eyes.

Jesse relieved some of the physical pressure of Randu's knee as she lifted her head upwards. Jesse pushed hard against Randu's strength because she realized she was seconds away from death. Randu had Jesse pinned down and his knife was inches away from her throat. Jesse felt Randu gain an advantage as the knife cut slightly through her first layer of skin. On pure instinct and desperation Jesse reached up and viciously scratched Randu in his eye doing extreme damage to his cornea.

Randu yanked his head back as he screamed in agonizing pain. In reacting to his injured eye, Randu pulled the knife away from Jesse's throat. There was a superficial cut slightly on her neck but Jesse had no time to think about it at that time. Quick with her hand, Jesse swung her knife and delivered a surgeon's cut on Randu's face that traveled from his temple to his chin.

Randu fell back and grabbed his face that was drenched in blood. He couldn't see the cut but he knew it was bad. He could feel the unbearable sting as the salt from his sweat seeped into his wound. Quick to maintain his composure, Randu jumped off Jesse and retreated backwards a few steps. Randu touched his face and looked at his bloody hand then saw Jesse stumble to her feet into a combative stance.

"Bitch your ass is about to die" said Randu, as he looked down at the floor where he could see his blood.

"Come on motherfucker, you ain't hurt, that's a bitch wound. I have a lot more in store for your sorry ass" Jesse taunted.

Randu started to walk circles around Jesse. He watched her brace her body and realized that it would be a dogfight Randu also realized that he underestimated Jesse's fighting abilities.

*****

Shane's body laid motionless and smoldered from Brenda's deadly cocktail. Butch did his best to push the stench of burning human flesh from his mind as the scent filled the entire warehouse floor. Butch looked over at Quincy who was engulfed by the loss of his friend. It was clear to Butch that Quincy's mind was no longer in the game. Regardless of all the drama, Butch realized that things were falling apart and he had to act fast.

"Hey partner, snap the fuck out of it! Your boy is gone!" Butch screamed at Quincy.

"No more fucking games! We get this bitch my way!" replied Quincy as he cocked the trigger on his assault rifle, and began to spray bullets in Brenda's direction.

On her knees and taking cover, Brenda could feel the quick breezes of bullets whiz past her head and realized that she was not in an ideal spot. Brenda grabbed her last cocktail and fired up the newspaper fuse. Dangerously it flicked in her hands as she waited for the precise moment to launch her home-made bomb.

"Partner listen to me! I want her as bad you, so let's be smart! She's not going nowhere because we have her ass boxed in, but let's do this right!" screamed Butch.

The flame of the newspaper got closer to the top of the bottle, and silence filled the air. Brenda tossed the cocktail in the direction of Butch and Quincy but this time, came up short as the cocktail landed on the floor which created a circle of flames.

"Not this time freak!" Quincy vehemently yelled as he took a deep breath, and dashed quickly to a nearby column that bought him closer to Brenda. Butch watched Quincy position himself as he began to fire in Brenda's direction.

Brenda knew that her position was not a good one. She decided that the only choice she had at that moment was to pick a column, and go for the kill throwing caution to the wind.

She gulped in a deep breath, reached behind her back, and removed her second glock. Brenda quickly spun on the balls of her feet and turned herself in the direction where Quincy stood.

Brenda made sure she got a good start and ran from behind the column towards Quincy who was unaware that Brenda came directly his way. Butch saw Brenda as she closed in on Quincy and took aim at Brenda's back. Just then Brenda let off rounds from her glock in Quincy's direction that shattered bricks on the column where he hid.

"Bring it bitch!" Quincy screamed as he squatted down to escape Brenda's shots. What Quincy didn't realize though was that he exposed himself on the other side of the column as Brenda continued to run in his direction. Butch was somewhat impressed at Brenda's ability but still fired two shots from his weapon. The first shot whizzed pass Brenda but the second caught her in the back left shoulder.

While the gun powder burned deep inside the hole of her wound, Brenda accepted the excruciating pain and continued her quest to make it to Quincy. Brenda lowered her body as she slid on the warehouse floor and stopped at the left side of the column with her gun pointed directly at Quincy. Paying too much attention to his right side, Quincy quickly turned to his left and stared directly at Brenda face to face.

"Fuck you!" was the only thing Quincy could muster out of his mouth as a wounded Brenda looked deep into his eyes.

"You wish motherfucker!" Brenda retorted as she fired her glock five times. Three dead center into Quincy's forehead and two in his heart. Brenda watched the large man fall backwards and crash hard onto the floor. Brenda quickly crawled for cover to examine her wound and to shield herself from Butch.

*****

"Come on little girl. I'm not going to hurt you, I promised right!" Zig yelled as he became very frustrated because of his inability to locate the little girl.

On her feet inside the closet, Penny felt the effects of the heat and dust that made her cough out loud. Zig's screaming came to a sudden stop as he tried to zero in on Penny's noise. Penny used the light that came from under the door and listened as Zig's footsteps got closer. Those loud thunderous footsteps stopped right in front of the door. Zig's feet were so big that the shadow from them eliminated the beams of light Penny relied on to see. The little girl was frantic as she darted her head back and forth in search of a way out. Not able to find one, Penny curled into a fetal position and did everything in her power not to scream.

"Where is that little girl? I have no time for this bullshit. I wish she would bring her ass out!" Zig said to himself obviously frustrated. Zig eventually walked away from the door in search of Penny. Inside the closet a sigh of relief engulfed the 9-year old girl as death eluded her once again.

Penny bowed her head and got ready to say the Lord's Prayer that Mrs. Joyce taught her. Penny bent her knees and folded her hands to pray when like a freight train crashing, the door violently swung open that revealed the six-foot two inch Zig Steel.

"There you are young lady" Zig said as he kneeled down in front of the terrified Penny. She stumbled backwards until her back was against the wall. Penny silently wished that the wall would suck her into another world like she's seen on her various Disney movies. She just wanted to escape from the mammoth beast in front of her. Penny remembered his ugly face because he was one of the men who killed Mr. Baker and Eunice.

Zig twisted his head from side to side like an animal in the wild. He studied the little girls' features for a moment, and then stuck his dirty hand out to stroke Penny's face which made her tremble even more. Zig tried to be calm and moved away from the door a little while he said, "Come out the closet sweetheart no one's going to harm you. I just want to look under your arm that's all okay?"

Penny remained still inside the closet not budging an inch. She kept her hands behind her back never took her eyes off Zig, who looked towards the exit door and wondered if his brother was alright. Penny held her hands so that her two little thumbs touched as she continued to stare at Zig.

"I said get the fuck out of the closet!" demanded Zig, as he lost patience with Penny.

Penny took small steps to exit the closet. Zig couldn't help but to smile as he saw part of the barcode tattoo under her right arm. With his large grimy hand spread open, Zig wiggled four of his fingers at Penny for her to come to him. Penny took another step forward and was two feet away from Zig almost out of the closet. The sun splashed rays on Zig's dark sweaty face as Penny smiled at Zig and in turn Zig smiled back at her.

"You see little girl that wasn't so bad, right? Now come on and let me see what's under that arm."

Penny nodded her head up and down then slowly removed her hands from around her back.

"Yes, that's it baby; you see I promised not to hurt you."

In a blink of an eye, Penny courageously presented, hidden behind her back, a can of mace. She stretched out her tiny arms, and with the use of her thumbs she pressed with all her mite. A long string of stinging liquid found its mark dead in Zig's eyes. Zig fell to the floor in pain as he frivolously tried to wipe the sting away. Penny kept the can but cautiously slid out the closet and scooted pass Zig's large body.

"Oh shit! My eyes! My fucking eyes!" screamed Zig as he reached out with his right arm and swung wildly nearly hitting Penny across her head.

Penny frantically looked around the large warehouse floor and spotted a door that read, "Exit", and quickly ran in that direction. Penny entered the dusty staircase, wiped a spider web away from her face and rushed upstairs not really sure where she was going.

*****

On the third floor Jesse bled from her right forearm and her left elbow, from the slices of Randu's knife. She stood in front of Randu and waved her knife from side to side. Jesse quickly moved to her left to avoid Randu's attempt to slice her stomach open. Not wasting the opportunity, Jesse found the outstretched arm of Randu, and sliced him across the wrist that created a deep nasty gash.

"Shit" Jesse said to herself, realizing that she missed Randu's main vein.

"Okay bitch, it's time for brute motherfuckin force!" retorted Randu as he swung faster and harder at Jesse as she backed away from him.

Jesse maintained focus on Randu, but was unaware of a wet spot on the floor. She suddenly fell backwards and landed hard on her back causing agonizing pain to radiate from her lower back up to her neck. While on the floor, Jesse saw her Beretta and the adjoining clip a few feet away. Somehow Jesse managed enough strength to quickly spin on her stomach and crawl towards her weapon. Aware of Jesse's intentions, an enraged Randu leaped on top of Jesse and proceeded to viciously slash at her back.

Randu did a "Michael Myers" and sliced Jesse's shirt to shreds, then noticed under her shirt she wore Kevlar shirt. In a savage rage, Randu quickly rolled Jesse on her back and straddled himself on top of her.

"Damn my shit is hard. I can dig into your ass right now, but your ass is gonna die instead!" retorted Randu as he held his knife chest high ready to plunge it in Jesse's throat.

In an attempt to protect her face, Jesse noticed something that put her in complete shock.

"Get off of her now!" screamed Penny as she ran and dived onto Randu's back in an attempt to bite and scratch him.

Jesse for the first time in a very long time was terrified by the situation at hand. Not being able to move her legs because of the weight of Randu, Jesse used all her flexibility to stretch out her arm and reach for her handgun. Randu still had the knife in his hand and was able to turn his head around to see who was biting his neck and shoulder. He noticed it was the little girl they had been looking for which fueled his anger. Randu reached with his free hand and grabbed Penny by one of her afro puffs. He violently yanked her off of his neck and tossed her across the floor as if Penny were a rag doll.

Randu turned his attention back on Jesse and punched her on the side of her face which resulted in a nasty bruise. Jesse absorbed the blow like a true champion as she taxed her muscles and ligaments to reach for her gun.

Randu grabbed Jesse's leg and yanked it forward in an attempt to cut her achilles tendon. However Jesse's quick thinking resulted in her shifting her leg as the debilitating gash caught her on her calf instead.

"Fuck!" Jesse screamed as her leg burned with pain. Jesse lifted her upper body halfway off the floor and was able to get a forceful punch into Randu's throat. Her vicious blow caused him to gasp for air and drop his knife. Jesse kicked with everything she had, and was able to move her body to the right so that she could grab her gun.

Randu gained his composure as Jesse slid most of her body from under him and went for the clip that was inches away. Jesse reached for the clip and looked at Penny who seemed to be in a trance.

"Penny get out of here! Wake up! Get out of here!" Jesse screamed as Penny didn't move. Quickly Jesse turned her attention back to the clip, but was pulled away by her right leg by Randu who resembled a crazed madman on a mission. In defense, Jesse swung the gun at Randu's head but missed by inches.

Randu looked down on Jesse and smiled revealing blood-soaked teeth. He reached for his knife when Penny made her move. Jesse wondered what the little girl was doing when she ran to her right side. Jesse couldn't believe what Penny was about to attempt.

Penny reached down and grabbed the clip that was on the floor. Penny showed no fear when she headed straight for Jesse, who seemed to be losing the battle with Randu. Jesse had the empty butt of the gun pointed upward in the air as Penny got closer to Jesse with the clip. Randu's mind began to play tricks on him as he couldn't believe what he was witnessed. It was almost like Randu had watched a movie in slow motion as Penny pushed the 16-shot clip into Jesse's gun. Finally he snapped out of the trance and reached for his knife when he heard a dreadful, 'Click'

Jesse pulled on the Beretta loading a bullet inside the chamber. She had the gun steady, aimed and loaded inches away from Randu's head. Jesse didn't blink an eye or show any remorse, as Jesse simply said to Penny, "Turn around baby"

Penny turned away from the scene and all she could hear was the explosive sound of Jesse's berretta as it sent bullets in Randu's skull.

Jesse pushed Randu's dead body off of her and commanded to Penny, "Stay right there! Don't turn around baby!" Jesse lifted Penny up and made sure she didn't see Randu's dead body. Jesse stared at the brave little girl who just saved her life. "Small Fry come with me!"

*****

Jesse stood in the stairway with Penny out of breath and exhausted over her battle with Randu. Jesse ripped her shirt in strips to make tourniquets to stop the bleeds on her leg and wrist. Jesse was physically a mess and could feel her face as it began to swell from the right cross Randu delivered to her jaw. Emotionally, Jesse didn't know how to feel. She considered Randu to be one of her best friends. Although she refused to show it, she was devastated about Randu's involvement in this whole scenario. However, the man who tried to take her life was not the man she knew and she was glad his fucking ass was dead.

"Small Fry I want you to stay inside this staircase, one flight below and don't move. If you see anyone besides Ms. Brenda or me, you run downstairs to the front door that will take you outside do you understand? Where's the mace Ms. Brenda gave you?"

Penny rubbed her hands together tightly, because of her nervousness, and answered, "I sprayed a big man with it when he found me in the closet. He was the man in my house that night! He killed Mr. Baker!"

Penny rushed to and hugged Jesse tightly around her waist. Jesse rubbed Penny across the face and promised, "Boo, just stay right there like I said. We'll be back."

Jesse looked in the direction of the gunfire. She adjusted the vest on Penny, and told the little girl to stay. Jesse carefully headed to the second floor of the warehouse.

Jesse cracked the door slowly and peeped inside. She scanned the area carefully then screamed "Brenda you here?"

Still behind the column sweating profusely, even in this very dangerous situation, the sound of Jesse's voice sent a soothing almost therapeutic feeling through Brenda's body. She felt as such because she knew her friend was alive.

"I'm here Jess! One went right through me! I stopped the flow for now. Three columns to your left you can see that motherfucker!"

Jesse stuck her head inside the door, she checked the area her partner mentioned, and sure enough she saw Butch. Unfortunately she's unable to get a good shot because of his position behind the column.

"All I want is the girl! Just give me the girl and we all walk away!" Butch pleaded Jesse.

"Brother, you had the option of rotting your ass in prison! But you fucked that up big time when you shot my girl! So get ready for your toe-tag because your ass is going to the morgue!" Jesse retorted.

Brenda attempted to peak around the corner of her column, but quickly ducked her head back as a bullet from Butch's gun whizzed past her face. Without looking, Brenda held her hand out and pointed it in Butch's direction, firing four times but hit nothing.

With frustration engulfing his face, Butch glanced at his watch and realized that time was running out. Behind him was the exit so he contemplated his next move. The second exit door just closed; which indicated to Butch was that the bitch was now inside. It was now two against one.

*****

Unaware that Jesse just entered the second floor, Zig was busy rubbing his puffy red eyes from the mace Penny accurately delivered. Aimlessly he walked to the staircase door and focused on his eyes then stopped suddenly because he heard someone who had sniffled.

Zig looked over the banister and saw a shadow that moved without direction. He removed his pistol as he took three more steps down the stairs in the direction of the noise when he noticed a small figure that stood at the top of the staircase.

*****

Jesse crawled on the floor with gun in hand as she grimaced in pain because her leg burned like hell. With her head to the ground, Jesse advanced a few more feet and was startled at the sight of the burnt dead body of Shane. Jesse experienced a flashback of the bodies she's seen while in the military, as she went around the crisp corpse and continues onward.

Butch listened carefully not for Brenda but for her partner as he crouched down and began to look in the direction of the exit where she had to enter. Butch scanned the large dirty room but remained vigilant because he still had Brenda to contend with. Butch turned his body slightly to the left and noticed three steel drums where Jesse had crawled behind.

In an instant the situation pushed through Butch's mind. How did he allow these two fucking broads, to out think him? Butch was cornered, two against one and just think a while ago he called his brother stupid. Butch thought how ironic it was because he felt like a stupid ass himself.

"Brenda do you have a lock on his ass?" Jesse yelled.

"If his fuckin' ass steps from behind that column, I'll peel his damn dome!" replied Brenda.

Butch contemplated the exit door again and asked himself if he could make it. He figured that it was his only chance to get away from those crazy ass females. The way the women had themselves hidden, he had no real good shot at either one of them. Self-loathing stepped into play again. Butch prided himself on his ability to get through any situation. Butch felt less of a man because for the first time and a while he felt hopeless. Butch surveyed the area again and noticed something important that he overlooked. The steel drums that sheltered Jesse had worn-out warning signs stamped on them that read; 'Flammable'

Butch looked back towards Brenda who he knew was injured. He fired twice at her not really concerned if he hit her or not, because Butch just wanted to cause a distraction. Butch again fired his gun this time at Jesse and in the process hit the drums that protected her which caused them both to leak fluid.

"Brenda that motherfucker is moving, take the shot!" screamed Jesse.

Brenda carefully peeked from behind her column, and sure enough she saw Butch's punk-ass run towards the exit. Brenda took dead aim when from her peripheral vision she saw a lighter fly through the air that headed right for the drums where Jesse hid.

"Jesse move baby! Get away from there! Hurry up!" Brenda screamed as she took her eyes off Butch for a split second which allowed him to escape. At that moment the lighter hit the floor and ignited the spilled liquid.

Jesse smelled the liquid and didn't think twice. She quickly jumped to her feet and ran towards the exit. On her way out she saw Brenda who continued to bleed from her shoulder. Jesse stopped to help friend get out of there. Brenda knew her partner well and commanded "Go! Don't look back! I'll be right behind you!"

"Brenda please! You know I'm not leaving you here! Put your good arm around my neck and let's get the fuck out of here!"

Brenda and Jesse ran side by side when the two liquid-filled drums ignited. Jesse turned abruptly as she heard from behind the exit door, "Jesse help me!"

Jesse grabbed Brenda by the waist and charged for the door. Like a bull she ignored the cut on her leg and rammed the door open. There was a thunderous explosion that released a ball of flames. The vibration from the explosion pushed the two women out of the door and into the second floor staircase.

Brenda and Jesse coughed and gasped for air as they both heard from a distance Penny screaming for her little life.

*****

Smoke poured out from the second floor window of the warehouse. Tut took notice of it as he made a right at Exit 13. He assumed this had to be the area where that officer spoke to Captain Gordon about earlier.

Tut watched as a tow truck removed a wrecked vehicle from the highway. Flares sat in the middle lane that was slowed by traffic and monitored by one state trooper. Tut proceeded off Exit 13 and couldn't understand how the black cloud of smoke that filled the sky was ignored by the trooper.

Determined to go straight towards the warehouse, Tut found his phone and speed dialed Jesse's cell to no avail as he waited for an answer but got none. Tut began to get closer to the secluded area as he could see from a distance two idle vehicles up ahead.

*****

Penny was all alone as she believed Jesse and Brenda were dead from the explosion. She knew they were upstairs and was sure those men killed them. Penny frantically began to cry as she ran towards the door that lead outside. In route straight for the door, Penny heard a door slam loudly.

Frightened to death, Penny mustered up the courage to turn around as she looked behind. All she saw was a fierce Zig in high pursuit who gained on her fast. Fear temporarily froze Penny right where she stood but she snapped out of it and quickly turned around to run towards the entrance door. Just a few feet away from the door, Penny came to an abrupt stop as her head jerked backwards because Zig had grabbed one of her afro puffs.

"I should cut your throat little girl! You are really pissing me off right about now! Didn't I tell you I wouldn't hurt you? I should kill your little ass!" Zig screamed as he rubbed a 10-inch stainless steel hunting knife across Penny's puffy red cheek menacingly.

Penny cried uncontrollably as she tried hard to break Zig's unrelenting grip…and to top matters off, Penny knew he was one hundred times her size.

"Please mister let me go! I didn't do anything to you, please don't hurt me!" Penny begged, as Zig continued to rub the knife up and down her face.

"My brother! You came through!" yelled Butch in glee as he opened the door and saw his brother with their prized possession. To Butch and Zig, the little girl had the power to alleviate twenty-five years of pain and suffering that they felt was unfairly bestowed upon them. Butch walked faster and never took his eyes off Penny who recognized him from her home that Friday.

Penny's heart felt as if it just fell into an abyss. Even though she was just a 9 year-old child, the little girl saw that Butch had bad intentions in his dark evil eyes.

"I want to go home! Please leave me alone, just leave me alone!" cried Penny as Butch continued to walk forward.

"Zig hold her arm up now!" Butch demanded.

With very little effort, Zig lifted the little girl's arm and revealed the red barcode tattoo. Butch checked the time for the noon deadline for the money transfer. His watch read 8:48AM. Just then Butch was startled because of movement in the room.

"Let her go, Motherfucker!" demanded an injured and bloodied Jesse as she held up Brenda who grimaced from her injured shoulder. Jesse, who lost her weapons while she escaped the explosion, coughed from the smoke still trapped on her lungs.

Brenda pointed her gun in Zig's direction with no idea how many shots remained in her clip, but knew all she needed was one and yelled, "Whatever the plan was my brother, it's not going down! I'm telling you to let the girl go. You've done enough to her already and the shit stops here! Let her go!"

Zig callously smiled at Penny and picked her up. He used her as a shield, and then turned to face Jesse and Brenda.

"Smart move my brother! Fuck them dykes, were in charge! They're not going to shoot with her in front of you! Come on Zig, I know another way out!" Just then everybody heard muffled sounds that came from outside. For sure the sound became more profound as it got closer. "

Shit come on Zig, I can hear the sirens. Somebody called the fire department! Let's go baby, we have it all now, it's over!" screamed a desperate Butch.

Zig turned to Butch and provided a smile upon his face as he bought Penny forward.

"They're not going to shoot little brother, now come on, time is running out!" Butch demanded.

Zig glanced at his powerful big brother who had always been in control, and was proud of the fact that he was the master planner.

Butch gave Jesse and Brenda a military salute while he proceeded to leave the building. Jesse and Brenda felt helpless because they couldn't risk Penny's life with an attempted shot in Zig's direction. Poor Penny no longer fought for freedom and wore a blank stare in her eyes.

Butch took a few steps forward then looked at Zig who had a strange expression on his face. Right at that moment, Zig quickly turned away from Butch, released Penny, and proceeded to push her in the direction of Brenda and Jesse.

Not thinking twice, Penny ran towards her two guardian angels. A shocked Butch fell slowly to his knees with his mouth gaped open and looked at his brother in utter disbelief.

Jesse looked at Penny and screamed, "Run baby run!"

Butch reached from behind his back, pulled out a weapon, and pointed it directly towards the little girls' head. In sheer pain, Brenda held her weapon with two hands and fired at Butch grazing the left side of his skull. That shot caused him to fall backwards and drop his weapon.

Penny ran and jumped into Jesse's arms while Brenda without hesitation took aim and fired at Zig but all she heard was a click of an empty weapon.

Zig looked down at his brother who bled from the face. Extremely angry, Zig grabbed his brother's gun and yelled "Why did you shoot him? I let her go!"

"Jesse go now!" ordered Brenda as she zeroed in on Zig who took aim at them.

The detectives and the young girl busted out of the entrance doors into the sun baked empty area and heard the sound of fire trucks. They turned their attention to a garbage dumpster where Jesse, Brenda and Penny ran for cover. Gunshots were fired in rapid succession that rattled the dumpster. .

"Run just run" screamed Jesse as she hopped on one leg and pulled Penny along with her.

Zig ran out the door with Butch draped over his shoulder and screamed, "I'll kill you all! You didn't have to hurt my brother!"

The women sprinted as fast as they could; when Brenda witnessed Zig help get Butch inside a black minivan. "Hurry up we have to get to a public place because he's going to come after us!" Brenda wailed.

They all continued to run past the fueled-out newspaper truck they used to get to the warehouse. Brenda and Jesse with Penny in tow ran painfully down the service road of the Major Deegan Expressway.

"Oh shit!" Jesse exclaimed as she gritted her teeth from the pain not only from the cut on her leg but also from the cramps on her side. What made matters worse; Jesse spotted a long black sedan that sped towards them.

Jesse and Brenda knew that they could not outrun the car so they quickly turned in another direction with Penny in an attempt to elude the car. Exhausted and unable to run anymore Jesse removed her knife and grasped for air.

Brenda placed Penny behind her and found a nice sized rock that she picked up. The two female warriors guarded Penny who stood behind them. Suddenly the long nosed vehicle's came to a halt and the locks on the doors popped up.

Jesse and Brenda were psyched for this encounter. Jesse held the handle of her knife tighter and Brenda slowly raised her good arm ready to throw the rock at whoever exited the car. Jesse's eyes widen at the sight of King Tut as he got out of the car.

"Come on everybody get in and let's get some help!" Tut ordered.

Tut tilted the front seat so they all could get in the backseat. Jesse hesitated before she got inside the car. Her eyes pierced Tut's eyes as nothing was said but much was communicated between the two of them. Jesse reached out her bloody hand and palmed Tut's face as tears streamed down her cheeks. Tut nodded his head and said, "I know baby, I know." Chills ran through both their bodies as Jesse got inside the car.

Tut put the car in drive and looked in his rearview window "I have to get you all to a hospital."

Taking a deep breath Brenda said, "No Tut we're going to my place, no public places yet because the hunters are still out there."

Tut nodded his head and drove off towards Brenda's house. Penny sat in between Jesse and Brenda and grabbed their hands squeezing them tightly as fire trucks whisked by.

Chapter Twenty-Eight
My Brother's Keeper

While the radio announced the multiple murders of the Baker family, Butch and Zig sat at the dinette table where they planned how they would get paid for their long-suffering lives.

After Butch bandaged his face, he turned off the radio and sat silently to stare at the black barcode gun. This was the same barcode gun that was supposed to be used on Penny to free Melvin's fortune. The clock on the wall that ticked made Butch crazy. Every second penetrated his brain. Every 'tick' reminded him that time was no longer on his side. The dream of the money escaped them with each minute that went by.

Zig sat silently and peeled away scabs on his hands, never saying a word since they entered the apartment.

"Zig did you wear your gloves while driving the van to the train station?"

"Yes, I did and I made sure to dump our clothes in the sewer too."

"Little brother, thanks for getting me out of that warehouse, that bullet just missed my skull" Butch said.

"Don't ever thank me for something like that Butch, because that's what brothers do for one another."

Butch wore nothing but compressed underwear, chuckled while he tapped his fingers on the table.

"Zig, remember that time I ate dad's fish sandwich that he was saving for the football game, and you took the ass whipping for me?"

"Yes, I remember it well Butch, you always pushed daddy to the limit, and I thought what the hell, let me take one for big bro."

Butch picked up the barcode gun and rubbed it as though it was a woman's breast admitted, "I miss them so much Zig it hurts like hell. This may sound crazy, but everything I was trying to accomplish was for them."

"Butch what we did was wrong and I was never a great scholar of the bible, but I can't remember when the last time I thanked God for anything. I know one thing for sure. The shit we've been doing and all the people we've killed guarantees our asses a place in hell. I'm sure our parents are not there" Zig honestly admitted.

"Zig, when did we get a fair shake when it came to this great fucking thing they call life? Our father busted his ass every day, ten hours a day, dealing with bullshit on a job that didn't feel his 'kind' belonged there. He went to fourteen banks almost begging for a fucking loan to put money down on that house. He wanted his wife and kids to know what a back-yard barbecue felt like. When those lowlife motherfucker's that we called relatives needed to pay their rent or light bills, I saw my father come out of his pocket."

Butch looked up at the white ceiling and did his best to hold back his tears while he continued,. "My beautiful mother helped the sick, wiped their asses, and fed them. She still came home and cooked six days out of the week making sure her three men were always taken care of. She always fought for us, even in school when they said we were not qualified to attend their prestigious private school. Moms came up there with rollers in her hair threatening to sue the shit out of them if they tried to fuck with the Steel Brothers. She was the best woman I ever knew."

Butch squeezed his hands together so aggressively that they began to burn. Butch no longer held back and allowed his tears fall.

"You are so right Butch; they went through hell to make sure we had the best. We lacked or wanted for nothing. Yes Butch, you are also right when you speak about the people in my opinion who used our parents; but you know what I remember more than anything Butch? I remember how my father looked up to the sky thanking his God for allowing him to be able to help his family members."

Zig gently palmed his brother's face and turned it to him so that he could look into his eyes, "My mother helped deliver a hundred and seventy-five babies in that hospital, also taught stroke victims how to walk and talk again.. She never once complained about her job, or how nasty it got, because she wasn't built like that. Butch, she was a warrior. Look at what we've let ourselves become. We have used twenty-five years of our lives to plan a massacre, when all we really did was plan our own demise. Butch, I love you until my last breath, but I can't do this anymore. If there really is a deep depth of hell, we mortgaged our souls there forever and ever."

Butch peered at his brother because he was perplexed and needed to know. "Zig, why did you let her go?"

"During the last few hours of our stakeout in the car, our parents came to me Butch, they came to me in all their glory telling me how wrong we were and how it wasn't too late to make a change. When I looked inside that little girls' eyes today Butch, I saw the eyes of our mother and those eyes read innocence."

"That motherfucker took the only thing besides you, that I loved Zig. On top of that, his fucking father tried to have us hurt. Now I am suppose to forgive and forget?" Butch asked.

"What else do we have Butch? It's over and I'm done because sooner or later they will begin their own manhunt. I mean we killed two cops man, don't think they're not two seconds off our asses?"

"Little brother listen to me. We still have about one hundred thousand dollars in cash inside the safe, plus we have the passports and apartment in Canada. We can leave tonight" Butch suggested.

"Butch, what do you mean tonight? What do you have planned for the rest of the day? How far do you think that money will get us? Don't you think those cops have every type of transportation watched? Listen I love you, but I'm done."

Butch wondered about his brother so he asked him, "So Zig, you're telling me that this is it, brother? You're going to forsake me with this decision you've made?"

Zig took a deep breath and turned to his brother, "Butch, for the last time, I'm finished and you will always be a part of me, don't ever forget that."

Butch retrieved the barcode gun and looked at his brother. Butch got up from his chair, walked to the refrigerator, and poured a glass of orange juice. He returned and gave it to Zig. "I'm going to take a shower and you're going to drink your orange juice. When I come out we will discuss a new plan, because that bullshit you're talking about doesn't make sense."

Butch watched Zig sip on his orange juice, and affectionately gave his little brother a kiss on the cheek.

Zig watched his brother walk away and took another sip of juice. He placed his glass on the table and sat back to relax in his chair. Suddenly and violently Zig was jerked right out of his chair and onto the floor. Butch wrapped a leather belt around his neck and squeezed with great force.

The brothers wrestled on the green tiled floor and Zig reached up with his large muscular arms in an attempt to free himself. Butch braced himself against the radiator and squeezed tighter. "Sit still baby brother, please stop fighting."

As spit shot from his mouth and his feet kicked over the dinette table, Zig's face turned fire truck red as he got woozier by the second.

"All you had to do was give her to me baby brother, I would have taken the fall", Butch cried out as his tears fell and heart pumped faster.

Still trying to fight, Zig was able to muster up a surge of strength and turned his head around to look into Butch's eyes.

Their eyes met, but Butch couldn't help but to cry out, "Oh God Zig I'm sorry! Please don't look at me! I'm so sorry baby brother."

Butch turned his head away and leaned against the radiator as he heard the last breath leave Zig's body.

The imprint of the radiator was on Butch's back as he loosened the thick black leather belt from around Zig's neck, dropping it on the kitchen floor. Butch sat next to his dead brother and held Zig's head in his hands while snot ran from his nose. Butch shifted his body which caused Zig's body to fall lifelessly to the floor. What's even more chilling was that Zig's eyes were wide open piercing at his unmerciful brother Butch.

Butch hovered over his little brother that he promised his parents to always care for. When they were little Butch bathed his brother and combed his hair. He taught Zig how to play 'skelzies' and how to make a 'slingshot'. Butch kicked anybody's ass who messed with his baby brother. They shared everything together, even the pain and sorrow of their parents' death.

Butch reached down and gently rubbed his hand over his brother's eyes closing them for the final time.

Out of touch with reality; a direct effect of Butch's brutal murder of his only brother, he began talking to Zig as if he was still alive.

"Come on little brother; let's get to your room so you can rest while I continue what we set out to do. Don't worry, they think they're safe but Butch has something for their asses."

He picked up Zig by his large tree branch arms and dragged him out of the kitchen and to his bedroom. Butch stepped over his brother, and walked back to the living room. He picked up the 8x10 picture that was taken back in 1980. It was a photo of him, Zig and their parents at Sears Department Store. Butch tried not to look at the picture but couldn't help himself as it seemed the eyes of his parents and little brother penetrated his dark soul.

In Zig's room was a hi-riser bed covered with a blue flat sheet, and white pillows. There were two beautiful pictures of flowers that hung on the walls, and his windows were adorned with matching blue curtains.

Butch used all of his strength to lift his brother's upper torso onto the bed first. Then the rest of Zig's body was gently shifted on the bed. Butch stared at the ugly black and blue mark around Zig's neck. Butch touched it gently as he lifted his brother's head onto his pillow. Butch leaned over his brother and gave him a final kiss on the forehead before he walked out. "They will remember the Steel Brothers." Butch promised as he slowly closed the door behind him.

Just a few feet down the hall, Butch entered his room where a black duffel bag sat on his bed. Butch unzipped the bag talking aloud, "I hope you can hear me bitch! Your fucking life depends on it! I hope your fucking ass is loved because everything I ever loved is in the next room and the fucking ground. You better pray they love you, because I ain't got nothing to lose no more bitch!"

Dressed with his black cargo khaki pants and a black shirt, Butch dons a bullet proof vest. Also in the bag, Butch pulled out two .45 automatic handguns checking them for ammunition.

"All everybody had to do was mind their fucking business and let us take what was rightfully ours, but no, everybody wanted to be a fucking hero! So in a few minutes bitch, we are going to see whose ass is the blackest! Do you hear me freak?"

Butch removed from the duffel bag a disposable cell phone and made sure that it was fully charged.

"I will finish what I set out to do, and no one including the Glorious One himself will stop me! Do you hear me, bitch? I know you fucking hear me!"

Butch walked over to his closet that he padlocked for security purposes. He gently tapped on the closet door and listened. Butch knocked a second time but a little harder and became angry because of the silence. With great force, Butch banged aggressively on the door again which caused the pictures on the wall to fall and shatter on the floor. He then stuck his ear to the closet door and inside there were sounds like a puppy that whimpered.

Butch pulled out of his pocket a ring of keys. He found a silver key and stuck it into the padlock to open it. Butch removed the lock and tossed it on the bed.

The door looked antique and had a doorknob made of glass. As a child Butch actually believed the doorknob was made of diamonds. Butch violently swung the door open as he pointed his gun inside. After Butch opened the door, the stench of urine and feces invaded his nostrils. Butch clicked on the closet light and observed discarded 'White Castle' containers and empty cans of soda sprawled all over the closet floor.

A small wounded hand wrapped in a bloody towel was raised to guard against the bright shining light and begged in a feebly pitiful voice, "Please don't kill me! Please!"

With absolutely no emotion or sense of concern, Butch demanded with a voice as cold as ice, "Get your stink ass up!"

*****

Tut drove Jesse, Brenda, and Penny down the Major Deegan. Since they wanted to go to Brenda's house, he got off the Fordham Road exit that connected them to Pelham Parkway East. It was so quiet in the car. all you could hear was the low hum of the engine, but each and every one of them had something on their minds.

Penny for example replayed in her mind everything that happened to her. Tears rolled down her cheeks because she knew her family was dead. Penny was also afraid because those bad guys were still out there and they wanted her. She hated Mr. Baker for putting that tattoo under her arm. All in all, Penny was sure of one thing, Jesse and Brenda promised not to let anything happen to her and they kept their promise. Penny definitely felt safe in their hands.

Brenda thought about her baby sister Vanessa. Even though she was her guardian since their parents died, Vanessa played a major role in the type of woman and detective she was today. It was almost like therapy for Brenda to come home to Vanessa especially after hard days on the streets. Vanessa induced normalcy to Brenda's life that was often riddled by the hardship of street crimes and all the drama that came with it.

Jesse could only think about the heroism of her dearest and close friend Tut. It blew her mind that when the chips were down he was there. When she was ready to give up, he was there. "When no one else was there, Tut came through for me." Jesse knew in her heart that she was the only reason he risked his life. Physically, Tut was a dwarf, but he stood ten feet tall to her right then. Jesse realized her heart opened wide for Tut today. Not because he single-handedly saved their lives, but because he loved her, he truly and unconditionally loved her. Jesse cried silently with that realization.

*****

Brenda, Jesse and Penny all hid in the backseat of Tut's car as he drove down Pelham Parkway towards Brenda's house.

"Tut two more blocks down on the right and you'll see a red brick detached house with little gnomes on the front lawn. That's my house. Hopefully there will be some police activity in place" said Brenda.

Tut looked into his rearview mirror and responded, "I still totally disagree with you two. You should let me take you to the emergency room. Jacobi Medical Center is like three minutes away."

"Tut baby, those cats are still out there and we have no idea where they could be. These guys could have moles planted everywhere. They had all their bases covered. The less we stay from public places, the better for now. Besides, my wound ain't so bad I can bandage up at Brenda's" Jesse said trying to convince Tut.

"Brenda, your wound looks pretty bad. How bad were you hit?" Tut asked.

"For some reason I don't think it went straight through like I thought earlier. It didn't penetrate; it only grazed my skin and took out a chunk of it. The bleeding stopped; I'll go to the hospital after we contact the Captain."

"Jesse and Brenda how's your friend back there?

Brenda touched Penny on her sweaty forehead and said, "We will explain in time Tut, but look ahead there's my house. Do you see anyone staked out in front?"

"No Brenda, I don't see anyone. What do you want me to do?"

Brenda pressed a button that opened her garage door. "Drive in and we'll go in through the kitchen door."

The deuce and a quarter pulled inside the neatly cleaned garage as the door quietly closed behind them.

*****

Jesse washed Penny's face as she sat catatonically. Tut helped Jesse by gently cleaning the abrasions on Penny's arms and legs with hydrogen peroxide.

"Jesse listen baby, I can see what you can't see and you need stitches for that gash on your leg."

"Tut, you can drive me personally to the hospital when this is over, but for now, just use the gauze pads; medical tape and ace bandage will you?"

Not liking the tone and tenor of her voice Tut does what Jesse demanded, as he listened to how she spoke to Penny.

"Small Fry how you doing Boo? You look like you had a rough weekend."

Closing her eyes as Jesse puts Vaseline on her face Penny, responded "I sprayed that man like you said I should Jesse. Those were the men who hurt Mr. Baker at our house. Are they coming back for us?"

"I don't know Small Fry but what I do know is that you saved my life today, and for that I owe you mine. I will never be able to repay you for what you did in that warehouse. You were brave and fearless, and you will always be my girl."

Jesse clinched her teeth from the pressure of the ace bandage that Tut wrapped around her thigh. She reached out affectionately with both arms giving the little girl a big hug.

"Well Small Fry it looks like our little journey is coming to an end. I promised you until we catch those bad guys, Brenda and I will protect you as if you were the President of the United States" Penny and Jesse chuckled but just a little.

Tut finally finished bandaging Jesse's leg and she put on a pair of jeans Brenda gave her. Tut turned his attention to Brenda and did a great job cleaning and bandaging her shoulder wound.

"Tut I'm sure I speak for all of us when I say thank you for saving our lives. We all were at the end of our rope when you showed up. Not right now, but when all this is said and done I want to know how you found us. Now we have to call the captain to let him know we are here safe and sound. But Jess let me ask you something? Weren't you here when Vanessa said Friday was her last day at her summer job?"

"Yeah Brenda, Vanessa told us last Wednesday when we were watching the movie. Getting back to the Captain, we need to call him. But first, let me give Penny something to eat"

"Come on, let's go to the kitchen there has to be something quick we can prepare for Penny" Brenda assured.

Everyone walked to the kitchen, and Penny took the opportunity to stare at Tut who walked behind everyone. Doing her best not to gaze, Penny quickly looked at Brenda's fish tank to avoid being detected.

"It's okay Penny, my name is King Tut, and yes everyone is taller than me. I must look very strange to you but you don't have to be afraid. Besides anyone who is a friend of Jesse and Brenda is a friend of mine.

"I'm sorry Mr. Tut for staring. Jesse and Brenda are my friends so that makes you my friend too!" proclaimed Penny.

Everyone took a seat at the kitchen table except Brenda. Jesse raided her refrigerator and brought out cold cuts, cheese, olives, and crackers. They all started munching on the goodies except Brenda. On her refrigerator was a yellow Post-It note that asked the question, "Are you hungry?, dial 917-555-1425." Taken back by the note Brenda felt uneasy.

"Jesse come here please" Brenda asked.

"Sure baby what's up"

Jesse stood next to her partner and read the note. She glanced back at Brenda and rationalized, "We just got the cold cuts out of the refrigerator, and everything seemed fine."

"Jesse that note was not there before and it's not in either of our handwriting. With all the shit that went on this weekend, I trust nothing or no one!"

Jesse walked closer to the refrigerator and opened the door slowly. Once the door was fully open, they surveyed the contents and nothing seemed out of the ordinary.

Jesse looked over at the table and noticed that Tut was playing with Penny. She grabbed hold of the freezer door and looked at her partner again. "You're probably worrying for no reason at all."

Brenda took a deep breath and nodded her head in agreement. Brenda watched Jesse as she slowly opened the freezer.

Brenda stood side by side with her partner as Jesse finally swung the door completely open. What they saw caused Brenda to fall to the floor in total shock.

Brenda and Jesse were taken back by the ghastly site in the freezer. Someone had removed all of the food in Brenda's freezer; all except the hideous package left behind. Inside the freezer, on a saucer covered with Saran Wrap, are Vanessa's ring and index fingers. Vanessa's high school ring was still on one of the fingers. The fingers turned a pale white from being inside the freezer.

Jesse got down on to the floor to help Brenda and demanded, "Tut keep Small Fry over there with you!"

Jesse held a distraught Brenda in her arms as she looked up at the refrigerator door and once again read the telephone number written on the yellow paper.

"Hold it together baby. We have to believe Vanessa is alive. You start thinking the worse, we lose our edge. There's no way she's dead! Brenda, we still have a chance, but you have to hold it together baby" Jesse pleaded to her best friend.

Chapter Twenty-Nine
The Switch

Twenty minutes passed since the gruesome discovery in the freezer. Brenda is comforted by Jesse, Tut and Penny who all watched her have a complete meltdown Brenda drunk a glass of water in an attempt to calm herself down when all of a sudden Brenda got angry. After she had stared at the refrigerator, Brenda jumped up from the table, grabbed her gun, and started to load it.

At that moment, Jesse held her hand gently and said, "If you lose your cool Boo she won't make it home today, that I'm sure of. Those men have bad intent on their minds, and the last thing we want is to trigger those bastards. We have to take some time to figure out how to get her back. Brenda, the first thing you have to do is get your head together girl, and dial that number."

*****

Stationed inside a smoke-filled room, using only the light from the sun, are Detectives Frank Cannon and Benjamin Jones, both in deep thought as they studied a thirteen page profile on Melvin Baker. On the dingy white wall are old newspaper clippings the officers were able to gather from the Internet. The newspaper had the story of a fatal accident that occurred in the Bronx, during the summer of 1981, right next door to Melvin's home.

Next to that clipping was today's three page story about the massacre of the Baker family. Thumb-tacked to the other wall was a one page article of the untimely death of long time attorney John Hatcher and his wife Candice, who plunged to their deaths off the roof of a luxury high-rise on Park Avenue.

The men simultaneously took puffs on their cigarettes while a somewhat distraught Captain Gordon entered the room drenched with sweat and with his collar opened at the neck.

"Guys, Detectives Simple and James are still out there with the little girl Penny. I have to believe that they are alright but I know they are in danger. Tell me something guys. Give me something to go on!."

Detective Jones put his cigarette out in the butt-filled ashtray and reported "Sir, twenty-five years ago, a then ten or eleven year old Melvin Baker along with his deceased father Donald were involved in a motor vehicle accident which killed a married couple; Pete and Simone Steel. According to the news clippings Melvin Baker, then a little boy, grabbed the steering wheel of his father's car that caused the accident."

Captain Gordon walked over to the wall and carefully studied the articles then asked, "Please tell me with your own ideas what I think you're telling me detectives."

Detective Cannon took a sip of warm ginger ale, then responded "We still have to dig a little more Captain, but we strongly believe the murders involving the Baker family was an act of vengeance. We say this because two of the only remaining Steel family members have been identified, sir. I bet the little girl that Jesse and Brenda are protecting was the only one that got away."

"Who did you say were the only remaining family members Detectives?"

Cannon shuffled through some papers and answered, "Butch and Zig Steel."

The time was 10:15AM and the Captain knew a little more about those allegedly involved. "Keep digging Detectives. Keep up the good work. Soon as you find more information, I want to be updated right away.

*****

Captain Gordon stepped outside. He walked around the corner to hide as he lit a cigarette. It's been ten months since his last one

Captain Gordon was really worried about Jesse and Brenda. He cared more for them, almost as if they were his own daughters. Gordon felt woozy from the first pull of nicotine as he summed the events in his head… "Jess and Brenda haven't called him yet, which meant they were still laying low. The perps are still out there and Jesse and Brenda's skills taught them to protect at all cost. Those motherfuckers could possibly be Butch and Zig Steel. Those bastards mean business and we have to find the girls as soon as possible…"

*****

Tut was in the living room playing 'Pitty-Pat' with Penny. Jesse was in the kitchen with an angry Brenda who paced back in forth across the kitchen floor. Brenda snatched the post-it note off the refrigerator door.

Jesse stepped in front of Brenda to stop her pacing, "Boo this is it, and remember what I said- No screaming or threatening tone. Listen to their demands, and I'll be on this cordless phone writing everything down. Are you ready?"

"Yes I'm ready" Brenda answered while she looked at the phone number.

Jesse kissed Brenda on the cheek and handed her the phone. Brenda then dialed the numbers. Brenda did her best to keep her composure because losing it could cost Vanessa her life. While Jesse listened on the other line, the dialed number rang three times before it was picked up

"You wanted me to dial this number?"

"What's your name?"

"My name is Brenda Simple."

"How much do you love your sweet smelling sister, Brenda?"

"I love her enough to exchange my life for hers."

"That sounds noble Brenda, but your life means shit to me. What I need to know is, do you love your sister enough to give up another's life so your sister can live?"

"Please explain to me what you mean."

"Brenda, do you take me for a fool?

"I said nothing about you being a fool. I asked you for clarity of what you asked me."

*****

Butch sat on his bed with Vanessa wrapped between his legs. He placed his big hand on her neck and squeezed hard almost suffocating Vanessa and asked, "Brenda is this clear enough?"

Butch placed the phone to Vanessa's mouth and commanded, "Vanessa say something to your big sister."

*****

Before Brenda could respond, Jesse ran over to Brenda and embraced her around her shoulders in an attempt to keep her calm.

"Brenda please come get me I'm afraid Bre..." Vanessa said weakly before she gasped for air as Butch squeezed Vanessa's slender neck, stifling any words she tried to get out.

"Brenda, at this very moment I'm choking the shit out of your sister, and I know for a fact all it takes is eight seconds of this shit to cause her to suffer brain damage. An additional thirteen seconds more would kill this bitch, so how is that for clarity?"

Tears ran down Brenda's face like a running faucet, she quickly answered, "Sir you have my attention, please don't do this."

"I know I have your attention. Remember; don't fuck with me because I don't have anything to lose. I just released your sister but her nasty ass is throwing up all over my clean floors. Trust me her ass will be cleaning this shit up. No more fucking games. I know the little one is with you, so put her fucking ass on the phone, right now!" Butch demanded.

Without hesitation, Jesse ran to the living room to get Penny when Brenda waved her finger in a 'no' gesture. Looking at her partner, Jesse knew this was totally wrong and against everything they knew as detectives, but she felt this is their only shot at getting Vanessa back. Jesse ignored it and retreated to the living room.

The phone in her hand, Brenda broke the silence "Sir, I want to assure you…

Butch cut Brenda off in mid sentence and yelled, "Bitch, the only thing you better assure me of is that the little brat is on her way to this phone!"

Quickly racing back to the kitchen, Jesse kissed Penny on her forehead and whispered, "Small Fry do what I asked and be brave okay?"

Penny nodded her head up and down which made her afro puffs bounce. Penny walked up to Brenda and reached out her hand for the phone. Brenda felt defeated, afraid, and helpless said, "I'm giving her the phone."

Penny put the phone to her ear and said, "Hello"

"Do you know who I am little girl?"

"Yes, I know who you are. You're the man that hurt Mr. Baker and the rest of my family, now you want to hurt me."

"Little girl, you don't know the half of it. But you know what, if we're both still around fifteen years from now, and you're feeling pissed about what I did, look for me. I'll be waiting for you! Now put Brenda back on the phone."

Penny handed Brenda the phone and walked over to Jesse who gave her a big hug. Brenda looked at Penny and turned her attention back to Butch. "Now how do I get my sister back home safe?"

"At ten-forty five you, your dyke partner and the girl will drive to an abandon fish market that's near the Bruckner Expressway. A black minivan will be waiting with your sister in the backseat. You will bring your car to the back of the fish market showing me the little girl, while leaving the keys in the ignition. At that point, we will take each others' vehicles and make the switch. Brenda, let me make something clear, if you call any cops and I see them, I promise you two things. I will die in a blaze of glory, and Vanessa's head will roll at your feet."

"I promise to do everything you ask, and there will be no police, but please, may I speak to my sister one more time?"

Butch paused for a few seconds then told Brenda, No bitch, you can't speak to her until this shit is done. But I want you to hear something."

Butch held the phone to Vanessa's mouth while he applied pressure to her amputated hand. Brenda listened helplessly as her baby sister screamed "Oh God, please stop! Brenda help me!"

Butch took the phone away from Vanessa's mouth and asked, "She is so dramatic, right? See you in a few. Remember no cops or her head will meet the same fate as her hand. You better not underestimate me or it will cost you Vanessa's life."

*****

Brenda clinched her hand so tight that her nails broke the skin in her palm. The other hand visibly shook with the phone in it. Jesse took away the phone from her friend and placed it on the receiver. "Brenda, we have five minutes to plan and execute, so pull it together sister."

"Jesse what are you talking about, that crazy motherfucker is going to kill my baby sister!"

"Brenda, calm down and trust me, because we have little time." Jesse called Penny and Tut inside the kitchen as the phone rang which made Brenda jump. Jesse checked the caller ID and she noticed that it's Captain Gordon's private line.

Jesse looked at everyone at the table, and instructed "Don't answer it."

*****

Butch packed the barcode gun inside a silver suitcase along with his laptop. He aggressively took Vanessa by her neck and dragged her to the door. Suddenly he stopped to look in on Zig who is asleep forever.

"The time has arrived little brother."

Vanessa, with a horrified look on her face soberly asked "You killed your own brother?"

Butch slapped Vanessa across her face leaving a nasty red bruise clarified, "No, I gave him peace bitch, but you I will kill!"

Butch closed Zig's bedroom door and got his suitcase along with Vanessa. The only thing on Butch's mind was collecting his twenty-five year old debt.

*****

It was 10:43AM and the sky was overcast with thick dark clouds that were ready to open up at any moment. The underpass of the Bruckner Expressway smelled awful as Brenda, Jesse, and Penny all sat in the backseat of the car on the scene.

The detectives saw the black minivan as it turned the corner, and Jesse grabbed Brenda by the hand, "Be cool and we'll get Vanessa back; but if you lose your cool Brenda, everything gets fucked up."

"Stop cursing Jesse!" pleaded Penny as she looked at the same black van.

"I'm sorry Small Fry, no more cursing" obeyed Jesse.

Brenda saw Penny's face in the rearview mirror, and admitted, "I swear I hate involving Penny in this Jesse, she needs to be at the precinct!"

"This won't last long so just have a little faith, and keep your cool. This is it, let's do this!" yelled Jesse as she watched the driver's side door of the mini-van open up.

Brenda told Penny with concern in her eyes, "Penny we are right here with you is that understood?"

Penny proudly stated, "I'm not scared Ms. Brenda."

Butch got out of his car and brandished an automatic weapon that he pointed inside the van at Vanessa.

"Let's get this over with, come on!" shouted Butch as he surveyed the area in search of any type of a police presence.

Brenda and Jesse got out of their car feeling for their guns just in case Butch was bold enough to try something.

"Let me see the little girl!" Butch demanded which simultaneously sent chills and anger throughout Jesse and Brenda's bodies. The detectives stood by the driver's side of the car as Jesse held a blue blanket in her hand.

"I want to see my sister!" Brenda demanded.

Butch looked at his watch, and then waved his gun which indicated to Vanessa to get out of the van. Vanessa did as she was told while holding her bloody and poorly bandaged hand in the air. It was apparent to both Jesse and Brenda that Vanessa was terrified.

The temperature and humidity made it feel like one hundred degrees, but Vanessa shivered as if she was in Alaska.

"Baby I'm here! Everything is going to be alright I promise! Brenda vowed.

"No bitch, don't tell her that! Nothing is cool until I say it is!" Butch yelled as he smacked Vanessa across her head and knocked her to the ground.

"Partner that's not necessary, let's make the switch and keep everything cool alright? You get what you want, and we get what we want!" Jesse said as she tried to calm an antsy Butch down.

"Tell her to get out the car and hold her arms up!" Butch demanded.

Jesse shook her head at Penny who got out the backseat of the car still wearing the oversized bullet-proof vest. Jesse leaned towards Penny's ear and said, "Hold your arms up for me baby."

The brave girl did exactly what Jesse told her to do. From a distance Butch's eyes zeroed in on the barcode tattoo. He was so obsessed that he got a hard-on from just the sight of it.

"Okay very good, make her get back inside the car!"

Brenda couldn't take her eyes off her panic-stricken sister. Penny got back into the car but before she closed the door, Jesse reached into the front seat of the car.

"Hey, what the fuck are you reaching for!" Butch wanted to know.

"Take it easy partner; I'm just getting her favorite blanket, that's all. She can't sleep without it!"

Jesse motioned to Penny to lie down as she covered her with the blanket. She gave her a kiss on the forehead. "Be brave for me Small Fry."

"Okay, I promise."

Jesse closed the door and stood next to her partner who never took her eyes off her defenseless sister. "Okay so now what?" Jesse asked Butch loudly.

Butch pulled Vanessa close to his side and demanded, "Move the fuck away from the car with your hands where I can see them. When I drive away you can take your partner's sister, but I swear to you if you try anything I will shoot this bitch were she stands do I make myself clear?"

"We understand you clearly partner. Look, we're moving far away from the car with our hands in the air!" Jesse responded.

Butch reached inside the car, retrieved his suitcase, closed the van door and started to walk towards the car and made sure he kept Vanessa in front of him. Butch walked cautiously to the awaiting car. He could hear traffic moving easily above his head on the expressway. Closer to Brenda's car, Butch looked inside and saw Penny curled up in a fetal position under her blanket.

Butch opened the car door and checked inside. He observed the car keys that dangled from the ignition. He looked to his left where Jesse and Brenda stood at a distance. Butch felt satisfied, so he pushed Vanessa violently from his side to the ground on her elbows and knees.

Butch still looked at the two women with caution, and threw his suitcase inside the car. Once inside Butch closed the door and started the engine of Brenda's car. "Stop your fucking crying little girl, all this shit including your life will be over in a few minutes."

The car sped off towards the ramp that led to the Bruckner Expressway. Brenda and Jesse ran towards Vanessa, who happened to look towards her left and was shocked by what she saw by an abandoned burned out car.

*****

Butch checked his watch as he got off the City Island exit. He glanced towards the backseat where Penny laid motionless under her blanket. Butch smiled at himself while he looked in the rearview mirror. Happy with himself that things were back in on track, he reached out to touch the suitcase that contained his laptop and the barcode gun.

"Stop crying back there! Once I get what I want, I will send you where I sent the rest of your family."

Butch made a quick right turn and drove past numerous seafood restaurants and fish markets that were surprisingly still closed. Butch surveyed the area and drove to the end of the pier where it was secluded.

Butch turned off the car and loaded up the laptop. He plugged in the barcode gun into USB port and waited. Finally Butch was able to log on for Internet access to complete the transaction. Butch removed an automatic weapon and checked it for ammo while he waited for the website to load up.

Butch sat the gun on the passenger side seat and wiped sweat off his face with a handkerchief. He quickly glanced back at Penny who shook uncontrollably under her blanket.

"I'm not what you think I am little girl. What I did to your family I know seems horrible and unforgivable, but I don't expect you to understand the pain your father caused me years ago. I also had a mother and father that I loved just like you loved yours. They were good people who would have done anything for anybody, including your father, but because of what I'll just call a chain of events, my life was changed forever. Little girl those chain of events cost me my family just like it cost you yours. I hope your parents loved and cared about you as much as my parents did for me and my brother. I took my own brother's life and I know I will suffer because of that unforgivable act. But if it wasn't for your selfish father, Melvin Baker, our paths would have never crossed, and my parents and my brother would be alive today. I know you are just a little girl and you have nothing to do with this vendetta, your only problem is that you were born in the wrong family. I was harsh with you on the phone earlier this morning but it's nothing personal against you. I have no time to figure out what's fair and just. My only job is to finish what I started."

Butch entered the code for the barcode gun and logged into his off-shore account. He knew the pending transaction of twenty-five million dollars would return to the Baker's account in two minutes and seventeen seconds.

Butch turned towards the backseat and calmly said to Penny, "Okay little girl I need for you to lift up your arm and when I'm done, I'll put you to sleep quickly."

Butch reached towards Penny and could feel her small body as it shook even more under the blanket. Butch showed some compassion and gently pulled back the blue blanket. He jumped backwards and smashed his back against the steering wheel.

The blanket still covered his legs as King Tut pointed an automatic weapon with a silencer attached to it. Butch was petrified, as he sweated profusely with his eyes wide as saucers. Aware that he couldn't reach the gun that sat next to him, Butch heard the voice from the laptop announce, "Your time has expired. Transaction incomplete" as a loud beeping sound filled the inside of the car.

Strangely Butch clearly saw out of the rear window the essence of his parents and Zig. Pete and Simone apparitions' ascended, as Zig's descended lower and away from their parents. That vision caused tremendous pain in Butch's heart and soul because he knew that would be the last time he'll ever see his family again.

"Checkmate, I guess" says Butch as he focused back on King Tut.

"For Penny", Tut said as he fired three times that sent two bullets inside Butch's head, and one in his mouth which caused brain fragments to splatter on the dashboard of the car. Butch slumped over on the front seats of the car, as Tut pulled from the waistband of his pants an unregistered pistol. From his pockets he produced a bag of pills and two thousand dollars in cash that he proceeded to spread throughout the backseat of the car. The intent obviously, was to make the scene look like a deal gone bad.

Tut adjusted his leather gloves, skull cap and the plastic around his shoes, while he inconspicuously exited the vehicle and walked towards the bus stop a few hundred feet away. Tut never turned around to look at the car. .

Tut thought to himself how grateful he was that little Penny was safe while Brenda had her little sister Vanessa home again, safe and sound. Most of all Tut was thankful that Jesse, the love of his life, was safe and unharmed throughout the ordeal. Whatever happened in the future between him and Jesse, Tut was satisfied to know that he played a major role in saving her life, so that she lived to see another day.

Chapter Thirty
Bruised But Still Standing

Finally the saga of Butch and Zig Steel was over. Brenda, Jesse, and Penny albeit physically and psychologically wounded, they walked away with their lives intact. Vanessa was back in the loving care of her sister Brenda, to live with their lives as it was meant to be-together. One of the most heroic and selfless acts during this whole ordeal was the involvement, quick-thinking, and willingness to sacrifice his own life was the courageous King Tut. Ode to his love for his best friend and neighbor Jesse, Tut was willing to give his life for her. That kind of love comes but once in a lifetime and he had it for Jesse without a doubt.

*****

Inside The Bronx North Central Hospital were Brenda, Jesse and Penny along with Captain Gordon and five heavily armed tactical policemen. They are wore black body armor with helmets and weapons in hands. Jesse explained the entire weekend to Captain Gordon. Jesse paid close attention when Dr. Paul Benson, an African-American neurosurgeon in his early fifties entered the waiting area.

"Ms. Simple, your sister Vanessa is resting comfortably under heavy sedation. We have reattached her two fingers, but because of the time that lapsed we are not sure if she will regain full use of them. Luckily by placing the fingers in the freezer, it adds hope there is still a chance for full function in the hand. Even with that Vanessa will still require intensive therapy."

Brenda, who received hugs from Captain Gordon and Jesse, was somewhat calmed when she asked, "Can I see my sister please?"

"Of course you can, Ms. Simple come with me" said Dr. Benson.

Before she walked with the doctor, Brenda felt a tug on her shirt. "Ms. Brenda, please tell Vanessa that I hope she feels better."

Brenda rubbed Penny's face and responded, "I will sweetheart, I promise."

*****

Detectives Cannon and Jones have worked the case gathering new information and leads. They were skilled and diligent as they read old news clippings that involved Butch and Zig Steel. From their very thorough investigation into the lives of the Steel Brothers, Detectives Cannon and Jones were able to extract important leads that related to the case. The detectives were relentless with assisting in the search of Jesse, Brenda, and Penny.

Detectives Cannon and Jones knocked on the Steel brother's apartment door as they responded to information obtained from Frank's cousin who had worked for Verizon for the past fifteen years. The detectives were able to track back when and where the brothers got their phone service.

After the conclusion of drilling the lock on the door, they all entered cautiously with their badges visible and guns drawn. Once inside the apartment, Detectives Cannon and Jones carefully opened doors throughout the apartment before they approached Zig's room. The detectives entered the room to discover a lifeless Zig Steel.

At that moment, Cannon dialed Captain Gordon while Jones called the examiner's office to report what they had found.

*****

Inside the hospital room, Brenda laid next to Vanessa and stroked her hair slowly while she kissed her on the forehead. Still groggy, Vanessa opened her eyes and was able to give her big sister a weak smile as she looked at her bandaged hand. Vanessa softly asked "Brenda is he gone?"

"Baby, you don't have to worry, I'm here and all I want you to do is rest.

"I can't feel or move my fingers Brenda", Vanessa said as she began to cry.

Brenda moved closer and cuddled Vanessa's head inside her arms. "Listen Nessa, I don't want you worrying about that. The doctor said it would be a while before sensation came back to your hand. Dr. Benson is very optimistic and. you have to think positive. Regardless how your hand heals, remember God spared our lives. Let's not let that blessing go unnoticed and praise the Lord for his mercy. Do you understand?" Vanessa nodded her head "Yes" and drifted back off to sleep.

*****

"Jesse, are you sure about the direction Butch Steel fled to in Brenda's vehicle?"

"Captain, he took off on the Bruckner heading north like I said. We planned on pursuing him but we felt the safety of Penny and Vanessa were more important at the time."

"Did Brenda have lo-jack on her car?"

"No captain, she didn't. Only my vehicle did."

"The press can't be held back anymore, Jesse. I need a report on my desk by tonight, and I mean a report with every detail. You got me?"

"Captain I understand, and you will, but I really think we need to put an APB on Steel, and get Penny to the nearest counselor. She has had a traumatic weekend and she needs help immediately."

Penny quickly stood up from her chair and retorted "Jesse, I'm okay I want to stay with you please!"

Captain Gordon lifted Penny and sat her on his knee. "Sweetheart, that won't be possible because we need to get you back to the station. Jesse will be there later to spend more time with you."

Very disappointed and visibly angered, Penny did something completely out of character. She sighed really loud, jumped off the Captain's knee and sucked her teeth. Jesse was shocked at Penny's behavior but understood why her separation from them would be hard. Jesse held out her hand to Penny and she grabbed Jesse's hand ever so tightly.

"Captain let me see how Brenda is doing, and we can all head back to headquarters. I won't be long, and I will deal with the press myself", said Jesse.

In agreement, Gordon answered, "Let's all go see Brenda and Vanessa together."

Jesse obtained Brenda's room number from the nurse station and proceeded to Vanessa's room.

*****

It was 4:30 PM and the precinct was in pure pandemonium, as reporters from television and newspapers were trying to convince the Captain to let them get a glimpse of Penny who was secretly being hidden inside the building. With the news of the Steel brothers along with the bodies found inside the warehouse, the media didn't let up on the pressure.

Lights from cameras flashed every second. All the channels had their news crews at the precinct. Jesse and Brenda along with the Captain were inside the conference room while they waited to make their grand entrance into the media room. Brenda reminded Jesse that she had to leave soon to get back to Vanessa at the hospital. They were all ready to absorb the questions from the "Hungry as wolves" media. Jesse, Brenda, and Gordon entered the room and took a seat as the frantic surge of questions began.

*****

After forty-five minutes of elapsed time had gone by, Captain Gordon stood to his feet and addressed the media, "Ladies and gentlemen you now know everything we have learned thus far. As this case continues to develop, updates will be provided to the media for coverage. You all have asked your questions, we need to continue our investigation. Right now I need to meet with two of our fallen officers grieving families. They died in the line of duty while working to keep our community safe. As I've mentioned it seems to me we have multiple sets of homicides focusing around the now deceased Butch and Zig Steel. At this moment consider this press conference over. We will continue to work vigorously on putting this whole case together. Furthermore, you will not be granted access to Penny Baker, Good day."

The press shouted out more questions at Gordon, Jesse and Brenda as they exited the media room to check on Penny, who was in the care of a social worker and a child psychologist.

*****

Jesse and Brenda stood behind the two-way glass and watched as Penny related to the psychologists how the detectives protected her from the bad men. Jesse looked on and couldn't help but be reminded how Penny saved her life. Grimacing from the pain of the cut on her leg which Brenda noticed, she stared at Jesse.

"Partner maybe you need to get that checked out."

Jesse never took her eyes off Penny and said, "Yeah, I will. I just want to make sure Penny's alright."

Captain Gordon walked up behind his two detectives as they observed how well Penny articulated the events. Gordon took in a deep breath and very softly admitted "I love the both of you like daughters and I will say this like a father. I have been on this force now for thirty years, and I have seen every tactic under the sun. You suckered Butch Steel today because he had Vanessa. When all this shit blows over, I know you will tell me how you did it. I also know Butch Steel didn't get killed in a drug deal gone badly. Like two good daughters, in time you will explain a lot more. You two have always busted your asses for this department and for me; therefore, I will stand by you no matter what. As far as I'm concerned, Butch and Zig Steel got what was coming to them, but there is no damn way you two are going to keep me in the dark. Even if it means we have to go to a deserted island where nobody can hear us but the almighty himself, then so be it. Girls, we have a couple of long nights ahead of us so as usual I need you on top of your game, but for now, Look out for little Penny, she has a heart of a lion."

The Captain walked away after he lovingly rubbed the shoulders of his two detectives. At that moment an emotional Brenda glanced at her partner Jesse and disclosed, "He always stuck by me when I was just a rookie and wet behind the ears.

"I know, Brenda. When I dropped my first body he let me sleep on his sofa and eat breakfast with his family. He told me a dead rapist would never be missed, but a surviving fifteen year-old could possibly grow up to be anything she wanted to be. He also told me to keep my head up and stand proud, because that's what warriors do. We'll be safe with him, that I'm sure of."

Jesse and Brenda continued to watch Penny speak proudly about them. Brenda reached out and hugged Jesse around the shoulder, while Jesse responded by wrapping her arm around Brenda's waist. They both stood quietly even though their gesture expressively said "I love you sister!"

Chapter Thirty-One
Never Can Say Goodbye

It was 7:35PM; Jesse and Brenda were in the large conference room and played with Penny. The social worker completed the paperwork of the state's decision for Penny's transfer to a children's hospital in Syracuse, New York. Penny clutched her teddy bear the desk sergeant kept safe for her while she played "Tic, Tac, Toe" with Brenda.

The social worker, Susan Blake was a blond slender built woman who was licensed and certified by the state. She's been in the business for over fifteen years. While Miss Blake straightened the papers out on the table she asked, "Detectives may I have a word with you in private please?"

The three women got up from the table, as Jesse tapped Penny on the head. "Small Fry we'll be right outside this door if you need us. Don't try to escape out the window, now."

Penny rolled her eyes at Jesse's comment and laughed. The three women stepped outside the room and closed the door behind them. Brenda stared at the woman with concern and said, "Listen, we already know Penny will be going up state, but we want full guarantee that she will be taken care of by the state. If she's not, excuse my French, there will be some shit."

"Detectives, I know in this short period of time you have formed a bond with this child, but please understand the state is fully capable of providing the mush needed counseling this child will need."

Jesse scratched her nose and glared at the social worker. "I understand you're just doing your job and following protocol. Don't minimize our connection to Penny as a simple bond. No Miss. Blake, we have the deepest damn relationship you'd ever know. What we shared in the past weekend, others will never experience in a lifetime. We want assurances where Penny is concerned. That little girl better not end up as an ordinary number in your system."

Ms. Blake looked at the two detectives and clearly observed that they weren't bullshitting. She took a deep breath and attempted to assure them otherwise.

Down the corridor being led by Captain Gordon were Chung Lee Wong and his partner Tommy Pang of the Sunrise Electronics Corporation. Along with them were two women, one oriental and the other African-American who were the men's legal representation.

"Jesse, Brenda and Ms. Blake let's all go inside because there has been a major change in plans", Captain Gordon advised.

The black woman sat her suitcase on the table and gave Penny a smile as she removed fresh court documents that she placed on top of the table.

Different people, strangers to be exact, had entered the conference room to determine Penny Baker's future. The little girl had been through a series of traumatic and violent events. Penny Baker was adopted by a family where her adoptive brother and sister at times treated her unkindly. Penny's adoptive father Melvin Baker used this little girl as a guinea pig and branded a barcode on her arm just like she was cattle.

All of this was done because of the one thing that was true about Melvin Baker; he was a selfish and self-centered man. Eventually Melvin saw the error of his ways and wanted badly to pull his family together. It was admirable that he wanted his family to be closer, but Melvin Baker paid a huge price for his years of egocentricity.

Today Penny Baker was the living recipient of twenty-five years of selfishness, pain, sorrow and greed. In her short nine years, Penny had endured trials and tribulations. Those closest to her can only pray for better days for the strong little brown-eyed soldier she became. Brenda Simple and Jesse James were Penny's biggest admirers. The detectives were uneasy about all the people who came out the woodwork on Penny's behalf. Brenda and Jesse knew one thing for sure-they were not going to let anybody fuck over Penny Baker.

"Detectives, my name is Chung Lee Wong, and this is my partner Tommy Pang of the Sunrise Electronics Corporation. The first thing we would like to do is thank you for your bravery and courage in caring for our friend Penny. We know this must come as a surprise to you, but Penny's father Melvin Baker, who we all valued and respected, was a major shareholder in the company. We knew the Bakers' very well, and spent many outings with them. We knew each other's families very well and my daughter had sleep-overs with Penny on many occasions. I want to assure you Penny's no stranger to our family. The horrible tragedy that happened to our friends deeply saddens all of us at Sunrise."

Tommy Pang cleared his throat and continued, "We have explained the long version to your captain and because of your deep connection to Penny we feel you need to know also. Melvin Baker was a smart man but our first initial impression of him was that he was sneaky and self-centered. Over time as we all got to know each other and learned each other's cultures, Melvin's demeanor changed to one of a team player at work and a leader at home. Melvin actually was a very caring man, who felt he didn't do enough for his family. Melvin planned a long vacation at Disney World to create a closer relationship with his family. Melvin was also a very calculating man as well, always trying to think ahead. What our attorneys' have in their possession is legal documentation, and an audio testament giving Mr. Wong sole guardianship of Penny Baker."

The lawyer opened up a folder that displayed a legal document signed by Melvin and a family court judge. Brenda and Jesse could do nothing but look at their Captain, then at Penny who does not seem too upset about the new developments.

"Captain this is too damn fast! No disrespect Mr. Pang, but do you have any idea what this girl has gone through?" implored Brenda

"Detective Simple, your concern and compassion is honorable but we can't imagine her pain and suffering. Please be assured that her healing will be with love and compassion from the Wong family."

The men looked at Captain Gordon who nodded his head as the oriental lawyer. The woman smiled and reached her hand out to Penny, who looked at Jesse who was obviously upset about her going with Mr. Wong. Jesse's hands were tied, unable to do anything as Brenda swallowed down a huge lump in her throat.

"Oh hell no, this shit ain't happening like this!" Jesse proclaimed as she moved towards Penny only to be blocked by the black lawyer.

"Bitch, you better get your skinny ass out her way!" yelled Brenda.

"Ladies, it's out of our hands! You have to let this go. Come on you two, it's time to be professionals; everything will work out for Penny", Captain Gordon declared.

Penny was led out the room and looked back at her friends with water in her eyes while she clutched her teddy bear. Ms. Blake stood in silence with Jesse and Brenda perturbed as the party of four, including Penny made their way out of the precinct. Jesse and Brenda hot on their heels are gently grabbed by the captain, as they watched Penny enter a grey Bentley stretch limousine.

Captain Gordon gently rubbed Jesse and Brenda on their backs while Jesse admitted, "This shit ain't right we didn't even get to say goodbye."

"It's time to start getting back to your routines detectives. Come by my office and we'll discuss it. Brenda, come on baby, aren't you going by to see how Vanessa is doing? It's time to move on. Penny will be fine" Captain Gordon reassured his detectives.

*****

It was Tuesday morning 10:36AM at the 46th precinct. Jesse was very upset that Captain Gordon ordered Apollo to be tranquilized and placed in an animal shelter. She tried to understand that it had to be done because Apollo was dangerously aggressive in they needed access to her apartment. It still didn't sit well with Jesse because Apollo was her baby and she loved him dearly. Jesse called the shelter earlier and was told Apollo had an allergic reaction to the tranquilizer and vomited a few times. The veterinarian gave him some medication that seemed to work. They told Jesse she could pick him up any time after three o'clock. Right after Jesse hung up the phone, Brenda walked in the office with two cups of coffee as she arrived from the hospital.

"How's Vanessa doing this morning, Brenda?" Jesse asked.

"She's getting more x-rays this afternoon, and she's scheduled for the occupational therapist right after."

"How's she feeling though?"

"You know Vanessa, she told me she's fine, but I know it's on her mind, and it will take some time for her to recover from this shit." Brenda worried.

Brenda gave her partner a large cup of coffee and eyed the almost three-inch thick report on Jesse's desk.

"Jesse have you spoken to Tut yet?" Brenda asked.

Yeah, we talked briefly but Small Fry was my priority and Tut was cool about that. We're getting together tonight to talk."

"Jesse, you know he loves you, and would do anything for you so what's up? He's really a good guy."

Never looking at her partner Jesse said, "Brenda, mind your damn business, please? We need to get our shit together because the drama ain't over."

Brenda took a sip of her coffee and looked intently at Jesse. She needed to know if Jesse missed Penny as she did. "Do you miss her Jesse?"

"I don't feel like talking about it right now…maybe later."

Deciding that she wouldn't push the issue, Brenda continued to look at the report when the sound of a knock on the door interrupted her.

"Small Fry!" Jesse yelled in surprise. Penny was at the door and had on a white designer jogging suit, white sneakers, and her hair was neatly braided. In top speed Penny ran into Jesse's arms. Behind Penny was Mr.

230

Wong and his eleven-year old daughter Chelsea. Penny waved Chelsea over and introduces her to the detectives.

*****

About forty-five minutes elapsed while Jesse and Brenda enjoyed their conversations with Penny and Chelsea. They all just finished their ice-cream when Mr. Wong indicated to Brenda it was time for them to go. Brenda put down her spoon and stood up from the table. Mr. Wong called Chelsea over so that the three of them could speak in privacy with each other.

"Come here baby" said Brenda as she placed her arms around Penny.

"Will you and Jesse come see me at my new house?" Penny asked happily.

"Small Fry, we are all family now, and we would love to visit you at your new house!" Jesse assured.

"We want to give you something to remember us by." Brenda removed her detective shield, placed the badge around Penny's neck and kissed Penny on the forehead. She then gave her a long hug, savoring the moment..

"You be a good girl, and I want you to stay out of trouble you hear me?"

Penny nodded her head up and down at Brenda while she smiled and asked, "Is Vanessa going to be okay? Is she getting out of the hospital soon?"

"She's doing fine and I think she will be coming home real soon. I'll make sure she knows you asked about her, Detective Baker."

Penny pulled away from Brenda and ran towards Jesse who got close to Penny's face.

Jesse looked deep in the little girls' eyes and said, "Anytime you need to talk about anything on your mind Small Fry you dial my number on this card. Just remember that your family loved you and are looking down on you, so you better make them proud, you hear me girl?"

With her soft brown eyes that would melt any heart, Penny softly answered, "I will Jesse, I promise."

Penny gave her friend a big hug while Jesse held on longer for safe keeping. Jesse knew Penny would be fine. She was a brave little girl. Penny survived the death of her family and the Steel Brothers who tried to get her. Penny's smile was as wide as the Mississippi River. Penny was moving on with her new life and most importantly she was happy.

Jesse released Penny and along with Brenda watched Mr. Wong and Chelsea hold Penny by each of her hands as they led her out the door. Mr. Wong stopped abruptly and turned to Jesse and Brenda to whisper in their ears, "You must not worry about Penny detectives because her father was well compensated for his ingenious projects. When little Penny turns twenty-five she will be able to provide a lucrative life for her future children and grandchildren."

From their office window, Jesse and Brenda watched Penny laugh and talk to Chelsea, while Mr. Wong was on his cellular phone. That sweet little girl had no idea that she was the future heir to the Baker fortune. Penny and her new family got in their car and drove off.

Jesse and Brenda heard the office door open then turned and faced Captain Gordon who stood at the entrance. "Detectives as of this moment you two are officially on two weeks paid leave of absence. Don't question me or look dumbfounded. Just get yourselves together, fill out the necessary paperwork, and clock out. We will talk in two weeks ladies."

They shook their heads in unison, "Yes sir."

*****

In the warm climate of St. Thomas, Jesse and Tut are laid back on the beach and sipped on Coronas. They both enjoyed the beauty of the blue sky that reflected in the clear water of the ocean. Jesse admired the exquisite engagement ring she accepted from Tut.

Jesse wore cargo shorts with a tank top to match. She looked over at her future husband and said, "This isn't going to be easy. I am not your average woman who follows the norms of married life. In my line of work there are no guarantees. Are you ready for all that Tut?"

Tut who wore shades, a straw hat and beige shorts, sipped on his beverage then responded, "Baby, I have been "Different" all my life. I've been ridiculed all my life. All I know is that the closest thing I have to a family are you and Apollo. So yeah, we are different in our own ways but we always respected each other's differences."

Jesse looked at her beautiful ring again and then at Tut. She had to be honest with herself and admit she's had romantic feelings for Tut for a while now. It felt wonderful to give into her love for him. While Tut laid in the sun with his eyes closed, Jesse felt flutters inside her stomach. The last time Jesse felt flutters was in the tenth grade when she kissed a fat but handsome kid named "Biscuit". Jesse leaned over and gave her future husband a long sensuous kiss on the lips. While she listened to ocean currents, Jesse buried her toes in to the warm sand and exhaled.

*****

232

Gnarles Barkley performed at a jammed packed Madison Square Garden. Fans screamed and had a great time at Summer Jam. Brenda and Vanessa were in the fifth row as they danced and sang along with the crowd. Brenda reached out and hugged her little sister around the shoulder and said, "I am so blessed to share this day with you Vanessa. God has been good to us and I will never stop thanking the Lord for our second chance.

Vanessa slowly lifted her hand and painfully wiggled her reattached index finger in Brenda's face, "That's another blessing Brenda. I can move my fingers! Those scary days are behind us and we have to move on. God has blessed us, so let's enjoy this day. One thing I want you to promise me? Please don't do your old dances here in the "Garden" I have an image to uphold!"

The two sisters busted out with laughter as Brenda jumped out of her seat and proceeded to do the "Cabbage Patch". Vanessa was so embarrassed; she sunk down in her seat and did her best not to be seen with Brenda.

Hey you! Yeah I'm talking to you. Did you really think it was over?
Let's have some fun together!
Go to the next page and read my alternate ending for
"Whatever It Takes"
When you're done please let me know what ending did you prefer by
contacting me at
WWW.Madboenterprises.com and click on the e mail tab.
Or visit
WWW.Myspace.com/madbo726 and let me know. While you're on my
page add me as a friend.
Finally if you've purchased "Whatever It Takes" on Amazon, please be so
kind and post a review.

From an author to a reader, thank you so much for your support. You
have no idea how good it feels to know that I have earned your support.
I really hope this is the beginning of a long and lasting author/reader
relationship.
God Bless and thanks again!!!
So with no further interruptions enjoy the alternate ending!!!!

The Alternative Ending

Jesse took Penny's hand and pulled her behind the silver metal door. Brenda squeezed off a few rounds at Butch and Zig who took cover behind four wooden cargo boxes. Jesse shielded Penny behind the door and told her, "Small Fry cover your ears!"

Jesse brandished a Beretta in each hand and fired what had to be twenty-five shots in unison at the Steel Brothers. She quickly discharged her clips and then reached inside her pocket for more ammo but grimaced from the serious knife wound she sustained earlier.

Butch, who was determined to get Penny screamed, "All we want is the girl! Just give us the fucking girl and we promise to let you leave!"

Brenda ripped the bottom of her shirt and tied it around her armpit to ease the pain of her arm. She checked her weapon then peaked from behind the door only to observe someone's knee protrude from behind a crate. She pointed out to Jesse the entrance doors that were located fifteen away. Jesse realized that Brenda wanted to make a run for the door. Jesse nodded her head in agreement while at the same time, she grabbed hold to Penny's vest and prepared to make their move.

Brenda still saw a knee that stuck out from behind the crate. Brenda took aim, licked her lips and fired, blasting the body part. "Oh shit Butch my knee!" screamed Zig as blood ran down his leg.

Brenda fired seven more shots in the Steel Brother's direction while she screamed "Move Jesse! Move!"

Jesse yanked Penny by the vest and dragged the little girl towards the door with one arm while she fired with the other. Brenda, who squatted in position, fired six more times just to make Butch duck for cover while Zig nursed his wounded knee.

Butch glanced from behind the crates and yelled, "Come on Zig get the hell up they're getting away!"

Zig moaned in agony as he got up from the floor. He used his muscle ripped arms as leverage to gain his balance. Butch wore a look of despair because he could feel his twenty-five million dollars slowly slipping away. Butch who was a muscular man himself reached for his brother and lifted him under the right arm pleaded, "Zig come on brother this is it! We can't let this happen, not now!"

Zig mustered up the ability to psychologically push the pain out of his mind and with pure determination said to his brother, "Come on let's go!" The two brothers hurry towards the exit doors and hoped their prey was still in sight.

Zig hopped towards the door while he left a trail of blood behind him. He checked the semi-automatic rifle and made sure it was fully loaded. Zig felt his brother's hot breath on his neck and yelled, "I see them inside the red car."

*****

Brenda frantically connected wires under the steering wheel of the car and hoped to get it started. Jesse squatted behind the open passenger door and waited for Butch and Zig to exit the warehouse. Jesse heard the sounds of sirens from a distance. Penny laid in the backseat and covered her ears. The gun fire had been traumatic for her and she was extremely afraid for Brenda, Jesse, and herself.

"Brenda come on shit hurry up!" Jesse screamed as Brenda stripped two red wires with her knife. She quickly tapped them together that resulted in sparks to flicker. Brenda pumped the gas quickly with her foot and prayed that one of the sparks would start the car's engine.

"Oh shit they're coming out!" screamed Jesse as she fired four times at the entrance door in made the brothers duck back inside.

"Come on damn it!" yelled Brenda as she pumped the gas pedal faster. All of a sudden she heard the engine as it began to putter.

Brenda twisted the wires together and tucked them back under the steering wheel. Jesse confident her partner would get the car started jumped in and commanded, "Let's go baby!"

Brenda spun the car towards the Major Deegan south ramp and took off. Brenda checked her rearview mirror and saw Butch and Zig as they ran towards their black minivan.

"Brenda we're going to Fordham Road near BBQ's. There's a police command station truck parked right in front of the restaurant!"

Brenda pressed her foot on the gas that caused the car to make a screeching noise as they headed south to Fordham Road..

*****

Zig tore his pants leg to assess the severity of the gun shot wound. Butch was in hot pursuit of Jesse and Brenda however he informed Zig, "There's a first-aid kit in the glove compartment Get it and work on your leg!"

Zig removed the first aid kit from the glove compartment and opened a bottle of alcohol. Zig took off his belt from his pants and placed

238

it between his teeth and bit down on it with great force. Butch was going ninety miles an hour as he headed for the Deegan right behind the detectives.

"Don't lose them Butch" Zig mumbled as the leather strap was inside his mouth. Zig took a deep breath as he poured the alcohol on his open wound. Zig's face turned red as the burning sensation intensified in the wound.

Butch saw his little brother as he fought the agonizing burn. At that moment Butch remembered the alcohol cleansing he gave Zig for mutilating himself. Butch focused back on the traffic ahead and decided to make his move. Butch noticed that Zig had begun to calm down when he reached into the cup holder and pulled out a semi-automatic weapon and yelled "Ok get it together Zig, take their car out!"

Zig checked to make sure the gun was fully loaded. Refocused back on the road Zig wondered, "Is she still alive? She's our bargaining chip Butch!"

Butch looked towards the backseat from his rearview mirror and answered "I made it so that she would be able to breathe and the window was cracked so she should be! If not then so be it but for now take them out!"

Butch passed a woman inside a SUV with her children. The brothers were one car and one lane away from Jesse and Brenda. Butch watched Zig as he strapped the belt around his bandaged knee then rolled down his window and yelled, "Come on Butch get me closer!"

*****

The ride on the Major Deegan was dangerously intense. Brenda peeked in her sideview mirror and saw that Zig had pointed his weapon directly at their vehicle. Brenda slammed her foot on the accelerator to increase their speed and informed her partner, "Jesse he going for the tires!"

Jesse quickly turned her body 180 degrees to the right and stuck her upper torso out of her window. She made sure she had a clear shot that wouldn't put any innocent drivers in jeopardy. Jesse fired two rounds at the radiator of the Steel Brother's mini-van and struck it dead on. Steam and hot water spurted out of the front of their vehicle. Zig answered back and fired two rounds at Brenda's car. The second shot blew out the left rear tire. Brenda almost lost control of the car as it was headed towards a concrete divider.

Jesse held the door handle while Brenda whipped the wheel to get the car under control. Brenda saw Jesse had lost her balance while she continued to hang out the car door window. So she controlled the car with one hand, while she pulled her partner back inside the car with the other.

"Oh God thanks Brenda! Small Fry are you okay?" screamed Jesse after she regained her composure.

"No! I wanna get out! Are we gonna crash?" screamed Penny as she continued to lie on the backseat floor.

"No sweetheart we are not going to crash but make sure you keep your head down!" Brenda ordered.

Brenda continued to drive when suddenly Jesse smelled smoke. Jesse checked the rearview mirror and saw that the mini-van spewed black smoke. Just then a driver in the left lane pointed to Brenda's back tire and then just as quickly pulled away from her.

Brenda checked her sideview mirror and shouted "Oh shit Jesse we're driving on our rims look at the damn sparks!"

While the exit got closer, Brenda acierated the car to get off the Fordham Road exit. The usual traffic was on Fordham Road and Brenda honked her horn furiously as ten or more cars waited at a red light.

"Get the hell out of the way!" screamed Jesse as cabs and passenger cars blew their horns in anger, not realizing that the women were cops. Brenda made a quick left and used the sidewalk to get through. Some drivers were pissed off, while others couldn't believe what they just witnessed.

*****

Butch's face enraged with anger as he refused to let Brenda get away from him. He turned on his windshield wipers to clean away the black sut that sprayed onto his windshield. Butch aggressively pressed harder on his accelerator because the temperature gauge told him that the car was too hot.

"Come on Butch we don't have much time people are beginning to go to work and this car doesn't have much life left!" Zig reminded his brother as the car radio read 9:27AM.

In pursuit of Brenda, Butch did the same and rode the curb to get through traffic. Butch observed Brenda head up a hill that leads to West Fordham Road. He picked up speed and yelled "Zig fire on them now!"

Zig stuck his hand out of the window and fired three times. He shattered the back window of Brenda's car. Bystanders on the street ran for cover. Sadly in the backseat of the car, with glass fragments all over her back, Penny Baker cried for her young innocent life.

*****

Jesse quickly jumped to the backseat to check on Penny. The little girl cried hysterically and was traumatized. Jesse wanted to sit and cuddle her but there was no time for that. All Jesse could offer the little girl was a pat on the back and words of wisdom, "Keep it together baby."

Jesse checked her clip and placed it back inside her gun. She returned fire and hit Butch's windshield. As they passed under the number 4 train, Jesse quickly ducked as Zig fired two more shots at their car.

"Brenda give me your gat!" Jesse demanded as she shot three more times which in turn knocked out Butch's headlights.

Brenda worried about the people going to work and school. The people run and duck out of harm's way as Brenda knew they were placing innocent people at risk as she did her best to get out of the populated area.

*****

"Fuck this! They're not getting away, what's mine is mine!" proclaimed Butch as he picked up speed. Sparks continued to fly from Brenda's car tire which hit Butch's windshield. Butch knew the girls' car didn't have much to travel on because the rim looked mangled and ready to fall off.

Inches away from Brenda's back bumper, Butch taxed the burnt out van for more power. He received it as he rammed them hard in an attempt to get the car to crash into another parked vehicle. While the two vehicles sped past Modell's Sporting Goods Store, Butch noticed that Brenda was ready to make a right turn onto the Grand Concourse. He refused to let her so he pulled parallel to her car and knocked them to the left instead.

"Zig listen to me! When I get even with those bitches you put bullets in their asses! If their car crashes so be it. All I need to do is scan the girl's arm, dead or alive!"

Butch attempted to get along side of Brenda's car but was forced to pull back because Jesse spotted them and without hesitation she fired shots that just missed Zig's head. People on the streets ran back inside the Citibank and 99 cent store for shelter. Zig heard sirens as they closer and yelled "Butch if you're going to do something it better be now, cops are right behind us!"

Butch took his brother seriously and fired three times from his front window. One of the bullets hit Brenda's other back tire causing her to lose control and jump the curb. Brenda, Jesse, and Penny crashed through the display window of Beat Street record shop.

"Grab that bitch Zig and use her as a shield! Trust me they won't shoot once they see her! Carjack one of these motherfuckers because the cops are coming. "

*****

Jesse rubbed her chest and spat blood from her mouth while Brenda held her banged up forehead from the blow of steering wheel. Brenda also busted her nose and broke her glasses. Jesse used every ounce of strength to regain her wits while still concerned about Penny, "Small Fry are you okay!" In the backseat, Penny was motionless as she laid on the car floor.

Brenda wiped the crimson colored blood from her face while she scrambled to find her weapon. She looked out the passenger side view mirror and saw Butch as he crept up on that side. "Jesse on your three! On your motherfuckin three! He's coming up on your door!" Brenda screamed.

Jesse turned her attention away from Penny and with all her strength; she kicked the backdoor open smashing it on Butch's chest. Butch winced in pain as he dropped his weapon and fell to the ground. Jesse reached across Penny and opened the other door. Up ahead Jesse saw the Footlocker store where she always bought her sporting good needs. Brenda crawled out of the car while blood continued to run from her nose. She picked up her gun that laid on the floor but wasn't sure of how many shots were left in the gun. Brenda didn't give a damn because all she needed was one for Butch's skull.

Brenda made it to the back of the car. She passed the tireless red hot rim that still sizzled at about 200 degrees fahrenheit. Brenda looked for Butch who she hoped was still on the other side of the car. Right up the street towards West Fordham Road, Brenda saw three marked police cars that approached in her direction as the sirens blared. Just then the back door swung open and Jesse and Penny were crouched down by Brenda's side.

"Brenda what do you see? Do you have a shot?" whispered Jesse as she surveyed their surroundings to make sure they were safe.. Jesse saw Zig as he pulled his brother towards the entrance of Dr. Jays clothing store. Jesse maneuvered her body to get to the other side without being seen.

Jesse had a visual on Butch's head. She raised her gun and was ready to squeeze the trigger when she heard, "Police halt! Put your weapons down now!"

Brenda shielded Penny, turned around, and saw four cops with guns drawn at Jesse. "Officers stand down! We're with you! We're detectives at the four-six, stand down and look at my shield!

Aggressively confident, Butch started to ramble on. "That's right motherfuckers! Listen to that bitch! Stand the fuck down and there won't be any shit!"

Brenda felt that Butch was an asshole with a lot of mouth. She slowly rose to her feet with her gun aimed dead on at Butch and Zig when her heart plunged into her stomach. To Brenda's horror, these heartless bastards had her little sister Vanessa. What's worse was that they used her as a human shield.

Jesse now ready to blast holes into the Steel Brothers was halted by her partner.

"Jesse no! Do not take that shot Jesse!" Brenda begged because Butch stood behind his brother who was shielded by Vanessa. The brothers carried very large duffel bags and a terrified Vanessa inside Dr. Jays.

More police cars arrived on the scene and only encouraged Zig more. He shouted "One step baby! Just take one step and I'll blow her brains in your lap! You think I'm bullshitting? Try me baby!"

Brenda raised both her hands up and stated, "Ok you got it" as she watched her baby sister get dragged upstairs to the upper level of the store.

*****

It was 10:05AM; the brothers were inside the store and used brute force to push workers and the manager to the upper level of the building. Butch glared out the window and saw the police were barricading Fordham Road within a one block radius. The idea was to make sure no one was allowed in or out. Butch knew that he had blown his one and only chance to accomplish what he had longed for the last twenty-five years. He turned to his little brother who held six people hostage at gunpoint.

"Do we have everything inside the duffel bags?" asked Butch while he watched the tactical truck pull up next to the pizza shop. Butch observed as the doors swung open and eight men dressed in black jumpsuits that held assault rifles exited. The officers ran in the direction of Captain Gordon who had arrived on the scene. The Captain was now in deep conversation with Jesse and Brenda who both received medical attention from EMS workers.

"Yeah we have everything that we'll need to hopefully get us out of here" responded Zig.

While Butch peeked out the window the telephone behind the counter had begun to ring. The store manager and his employees were fearful for their lives and prayed silently to themselves to get out safely. The phone continued to ring when Butch said, "Ladies and gentlemen this call is probably about all of you. The NYPD wants to save your lives but the Steel Brothers don't give a fuck about any of you. So follow instructions and don't let me have to blast any of you, understand?"

"Butch you need to get away from the window, sharpshooters are out there" Zig advised as he rubbed the barrel of his gun across the face of a badly shaken Vanessa.

Butch realized his brother was right so he motioned for the people to go sit by the sneakers section. The phone rang again and Butch answered it on the tenth one, "Before you say anything I need to know who are you and can I trust you on your word? Captain Gordon I don't want to hurt anyone in this store, but I promise you if my instructions are not followed, I'll kill every one of them one by one. What I want is very simple, and that is for you to supply me with a car with a full tank of gas, along with your men giving us room to drive away."

Butch quickly turned his head in anger because Zig hit the button that terminated the call. "What the fuck did you do that for?"

"Butch, in two minutes he'll call back so before he does, I need you to listen. It's over brother, I accept that now. There is no way that man is going to pull his men back and let us walk out of here. We had two of his fellow officers murdered earlier this morning, which puts every cop out there on full alert to make hollow points enter our asses."

Zig finally let go of his unrelenting grip on Vanessa's neck and continued, "Butch all the shit we did and the havoc we caused gained our asses a one-way ticket to hell. No amount of money in the world is going to change that fact. The only way out of this will be in body bags, not a getaway car. Butch throughout this shit you've been the leader. At this very moment I'm taking over and we will go out in a blaze of glory. I refuse to let us rot in a fucking prison. When the commanding officer calls back, you tell him this shit will be over in thirty minutes as long as he promises to keep his men back."

Butch stared at his younger brother and realized that it was really over. It was time for Butch to listen and acknowledge what his brother had just expressed. The road may actually end here today and Butch also knew it was time to go out of life the way they lived it, hard and alone.

The phone rang again and Butch picked it up, "We promise to come out with the hostages in thirty minutes as long as you keep your word not to do anything stupid. Very good, we'll see you soon."

*****

Absolutely drained but shielded behind a police car with their Captain, Jesse and Brenda looked at the red LCD numbers on the dashboard. It had been thirty minutes since the Steel Brothers promised to come out with the six hostages. Jesse looked to the sky and saw that there were four helicopters from the major news networks. There were also news vans that broadcasted the whole situation live on television.

There were exactly twenty marked police cars parked perfectly next to each other. Four police officers dressed in riot gear used the cars as shields. On the roofs positioned tactical snipers equipped with high powered rifles waited for their command.

On the scene Chief McIntosh just arrived and ran towards Jesse, Brenda and Captain Gordon. "Remember what I said Captain. We stand down until those hostages are out here, inside a police vehicle, and driven to safety."

Never taking his eyes off the entrance of Dr. Jays, Captain Gordon simply replied, "Yes sir."

Jesse squeezed Brenda's hand and whispered, "Sister you have to believe Vanessa is fine baby! In a very little while she will be in our arms feeling all our love."

*****

Inside a police command station truck three blocks away and surrounded by four heavily armed officers, Penny coddled a warm unopened soda. A bandage on her forehead and a dirty face, she tugged on the pants leg of one of the officers, "Is Jesse and Brenda alright sir?"

The officer, a white man in his thirties with a crew cut and a body like granite, kneeled down to Penny and answered, "Yes sweetheart, soon this will be over and you will be able to see your friends."

*****

Captain Gordon observed the anguish on Brenda's face. All of a sudden he saw her facial expression change. The Captain turned his attention towards the entrance door of Dr. Jays. All six hostages were led in single-line with their hands up in the air. The hostages all looked frightful as tears streamed down their faces.

A mini microphone in his possession that sat on his jacket collar, Captain Gordon calmly instructed, "Everyone follow my order to the letter, and stand down until the hostages are free from harm, over".

Sweat formed on the Captain's head as he watched in silence. The six hostages were five feet from the entrance door. Meanwhile, Brenda held on to Jesse's hand tightly, fighting back tears because there was no sign of Vanessa anywhere.

*****

The hostages took baby steps toward freedom, their bodies shook uncontrollably. Inside, the Steel Brothers kept their minds on the task at hand. They wore from head to toe ceramic armored body armor insulated with triple blended Kevlar. Their bodies were cooled as the suits allowed air to enter.

Butch held his AK-47 assault rifle when his mind began to play with him. To his left, Butch swore he saw his mother Simone as she mixed a big bowl of blueberry pancakes batter. To his right, he watched his father Pete on the couch as he laughed at a rerun of "Sanford and Son" and shared Oreo cookies with Zig.

Zig pulled back his safety latch and looked at his brother. He remembered how Butch taught him how to catch a football. No matter how long it took him, Butch never lost patience with Zig. Butch always encouraged him to hold on to the ball and praised him when he did well. The brothers remembered the good times; but that life was lost to them the day Melvin Baker killed their parents.

*****

The hostage negotiator crept towards the store front entrance. He waved with both hands for the six hostages to follow him. The negotiator saw something move in his peripheral vision. When he turned to look, the panic stricken negotiator hollered, "No! Get down!" Deep in the "Big and Tall" section of the store echoed bullets and flashes of light. Hostages dropped to the ground like flies and the hostage negotiator took one dead center in the skull. Blood was splattered everywhere. Flesh was ripped away from the innocent victims who thought their ordeal was finally over.

Sadly the hostage negotiator had only been married for two years and his wife just gave birth two weeks ago to their first child named Samantha.

In utter disbelief, Captain Gordon grabbed his head and tried to process what he just witnessed. Immediately, he pulled out his service revolver and pointed it towards the entrance door. Brenda had tears of anger that rolled down her checks, burned with rage as she looked at the carnage in front of the store. Jesse without thinking ran from behind one car to another car with the hope to get a better angle on the crazy motherfuckers inside.

246

Clearly frantic by what just happened, as spit shot from his mouth Gordon screamed into his radio, "Fire on my command!"

On the roof tactical cops burned with fury as they looked down on their fallen comrade. They salivated for the moment when their captain would give the order.

Forty uniformed cops most of who were working hard to hold back their tears, pointed their 9mm weapons at the entrance door. The helicopters above zoomed their cameras at the entrance door. Either they had elephant balls or absolutely no respect for the NYPD, the Steel brothers exited Dr. Jays dressed in black while they defiantly stepped over the dead victims' bodies.

"Take those motherfuckers out now!" Gordon commanded. On that order bullets blasted off and filled the air with the smell of gun powder. Fordham Road was definitely a war zone.

Butch exited the building and was immediately hit with about thirty shots all at once. The bullets were mostly from 9mm handguns which only made his body jerk to the left. Butch returned fire at a car and knocked out its windows. The bullets hit a female cop in her arm and chest. The woman fell to the ground and screamed in pain. Her partner, a Spanish officer, ran from behind his car in an attempt to pull her to safety and was hit in the head. A huge chunk of skin, skull, and brain flew two feet in the air and landed on the ground. The heroic officer died instantly.

Jesse experienced a flashback to one of her "Recon" missions during active duty in the military. She laid flat on the ground and locked in on Butch's knees. She fired six shots and hits them dead on but they had no impact as Butch continued to walk slowly towards the corner about forty feet away. Jesse spoke to her partner from a transmitter, "Brenda they have on body armor, go for the throat!"

Zig who was crouched down behind a parked car in front of Burger King fired a succession of bullets at two police vehicles that shielded eight cops who returned fire. Zig loaded another clip inside his rifle and quickly ran from behind his car and towards the officers. The officers were caught off guard as they reloaded. They were attacked by Zig which resulted in three fatalities and two critical injuries.

Zig looked up towards the roof of Foot Locker where he saw two sharpshooters. Zig raised his gun to fire when he was hit by seven bullets. The impact knocked him down towards the sidewalk that caused him to lose focus on the men on the roof. Zig started to back up towards the entrance of Burger King and fired a shot at Captain Gordon that just missed his head.

Brenda grabbed the Captain and pulled him to the ground. She fired seven shots in succession from behind the police car hitting Zig dead on his stomach but the bullets didn't penetrate the armor. Brenda watched Zig enter the empty restaurant and fired one more time that hit him in the chest but also had no effect.

While twenty more police cars arrived and blocked off the Grand Concourse, Butch fired in their direction. His attention was diverted as he took six shots from Jesse. Butch's eyes connected to Jesse's immediately. While both stared at each other for a brief moment, Butch lost his balance because of shots he took from uniformed officers.

Shots came from all directions. Butch decided to enter the Optical City Eyeglass store. He took cover behind the counter to reload and figure out how to get close to his brother.

While the two assailants were out of sight, Captain Gordon ordered an officer to bring a car over to gather the injured officers. Both the Captain and Brenda loaded the injured into the backseat. After they loaded the last officer Brenda slapped the trunk and the car sped off east of Fordham Road.

*****

Inside Burger King, behind the counter, Zig reloaded his rifle while he checked his armor to make sure everything was in tack. Zig peaked from behind the counter and saw that more police cars had arrived and more officers had been deployed. Zig realized that his brother was alone out there and was not sure if Butch was injured or not. Zig lifted his mask to stick a piece of gum in his mouth, grabbed his rifle, and hopped over the counter to head back out into the street.

*****

Butch surveyed the scene from the eyeglass store. He felt his chest and wondered why it was so sore. He tried to put it out of his mind but couldn't help but to wonder if the armor had begun to break down from all the shots he had taken. Refocused, Butch reloaded his assault rifle and took three deep breaths before exited back out to find his baby brother.

*****

"Jesse let me ask you a question okay? Are the city pools closed down yet?" Brenda asked through her microphone.

"I don't think so Brenda I believe they officially close down next Friday, why?"

"I think I know how to take these motherfuckers out Jesse.

The Captain was mortified at all the blood on the street, helicopters that hovered above in the sky, and the sad looks on his officers' faces.

248

Gordon looked at Brenda and stated, "Brenda tell me what you need and I'll get it for you."

"Captain I need you to get two tankers of chlorine here as fast as you can. Once those bastards come out, we'll keep them neutralized and fixated in the area. I have a plan but we have to move fast!"

Gordon got on his phone and contacted the Parks and Recreation Department. Brenda reloaded her guns and got ready because to her right she observed Zig as he exited the restaurant. "Captain here we go!"

On one knee Jesse had an assault rifle that she got from the tactical truck. She had her eyes glued to the eyeglass store where she witnessed Butch jump over the counter ready to make his grand return. Quickly Jesse grabbed her transmitter and announced to Brenda, "Okay this is it Brenda, let's give these motherfuckers a lullaby."

Zig exited Burger King with his rifle in hand. He scoped the area frantically and looked for his brother. The street was quiet but the intensity was deafening. At least sixty heavily armed police officers watched and waited for Captain Gordon to give the command to fire. Zig now made his way towards Butch who stood on the corner of Fordham Road with no place to go. Butch was blocked in by at least ten police cars with twenty officers all ready to blow his brains out.

Butch saw Zig and gestured to him to raise his rifle. Gordon with his mouth near his transmitter whispered to the leaders of each unit, "Everyone stand down and wait for my command, but under no circumstances do they walk out of this perimeter."

Every officer's finger was on their trigger, itching to fill the Steel Brothers with hot metal. The officers followed their orders and did as they were told. The street had a very eerie feeling due to the silence. Butch moved towards his brother and couldn't help but to rub his chest because of the soreness.

Jesse with her eyes dead on the gesture said to herself, "The body armor is weakening on his ass. One of those bullets penetrated. He's vulnerable and I'm going to pounce on that ass."

Butch and Zig stood side by side in front of Beat Street record store. They seemed to be holding a regular conversation in the mist of all the drama that went on. While the brothers stood in the street, the roar of loud engines was profound as it made its way up Fordham Road.

The two blue tankers approached the blocked area. Butch and Zig were baffled and weren't quite sure the purpose for the trucks. One thing the brothers did know for sure: The end was near. Zig tapped Butch on the shoulder and screamed through his mask "Hell or heaven I love you like no other!"

Butch stared at his younger brother through his green colored goggles, gently placed his hand on Zig's shoulder and boldly stated, "It was well worth it! Today they will never forget the Steel Brothers!"

The defiant brothers gripped their assault rifles, positioned their bodies in a squatted stance, and aimed toward the tankers that moved closer.

Captain Gordon screamed into his transmitter, "Do not let them fire at those tankers! Ready, Fire!"

On that command bullets rained down upon Butch and Zig from all directions as the sound of shots could be heard all the way to 183rd street and the Grand Concourse. The force of the fire power knocked the Steel Brothers backwards. Zig fell to the ground and grabbed his hand which had been partially blown off. Butch saw Zig go down after he took a bullet to the hand. In retaliation, he fired about sixty shots back at the officers. Fatally Butch hit a white female cop in the head leaving her brains splattered on the ground where she laid.

"Oh shit! Captain now! Wet um up now!" screamed Brenda as she watched Zig stumble to his feet and take three shots to the leg that ripped part of his armor gear.

"Do it now!" screamed Gordon as he watched the tankers that were controlled by hydraulics point large hoses at the Steel Brothers. Forceful and strong streams of chlorine were aimed directly at Butch and Zig. The high powered streams hit them with a vengeance and knocked them along with their weapons to the ground.

Brenda saw that Butch and Zig were soaked and coughed uncontrollably on the ground. She yelled at the Captain, "We got them sir! Their asses are finished!"

Jesse slowly came from behind the vehicle with her gun cocked and ready, "Stay down! Don't move!"

Brenda saw Jesse as she ran over to the fallen assailants. She quickly left the Captain and rushed to assist her partner. Both of the brothers struggled to make it to their feet. Zig gained his composure quicker than his brother and lunged for his weapon a few feet away. Jesse responded and fired three times that pierced Zig's side. What others didn't know that Brenda knew was chlorine weakens the body armor material known as "Kevlar" which makes it vulnerable to breakdown and easier gain penetration.

Like holes in a water barrel, Zig fell to the ground as blood poured out of his body. Zig took quick and short breaths as his heart rate slowly decreased. The captain waved his arms frantically to the other officers on the scene to stand down. Captain Gordon trusted that his female detectives could handle themselves, but the father in him made him cautiously send two officers over for back up.

Butch regained his composure and crawled on top of his brother. In a weak and sorrowful voice Butch said, "Please no more."

Butch lied on top of his brother's chest and felt as his breath got shorter as his life was about to end. Zig looked into his brother's eyes and mouthed, "I love you." Butch could literally hear the "16 grams" leave his little brother's body. Zig Steel was dead.

Butch stared at Brenda and Jesse as they pointed their weapons at him. He then looked down at his brother and closed his open eyes.

"Where is my sister? What have you done to her?" pleaded Brenda who didn't want to kill the fallen Butch.

"Any way you look at it, you're leaving this scene in a box. That's choice you made and honestly I really don't give a fuck", said Jesse who stared at Butch coldly

"Tell us right now where Vanessa is and I promise to do your ass quick" Jesse promised.

Butch caressed Zig's face then looked at Jesse and Brenda with a devilish grin then reached for his waistband.

"Please don't do it. Just tell me where my sister Vanessa is." Brenda begged the heartless Butch while she added more pressure to her trigger.

Butch threw caution to the wind and reached for his handgun. Brenda fired twice and struck Butch square in the chest. The impact knocked him backwards onto the ground next to his brother. Brenda fell to the ground and grabbed Butch by his face while blood gurgled from his mouth. "Where's my sister you sick son of a bitch! Tell me now motherfucker!"

In his last seconds of life, Butch showed no remorse as he spat up blood that hit Brenda's shirt. He looked up at Dr. Jays and whispered his final words, "Your sister... goes... boom."

Brenda clearly understood what Butch meant; she slammed Butch's head down so hard it hit the ground with a loud thud.

Quickly Brenda jumped to her feet and took off inside Dr. Jays. Jesse was inches behind her along with three other officers.

Officers rushed to the dead bodies of Butch and Zig while Captain Gordon yelled, "Jesse and Brenda what the hell is going on?"

En route Jesse turned to a fellow officer and demanded, "Get the bomb squad here now!"

Not aware of the full details, but trusting Jesse's judgment Captain Gordon shouted, "Does anyone here have experience with explosives? Speak up now please!"

Immediately Gordon spotted an officer sprint towards his direction. A female Spanish officer named Lucy Delgado, a nine year veteran who worked in the bomb squad three years ago. She transferred out of that division because she failed to defuse a bomb inside a store that killed hostages in Queens.

Lucy, a short but well put together woman sported short black hair, is given a path by her fellow officers until she was face to face with her Captain.

"I got no speeches Officer Delgado. All I want to know is are you up to this, Yes or no?"

Delgado fought back the images of her last failed bomb encounter, and answered, "Yes sir."

Gordon grabbed the officer's arm and ran inside the store. Not before he delegated a task to Lieutenant Tony Hicks. "Hicks you are in command of this scene! No one in, no one out! Get the paramedics out here to clean up those bodies. Also, call CSI right away!"

Saluting his commander, Hicks responded with confidence "Yes Sir!"

Gordon and Delgado ran up the stairs and spotted Jesse and Brenda who stood near Vanessa. The officers got closer to the scene and noticed an explosive device wrapped around her body.

Gordon looked at Brenda who rubbed her baby sister's head in an attempt to keep her calm. Lucy saw a small LCD clock taped to Vanessa left thigh that counted down 2:35, 2:34, 2:33…

Brenda I need you to let Officer Delgado get over there and stop that timer."

Lucy surveyed the various wires that surround the young woman and noticed a block of C4 that was taped to her right thigh. 2:22, 2:21, 2:20….

"Brenda you have to move back. Let this woman do her job!" ordered Jesse who looked into Vanessa's eyes and could clearly see she was terrified.

Captain Gordon gently pulled Brenda by the arm towards him so that Lucy could go to work. On her hip Lucy had a "Leatherman" utility knife that she began to open.

Jesse ran over to a rack where she grabbed a Nike tee shirt and gave it to Lucy and said, "For your face."

Lucy thanked Jesse then patted her head while the clock read 2:01, 2:00, 1:59… Jesse took two steps back and huddled next to Brenda and promised, "I'm here baby and I'm not going anywhere."

Lucky to have small fingers, Lucy began to trace the blue and yellow wires that were hooked to the clock that read 1:50, 1:49, 1:48…following the path of the wires Lucy watched them take different directions. The blue wire went to a switch that's wrapped around Vanessa's right wrist and the yellow wire went to another switch that's wrapped on her left wrist. Lucy kept the time focal in her mind, and looked up at the clock that read 1:39, 1:38, 1:37…

Quickly Lucy opened her knife and pulled out a set of miniature scissors that were attached. She stared at the two switches around Vanessa's wrist. Lucy fought back the anxiety from the last bomb incident in her head and checked the time 1:21, 1:20, 1:19…

Brenda tried to get closer to her baby sister but was restrained by Jesse and Captain Gordon. They forced her to stay with them and not interfere with Lucy. "Come on man let me go! She needs me shit!" cried Brenda as she was not allowed.

Lucy took a deep breath and gently grabbed hold of the blue wire while she positioned her scissors around the thin piece of insulated metal. Lucy looked at Vanessa and nodded her head as to say "Here goes" while the clock ticked down 1:00, :59, :58… Lucy slowly began to snip the wire when she suddenly noticed a black wire attached to a small detonator. This device was hidden under Vanessa's shirt sleeve.

Utilizing the knife, Lucy carefully cut the shirt sleeve open. She noticed that the wire went up Vanessa's arm and through her bra. The LCD screen now read, :50, :49, :48… as Lucy with sweat beads on her forehead carefully cut the buttons off Vanessa's shirt that revealed her upper torso.

Lucy followed the wire that went under the bra and around Vanessa waist and saw that the black wire was stuffed behind the block of C4 that was taped to Vanessa thigh. The seconds counted down, :33,:32,:31 as Lucy cut away the tape from Vanessa's pants and not the tape on top of the C4.

Brenda was terrified at the possibility of losing her sister. Vanessa looked at Brenda and mouthed silently to her "Get out."

With wet jet red eyes, Brenda silently responded "Hell no!"

Lucy gently pulled the block of C4 away, and could hear the noise of the tape as it peeled away from the fabric. The time dangerously counted down, :20, :19, :18. Lucy held the block of C4 in her hands and was careful not to pull the blue or yellow wires which served as contacts. She was positive that the black wire was the fuse to detonate the bomb. Lucy grabbed hold of Vanessa's hand while the clock read: 12, :11,:10. Lucy positioned her scissors on the black wire, closed her eyes, and let her past failures go. Lucy squeezed down on the scissors snipping the black wire and opened her eyes and saw that the clock stopped at: 07.

Lucy carefully detached the two remaining wires from the C4 and confiscated the explosive putty appropriately inside a shirt. Lucy fell backwards and landed on the floor and praised, "Thank God it's over!"

Brenda broke away from Jesse and Gordon and ran to Vanessa. They hugged each other and cried uncontrollably. Brenda was grateful to God and Officer Delgado for saving her baby sister's life. Jesse and Captain Gordon picked Lucy off the ground and commend her for an excellent job.

Jesse said happily, "Delgado, you held it down sister! Thanks for saving my family." The two women embraced each other.

*****

Jesse and Captain Gordon walked closely behind Brenda and Vanessa. The sisters found it hard to let go of each other as they held hands. Jesse looked up the street and saw her "Sweet Face" Penny who stood next to Lieutenant Hicks.

Penny looked up and watched as Vanessa was helped into an EMS van. She ran over at top speed and hugged her around the waist and said, "Hi Vanessa, I'm glad you're okay."

Vanessa allowed herself to smile then responded before she entered the van, "Me too Penny, me too."

Jesse held Penny by the hand and took her away from the crime scene. Jesse looked back and watched as Butch and Zig Steel were placed inside body bags and loaded into a van. They would be toe tagged and buried in Potter's Field.

Jesse exhaled and wholeheartedly said, "May your souls never find peace."

So here we go again, just like my first novel *The Mouse That Roared!* If my second novel *Whatever It Takes* was made into a motion picture here are my star picks:

Butch Steel	Idris Elba (Stringer Bell "The Wire")
Zig Steel	Terry Crews (Everybody Hates Chris)
Jesse James	Gabrielle Union (Bad Boys 2)
Brenda Simple	Sanaa Lathan (Alien vs. Predator)
Penny Baker	Dee Dee Davis (Bernie Mac Show)
Vanessa Simple	Meagan Good (Waist Deep)
Melvin Baker	Kristoff St. John (The Young and The Restless)
Joyce Baker	Chrystale Wilson (The Players Club)
Pete Steel	Clifton Powell (Dead Presidents)
Simone Steel	BernNadette Stanis (Good Times)
Karen Steel	Paula Jai Parker(Hustle&Flow)
King Tut	Tony Cox (Bad Santa)
Capt. Gordon	J.K. Simmons (Spiderman 1, 2 & 3)

Let me know what you think!!!

For more information and upcoming publications, or to tell me what your picks are for the "motion picture", you can contact me at

Dwayne Murray, Sr.
Madbo Enterprises
1444 East Gunhill Road, Suite 32
Bronx, New York 10469

Or visit my website at:

WWW.MADBOENTERPRISES.COM

Click on either my guestbook or email address, I would love to read your opinions about the book.

Or

Let's be friends. Hit me up at

WWW.MySpace.com/madbo726